Also by Bernadette Strachan

THE RELUCTANT LANDLADY
HANDBAGS AND HALOS
DIAMONDS AND DAISIES

About the Author

Little White Lies is Bernadette Strachan's fourth
novel. Bernadette was born in Fulham, London
into an Irish Catholic family. Before becoming
an author she ran a wool shop, produced radio
commercials, and was a voiceover agent repre-
senting many household names. She is currently
writing a stage musical with her husband,
Matthew. They have one daughter, Niamh.

Bernadette never eats carbs during the week.

Bernadette Strachan

Little White Lies

HODDER

First published in Great Britain in 2008 by Hodder
An Hachette Livre UK company

1

A CIP catalogue record for this title is
available from the British Library.

ISBN 978 0340 95313 6 (A)
ISBN 978 0340 89805 5 (B)

Typeset in Sabon by Palimpsest Book Production Limited,
Grangemouth, Stirlingshire

. Printed and bound by Clays Ltd, St Ives plc

Hodder & Stoughton's policy is to use papers that are natural, renewable
and recyclable products and made from wood grown in sustainable
forests. The logging and manufacturing processes are expected to
conform to the environmental regulations of the country of origin.

Hodder & Stoughton Ltd
338 Euston Road
London NW1 3BH

www.hodder.co.uk

This book is for
Penny-and-Steve-on-a-bike,
with my love

One

Billie Baskerville was running away. Again.

Last summer she ran to her parents' bungalow, but that hadn't been far enough, so now she'd pulled on her trusty trainers and run all the way to the sea. Drizzly, dozy Sole Bay, a fly speck on the East Anglian hump of England, was to be her Fresh Start. Those capitals are important. Billie's Fresh Start would save her from her mother's histrionics, her brother's disapproval and her father's cravats.

On the threshold of Barbara's Brides, Billie finally stopped running. She was dismayed. Not the sort of girl to be easily dismayed, Billie was optimistic, resourceful, with a sincere belief in the restorative powers of the oven chip, but even she had to admit that the imaginary roll of drums she'd awarded this moment didn't seem merited. The shop was dimmer, dirtier, and more neglected than she'd expected. And she'd expected it to be pretty dim, dirty and neglected. Great Aunty Babs' letter, now crushed at the bottom of Billie's chain-store interpretation of a Gucci holdall, had been frank: '*It needs a little TLC, deer. But don't we all?*'

The building looked like Billie had felt for the past few months. A little TLC wouldn't do it: the place needed bull-dozing. The original shop front was handsome enough, with its twin bow windows curving out into the narrow street like a cantilevered Edwardian bosom. They flanked a recessed door, approached by a porch whose tiles were almost invisible under a thick overcoat of dust. The windows, unlit, presented two lopsided mannequins, like tipsy hookers in Amsterdam's red-light district. One, headless, was naked except for a lace glove, and the other, her jaunty red wig obscuring an ineptly felt-tipped face, modelled a nylon crinoline whose Daz whiteness had long ago faded to the colour of freshly exhumed bone.

1

Taking all this in, as her bruised but hopeful heart descended in some slow internal lift to her feet, Billie didn't notice the door opening.

'You must be Billie!' sang the girl in the doorway. So dotted with freckles she could have been a Dalmatian, the stranger had the bright eyes of a Disney character and the kind of swingy, shiny, red-gold hair promised but rarely delivered by shampoo commercials. Her smile reached her eyes and beyond, as if there wasn't quite room on her face for it. 'Come in, come in!' she squealed, doing a good impersonation of somebody who'd been waiting for Billie and her tattered luggage all her life.

Stepping into the shop, its dark interior every bit as grubby and forlorn and downright Addams Family as its exterior promised, Billie suddenly felt what her Great Aunty Babs might have described as 'queer'. It was as if she had been blessed with X-ray vision. Standing in the middle of the sticky floorboards and ignoring the beaming girl, Billie could see right through the brown paint, the woodchip, the stock flown in from the 1970s Soviet Union. She could discern the room's elegant bones, the beauty of its panelling and the effortless perfection of its proportions.

It was unexpected, this fluttering in her chest, as if a pigeon was trapped in her Wonderbra. This was Billie's first real excitement since she'd fled home to the family mock Tudor corner plot last August.

Maybe, Billie marvelled, as the freckled girl fussed about, hanging up Billie's jacket and taking her bags, the fluttering was more than mere excitement. She shook herself. It couldn't be love at first sight with a decrepit, mouldering ruin of a shop. It was absurd and Benny Hill-like, like a busty teenager lusting after a toothless pensioner.

Besides, Billie had fallen in love at first sight once before and that had caused more uproar than a kangaroo at a funeral. It was the reason she'd laced up those trainers again. 'You must be Dot,' she smiled at the girl, remembering her manners. 'According to Great Aunty Babs' letter you keep this show on the road.'

'Oh, well,' blushed Dot, 'I wouldn't say that.'

Looking around her, neither would Billie. The premises were

obviously rarely troubled by Hoovers, dusters or, she suspected, customers. Dot's own outfit was also slightly dusty, being the kind of tie-dye dress that invariably smells faintly of incense. Garnished with cheesecloth scarves and an armful of the kind of jangling metal bangles that turn skin green within thirty seconds, Great Aunty Babs' assistant was pure hippy: cut her slender frame in half and it would say 'Peace and love' all the way through, like a stick of Glastonbury rock. Hippies made Billie come out in hives, but something about this sunny girl made Billie answer Dot smile for smile, customised Doc Martens notwithstanding.

Deep down, Billie rather envied girls like Dot, who wore exactly what they liked and looked comfortable in it. A slave to trends, Billie hitched a lift on every bandwagon going. She'd persevered with baseball caps even though the effect was less Posh Spice and more ASBO, and she owned so much fake fur she suspected her Top Shop bomber jacket had pupped. With an unruly bosom and unrulier hair, Billie had never cracked dressing to flatter her good points, whatever they might be.

They weren't her legs – a touch too short, a touch too healthy – nor her hair. Kind friends might say 'Sarah Jessica Parker' but they were thinking 'sci-fi candyfloss'. Her bottom didn't qualify as a good point either: handy for keeping her warm on bus-stop benches, it brought to mind a bag of spanners when introduced to Lycra.

If pressed, Billie *might* admit that her eyes were the sort of sea green that could make men look twice, or that her curves erred on the right side of Rubenesque, or that her idiosyncratically wonky teeth were charming. But you had to press very hard indeed.

Dot, serene in her boho uniform, was burbling on, in a way that was clearly typical of her. 'Babs has arrived safe and sound in Sydney. Her pen-friend picked her up at the airport.' She flashed her eyes. 'Terribly handsome, apparently, and ever so good for eighty-four. He's driving her into the outback.' Dot frowned. 'Or should that be *out* to the outback . . .'

Nipping into this gap, Billie asked, 'Do you mind me coming to look after the shop while she's away?' It was only polite to check. 'After all, I'm sure you could manage on your own.'

'I so couldn't!' hooted Dot, obviously tickled at the notion of 'minding'. Her laugh was a rusty throttle, unexpected from such a waif. 'I'm hopeless! I'm worse than Babs, and that's saying something!' After this frank self-appraisal for her new boss, Dot suggested, 'Tea?'

The electric kettle was as battered as the shop. As it coughed itself to a climax, Billie followed Dot on a tour of her new fiefdom. Her elderly relative had a weakness for dark-brown gloss, and it covered everything that the woodchip didn't. A narrow, treacherous staircase at the back of the shop led up to the chaotic stockroom, stuffed with aged white dresses, folded over like weary ghosts. Beyond these stairs, on ground level, was an unfeasibly dinky loo, possibly salvaged from a doll's house, and an equally teeny kitchenette, home to a collection of tannin-streaked mugs given away free by stationery companies, and a tea towel that had last been rinsed when Billie was a virgin.

'Babs is very particular about our stock,' Dot was saying. 'She likes to feel we have something for everyone.'

Everyone, thought Billie, with a man-made fibre fetish and a secret desire to be mistaken for a Russian prostitute. The shop floor was crowded with rails, which in turn were crowded with the ugliest selection of wedding dresses Billie had ever seen. She was no fan of weddings, but even the most dewy-eyed romantic would find little inspiration in Babs' dingy cream puffballs and day-glo sheaths.

'We write all the signs ourselves, to save money,' boasted Dot happily, gesturing to a creased piece of inside-out corn-flakes packet that invited the browsing punter, in thick red strokes, to 'FINNISH OFF YOUR OUTFIT WITH A TIARAR'.

'Very, erm, effective,' murmured Billie, wondering which of the pair was the illiterate cheapskate. Probably, she concluded, her great-aunt: the letter in her bag ended jauntily: '*Yours, until we meat again.*'

Satin slippers, now a tide-marked grey, slumped in corners waiting for the right foot to come along. Creased veils sat in a spooky glass cabinet, watched over by a white glove on a dummy hand which seemed to be making a rude gesture out at the shop floor. 'Don't tell me that's the till?' Billie backed away dubiously from the mahogany and brass monster that dominated the counter.

'Isn't it marvellous?' Dot seemed carefully programmed to miss the point. 'Completely original. No horrid computery bits, so it's easy to operate. Although,' she added, 'you do have to convert everything into pounds, shillings and pence and back again. Oh, and don't open it!' she warned suddenly. 'Jenkins is asleep in there.' She responded to Billie's dumb look. 'My mouse. He's not been well.'

Billie paused. She could have said, 'A mouse?' or, 'Sorry, I thought you said "my mouse" for a moment there,' or even, 'Goodbye. You're mental.' But she simply nodded. This girl was unusual, and would take some getting used to, but she was making Billie's antennae twitch. Clambering out of the self-dug crater that Billie had lain in, shell-shocked, for the past year, she needed a friend, and some instinct was telling her that Dot might be it.

The warm tinkle of the old bell over the door announced a newcomer. Out of the dusk of Sole Bay materialised a tiny woman in a formal coat that had seen better days. White-haired head resolutely down, she negotiated the forest of disgusting dresses.

'Annie,' whispered Dot. 'Our most loyal customer.'

As amazed at Annie's existence as she would have been if a unicorn had wandered in, Billie beamed at her.

The wide smile seemed to unnerve the elderly lady who halted, flustered, beside a strapless monstrosity in peach sateen. 'Am I intruding?' She asked, in a high, fluting voice steeped in genteel timidity.

'Of course not, Annie,' said Dot. 'This is Billie. She's Babs' great-niece, and my new manageress. Tea?'

'Oh goodness, no.' Annie responded as if bestiality had been mooted. 'Just the usual, please, my dear.' She held out a small notebook.

Taking it from her, Dot removed a fiver from between its pages, scribbled in it, signed it, and handed the notebook back. 'See you next week.'

'Goodbye,' said Annie, carefully, as if she'd just learned the word. The shop bell jangled again as she left.

'One day,' mused Dot, 'she'll accept a cup of tea from me.'

'What was all that about?' asked Billie.

'Annie's saving up for a wedding dress. She's been bringing in a few pounds every now and then for quite some time.'

'Is the dress for her?' Billie was intrigued, even if Dot seemed to find this perfectly normal. She was touched, too. The woman had seemed vulnerable, despite her dated, formal demeanour. 'She's a bit . . .' There really was no other word for it. '*Old*, to be buying a wedding dress.'

'I suppose she is,' admitted Dot, incuriously, as she tweaked a faded frock. 'Have you noticed our anti-shoplifting technology?'

Billie had. Pinned to one of the two changing cubicles was a Polaroid of Dot, assuming an unconvincing cross expression, above a sign that read 'MAKE SURE YOU PEY FOR THAT YOU NAUGHTY OLD THING!'

'And, of course,' said Dot, swelling with pride, 'there's our Gallery of Happiness.'

A pinboard over the baroque register was studded with yellowing wedding-day photographs. Fat, thin and in-between ladies in white grinned down at them, gripping bouquets and sprays and single stems, accompanied by posses of bridesmaids and flower girls and pages and best men and matrons of honour and, of course, the occasional groom whose face seemed to be sending out mute cries for help, like a hostage in a strangely ornate and well-dressed kidnapping. Billie could almost smell the hairspray. 'Mugs,' she whispered, sadly.

'Sorry?' Dot evidently thought she'd misheard.

'Nothing.' Billie felt ashamed. Now was not the time to lay her personal history on this friendly girl. Longer than *Ben Hur*, and rather less interesting, The Story could wait. 'Dot, enough about the shop. Tell me about *you*.'

'Oh. Ah.' Dot seemed wrong-footed, as if she was unaccustomed to talking about herself. 'I work here. But you know that. I love animals. I believe in reincarnation, you see, so that worm you tread on could be your great-grandfather. And I like poetry.'

Billie didn't like poetry. It scared her. She could recite snippets of her GCSE requirements, and might recognise Pam Ayres in the street, but would never willingly pick up a poetry book. 'Music?' she asked, hoping that she'd found somebody to share day-long Robbie Williams/Abba/Kylie fests with.

'I *love* music,' confirmed Dot. 'Especially folk. I come from a long line of Morris dancers on my dad's side.'

There being no answer to that, Billie said, 'Boyfriends?'

'Oh, boy*friend*.' Dot stressed the singularity of her beau. 'I live with Jake.' Inner lighting clicked on behind Dot's eyes, and she assumed a look of such bliss that Billie took a step backwards. 'He's wonderful. An artist. So talented. A genius. I'm so lucky, so very lucky.' She paused, before sighing, 'We're very much in love.'

It was an avalanche of romance. Billie wanted to pick the pink marshmallow out of her hair. 'That's nice. Getting married?' It seemed an appropriate question to ask in their surroundings.

The inner light flickered. 'No. But I'm sure he'll marry me one day.'

That phrasing struck Billie as peculiar. A modern female might be expected to say '*We'll* marry' rather than use Dot's passive language. 'Wouldn't worry about it,' Billie smiled, with a conspiratorial wink. 'It's overrated, you know.'

'Are you married?' asked Dot.

'Jesus, no.' That came out very fast, very scornful. Billie hated the acid that had crept into her tone since last summer. 'I mean, no,' she repeated, more gently. 'Not really my cup of vodka. I'm single. Very, very single. About as single as you can be without being a dead nun.' She paused, before saying with the eager horror of a serial killer confessing all to the cops, 'You might as well know from the beginning, Dot. I'm anti-weddings.'

'Oh.' Dot jumped, then eyed her disbelievingly. '*All* women like weddings.'

'Not this one. I'm allergic.' With a wicked look, Billie teased, 'We're a fine pair to run a wedding shop. One immune to the lure of a white dress, the other living in sin.'

'We'll do alright.'

Hoping that Dot's calm confidence was contagious, Billie settled into a spindly chair, then hurriedly stood up again when it swayed dangerously. She followed Dot into the kitchenette and accepted a cup of tea from her. It was, Billie noted approvingly, a *good* cup of tea: this boded well. Wandering back to the shop floor, she asked, 'Do you have bank stuff and keys and that for me?'

'Oh yes. Of course. Babs set up an account for you.' Dot rummaged in the curtained shelves beneath the glowering cash register, and produced a pile of bank bumph. 'You can pay me, and yourself, out of the account.' Looking around her, Dot added, 'She thought you might like to make a few improvements, as well. Although I can't see how.' Dot shrugged her shoulders. 'We like Barbara's Brides the way it is, but Babs said you're to have a free hand with it. Is there anything you'd like to change?'

Instead of baying 'EVERYTHING!' into that shining face, Billie marvelled at how unbusinesslike the two women were. And how much they loved this shop, and each other. 'What's the turnover?' She asked, having learned the word in a book called *Shopkeeping for Dummies* on the train journey.

'The . . . ?' Dot looked bemused, like a Neanderthal faced with a microwave.

'Customers,' Billie simplified it. 'How often do you sell a dress?'

'Ah. Hmm.' Dot pouted. 'Let me see.' She wrinkled her nose. 'We sold a dress in January. No. I tell a lie. It was November.'

'*A* dress?' queried Billie, grasping her mug a little harder. Maybe the ozone had clogged her ears. 'Last November?'

'Yes. And somebody bought a marked-down veil for a hen night the other week.'

'I see.' So there was no turnover. How on earth did Great Aunty Babs sustain this place?

As if she'd read her mind, Dot said comfortably, 'Babs often laughs it's lucky she doesn't rely on the shop to keep her.' She gently pulled open the till's cash drawer to peek at Jenkins, snoring on a luncheon voucher. 'The husbands left her well off, she says.'

Ah. The husbands. Just one of the reasons Billie's mother regarded Great Aunty Babs as a geriatric Antichrist. Babs' history (or 'career' as Nancy Baskerville termed it) of marrying wealthy gents in the twilight of their days (or 'last legs' if you were Nancy) had raised eyebrows at family gatherings. There had been three husbands, each older, more doddery and with more capital than the last. They died happy, and with airtight wills.

'Do you mind me asking what you take home?' Billie braced herself. Even an angelic being like Dot would need money for rent, food and a new handbag every now and then. The sum Dot named made Billie gasp: it would barely have kept her in tights. 'Is that all?'

'Oh, I'm not materialistic,' said Dot, airily. 'Jake has taught me to reject the false promises of capitalism.'

'Is that so?' Billie wasn't strong on political theory, although you couldn't beat her on *Hollyoaks*. Her voice unravelled into a yawn, and she bent to gather up her belongings. It was five thirty, closing time, and outside Sole Bay was already dark. 'I'm ready to drop now, Dot. It's been a lot to take in.' She gathered up her bag and her laptop, from where they lounged by the shop door. That innocuous computer carrycase contained a ticking bomb which had plummeted, unannounced and unwelcome, into her email in-box two weeks ago. A whole fortnight of mustering her courage to read it had got her nowhere: Billie clearly had to work on her mustering skills. Glowing as if it contained kryptonite, the little computer taunted her: it knew she'd run out of excuses and that tonight, on the threshold of her Fresh Start, Billie would finally read *that* email. 'Do I reach the flat through the stockroom, or is there an outside entrance?'

'Flat?' Dot looked perturbed. 'What flat?'

This wasn't in the realm of expected answers, and Billie was thrown. '*The* flat,' she repeated stupidly. 'Upstairs.' Panic coughed and announced itself. 'Great Aunty Babs' flat. The one she said I could stay in.'

'Oh. Oh no.' Dot's distress gained momentum. 'Oh no no no no,' she wailed. 'Babs lives on the front, but she's let out her house to a German family. They'll be neat, she thought. There's no flat upstairs, just the stockroom. Unless Babs meant you could sleep on the camp bed.' Dot seemed unconvinced by her own theory. 'But it's all bent. And it's freezing at night. And a pigeon kind of lives up there.' She paused, before saying emotionally, 'And he's not been himself lately.'

9

'I get the picture.' Billie exhaled slowly. She'd misunderstood her aunt's written ramblings. 'Where's the nearest hotel? The nearest *cheap* hotel,' she added, aware of her purse's shortcomings. This setback was a blow, but Billie squared her shoulders. She could do this. She could drown out the family chorus of doubt and dread, she'd find a way to make this Fresh Start work. Anything, *anything*, was better than another evening watching her parents rehearse their latest amateur dramatic roles in *Chicago*: she would rather sleep in a wheelie bin than witness her mother's galumphing shimmy shake once more.

'You can stay with us!' The inspiration prompted Dot's widest grin yet. 'In Jake's cottage.'

'Oh, I couldn't . . .' Billie's fight was feeble. An artist's cottage sounded cute and comfy. And cheap. She imagined downy beds, an open fire, gentle conversation.

Practically jumping up and down in her Doc Martens, Dot insisted she could. 'Look! Here's Jake now!' she sang delightedly, as the door opened to admit a tall, lean man. She took his hand. 'He'll persuade you. Jake, meet Billie. She's going to stay with us for a while.'

Gangling, stooped and pale, Jake had babyish curls of translucent, somehow greenish, blond. His face was taut and guarded behind a surprising beard. Young men these days tend not to have beards. Perhaps, mused Billie, he kept budgies in it: it was certainly roomy enough.

Hooded eyes the colour of pondwater met Billie's and a bolt of antipathy so vehement that she half expected it to be visible crackled between them. Her decision was made. 'Honestly, it's fine. I'll go to a hotel. I don't want to be any trouble.'

'Tell her, Jakey.' Dot was evangelical now. 'We'd love to have her, wouldn't we?'

Still silent, Jake regarded Billie with rude frankness, as if she was a second-hand Ford Fiesta he considered overpriced. Dressed in an eclectic assortment of second-hand garments that would guarantee a fancy-dress first prize as The Artful Dodger (or The Pretentious Tosser), he pulled his military greatcoat around him and finally said, 'OK.'

'Please,' Billie tried not to beg. 'Just point me at a hotel.' This man smelled of cabbage and something told Billie that his cottage would have no downy beds. His beard appeared to be moving.

'No, no, you can have the spare room,' Dot insisted, leaning on her scarecrow-ish swain. 'As long as you don't mind sharing with Mrs Fluff.'

'Mrs . . . ?'

'Mrs Fluff. Our cat,' Dot enlightened her. 'Well, our baby, really.'

Next to cats, Billie's deepest dread was of cats that were babies 'really'. She sensed Jake's spare room creeping nearer, and she flailed, looking for escape. Help came from a surprising quarter.

'I know of a place you can stay.' Jake had an impressive assortment of speech impediments, and he spoke low, so that Billie had to lean in to hear. 'It's beautiful. It's free.' He paused. 'But you might be too narrow-minded and bourgeois to appreciate it.'

'Try me,' said Billie.

Two

Like Marmite and Barbra Streisand, beach huts divide people into two distinct camps. You either love them or you hate them.

Billie loathed Marmite and the way it made her breath smell of the undead; Ms Streisand's heavy-handed way with a ballad gave her the dry heaves; but she loved beach huts. She was mad about their cheerful décor, their dinky dimensions and their unabashed kiss-me-quick vulgarity.

Mind you, she'd never considered living in one before.

'You can't. I won't allow it.' As adamant as somebody who weighs less than a toddler can be, Dot was horrified. 'You'll never fit all your things in there.'

Hunched in the sleet-lashed dark of the March early evening outside the chalet, Billie jiggled the bag and laptop in her arms. '*This* constitutes my things.'

'Looks like you fled from a burning building,' said Jake under his breath.

Glancing sideways at him, Billie wondered if he had any notion how close to the truth he was. 'It's so pretty,' she murmured, taking in the jaunty blue and white stripes of the tiny hut, and the slope of its roof, and the geraniums on its abbreviated deck. 'Herbert's Dream II' announced the hand-painted nameplate: not for Great Aunty Babs the banality of 'Dun Roamin' or the whimsy of 'The Haven'. Who, wondered Billie, was Herbert? And what had he dreamed of, not once but twice? 'Herbert?' she queried, aloud.

'Oh, some ex-husband,' explained Dot, impatiently. 'The last one, or the second to last. He had a racehorse called Herbert's Dream, apparently.'

'Hence the two.' Billie nodded, satisfied.

'Never mind blinking Herbert, there's no electricity!' Dot was yelping. 'And no running water! You'd have to use the public loos!' She upped the cajoling when there was no change in Billie's smitten expression. 'What about a telly?' She attempted sternness, but it wasn't her forte: Dot's voice was calibrated for cooing at kittens. 'I never watch it, but I think you might.'

Ignoring the worrying questions Dot's certainty threw up about her mental resources, Billie bluffed, 'Going without television will be refreshing. I can read, and . . .' Actually, panicked Billie, what *would* she do without her *Corrie* chums, her *Sex and the City* gal pals and those irrepressible Eastenders with their cockney japes (incest, cocaine deals, gangland killings)? 'And, erm, embroider,' she claimed wildly, nimbly inventing a Victorian alter ego.

Scrabbling for inspiration, Dot found it close to hand. 'The hut is practically in the sea!'

That was the wrong argument to choose. 'Yes, it is, isn't it?' Billie unfurled a half smile. The line of huts sat where Sole Bay dwindled into the surf, at the foot of broad concrete steps leading down from the promenade. Only a few hundred yards of pebbly beach separated Herbert's Dream II from the North Sea. 'Practically in the sea,' repeated Billie dreamily. Scared of weddings but unafraid of sleeping with her feet in salt water, she told Dot and Jake, 'I've always loved the ocean,' as a cheeky breeze unravelled her hair like knotted knitting.

With a flourish, Dot played her trump card. 'It's illegal to live here,' she declared, arms folded against the insistent attentions of the wind. 'Babs' lease only allows daytime use. You could be arrested. And locked up.' She warmed to her theme. 'And you'd be in the papers. And you'd be—'

'Burned at the stake?' smiled Billie, whose decisiveness came in handy at times like this. 'I've made up my mind. Dot, I know you're looking out for me, but please don't worry.'

'But my gran's friends with the local bobby . . .' said Dot, miserably.

Jake spat, 'Pig lover,' and curled his lip.

Ignoring him, Billie slipped an arm around Dot's shoulders. 'This is my home for the time being. It'll be alright. Somehow.' She felt exhilarated, like the time she'd tried paragliding on holiday. Hopefully this venture wouldn't end with Billie crying and covered in jellyfish, trying to find the Greek for, 'Please remove this sea urchin from my bra.'

In lieu of the more traditional alarm clock, two gulls the size of spaniels woke Billie the next morning. Raucous as the dregs of a hen night, they swapped seabird gossip on the window sill.

Disoriented, Billie gripped the duvet as her ragged, drowsy thoughts rearranged themselves. She came to and realised that the gulls weren't monsters, and the duvet wasn't a duvet: it was a crochet blanket in toning shades of sludge donated the night before by Dot.

The sun bounced off the sea, in through the tiny uncurtained window to illuminate every corner of the whitewashed hut as brightly as a searchlight. Wincing in the glare, Billie made a mental note to organise curtains.

Swinging her legs out of the camp bed rescued from the stockroom, Billie found herself on her knees with the bed closing on her back, like a turtle. She made a mental note to organise a decent bed.

Ten more minutes prompted ten more mental notes. Billie's new home needed, in no particular order, somewhere to wash, somewhere to cook, somewhere to sit, and somewhere to stand and howl when the absurdity of it all got too much for her. She imagined her parents' reaction to her new address: the keening would be redoubled, and the prophecies of ruin and despair and dying alone without face-saving husband or mortgage would be trotted out. Unable to frown since her recent facelift, Nancy Baskerville would attempt one of those disturbing gurns that were intended to denote maternal disappointment but, thanks to Harley Street, suggested severe constipation. Shame, then, that Billie's mobile refused to work in the hut, and spreading the word would have to wait.

Scavenging a Bounty from her bag, which could usually be relied upon to supply an overlooked chocolate bar from its innards, Billie surveyed her home. The economical white wooden space was, at most, one Nigel by two Nigels. Nigel had been her first boyfriend, a dull fifteen-year-old, bad at kissing but obligingly good at insane jealousy. He'd been exactly six foot tall (most of it spots) and, ever since, Billie had found imagining a row of prostrate Nigels to be a handy way of calculating distance.

The beach hut was calm, it was cute, and the gentle shushing of the waves was a welcome substitute for the lupine howls of her mother 'getting into character' as Roxie Hart. Bare and white, the room suited Billie's state of mind. She was a clean page, waiting for life to scribble on her again. She had, Billie promised herself urgently, packed away the pain of the last few months for good. She would be sensible, careful, wise. She would *not* be – she recalled her family nickname – Batty Billie.

Stretching, her limbs felt looser. Perhaps it was Billie's imagination, but she chose to believe that the sea was already working its healing magic.

'It's basic,' Billie told the seagulls, as she locked the padlock of the door behind her. 'But it's mine.' She threw in an, 'All mine!' and a throaty horror-movie chuckle for good measure.

A door two huts down banged, and Billie jumped, suddenly remembering her fugitive status. Standing on the step of a pristine hut was a tall, fair man, his features blurred in the glare of the sun, and his white-blond hair glowing like a halo.

'He's seen me.' Billie tried to look nonchalant. She couldn't do Nonchalant very well, so she tried Cocky. When that, too, fell flat she opted for Furtive and scuttled up the steps. She looked back, shading her eyes with her hand. The man had gone.

Clear, watery sunshine drenched the small town of Sole Bay as Billie walked to work. The blues and whites and pinks and creams of the houses and shops suited this mild weather perfectly. Her four-minute meander through the awakening streets contrasted pleasingly with the sweaty commute she'd endured until two days previously. Struggling to secure a sticky velour seat on the bus, Billie had started every day in her snot-coloured suburb in a foul mood.

Today, though, Billie found herself nodding a cheery, 'Good morning!' to the people she passed. The town affected her that way, as if she'd been rinsed in the waves overnight, and woken up not as a grubby Londoner, with bad manners and a permafrown, but as an extra in a gentle black and white comedy of English country life.

Sole Bay was a place out of time. A genteel hand stopped the clocks in the 1950s: the idyllic photogenic 50s, when kindly shopkeepers slipped gobstoppers to kiddywinks, not those other horrid 1950s when pregnant teenagers were disowned and women weren't allowed orgasms in case it gave them fancy ideas.

No, Sole Bay was a pocket of charm and Englishness, the exact geographical equivalent of Margaret Rutherford. Its narrow streets veered off the cobbled main square at crazy, pre-town-planning angles, and Billie took a wrong turning or two before she discovered Little Row, where the shop waited for her.

Barbara's Brides squatted dead centre in a sedate strip of genteel, prosperous businesses. To the right was a proper butcher's, cool and dim with sawdust on the floor. A red-faced man in a striped apron, perfect casting for Kindly Butcher, winked at Billie as she glanced in. She tittered, and allowed herself a private preen, even though the butcher made her Gramps look hot. When a girl has been shrouded under dust sheets for the best part of a year, she appreciates any and all winks.

On the other side of her great-aunt's establishment was a picture-perfect sweet shop. Home-made fudge peeked out provocatively through the Georgian-style mullioned window. Its sugary charms weren't lost on Billie, who leered in like a lecher in a lingerie department.

'Sweet tooth?' asked a voice from the doorway. A chubby lady, somewhere between sixty and a thousand, stood in a floury apron sweeping her porch.

'Not really. Kind of.' Billie's sweet tooth, like her tendresse for Simon Cowell, wasn't something she readily admitted to, despite the fact she'd once had an out-of-body experience by the Pick 'n' Mix.

'Taste that.' A cube of fudge was produced from the woman's pinny pocket and held out between sugared fingers. 'Just made it. New recipe.' Her hair was Elvis black, although the style owed more to the Bride of Frankenstein.

Billie made an entirely new sound: vowel-less and fruity, it was impossible to translate but denoted dangerous levels of bliss.

'You the great-niece?' Billie's new neighbour looked her slowly up and down, not unkindly.

'No secrets in this town, are there?' laughed Billie.

'You'd be surprised.' The woman didn't laugh. Her round face was doughy, and her eyes were like two raisins sunk in it. Raisins don't usually glitter, but these two certainly did. 'Nowt like Babs, are you?'

'Not really.' Billie shrugged apologetically. 'Sorry.' She held out her hand. 'I'm Billie.'

The woman took her hand and shook it heartily. 'Zelda,' she said, sucking another piece of fudge. Her sweeping resumed. The interview was evidently terminated, for Zelda had started to sing to herself, a falsetto, East Country-accented version of 'Don't Cha Wish Your Girlfriend Was Hot Like Me?'

The handwritten 'Clossed' sign was still showing on Barbara's Brides' door. Billie had a quick game of push-me-pull-you with the big rusty key in the old lock, before falling in and wading through the pizza delivery leaflets, invitations to take out a nought-per-cent credit card, and a pamphlet for a donkey sanctuary addressed to Dot. Righting herself, Billie switched on the lights, noting how little impact they made on the soupy gloom at the back of the shop.

Swinging her laptop up on to the counter, Billie unzipped it slowly. She'd run out of excuses. The lack of electricity in Herbert's Dream II had given her a reprieve for the night, but it really, truly, honestly was time to confront her email.

'Morning!' Dot, all bangles and hemp, clattered in on rainbow-coloured clogs.

'Morning,' echoed Billie. Tucking away the laptop, she told herself piously that she needed privacy to read the email.

'Your crash course in wedding-dress shoppery starts here,' beamed Dot, as she held up one forefinger. Slowly, she pressed down on the switch of an ancient radio on a high shelf. 'East Coast FM. Always on in the background,' she explained, as a Beatles track tinnily filled the room.

'Right.' Billie nodded. She nodded again when Dot picked up the kettle and filled it sl-o-wly from the tap, as if Billie might have been new to the complex world of the cuppa. She nodded again when Dot held up a tea bag, displayed it from all angles,

17

and then placed it in a chipped mug with all the care of a bomb disposal expert.

It was going to be a long day. Remembering to nod and say 'Got it' at intervals, Billie's mind wandered as Dot pottered about, putting the change (and the mouse) in the till, primping the tired stock and waking the shop up for the day ahead. Rescuing Great Aunty Babs' letter from under the stratum of make-up, mobile, magazines and sweet wrappers in her bag, Billie looked it over again.

The letter had arrived out of the blue. Kept apart by her mother's disapproval, Billie and her great-aunt hadn't met for ten years. Postcards had been exchanged, and Billie could rely on her birthday cheque for two pounds and fifty pee, but this chatty, intimate letter had been a surprise.

'*I'm being very cheeky,*' Great Aunty Babs had written in her meandering hand. '*But if you cud take some time out of your bizy life to help me, I'd be so greatfull.*'

'Bizy.' Huh. How Billie had snorted the first time she'd read that at her desk in the telesales office. Since last summer Billie's bizy life had been one long round of banging her head against the wall trying to forget last summer, to a backdrop of her mother's suggestions that she go on a diet, try Botox, buy a smart raincoat.

To earn some running-away money, Billie had taken a job so dull that a letter from an OAP counted as kicks: she flogged double-glazed conservatories over the phone, extolling their virtues from a laminated list as if they were the Taj Mahal rather than glorified lean-tos.

By contrast, her great-aunt's life had sounded packed. '*I long to meet an Australian gent I have been corisponding with,*' Great Aunty Babs had explained, the girlish breathlessness leaping off the page. '*I have high hopes of Colin, so I may stey for six months,*' Great Aunty Babs' vagueness was the stuff of Baskerville family legend. '*Or longer. Or less. Or forever. Cud you help me out and look after the shop? I can pey you, and you'll have a free hand with any improovments. Your the boss! If you say yes, it would be a lifeline.*' She'd underlined that last word three times.

Does a lifeline work if there's someone pulling at both ends?

Suddenly the A5 Basildon Bond had morphed into Billie's passport to her Fresh Start.

Trapped in uncharted suburbia, wearing a telephone headset straight out of *Star Trek* in an air-conditioned, fluorescent-lit box with carpet tiles on the walls, Billie had yearned for beauty. And adventure. And a reason to get out of bed in the morning.

Folding the letter into its well-worn creases, Billie looked out at Little Row as Dot handed her a cup of tea. Perhaps this windswept, sun-tickled, generous little town was offering her all these things.

'It's time we dressed that poor bint in the window,' said Billie decisively, taking her first step as fledgling manageress.

'Okey-dokey.' Dot stepped up into the window display. 'What shall we put her in? A nice shepherdess gown?'

There's no such thing as a nice shepherdess gown, but Billie kept her heresy to herself, and plucked a simple white nylon shift off the rails. Just carrying it across the shop floor made her hair stand on end; it could easily combust during the first dance. 'Let's try this.' She clambered up beside Dot, and they began to dress the naked mannequin.

The dummy fought back. Those long hard fingers were vicious. 'Now!' gasped Billie, holding back the harpy for Dot to push its arm through a sleeve.

Pulling the arm off, Dot staggered backwards, ploughing into a pyramid of confetti boxes.

'This means war!' Billie was quite enjoying the fray, but the ting of the bell above the door stopped all the action in the window.

A heavy-hipped, middle-aged woman with a perm was grinning coyly up at them. Knowing that paying customers were rarer than guitar-playing chickens, Billie smiled back, then looked to Dot, who looked right back at her.

'Your customer, Miss Billie,' she said gently, a faint challenge in her blue eyes.

'Of course, Miss Dot.' Taking up the gauntlet, Billie clambered, heavy-footed, out of the tangle of limbs in the window. 'How can I help?'

'I'm getting married!' the woman told her, unnecessarily. 'Look.' She waggled a diamond the size of a distant full stop at Billie. 'Me! Imagine.'

'Congratulations,' said Billie. From her lips it sounded ever so slightly like 'Condolences': her allergies would have to be overcome if she was to make a go of Barbara's Brides. She shot a look at Dot for support, but she was sitting in the debris of the window reading a leaflet about a hedgehog hospital. 'When's the big day?' This seemed like a sensible, practical question.

'As soon as I can get over there.' The woman paused for effect, before saying in a determinedly casual way, 'He's from the States, you see.' She paused again. 'He's American.'

'Yes. I suppose he would be.' Selling wedding dresses might not be as straightforward as Billie had hoped. 'Any idea which style you're after?' she asked, hoping that the customer preferred the dated, the hideous or the downright Barbara Cartland, as that was all the shop had to offer. When her question provoked a blank, almost scared, response, Billie suggested helpfully, 'What kind of dress does your fiancé like to see you in?'

'Oh, he's never seen me.'

'But . . .' Billie flashed a look at Dot: engrossed in her leaflet, she seemed to be crying. 'Then, how . . .'

'We met on the internet.' Eager to chat, the woman leaned her elbows on the counter. 'I knew immediately he was the one. I've written to other men on Death Row but none were as sensitive, as thoughtful, as interested in *Emmerdale* as him.'

'Death . . .' Billie had lost the knack of ending her sentences.

'Yes. Maybe you've heard of him?' Animated with pride, the bride-to-be said encouragingly, 'The Mississippi Mutilator? I just call him Len.' She looked wistfully into the middle distance for a moment. 'My Len.'

After a surreal half-hour, the bride-to-be bounced off in her stretch denims carrying a magnolia terylene drop waist that fitted her like a (rather nasty) glove and needed no alteration, and a surprisingly pretty diamanté headdress.

As the door clanged shut, Billie punched the air. She'd made her first sale. And to a serial killer's fiancée. She swivelled round to Dot. 'Have you ever heard anything like it?' she gasped. 'I could hardly believe it.'

'Me neither,' sniffled Dot, dabbing at her eyes. She held up a picture of a hedgehog with a plaster on its snout. 'All the suffering in this crazy old world of ours.'

Billie frowned at Dot. For quite a long time. Perhaps there was something in the Sole Bay water supply. Perhaps soon Billie would date mass murderers, and sob over pictures of under-the-weather woodland creatures.

Perhaps she'd even learn to love weddings.

Nah.

Three

It was an anniversary of sorts. A whole week had passed since Billie had jumped feet first into the world of weddings. A celebratory pasty had been bought from Mr Dyke the butcher to mark the occasion in the best possible way.

'He makes a mean pasty, that Mr Dyke,' mumbled Billie through greasy lips.

Watching her sorrowfully, her vegeterian assistant – who apologised to quark before eating it – said, 'There's been a Dyke in Sole Bay for generations. This town is built on Dykes.' If she was aware of her pile-up of double entendres, she didn't show it. 'You can trust a Dyke.'

'Indeed,' giggled Billie, whose tastes in food and humour were similarly lowbrow.

'Although,' began Dot, in an undertone, lips pursed, 'he is a bit of a one.'

'A one?'

'A *one*,' said Dot, suggestively. 'Kept a few beds warm over the years, according to my gran.'

'The butcher?' Billie was incredulous. 'But he's got ruddy cheeks and a round tummy and a handlebar moustache.'

'He's a beast,' whispered Dot, emphatically.

'He's a cute old fella.'

'He's a hound. Had everyone. *Everyone*.'

'But . . .' Billie wasn't sure she wanted to hear this about her cosy new town. 'He's married.'

'Poor Zelda had—' Dot peered out of the door and lowered her voice when she realised that Zelda was outside, washing her shop windows and warbling 'Smack My Bitch Up'. 'Poor Zelda had her heart broken by him years ago. Nobody knows exactly what happened, but people say that's why she's the way

22

she is.' Dot shook her head sadly. 'She's been driven wild with sexual jealousy.'

Billie had to protest. 'Zelda? She wears surgical stockings!'

'Evidently, they are no barrier to passion,' said Dot, sagely.

'I don't know if I can look his meat in the face again,' sighed Billie.

And there the double entendres ended for the time being, as Billie's mobile chirped at her from across the room.

Temperamental as a coked-up supermodel, and similarly picky about where it deigned to work, Billie's phone didn't like the reception in Herbert's Dream II, in the front of the shop, the back of the shop, the yard, the stockroom or the street. Apparently it *did* like the reception where it sat, balanced on a pile of 1980s bridal magazines.

'Oh. *You*.' Ashamed at her own disloyalty, Billie was reluctant to pick up when she read her caller ID. Blood is thicker than pasty, however, so she pressed a button and said a cheery, 'Hi, big bro.' It was advisable to sound cheery around Sly: he homed in on misery like a cruising vulture and liked to pick it apart. At length.

'Sis,' cooed her brother in the silky, would-I-lie-to-you tone he'd cultivated since setting himself up as a motivational guru. 'I'm worried about you.'

This was a standard opener. Sly claimed to worry about everybody, from his nearest and dearest to bus conductors. Billie had long ago rumbled his global concern as an expert way of opening people up. Opening people up was a vital part of Sly's trade. 'Why?' she asked, dripping innocence. 'I'm fine.'

'Mum and Dad are worried, too.'

That meant that Mum was worried – very vocally – and that Dad had nodded over the top of his newspaper. 'I called her last night and told her everything was great.' Billie's teeth were starting to grit of their own accord.

'She tells me you're living in a shed?' Sly sounded baffled, like a *Daily Mail* subscriber encountering a Goth. 'You can understand why we're worried.' Billie could almost hear him cocking his head to one side, a considerate, yet wise, Labrador. 'Are things really that bad?'

No, Billie longed to yell. *They're that good!* 'It's not a shed, it's a beach hut, er, house, kind of thing.' She could have told her brother that she felt liberated and feather-light, that she was sleeping well for the first time in a long time, that feeling was returning to various numb parts of her. Billie didn't tell him any of these things, because she couldn't find words he would accept. Perhaps they weren't minted yet. She contented herself with, 'I'm enjoying myself, honest.'

'So you're going ahead with this whole shop stunt?'

Stiffening, Billie launched into what she could remember of her yoga breathing. (She'd only gone to one lesson, scared off by the sight of so many leotards.) She threw back her shoulders: conversations with Sly left her hunched like a Grimms' fairy-tale witch. 'Yup.' Years of deference to her older brother, the Goldenballs of the Baskervilles, meant she could never defend herself properly. Why, she longed to ask, was it a *stunt*? Why the contemptuous language?

'Are you sure it's healthy?' Healthy was one of Sly's professional buzzwords, along with 'nourishing', 'positive', and 'major credit cards accepted'. 'With your unfortunate history?'

'Yup.'

'Mum tells me the shop is a mouldy old dump off the beaten track.'

Unable to argue with that, Billie simply said, 'Well, I like it.' Then she surprised herself by saying, 'It feels like home.' She glanced across at Dot, who was up a ladder rearranging garters on a high shelf. Dot wrinkled her nose down at her.

'I'm coming up to the back of beyond to see for myself,' announced Sly. He announced everything, like a newsreader.

'It's not the back of beyond,' protested Billie. 'It's got a Tesco Metro.'

'Hey! Does your shop have a workforce?' asked Sly, as if inspiration had struck.

'It's got a Dot, if that's what you mean.'

'Tip top. We'll hold an Inner Winner (trademark applied for) seminar!'

'Noooo!' Billie reacted as if her brother had offered her a nice cup of sick.

'It's on the house, don't worry,' said Sly, magnanimously.

'My seminars are proven to improve productivity one thousand per cent.'

One thousand per cent of almost nowt is still pretty small, but Billie managed a weak, 'Thank you,' because she was that kind of girl.

'No need to thank me. What are families for?'

Billie braced herself. One of Sly's aphorisms was galloping towards her.

'They're forever.' Sly made sure his smile was audible. '(Copyright applied for.) Bye.'

Stepping daintily down from the ladder with dust in her fringe, Dot said in a gentle voice, 'You look ever so churned up. Shall I make you a cup of chamomile tea? Or perhaps you'd like to cuddle Jenkins for a while?'

'Not really.' Billie had sneaked a good look at Dot's mouse: he only had one ear and his tail was frayed. 'Thanks, though,' she added hastily, busying herself with tidying the dog-eared magazines as she slowly came off the boil.

Families in books or on television 'supported' each other. They 'were there' for each other, they were 'what life is all about'. Why, then, did any contact with Billie's kin make her feel as clenched as a handknit emerging from a boil wash? It had been impossible to express herself to Sly, as if somebody had nipped in and neatly gagged her while she was on the phone.

The anger Billie felt was ugly, and unwelcome, and had to find an outlet more appropriate than slamming out-of-date magazines on top of one another. A killing spree in Sole Bay would only annoy her new neighbours, so instead she reverted to the yoga breathing, which led to a protracted coughing fit. Dot slapped her heartily on the back, which was far more uncomfortable than the coughing fit, but as the dowdy shop swam back into focus, a new determination sharpened up as well.

Billie would show them. She'd make a go of this. More than a go of it, she'd make a success of Barbara's Brides. Her mother and her father and her brother would have to admit that, for once, Billie had done them proud. In her mind's eye, as she stood sipping the water Dot forced anxiously on her, Billie was starring in a miniseries about the struggle of one dynamic, beautiful woman to build an empire of groundbreaking wedding-dress shops: her wardrobe was by Stella McCartney and her face was borrowed from Sienna Miller.

More realistically, a lower-key plan was crystallising: its midwife was Sly's disapproval. Too nervous to share her schemes with Dot just yet, Billie finished her water and stared out of the window.

Immediately, she wished she hadn't. Staring right back at her was a tall man, his legs superlong in black jeans and his hands stuck in the pockets of his leather jacket.

Hastily transferring her gaze to a damaged thong reduced to sixteen pence (and still overpriced), Billie shivered. He was the guy who'd spotted her that very first morning, who'd ensured that she now nipped up and down the steps to Herbert's Dream II like a lumpen cat burglar. She dared a glance out of the window.

He'd gone. But the fear he'd provoked lingered. That tall, blond man had the power to have her evicted from her niche. His eyes, she couldn't help noticing, had been blue. *Very* blue. Beautifully blue, some might say, if they weren't scared shitless by them.

Two more pounds were dropped into the tin allocated for Annie's fund. Once again she politely refused tea, and seemed terribly embarrassed by Billie's attempts to chat about the improving weather, looking this way and that as if searching for an escape.

After she left, in her dignified shabby coat and clutching one of those massive handbags elderly ladies wield like shields, Billie said approvingly, 'What a nice old girl.'

'Huh!' Zelda's sour honk from the corner startled Billie. She hadn't seen her neighbour come in, nor heard the shop bell. 'Why do old people have to be *nice*? Nobody expects youngsters to be nice,' she cawed, one false fingernail toying with a lock of unlikely black hair. 'I was never nice, and I don't intend to take it up now.'

Smiling indulgently, Dot insisted, 'Oh you *are* nice, Zelda. You're lovely.'

Who, Billie wondered, would be considered less than lovely in Dot's universe? Jack the Ripper? Vlad the Impaler? Or would Dot argue that they were misunderstood and needed a cuddle? 'We like you just the way you are, Zelda,' she laughed. Zelda was omnipresent, like God and Lulu, as much a part of the fixtures and fittings of Barbara's Brides as the flammable dresses.

'How's that Jake treating you, darlin'?' Zelda asked Dot.

'You know Jake,' answered Dot dreamily.

'That's why I'm asking,' growled Zelda. 'If he doesn't do right by you . . .' She left her sentence unfinished, but managed to induce visions of mediaeval martyrs being boiled alive in oil in Billie's mind. Zelda's attention was diverted, suddenly, like a cat being distracted by a sweet wrapper dangling on a piece of string. 'Hey! You!' she shouted, darting into the street. 'MANEATER!' she howled, at the slowly disappearing back of an anorak on a shaky mobility vehicle.

The door shuddered shut behind Zelda, and Billie looked over at Dot, who, as usual, had light to shed.

'A love rival,' she explained. 'Mrs Davis has been linked with Mr Dyke in the past.'

'A love rival on a mobility vehicle . . .' Billie turned the notion this way and that.

'It's NFSB,' said Dot. She paused, before elucidating. 'Normal for Sole Bay.'

Surprising herself, Billie shadowed Dot, greedily hoovering up every detail of running Barbara's Brides. Such motivation was new to Billie. Back at the telesales office she'd always been the last back from lunch, Quavers shards down her front, and the first to sprint through the door on the stroke of five.

She knew why she was so keen. The reason was the only thing that had ever motivated Billie: love. Billie was in love with this neglected old treasure and had stopped trying to talk herself out of it. Her feeling for the shop was the rocket fuel for her new plans, plans she still hadn't shared with Dot.

Billie's fears that nobody ever crossed the threshold were unfounded. Locals popped in all the time. They chatted, they drank tea, they doled out home-made biscuits, they sat on and creased the stock, they drew moustaches on the brides in the magazines. Almost the only activity they didn't indulge in was buying.

Dot trotted through the rudiments of bookkeeping, which involved handwriting receipts, skewering them on a spike and then losing the spike. Filing was confusing. 'Why,' asked Billie, 'are the water rates under T?'

'T for taps,' explained Dot, kindly, as if dealing with a simpleton.

'Of course.'

The last stocktake had been in 1999. Filed under D for Dresses, it made chilling reading. Only forty gowns had been sold in the intervening years.

The two plump ladies who did the alterations dropped in with some undercooked flapjacks, to tell Billie how much they disapproved of Great Aunty Babs' practice of holding a sizable stock of ready-to-wear dresses for the last-minute or impatient bride, an idea which struck Billie as unusually sensible.

She was less impressed with the 'fibbing tape', a special tape measure for the larger customer, which took two inches off all vital statistics. 'That's treating women like silly girlies,' protested Billie.

'We're protecting them,' corrected Dot, placidly.

'Who says they need protecting? If they ate the cakes they can face up to the inches. Why does everybody assume that women's brains dribble out of their ears the moment a wedding is mentioned?' Billie harrumphed, pushing the fibbing tape to the back of a drawer. 'Perfect weddings are just another stress, another impossible ideal that we can't live up to.'

'Well, I love weddings,' said Dot, happily.

The half smile told Billie that Dot couldn't quite believe her, as if deep down anybody with half an ovary felt the tug of the aisle. 'I loathe them,' she said, emphatically. 'Weddings are an evil scam, designed to shackle you forever to some git you met at a nightclub.' She sped up, warming to her theme, perhaps goaded by Dot's look of horror. 'I mean, why should we change our surnames? Don't women's surnames matter? Why do we agree to lose a third of our body weight and truss ourselves up in white lace? Why do we put ourselves into debt so that uncles we've never met can cruise the buffet in a stripey marquee?

When did love become big business? What's so bloody special about a white dress anyway?'

'Right. OK.' Dot cowered, busying herself with a partner-less, elbow-length glove. She seemed at a loss for what to say. 'So you really don't like weddings, then?' she said, eventually.

'No.' Billie, ashamed for dumping such vitriol at Dot's clogs, apologised. 'Sorry, Dot. That rant sounded very bitter. Ignore me.'

'I reckon you'll give in and get married,' persevered Dot. She was, Billie had come to realise, a persevering perseverer. 'One day. Bet you.'

'I promise that if I ever get married I will hand you a million pounds.' Billie knew her future earnings were safe. 'In cash.'

'Ooooh!' beamed Dot, as gleeful as if the money was already in the bank. 'I'll open a badger sanctuary!'

Marvelling at the differing ways to blow a million – Billie's own dream scenario involved a sports car, a mews house and a forthright offer for a few hours of George Clooney's down time – Billie began to listlessly rearrange a rail of squeaky man-made fabric dresses. One stood out as a real Babs special. It was a nightmare of ruffles and bows and flounces and frills. Billie had never used the word 'furbelows' before, but she suspected there might be one on this dress. 'Look at the state of this,' she laughed, holding it against her for Dot to see.

Usually reliable for a giggle, Dot was straight-faced. 'Can you honestly say,' asked Dot, gazing penetratingly at her boss, 'that you've never even fantasised about what you'd wear at your own wedding?'

'Well . . .' Billie shoved the hanger back on the rail. Perhaps it was time for Billie to tell Dot her story. *The* Story. The one that defined her these days, much as she kicked against that fact. 'I didn't just fantasise.'

'You had a wedding!' Dot squawked, straightening up. 'But you said . . .'

'I said I'm single.' Billie straightened the pleats on an obnox-ious number in off-white velveteen.

'So . . .' Dot trod carefully, a pained look on her face as she groped her way along the facts, reminding Billie of her grand-mother watching *CSI*. 'So, you're divorced?'

'Nope. The Story's better than that.' Billie conjured up a pallid smile. 'Pin back your ears. This is a classic,' she said ruefully. 'My wedding day went like clockwork, Dot.'

Dot gasped. She really was an excellent audience.

'The twenty-third of August last year. A Thursday. James's parents' anniversary. A soppy touch. Very James. There was a bit of moaning from the guests about having to take a day off work. Our local church was garlanded with lilac and white flowers. The wedding had a theme, see. Lilac and white.' Billie shook her head, amazed that she was capable of having not only a wedding, but one with a theme. 'It looked stunning. My mother's new facelift hadn't quite settled down – she still looked mildly startled at all times – but she looked stunning, too. And, somehow, so did I,' said Billie wonderingly, remembering her reflection in the long mirror of her five-star hotel suite. 'God knows how, but the make-up artist had somehow given me new skin. I'd lost pounds to get into a vicious brocade monster of a dress that laced up the back and cut off my breathing, but took years of sitting on my bum off my bum.'

Billie sank into the rickety chair. 'My dad's speech had been edited down to forty minutes, and we'd persuaded him to ditch the slide show and most of the Venn diagrams. The bridesmaids were overexcited. My brother was ushering for all he was worth. Only one detail fell short of the required perfection.' She turned a grubby veil over and over in her hands. 'No groom.'

'He jilted you!' Dot put a hand to her mouth, as if she was watching a horror film. 'At the altar?'

'Not quite. It doesn't even qualify as your archetypal jilt.' Billie attempted a laugh, but it came out as more of a Jenkins-style squeak. 'There was a note, just before we were due to leave for the church. Cold feet, all the way up to the neck. No real reasons, just excuses. And a few accusations. None of them founded on anything. But there was a desire to run, to be free, between every line. All of a sudden it was as if we'd never been in love at all.' Billie's brightened expression wouldn't fool a cat, let alone a sensitive soul like Dot. 'All for the best really. I mean, if a person can do that to you, they're not really marriage material, are they?'

Dot wasn't reflecting the change in tone. The poor girl looked fresh from a screening of *Bambi*. 'Now I get it,' she said softly.

'Weddings are just a con, a charade, an excuse to part gullible lovebirds from their money.' Billie tossed the veil into the air for punctuation, and it spiralled slowly to the brown floor-boards as Dot had the last word.

'If you really believed that,' she said carefully, as if exploring a patch of Sole Bay studded with landmines, 'you wouldn't love this place as much as you do.'

Shutting up shop, Billie gingerly shooed Zelda's cat from her porch. A malignant black bathmat, the grumpy feline boasted a catalogue of ailments that included ticks, scurvy, rickets and the odd phantom pregnancy, which was rare in a tomcat. Dot referred to him as 'courageous', or 'an old trooper', but Billie preferred 'smelly' as a catch-all description.

Raven, who didn't take kindly to being shooed, glared up at Billie with glowing orange eyes, and stayed where he was.

'OFF!' shouted Billie, refusing to be bested by what looked like an abandoned hat. Eventually, she stepped over him, glowering down. 'Who do you think you are?' she hissed at him.

The look that Raven gave her suggested that he knew exactly who he was, thank you, and what's more, he knew all about *her*. Billie couldn't quell the foolish thought that Raven knew what a coward she was. Somehow, the flat-faced cat knew that once again, she had carefully put away her laptop without reading James's email.

Four

Like a bemused victim of Trinny and Susannah, Herbert's Dream II had been made over. A fortnight had transformed him from a drab bachelor to a jaunty hut-about-town.

The entire innards had been painted with a job lot of brilliant white. A blitz on Sole Bay's charity shops has furnished it with change from a twenty-pound note. Arranging a mishmash of striped and flowery cushions on her new, narrow but comfortable, wrought-iron bed, Billie thanked God for the out-of-touch matrons who ran charity shops: they had never heard of shabby chic and priced accordingly.

The challenge was to shoehorn in mod cons without obliterating Herbert's seaside-y charms. A 'rescued' deckchair was recovered in chintz. A second-hand camp table, fresh from a career of facilitating OAP picnics in lay-bys, supported a camp stove. Beneath the table sat a washing-up bowl and a washing-Billie bowl, their bright colours contrasting cheerily with the gingham curtains Dot had run up.

Billie's scant collection of clothes hung around the walls on hooks, Shaker style. Or can't-afford-a-wardrobe style. Her jeans were spreadeagled by the door, and a smock dangled over the deckchair.

A water container squatted alongside the table. Filling it from the communal tap was a chore that Billie had come to dread. Hobbling back over the pebbles, the container banging against her shins, she imagined bystanders doing double takes and hissing, Sherlock Holmes-like, 'Hold hard! Isn't that a mighty large receptacle for an individual permitted to use the premises for recreational purposes only?' That container was a pitiless tyrant, and the fraught, bruising forays to the standpipe punctuated Billie's schedule the way reality shows once had.

Battery-operated lanterns slung from the beams cast a

forgiving amber light over Billie as she read herself to sleep each night, from her new library of second-hand books. Fear of encountering a bogey on each page couldn't spoil the contrasting delights of Jane Austen and Jackie Collins.

Now that she had a modicum of comfort (cross-legged midnight scampers to the public loos aside), Billie relished returning to her kooky little haven after a day of toil at the Barbara's Brides coalface. Two weeks into her Fresh Start, she was still comparing her journey home through Sole Bay with the assault-course commute back at her parents'. She had swapped a dark walk home along deserted streets, looking over her shoulder and imagining burly ne'er-do-wells in the bushes, for a trot past candy-coloured house fronts, guided by the swishing petticoats of the sea. Lights came on in the houses as she passed them, painting small square patches of pavement, as the lighthouse further down the coast swept its paternal gaze over them all every few seconds.

Reaching the broad steps that led down to the darkness of the beach, Billie looked left and right, studiously casual and screamingly obvious. With scant acting skills inherited from her mother, Billie minced down the first two steps as if she didn't have a care in the world, then broke into a gallop on the second two.

After a brief tussle with the padlock, Billie was in, and soon the kettle was whistling unselfconsciously, unaware of its criminal status. Observing all her homecoming rituals, she switched on the lanterns, turned on East Coast FM and clambered into her pyjamas. The evening phone-in about a recent report that caravans cause cancer swirled about the hut unheard as Billie lay back on her charity cushions with a soothing mint tea to contemplate her bedtime reading.

No Regency coyness or bonkbuster knicker-ripping tonight. Billie had sought out Sole Bay's library earlier in the day and, after making Annie jump out of her zip-up tartan boots with a whispered 'Hello!' in the romance section, had used the facilities to print out James's email.

Even the most dedicated coward has to give in and face the music sometime. Billie was a noted coward, her craft honed through long years forging notes for the PE teacher (her periods were eligible for the *Guinness Book of World Records*), telling boyfriends it wasn't them it was her (even though it was *definitely* them), reassuring her mother she didn't look too old at fifty-eight to play Sandy in *Grease*, and avoiding her rear view in those cruelly comprehensive movable mirrors shops see fit to install in their changing rooms these days. But that was the old Billie.

The new, businesslike model faced up to things. Folded in her hand, the printed-out email looked innocuous. It could have been a shopping list, or a note to say, 'GONE TO BINGO. YOUR DINNER'S IN THE DOG.'

Opening it, she winced. The title in the subject box was 'Sorry'. Just a short word, but it towered over Billie like Ayers Rock. A 'sorry' email usually arrived when somebody had to cancel lunch, or they'd lost the tattered Marian Keyes she'd lent them: it couldn't begin to cover what had gone on between Billie and James.

Billie was nonplussed, and she much preferred being plussed. With a tiny mew she dipped her toe in the freezing water.

> Hi there. How's tricks? Long time no see!

Billie reread that first line. James was addressing her as if they'd once attended an Esperanto evening class together. She swallowed. The 'sorry' of the title turned out to be punily anti-climactic:

> Sorry I haven't been in touch!

'Eh?' thought Billie, dumbly. Of course he hadn't been 'in touch'. The break-up had been bloodier than *The Texas Chainsaw Massacre*. Those exclamation marks made her pout. James loathed them, yet here he was scattering them willy-nilly. Billie read on, the suspicion dawning that her ex-fiancé had swapped his sober, accountant's personality with a surfer dude.

> I've joined a gym! Yes, me! I pump iron and feel the pain and generally make a tit of myself on all the scary expensive equipment. Afterwards I go for a curry and down a few beers – that's what you're meant to do, isn't it?!

Here the slew of exclamation marks abruptly stopped. Perhaps there was a hole in the bottom of James's exclamation-mark bag.

> I've got a new job. Won't bother telling you about it because it's every bit as boring as my last job, and your eyes used to glaze over whenever I used the word 'work'. I get more money and a comfier chair and the post boy thinks I'm important, so that's good enough for me. *Still* haven't got around to fixing the boiler – the shower continues to belch out five seconds of boiling water, before going stone cold. *Still* haven't gone to New York. But I did get to the Isle of Wight for a mini-break. Does that count?
> And you? Still flogging conservatories? Can't see that somehow . . . How are your folks? Still crazy as ever, bless them?

Bless them? James had never, ever blessed her family. Neither had he used the word 'crazy' about them in a jocular, gosh-aren't-they-funny way: he'd used it in a perfectly serious, can't-we-get-them-looked-at way.

> Are you still reading this? Hope so. I've got this mental image of you brandishing a crucifix at the screen and bellowing 'BEGONE SATAN'. It's taken me weeks to pluck up the courage to write this, and you've probably (very sensibly) deleted it without reading it. So I'm languishing in your wastebin icon, along with all the spam emails from strangely named folk offering you Viagra or a foolproof way to become a millionaire by sending all your money to Nairobi. Oh well. You thought I was quite nice once. And I rather liked you. The odd email can't hurt. Can it?
> James

Like one of her experimental stir-fries, that email took a while to digest. Newsy and breezy, it didn't do justice to what they'd been through together. It was as if Hitler had texted Churchill to suggest nipping out for a pint.

Restless, Billie wrapped herself in one of her knitted blankets and wandered outside. Her bottom insulated by an ancient cushion, she sank on to the pebbles. The sea would make things better. The sea always made things better.

Billie stared back at the town. Lights showed behind curtains where stable people with normal lives sat down to blameless dinners. And here I am sitting in the dark, she thought raggedly.

Even with a gun to her head, Billie could never, ever compose an email like that to James. The James-shaped box in her head was bulging and messy, with a warning not to open until 2048. Their almost-wedding day had bent her out of shape, transforming James into a not-actual-size presence in her life. When his name was mentioned she blinked and twitched as if she had Tourette's of the heart. She never wanted to see him again, never wanted to reprise that particular and peculiar pain. In a strange way this distaste showed James the appropriate respect: it was the only possible response to the magnitude of their shared drama.

James was evidently made of sterner, or weirder, stuff. He was over her. He could talk to her as if she was a nice girl he'd once known, not somebody he'd last glimpsed on the deck of their very own *Titanic*. No doubt he saw her as a blip in an otherwise successful life.

Billie didn't relish being a blip. She turned needily to the sea, gazing out at the darkness, the slide show in her head supplying the light and colours.

He was laughing at her. Even from this distance she could tell. That tall, yellow-haired bloke was laughing at her from the deck of his beach hut as he leaned his lanky frame against it.

He knew. He definitely knew. Hair dishevelled, heart pumping, Billie tore up the steps and plunged into the warren of streets that made up Sole Bay. One phone call to the council and her Fresh Start could be thrown off course. Her lonely vigil on the beach last night had made her more, not less, determined to keep on track. She would trundle on until James was a speck in the distance, a small landmark on an outdated map.

She risked a look back. Shit. He was still looking. And laughing. He was certainly handsome. She'd never gone for that peroxidey, punky look, though. Just as well. It wouldn't do to fancy your nemesis.

Passing the pock-marked market cross Billie half smiled. She had a nemesis. It felt rather glamorous.

Billie was early, but Dot was even earlier. They kept the 'Clossed' sign up as they supped their instant choco-crappo-low-cal drinks that tasted of dust.

'Fancy joining us for Sunday lunch?' Dot's even little teeth flashed over her mug.

The correct answer, given Jake's inevitable involvement, was 'No' or perhaps even 'Dear God, NO!' but Billie was well brought up and managed, 'I'd love to.' She was interrupted by a loud banging on the locked door. 'Oh Gawd,' she muttered, quickly turning away from the rough-looking teenager rapping angrily on the glass. 'I don't like the look of that one. Ignore her.'

Already halfway across the shop, Dot was saying delightedly, 'It's our Debs!' and then the furious girl was in.

'Where's Babs?' The newcomer was a formidable sight, her cannily bright eyes slanted into half-moons by the pull of her vicious ponytail, and her meaty legs grazed by her stonewash denim mini. 'And 'oo the fuck is she?' She pointed a growing-out nail extension at Billie, who shrank slightly, like a slug who's been threatened with the salt cellar.

Dot told her, 'That's our lovely Billie,' regarding the girl with misty fondness as if she was the local lady vicar and not one of the scariest examples of British girlhood that Billie had seen since she'd last witnessed a fight in a pub car park. 'Babs has gone away for a while. This is her great-niece.'

Something in those coldly analytical eyes told Billie that Debs didn't think Billie was all that great. 'Are you a . . . past customer?' Billie sounded doubtful. Not only were Babs' customers an endangered species but this nose-studded Amazon didn't seem the marrying kind.

'You what? I'm your fucking Saturday girl, you gibbon.'

The gibbon was taken aback. 'But I don't have a . . .' She noticed Dot's freckles darkening in a blush. 'Ah. I do. And it's *you*,' she finished, dragging up the end of the sentence and the corners of her mouth. She felt like a new prisoner being introduced to the lifer who ran her cell block. Extra-careful politeness seemed the best way to handle somebody so large and so malevolent. 'Brilliant! Great! Glad to have you on board!'

Unimpressed, Debs tore off her squeaky nylon parka. 'I go

37

for two weeks in Faliraki and everything's changed.' She cracked her knuckles, and both Billie and Jenkins jumped.

According to Dot, Debs was their good-luck token. 'We've never had so many customers!' she whispered, thrilled, as they watched a fidgeting woman and her daughter paw the dresses.

Dubious about Debs' magical qualities, Billie suspected the recent trickle was due to the dusting and the hoovering and the removal of dead flies from the window display. 'Is Debs OK?' she said, in an undertone. Snippets of her Saturday girl's sales patter had reached her ears – 'No way. Rubbish. You're never a size fourteen, love' – and she was feeling uneasy.

'She's a diamond,' Dot assured her. 'Come on, let's help these ladies choose.'

Swallowing her doubts about the wisdom of sleepwalking up the aisle to manacle yourself to an under-qualified Prince Charming, Billie matched Dot coo for coo as the two women tried to choose a dress.

Crumpled with anxiety, the mother's mantra was, 'I just dunno, love,' as her daughter paced the floorboards in frock after frock. 'I think I preferred the one with the lacing at the back.'

When the long-suffering girl clambered once more into the one with the lacing at the back, her mother put her hands to her head. As if she'd just heard she had to solve world poverty and had half an hour to do it, she wailed, 'I just dunno! What about the strappy one?'

'The first one you saw? An hour ago?' Billie double-checked. 'I dunno!'

Some psychological sleight of hand was called for. 'I shouldn't really be doing this,' Billie began, her low-key delivery grabbing the two women's attention. 'But something tells me I can trust you two.' She was silent for a moment, semaphoring 'deep thought' by means of putting her finger to her chin. 'We have a dress in the stockroom that isn't on the rails yet.' She ignored Dot's frank bafflement. 'It's unique. It's . . .' She looked to the ceiling for the right word, a fervent look on her face. In a deep register she finally announced, '*Stunning*.' She looked from one customer to the other, gravely. 'You must tell nobody that you have seen this dress. Nobody! I could get thrown out of the

Grand Association of Wedding Dress . . . er . . .' She rebooted herself. 'Procurers just for showing it to you.' Clicking her fingers, Billie commanded imperiously, 'Miss Dot! The dress!'

Luckily Dot had cottoned on and snatched up the first dress she saw in the stockroom. A simple design in white with organza sleeves, it had avoided the ugly stick that had walloped so much of Great Aunty Babs' stock but it fell short of stunning.

'Oh God!' moaned the older woman, as if somebody had just brought in a boy band, sedated, on a trolley. 'That's the one!' she squawked.

'Yes!' Yes!' Her daughter tore at her zip in the middle of the shop floor. 'I have to have it, Mum. Stu will die.'

Shortly the two women left, grinning like television evangelists, and the magical dress was folded up and ready to go to the alteration ladies.

Channelling Dick Emery, Dot chided, 'You are awful, Billie.'

'It was the nicest dress in the shop!' Billie defended herself stoutly. 'They believe they have the best dress in the world and, apparently, Stu will die.' She tucked a scratched patent mule on to a shelf. 'It's just one more little untruth on the way to the altar. It's less of a lie than promising to love someone forever.'

'I'm not listening.' Dot popped the cups of a threadbare satin bra over her ears. 'I believe in love. I believe in marriage. I—'

Interrupting this pink torrent, Billie raised one 44G cup to ask, 'Do you believe in nipping next door for a sausage roll? I'm starving.'

'No spirit of romance,' tutted Dot, setting off for Mr Dyke's.

'Strange, that, for somebody whose WEDDING DAY ENDED IN THEIR OLD SINGLE BED AT THEIR MUM'S!' Billie hollered the last bit. Sometimes she had to remind Dot of The Story. And herself. Because the customer really had looked beautiful in the dress. Funny how a length of white fabric could make you rethink all your hard-won knowledge.

'I don't do washing up,' stated Debs baldly.

During that long Saturday she had told Billie she didn't do errands, she didn't do tidying and she didn't do smiling.

'I presume you do getting paid?' Billie held up a couple of tenners.

'Yup.'

The tenners were snatched and stuffed into a bum bag. It seemed an opportune moment to warn the girls that they would have to attend her brother's team-building seminar.

'Semin-what?' snapped Debs suspiciously. 'Will it hurt?'

'Sly's never lost a seminarian yet,' Billie reassured her.

'What does Sly stand for?' asked Dot as Debs swayed out of the shop on her Ugg boots, plucking like a harpist at the gusset trapped deep in her bottom. 'Is he a Sylvester, like Sly Stallone? I've always liked him,' she added dreamily. 'Lovely hair.'

'Not exactly.' Billie hesitated. She might as well tell her. 'Actually, Sly was named after the character my dad was playing in the am-dram production when my mum fell pregnant. Just like me. Mum was playing Mina in *Dracula* when she found out she was expecting, hence . . .' Billie tailed off.

'*Wilhelmina*.' Dot nodded knowingly, sympathetically, with a slight wince. 'So what was your dad playing?'

'Well, it was a daring modern-dress version of *Peter Pan*, set in an office block. Dad was one of the pirates.' She paused, letting Dot get there on her own.

'Oh.' Dot looked chastened. 'Slightly.' She gulped. 'Oh dear.'

'Oh dear indeed,' agreed Billie. 'Sly changed his name by deed poll as soon as he got to secondary school. There's only so many beatings with a damp towel a boy can take.' She yawned. 'Time to go home, Miss Dot.' Switching off lights, Billie asked wryly, 'Any more members of staff to come out of the woodwork? Or is Debs as bad as it gets?'

'Babs is very fond of Debs,' said Dot, looking reprovingly at Billie. 'One of the last things she said was to keep an eye on her. She's got a heart of gold.'

'And a face of granite. She scares me.'

'She wouldn't hurt a fly. Well,' Dot rethought that statement. 'Apart from the vicious wounding and the aggravated assault and the time she threw a typewriter through the chip-shop window.' Perhaps it was the rigid look of fear on Billie's face that made Dot add, soothingly, 'But that's all behind her since she gave up the alcopops.'

* * *

April was too early in the year to expect the lavender dusk to be warm. Billie sped up as she neared the sea, pulling her cord jacket tightly around her. That padlock was a moody bugger, and Billie unleashed a few choice words as she battled with it. 'Bums,' she muttered. 'Willies.'

'SSSSH!'

The hiss had come from the beach behind her. She span round. At this hour the row of huts were deserted. The wind whipping her hair over her eyes, Billie squinted. The darkening shore was empty. Did murderers shush before they pounced, she wondered? Did ghosts? The key slipped from her fingers and she scrabbled on the ground.

'Need a hand?'

Jerking upright, Billie looked wildly around again. There was a figure standing in one of the weather-beaten boats that lay around the beach like abandoned slippers.

'I'm fine, thanks,' mumbled Billie, recognising him. It was that distinctive punky guy again. Her nemesis. She turned her back on him, sensing him clamber out of the boat and amble towards her.

'You should be careful,' he said, his voice a London drawl full of lazy life. 'Somebody might see you.'

'Doesn't bother me.' Billie, whose heart was pounding and who was very bothered indeed, cursed the key for getting smaller and her fingers for getting thicker.

'But you're breaking the law, love, aren't you?'

Billie gave up with the padlock, cleared her throat in readiness for a damn good scream, and faced the man. He was nearer and more distinct, although he stayed down on the pebbles. He was very tall, and very slender, and his eyes were locked on hers like a laser beam. 'Am I?' she asked innocently.

'You know you are, you dirty little squatter, you.' His tone was unreadable. Light, mocking, it seemed to lack spite but he didn't let her off the hook.

'It's a fair cop.' Billie smiled, and her lips stuck to her teeth. This man could turn nasty. Or he could make a joke of it all. She stayed silent, allowing him to take the lead.

'I've always wanted to say this, so bear with me.' The stranger cleared his throat and ruffled his already spiky hair.

'Blackmail's an ugly word.' He grinned happily, showing very white teeth.

Billie noticed that his molars were pointed. Vampiric, even.

'You leave me no choice,' he went on. 'Unless you come out for a drink with me I'll be forced to, how does one put it? I'll be forced to *squeal*.' He folded his arms. 'How about it?'

'Erm . . .' Billie wondered if he meant it.

'If you're wondering if I mean it—' That startled her. 'I always mean it.'

Years of conditioning had prepared Billie for this moment. *Don't talk to strange men*, her nursery school teachers had warned. Her mother had related grim fables of girls who accepted a Werther's Original in the street and ended up in a harem. Nobody, she reasoned, had ever mentioned blackmailing vampires. She risked a half smile.

'I was right about you.' With this open-ended compliment, her nemesis approached her. 'I'm Sam, by the way. I know your name. We blackmailers pride ourselves on that kind of detail. Next Friday. Eight o'clock. Here.' He stopped, and held out an elegant hand. 'Deal?'

I must be mad, thought Billie. But, 'Deal,' she said, and took his hand.

Five

'Mmm!' Billie sniffed the air as Jake dragged the door of the cottage open. Like everything else in his house it didn't quite do the job it was designed for. 'Something smells . . .' There was no polite word to cover the scents wafting towards her, so she left the sentence dangling and hung up her jacket on a coat stand fashioned from rusty drainpipes. 'What's the roast?'

Rolling the R with relish, Jake exploded. 'Rrroast?' he roared. 'You came here expecting a celebration of death?'

'Well, perhaps a chicken,' mumbled Billie, feeling like Hannibal Lecter in drag. 'It *is* Sunday.'

Loftily, Jake told her, 'We don't eat and kill our friends in this house.'

Even though she, too, had vegetarian leanings (easily compromised by the promise of a chop) Billie bridled at his pomposity. 'I'll go and see if Dot needs any help.'

Heading for the back of the house, Billie squinted into the gloom of the no-mod-cons kitchen. As she'd suspected, the romantic-sounding artist's cottage was created in Jake's image. The tiny two-up two-down near the front was chaotic, dirty and belonged to another era, just like Jake's beard. Half-finished canvases of sludgy khakis and browns loitered in every room, fighting for space with the bulky furniture. Unsettling artefacts lurked everywhere. A papier mâché badger bared its teeth at Billie as she passed, and she shuddered at a bald rag doll, lying across an open, mouldering encyclopaedia. The effect was the opposite of relaxing, and Billie was glad to see Dot's radiant little face in the murk.

'It's dark in here,' commented Billie, handing over a bottle of the off licence's second-cheapest Australian white.

'Jake painted the windows black a while ago,' explained Dot.

43

She seemed to find nothing strange in this. 'Said the sunlight was evil.'

'Right.' Billie stared into the pot of gloop that Dot was stirring on the blackened Aga, trying to avert her eyes from the mantrap on the dresser. 'What's for lunch?'

'Nettle soup to start,' Dot told her. 'Wine?'

'*So* yes.' Billie sat down heavily at the table. On her way to the house she'd wondered whether or not to tell Dot about the handsome blackmailer. As she'd kicked open the garden gate made from welded spoons, Billie had decided against it. Any sensible human would try to dissuade her from going on a press-ganged date, and Dot fitted that description, despite the mouse chum and the cabbagey boyfriend. The stranger scared her, but he intrigued her, too. The old Billie might be dead, but she wouldn't lie down just yet.

'Try this.' Dot handed her guest a foaming glass of wine poured from an unlabelled urn. Gasping, Billie raised it to her lips, barely listening to Dot's description of the wine until she heard, 'Jakey makes it in the bath. With his—'

'DON'T SAY FEET!' yelped Billie, slamming the glass down on to the table. The table, being a recycled toilet door, took her mind off the wine. The plates, all stamped *Lower Brockington Insane Asylum* took her mind off the table. The cottage was a multilayered nightmare, a sticky spider's web of Jake's obsessions and vanities. Dot, with her peachy skin and swingy hair, was utterly out of place there, like Snow White sharing a squat with Pete Doherty.

When the swampy soup was set out, Jake joined them. Half man, half Dyson, he noisily slurped up his portion.

Perched opposite Jake on a fourteenth-century birthing stool, Billie learned a lot about him. Over a main course of salad and a slab of tofu so rubbery it could have come straight from a glamour model's breast, Billie discovered that he didn't believe in the establishment, money, status, blinkered suburban values or God. Evidently he did believe in talking incessantly. Reading between the lines it was also clear that Jake had never believed in paying his way, lifting a finger, listening or combing his hair.

But Dot believed in Jake. Billie watched her gaze, rapt, at her shambling boyfriend as he pontificated about everything from Jonathan Ross's suits to global warming. He didn't repay the compliment. Oblivious to Dot's hard work in that wreck of a kitchen where the sink was made from a horse trough and the saucepans may have belonged to Jesus, he sat on his bony behind throughout, even when Billie attempted to shame him by offering to wash up.

Proficiency with a tea towel was a prerequisite for any man expecting a season ticket to Billie's downstairs. Suffragettes had thrown themselves beneath the hooves of horses for her: the least she could do was avoid men who believed women were genetically adapted to hoover. Early on, there had been tussles over the division of labour with James: the ugly scenes over the toilet brush had shamed them both until they'd hired a cleaner.

Rinsing the madhouse crockery, Billie broached a subject she'd been dreading. 'Dot, I've had an idea. A big idea.'

'Hmm?' Dot looked at her encouragingly as she dried a teapot with what looked like Gladstone's long johns.

'I phoned Great Aunty Babs last night, and she's agreed.' The crackly phone line, proof of Billie's ruinous karma with all things electrical, had reduced conversation with her great-aunt to shouts and 'What?'s but she'd been given the go-ahead by her game relative. 'Now all I need is your blessing.'

'Sounds serious.' Dot put down the asylum teapot, and turned her honest little face to her friend.

'Barbara's Brides is going to be reborn.' In her excitement, Billie tripped over her words, catching her breath as she raced through her plans to an increasingly wide-eyed Dot. 'I'm going to rip it all apart and start again. The whole place will be brightened up, refreshed. All the old stock will go. There'll be elegant, funky new dresses and shoes and bags and veils and underwear and *everything*. It will be modern, and clean, and inviting, but with all the charm of the past.' She answered Dot's frown with one of her own. 'Well? Are you in, Dot?' she asked, fearfully.

Looking slightly shell-shocked as she leaned against the trough, Dot didn't reply straight away. The pause nibbled at Billie's shaky composure.

Outlining her ideas, Billie had realised how central Dot was to the whole venture. This frail, tie-dyed girl was the shop's link with the past, and with Great Aunty Babs. As Billie studied Dot's pretty face with the sort of attention she had never given her college work, she acknowledged a more pressing, far more personal, reason for needing Dot.

As long as Billie had been on kissing terms with James, the two of them had fulfilled each other's needs in every way. Ticked every box. Tickled every G spot. He was the boiled egg to her soldiers, and she was the fries to his Whopper. It was only after he'd disappeared like free drinks at a student bar that Billie had discovered the big, girl-shaped gap in her emotional life.

It was a harsh way to learn such a simple lesson. Billie's naïve belief in the fake stability of romance had led her to neglect the women in her life. There were 'mates', of course. Billie had no shortage of people to call, but the resulting nights out tended to be big on cackling and short on conversation, centring on the relative merits of passing blokes' behinds. Now, Billie was as ardent a connoisseur of the male sitting-down parts as the next girl, but she'd found herself longing for somebody to confide in, and listen to.

The one girl that Billie had been close to during her engagement had stayed firmly on James's side of the border when hostilities broke out. Jackie had known and kept all their secrets, and Billie had come to rely on her irreverent take on things. Waving sadly from the other side, Jackie had retreated after a few stilted meetings for coffee, a casualty of war. Now Billie needed somebody to talk to, and, if she was honest, to care about.

This pause was a big one: the Royal Albert Hall of pauses. Dot was staring into the middle distance as if it contained a recipe for non-fattening cream teas. 'Are you in, Dot?' asked Billie again, with even less confidence.

'Course,' said Dot, easily. 'Sounds like fun'.

'Fun?' queried Billie, anxious that her assistant had heard properly. 'A complete refurbishment? On very little money? The whole place stripped and painted? New stock? New everything? Just the two of us doing all the work?'

'Yeah,' nodded Dot. 'Fun.'

Hmm. Billie would have to educate Dot about fun. It was traditionally found around wine bars and sweet shops, not up ladders. A thought struck her. 'Where are the portraits of *you* around here?' She'd seen plenty of half-finished, muddy faces looming out of canvases, but none that reminded her of Dot's piquant little mush.

'Oh, there aren't any.' Dot shrugged, not quite disguising the discomfort she obviously felt. 'Jake doesn't see anything special in me. I'm just ordinary. Not like you.' She twiddled a strand of the strawberry-blonde hair that gleamed like a hostage sunbeam in the grotty room.

'He's a better manipulator than my brother, and Sly's a professional,' sighed Billie. She lifted Dot's chin with one forefinger. '*I* see something special in you, Miss Dot.'

And she did. She saw a friend.

Eyes glistening with tears, Dot said sadly, 'Oh it's heartbreaking.'

Billie ignored her. This atypical callousness had developed witnessing Dot blub over many things, including a guide dog ('He's like Gandhi!'), a radio news item about a school bus that had got lost on the way to Alton Towers ('If only I could hug them all!') and Jake's talent ('Oh my God, that portrait of Bruce Forsyth painted entirely with soy sauce is so . . . *meaningful!*').

'It's not heartbreaking. It's about bloody time,' huffed Billie, as another unspeakable dress joined its miserable compatriots on the shop floor. This brutal clearout was the official start of the refurbishment. They'd rushed round to the shop as soon as the last plate was put away (in a selection of Victorian hat boxes, naturally) and now a meringue mountain, a kind of wedding-dress slag heap, obscured the light from Barbara's Brides' windows.

'Such a shame,' murmured Dot, tenderly placing an off-white, off-the-shoulder, off-the-scale-disgusting creation on the pyre.

'Good riddance, you mean,' snorted Billie robustly. She marvelled at the price tags as she consigned white frock after white frock to its fate. 'Why do little girls dream of growing up to wear one of these? Is it something they put in the sugar-free Ribena? You can get a fortnight in Magaluf for the same money.'

'It's a dream,' said Dot, with appropriate dreaminess. 'You can't put a price tag on a dream.'

'No, but you can pay a man with a trailer to take it to the dump.' Billie's gaze fell on a small trunk she hadn't spotted before. 'What's in that box? More of these monstrosities, I suppose. Let's get them out so we can put them down humanely.'

'Those are *really* old stock,' Dot told her. 'Babs didn't consider them trendy enough for her clientele.'

Intrigued at the thought of designs too dowdy for Babs, Billie surfed over the doomed wedding dresses to open the trunk. 'But these are beautiful . . .' she gasped, unearthing gown after gown, like a burrowing animal. 'Feel the fabrics!' The velvets and silks and crisp cottons were balm after handling Barbara's preferred nylon. Tiny covered buttons inched up the backs of expertly pleated and tucked dresses. Understated and chic, the curiously timeless designs contrasted strongly with the dog's dinners that had crowded the rails. 'Ooops.' Billie's heart sank as her finger poked through a moth hole. The dresses were showing their age.

Of the twenty-two creations in the trunk, only three were still intact. Tiny labels, surely sewn in by fairies, read 'Ruby Wolff'. 'Old Ruby knew her stuff,' pondered Billie, elbow-deep in sensual fabric.

Dot found a receipt, yellowed and crumpled. 'Look at the old-fashioned curly handwriting. According to this, Ruby lived just around the corner. Twelve Richmond Villas.'

'These must be forty years old at least. See how this moves.' Billie held a simple white velvet dress, luxuriously lined in silk, in front of her. 'I'll stick this in the window when we reopen.' Holding it to her body, she did an experimental swish. The fabric moved like water.

'Shame you hate weddings so much.' Dot put her birdlike head on one side. 'White suits you.'

'Makes me look drawn.' Billie folded the dress brusquely, as if it had scorched her.

'No. It suited you. You lit up when you looked in the mirror,' persisted Dot, whose cheesecloth smock hid a spine of steel. 'Even you can be seduced by a white dress. If you're not careful.'

Winded by Dot's insight (Billie liked to think she was mysterious, unaware that she displayed her emotions like floodlit kebab-shop signs), Billie plonked a veil on her head and simpered, 'You've seen through me. I admit it. I'm just waiting for Mr Right to come along.'

A loud knock on the door made them jump, and turn, like two meerkats.

'Afternoon, ladies, I'm Mr Wright!' bawled the toothless old man, his creased and filthy face pressed against the glass.

Eyes wide and mouths wider, Dot and Billie stared at each other for a long second before collapsing among the wedding dresses, gripped by the kind of hysterical laughter rare outside toddler puppet shows.

'Coming, Mr Wright,' gasped Billie, her chest sore, as she crawled across the shop on all fours. 'I'm been waiting for you!'

As Ernie Wright, Sole Bay's premier odd-job man, hauled away the rejected dresses in a trailer that stank of mackerel, Dot and Billie recovered enough to self-prescribe Magnums.

Sunday, drowsy and idle, had emptied Little Row. Alone now in the shop, savouring the sense of promise in its bare rails and shelves, Billie tacked up the last page of newspaper to the windows. Nobody would be permitted to see in for two weeks, until Barbara's Brides was reborn. The schedule she'd blithely concocted lying in her little iron bed now scared the bejaysus out of her, but Billie was determined to stick to it.

Locking up and scurrying past Dyke's, Billie hoped she wouldn't run into her blackmailing beau. He was a thing of the night, and he could slip out of the shadows at any moment. Billie picked up the pace.

The 'date' now loomed large. All her fears magnified by the darkness, Billie regretted her recklessness. Even a normal date, with a normal man, with normal hair would be daunting: she was still raw. Despite the niche she'd found in Sole Bay, Billie felt apart from people. As if she had a secret tattoo hidden in her hairline, Billie was alien, *different*. A night out with a man, perhaps a few drinks and a meal, was as absurd a concept to her as a suggestion that she use stilts for the rest of her life, or dress as a poodle.

It hadn't always been like this. Billie used to regard love and romance as a kind of adventure playground: she'd swung on the ropes more than most. Speed-relationships were her speciality. Billie had snogged, dumped and described genitals in lurid detail to her friends at the stage when most other girls were coyly exchanging phone numbers.

And then James happened.

Marooned at the dreariest party yet thrown by any human, Billie had been eating her own weight in cocktail sausages while concocting an excuse to offer her host ('I've just had a most urgent phone call from the hospital and apparently everybody I've ever loved has been involved in a horrific lawnmower incident') when James introduced himself. The tall tale had been forgotten, the proffered blood-temperature white wine accepted, and soon the bedsit around them, furnished with third-hand Ikea, had transformed into a Versailles ballroom. The resolutely single, party-loving, commitment-dodging Billie had fallen like a fridge into a swimming pool.

'And look how that ended,' she reminded herself. Only just discharged from the emotional equivalent of intensive care, all Billie's injuries resulted from that plastic cup of wine. If she'd said, 'No, ta,' left the party and dug out her *Smack the Pony* boxed set, she'd be a different person now: unscathed, healthy and far too busy snogging and giggling to take over an elderly relative's ailing shop out in the sticks. Love had manoeuvred Billie into a position where swapping lives with a pensioner was attractive. Love was dangerous. It came with strings attached, and like the conservatories she'd sold, the small print was invisible to the naked eye.

The wind off the sea was cold and wet tonight. It smacked Billie round the chops as she approached Herbert, and she was glad of its bracing directness. She'd been toying with the notion of replying to James's email, but tonight's trot down Memory Lane had made her mind up. Memory Lane is a one way street: there was no going back.

Six

Blanked-out windows hid frantic scenes from Little Row, of a screaming Dot executing perfect figures of eight on the hired sander, and Billie acquiring a bruise shaped uncannily like the Tube map of Greater London when she fell off the ladder. Perhaps it marked the start of the seven years' bad luck she'd won prising a pockmarked mirror away from the wall.

The ambitious scheme was great on paper. Barbara's Brides would be a cool white space, with distressed floorboards and recessed lighting. The panelling and the counter and the cornicing would be born again under a few coats of slick white paint. 'A virgin cube,' Billie murmured to herself, breaking open a packet of sandpaper.

It was the first packet of many. She'd envisaged herself wielding a dainty brush, her hair caught up in a scarf with a cute smudge of paint on her nose. The *Reader's Digest Book of Home Improvement* spoiled that fantasy. Preparation was everything, it preached, neglecting to mention that preparation was also back-breaking and boring. And endless. Billie's fingernails were the first casualties as she attacked the acres of brown paintwork with the sandpaper. Wilting, her nose pressed to a Nigel's worth of poo-coloured skirting, she vowed never again to open a letter from a distant relative.

As for removing Great Aunty Babs' beloved woodchip, this was the novice decorator's version of the Vietnam War: it was sordid, the enemy was tenacious, and a long struggle produced no clear winner. Even the placid Dot admitted to having dreams about lobbing hand grenades at the papery acne on the walls.

A vision in Billie's head kept her going, even when she was crying with exhaustion and Dot was face down in a pile of dust sheets. It was a vision of 'her' shop, of the regenerated Barbara's Brides. White, clean, brand new and full of hope: she rejected the armchair philosophy that the shop was an allegory for life post-James.

Barbara's Brides needed her. It gobbled up all the energy she flung at it, and demanded more. This process was long overdue. In her more poetic moments, usually hard on the heels of a flirtation with a wine box, Billie fancied she was rescuing the building from drowning. And if, in the process, it rescued her right back, that was a bonus.

They didn't toil entirely alone. Annie came in to add two pounds to her dress fund, and found herself sanding a tiny patch of woodwork in her hat and coat. Determined attempts by Billie to unravel her were stonewalled expertly, although she did smile when Billie thanked her, adding, 'I'm sure you must be very busy.'

'No, dear,' Annie whispered. 'I'm not busy.'

Jake, too, helped out in his own special way, by sketching them. 'Hold that pose!' he shrieked up at Billie as she stood on the counter to reach a cobweb. 'That expression!' he lisped, rapturously. Whipping out a pad from somewhere in the folds of his tweed cape, he began to sketch frantically. 'My God, your face,' he breathed. 'The planes are magnificent. Such majesty.'

Despite herself, Billie blushed. She held her head very still but looked unimpressed, as if artists were struck by the majesty of her expression every other day.

'Incredible,' purred Jake, his tongue sticking out as he drew.

Feeling exposed, Billie swallowed hard, unwilling to admit to herself that she was enjoying his adoring scrutiny.

'Do you want me to put the moustache in?' he asked.

Thinking properly and clearly, without the blare of the television to distract her, Billie had come to the conclusion that Barbara's Brides could actually turn a profit. It was the only wedding shop in Sole Bay, after all. In fact, it was the only wedding shop for miles, apart from an uninspiring establishment in Neeveston shopping mall that betrayed its origins as a seafood cash and carry. That meant that there was a scrum of potential customers out there who didn't even know that Barbara's Brides existed.

Pulling off her interior-designer hat for a moment, Billie had tried on her PR hat for size: it was a little too big, and the sequins didn't suit her, but she came up with some ideas. Leaflets were hastily printed at the Kall Kwik on the high street, and sat in a conscience-pricking pile by the shop door. Dot's aunty, who ran the biggest paper shop in Sole Bay, slipped one into every bridal magazine, and Dot cruised the surrounding villages in her Robin Reliant, placing ads in newsagents' windows.

The Barbara's Brides PR machine was cranking into gear. Slowly.

Limping to the butcher's on Friday morning, Billie was in search of a savoury snack to blot out the pain.

'My favourite young lady!' beamed the butcher, his red cheeks bulging.

Now that Billie knew of the passions lurking beneath his matter-stained apron, she responded with a prim, 'Good morning.' Wary of Mr Dyke these days, she checked the way he handled tripe for signs of sexual deviance. As she browsed the pasties, reassured by their meaty bulk, another customer came in.

'Good morning to *you*, Mrs Davis.'

Something in the butcher's voice made Billie look up, surreptitiously. A note of something more than gallantry had entered his tone.

Tittering, Mrs Davis, regally seated on her mobility vehicle with a three-legged Yorkshire terrier tucked in at her feet, responded with a girlish, 'What have you got that's tasty?' and a toss of her foldable rain hood.

Positioning herself by the sausages to get a grandstand seat for this transaction, Billie sneaked a look at Mr Dyke.

Rolling his moustache with a cold, clean finger, he was saying, slowly, 'Let me see now, Mrs Davis.' He bent over his meats, then looked up through his lashes at her. 'I seem to recall my pudding always goes down well with you.'

Pretending to study mince, Billie hugged herself. She was in eavesdropper's heaven.

Dentures whistling only slightly, Mrs Davis whispered, 'Oh, a length of your pudding sets me up for the day, Mr D.'

Billie froze. Mr Dyke was holding up a foot-long black pudding in an indisputably saucy manner. Good God! The man was waggling it! She picked up and dropped a pre-packed mixed grill in her confusion.

And now the lady on the scooter was laughing coquettishly, before it turned into a protracted smoker's cough. 'Just eight inches now,' she choked.

This was quality banter. Billie had parachuted into *Carry On Butchering*, and couldn't wait to report to Dot. Another customer joined them, blocking the light from the door. Billie saw the shadow cross the butcher's face, and in a very different voice, he said, guardedly, 'And what can I do for you?'

'Oh, I think you've done enough.' Zelda, her hand-knitted cardi held together by a cat brooch, stalked across the black and white tiles of the floor. 'And you, Mrs Davis,' she snarled, looking down at the little woman on her vehicle. 'I would have thought your pudding days were over.'

'Ooh. Perhaps I'd better . . . just a cutlet, Mr D,' muttered Mrs Davis, trying to restrain her little dog who was growling like an unattended hairdryer at Zelda. 'Shush, Peter!' she begged, avoiding the fudge-maker's eye.

Parcelling up a cutlet, Mr Dyke asked, resigned, 'Did you actually want to purchase something, Zelda?'

'Yes, *Mr D*,' taunted Zelda, dipping into her apron pocket for some fudge. 'A nice bit of sirloin for Raven.'

'You spoil that cat, Zelda,' murmured Mr Dyke mildly.

'He's no ordinary cat,' said Zelda, defiantly. She noticed Billie. 'Alright, my lovely?' she asked, with genuine warmth, before turning back to the butcher to issue a haughty command. 'Put it on me slate.' Zelda sauntered out, humming 'Anarchy In The UK' and passing just a touch too close to Mrs Davis's tiny trike.

Through a hail of puff-pastry crumbs, Billie relayed the little scene to Dot, who sat nibbling a falafel baguette as if it was real food. 'Mad as cheese, that Zelda,' ended Billie, fondly.

'Don't ever get on her wrong side,' advised Dot, with one

of those worldly asides that had stopped surprising Billie. 'Has the evil eye, according to the old folk.'

'What? Like a witch, you mean?' Billie demanded clarification. 'Never. They did away with them when they brought in high-rise flats and instant custard. There's no room for a witch in the modern world.'

'But this isn't the modern world,' Dot reminded her, calmly. 'It's Sole Bay.'

'True.' Billie was sobered by that thought, sitting down on the bottom stair and sending up a mushroom cloud of dust. 'I still can't believe Zelda is a witch. Surely somebody with supernatural powers would do a better job of dyeing their hair than she does.'

'She was always very sweet to my mum,' said Dot, looking at the denuded wall but seeing past it.

'Oh, Dot, I didn't know. Is your mum . . .'

'Yes. A while ago,' nodded Dot.

Billie could sense she didn't want a kind word: those kind words can break a carefully constructed dam. She stayed quiet until Dot spoke again.

'Sometimes I think Zelda could sense it.'

'Could sense what?'

'About my mum.' Dot turned to her. 'My mum was abandoned on the steps of Sole Bay vicarage. She was wrapped in a little blanket, with a biscuit in her hand. The vicar gave her to his cleaning lady.' Dot paused to frown. 'Adoption laws must have been more relaxed in those days.'

Fascinated, Billie probed. 'Did she ever find her real parents?' She thought for a moment. 'Your grandparents?'

'No, never,' said Dot, sadly. 'The cleaning lady was horrible. Used to hit her with her mop.' Dot shrugged. 'There's a whole chunk of my family missing,' she admitted, making it sound as if they'd all disappeared en masse after popping out one morning for the paper.

'I wish my family would go missing,' muttered Billie into her greasy snack.

'Sometimes Mum would get very sad,' said Dot simply. 'So me and Dad were always extra nice to her to make up for it.'

Unsure whether she was meant to feel like a heel for complaining about her family, Billie got on with doing just that.

'This is a surprise,' said Nancy Baskerville, archly. 'A phone call from my runaway daughter. What brought this on?'

Explaining about cleaning ladies hitting little girls with mops would take too long: 'I just wondered how the first night of *Chicago* went?'

'A triumph,' said Nancy, blithely. 'Your father's groin trouble came back during his solo but nobody noticed. The *Surbiton Enquirer*'s drama critic called me, oh, what was it?' Nancy wasn't a good enough actress, despite her years of am-dram, to pretend she hadn't learned the accolade by heart. '*A rare gem in a suburban setting.* Pity you couldn't be there, darling.'

'I'll come to the next first night,' promised Billie recklessly. She paused, waiting for a question about the shop, about the hut, about her state of mind.

'When are you coming home, sweetheart? We worry so.'

'I know, Mum,' sighed Billie. 'I know.'

Saturday arrived. Another day of sanding and scraping and undercoating and dealing with electricians as if she knew what they were talking about, it was also, possibly, Billie's last day on Earth if her date turned out to be a psychopath.

Keeping such thoughts to herself, she toiled alongside Dot all morning. They were still at the stage of the job where everything looks much, much worse than it did at the beginning. A stage where even a visit from Jake was a welcome diversion.

When he turned up on the doorstep, Billie assumed that he was en route to a carnival, but Dot's lack of surprise could only mean that Jake habitually strolled about the town in polka-dot trousers, chef's jacket and a tricorn hat. 'I brought lunch,' he told them.

'Oooh, thanks.' Billie softened towards him. Tending to the needs of her demanding tummy was a sure way to her heart, and she wondered if she'd been a little hard on old Jake. She sniffed the air expectantly: was there a faint whiff of chip about him?

'Apples!' trilled Dot, as Jake whipped out three from his pockets.

'Apples,' echoed Billie forlornly, trying to look grateful.

'Orbs of life,' Jake corrected them, his eyes gleaming. 'The perfect fruit. The circle of completeness. Eve's tainted and irresistible offering to Adam.'

There was a lot more in this vein. By the time Billie was picking the pips out of her teeth, Jake was eulogising his shrivelled Golden Delicious as 'a symbol of female lust through the ages.'

'No cake?' she butted in.

Carefully placing his apple core on a wet newly painted shelf, Jake opened his mouth, possibly to hold forth on the subject of cake as an allegory of female something or other, but his words were lost in a sudden commotion from outside.

The street was hidden to them, thanks to the newspaper stuck over the windows, but the hectic screams and shrieks had both Billie and Dot racing to the door.

Avoiding their toes by centimetres, Mrs Davis sped past, hollering, on her mobility trike. Flames followed her, lurching out of the shopping basket strapped neatly to the back of her vehicle. Zigzagging across Little Row, belching fire like a dying Spitfire, Mrs Davis was hysterical.

In marked contrast, Zelda, leaning on the door jamb of her fudge shop, was calm.

To Billie's eyes she looked smug. And guilty as hell.

Bewildered passers-by gawped at the pensioner, lurching up and down the narrow street at a speed surely never attempted by a mobility vehicle before. Mrs Davis's screams were incomprehensible, but, as Zelda languidly pointed out to whoever was interested, 'She ain't happy, is she?'

Dot bent to scoop up Peter, Mrs Davis's three-legged terrier, who had presumably been flung from the speeding trike for his own safety. 'Don't look!' she advised, pressing his agitated snout to her boiler suit, as his mistress bounced past on the cobbles, her groceries blazing.

A distant jangling, like panic set to music, sounded, and Billie stood up straighter. A fire engine. That meant firemen. She looked sideways at Dot: despite her distress on Mrs Davis's behalf, Dot was smoothing down her hair and licking her lips.

As a red fire engine turned gingerly down the narrow street, a striped blur raced out of the butcher's. Mr Dyke, his apron askew, bolted after his customer, who was now wailing, her hands off the wheel and covering her face.

The engine drew up, wheezing hard, and figures in yellow and blue leaped down. It's hard to concentrate on anything else when tall men in helmets have arrived, but Billie's attention was diverted by Mr Dyke.

As Mrs Davis's crazed trike turned back on itself, heading for the small crowd of onlookers, the butcher made a heroic leap and got a toehold on its footplate. He balanced, one hand on the wheel, the other on the canopy, like those sexily non-chalant boys who operate fairground dodgems, and managed to turn off the ignition.

The little scooter screeched to a halt, as firemen galloped towards it with foam extinguishers. Mr Dyke, as if starring in a movie called *A Butcher and a Gentleman*, folded Mrs Davis into his arms and tenderly lifted her out. With her white perm standing on end, Mrs Davis made an unlikely Debra Winger, but she clung to her hero until he deposited her carefully on a chair provided by the tea room opposite.

A low growl sounded close to Billie, and it wasn't Peter. Zelda was pawing the ground like a bull, a dangerous sparkle in her black eyes.

'Zelda,' said Billie, warningly, and reached an arm around the old lady's shoulders: she was in enough trouble if Billie's suspicions were correct. 'Leave it.'

Little Row breathed again. The shopping basket was a damp, sudsy mess of burned Brillo Pads and cornflakes, pored over by firemen. Mrs Davis was reunited with Peter, whose three-legged dance of joy was moving if you were Dot, slightly hilarious if you were Billie.

Pulsing with fury, Zelda was glaring at Mr Dyke. In a deep register, she muttered, 'Curse that man.' Her eyes were shimmering, and Billie tightened her grip around her shoulders, remembering Dot's tale of Zelda's powers. Billie looked closer: Zelda's eyes were full of tears, not hate. Billie was touched by

Zelda's distress, but before she could say anything a male voice was asking her, 'Is she yours?'

The tall, broad, and unfeasibly handsome fireman gestured at Zelda with a laconic movement of his thumb.

'No,' said Billie, stiff with self-consciousness under the scrutiny of two eyes as dark and desirable as cheap chocolate. 'Well, kind of. Zelda's my neighbour.'

'Right.' The fireman, who'd started off so assertively, coughed. His face was flooding with red, as if somebody had whispered the rudest joke ever into his ear: his, Billie couldn't help noticing, perfectly shaped ear, around which a stray brown curl had snaked. He turned to Zelda, who had wilted slightly now that the action was over and Mr Dyke had guided the still gibbering Mrs Davis into the butcher's. 'I don't know what went on here, and we're not going to ask too many questions. But do I have your word you won't waste our time again, love?'

It could have been a nod, but it could equally have been a shrug.

'Zelda!' admonished Billie, admiring herself for being so firm with a suspected witch. 'Does he have your word?'

'Yes!' spat Zelda angrily, before relenting slightly. 'Sorry, dear,' she said, looking the firefighter in the face for the first time. 'You're good boys.' She took him in properly, then turned to Billie. 'A looker, ain't he?'

The looker, whose blush had faded slightly, turned back to Billie. 'And your name?' he asked, brusquely.

'My name?' repeated Billie, surprised.

'Yes. Just for, erm, the paperwork.' The fireman bit his lip.

For some reason this simple gesture made Billie's thong, beneath her grotty boiler suit, flutter. 'I'm Billie Baskerville,' she told him, wishing she didn't have white gloss in her eyebrows.

He raised an eyebrow. 'Good name.'

Never had such a lukewarm compliment caused such tumult in the pants of the recipient. The fireman was flirting with her: a scene straight out of Billie's porniest daydreams. 'Thanks,' she muttered. Out of practice at talking to 'lookers', she floundered. 'Anyway,' she heard her disloyal lips saying, 'Better get Zelda indoors.'

Steering the protesting arsonist into the chaos of Barbara's Brides, Billie reminded herself, quite sternly, that the shop demanded her fidelity. Fancying a firefighter would be two-timing.

Which made her a two-timer.

Seven

Her date was on time. Sunglasses on despite the dark, he lounged, long legs crossed at the ankle, against a powerful-looking motorbike near the top of the steps that led down to the beach huts.

Self-consciously, Billie patted her hair and tugged at her waisted cord jacket as she approached him. She could tell he was staring at her from behind those dense shades, taking in the jeans and shirt and flattie pumps: could he tell she'd chosen clothes she could run away in? 'Hi,' she said, insouciantly, as if meeting dangerous men in indecently tight trousers was a habit of hers.

'Hi yourself.' That wide mouth smiled, and creased Sam's broad, strongly drawn face into a welcome, rendered wolfish by those razor-like canines. 'Hop on.'

'On?' queried Billie, uncertainly. 'Hop?'

Tossing her a helmet, Sam nodded. 'I'm rescuing you from Sole Bay. The pubs here are hopeless. I can't take another horse brass.' He took off his glasses and unleashed those blue eyes of his. They were beautiful, the kind of eyes that would make him a shoo-in for serial-killer roles. 'Come on, don't make me ring my contact in the council offices,' Sam threatened.

I shouldn't be doing this, thought Billie, swinging a leg over the bike.

It was like flying. Noisy and bullish, the bike roared through the lanes where Sole Bay petered out into countryside proper. A tight fist of adrenaline stole Billie's breath.

Sam was in tune with the motorbike, taking bends fluidly. Ironically, Billie felt safe, perched like a monkey behind her abductor. The outskirts of Neeveston, the nearest big town, materialised under their wheels and soon the suburbs yielded to the urban clutter of car parks and high-rises and deserted malls.

All, Billie couldn't help noting, prime murder sites.

For a girl who'd spent months in self-imposed purdah, mewling in her parents' spare room, wedged between last year's Christmas decorations and a suspiciously pristine exercise bike, this sudden flurry of male attention was all a bit much. Billie had sworn off men, but the gods of romance had just sniggered over their ambrosia. They were out to get her, she reasoned, arranging for a fireman with eyes of pure Cadbury to flirt with her one day, and a peroxided psychopath to whisk her off the next.

The street they stopped in looked deserted, its paving stones stained Lucozade yellow by the street lights, one of which flickered on and off above Billie's head.

'This is us, Billie-pops,' said Sam, taking her helmet. 'That door, there.'

That black, blank, anonymous door beyond which was . . . what, exactly? Billie hesitated, but Sam guided her firmly towards the door with a hand on her elbow. He pressed a bell, the door opened, and they were ushered into the low lights and velvet seating of a members-only club.

Relaxing, Billie hypothesised that this busy, buzzing, über-trendy venue was an unlikely murder scene. Cocktails were brought to their perspex table by Dolce & Gabbana-clad staff. In a smoked-glass mirror wall opposite, Billie could see that although the helmet had flattened her hair into a novel style that brought to mind a knitted snood, she looked stylish enough to complement her chic surroundings. Beside her, Sam's broad shoulders filled out his misleadingly casual tee – Billie knew that the simply cut top had cost more than Dot took home at the end of a week.

'Cheers.' Sam lifted his glass to her, a mocking look in his eye that seemed to be his default setting. He was a glowing, healthy, alpha male, radiating confidence and certainty. Somehow all that physical energy powered a slow, lazy and bitingly wry demeanour.

'Cheers.'

'You're going to be my girl, Billie-kins.'

Aaaargh. Anticipating having to repeat all this later to some bored WPC with a clipboard, Billie began to stutter. She wasn't good under pressure (she wasn't great without it), and the words tumbled out like water from a burst pipe. 'Hmm. Well. Now. Ah ha. The thing is. Oh God, Sam, are you mental? I mean, are you going to kill me, at all?' Clocking the lifted eyebrow which was as close as that laconically handsome face could get to astonishment, she raced on. 'No, you're not, are you? But you might tell on me. Well, do it then. I'll move out of the hut. Because I'm not ready for a relationship. I'm not looking for one.' Here, the tall fireman popped briefly into her head and was smartly ushered out again. 'I'm sorry, but I don't fancy you,' she gulped. 'You're gorgeous and everything, but I don't want . . .' she slowed. Sam was biting his lip in a way that usually denotes a suppressed guffaw, '. . . a boyfriend,' she finished, spent as a balloon after a four-year-old's birthday party.

After a respectful silence filled only by the lounge grooves on the club sound system, Sam began again, calmly, smirking only a little. 'Darling,' he said, taking her hand in his. 'I. Am. Gay.' He stared closely at her. 'You really didn't notice? I'm gay. As gay as gay can be. I'm gayer than the man who bummed the world's gayest man. Any gayer and I'd be straight. I'm so gay I make other gays homophobic.' He paused, perhaps enjoying the shades of mortification, embarrassment, regret and acute desire for alcohol chasing each other across his companion's features. 'And please don't say *relationship* out loud like that without warning me. I'm going cold turkey, and I'm looking for a mate.' He pointed at her. 'That's where you come in.'

'But you said you want me to be your girl,' insisted Billie pedantically. Her case pivoted on this: without that detail she was a schmuck. A schmuck with snood hair.

'Down your drink.' Sam had the air of a man who expected to be obeyed. Under the eternal teenager clothing, he was a proper grown-up. 'I do want you to be my girl. You're different.' He magicked another round from the staff who seemed to know his needs. 'You don't fit in at Sole Bay.'

Bridling, Billie disputed this. 'I bloody do.'

'Not really. Your jeans are at least two seasons ahead of the trendiest bird in the place. You appreciate a dry Martini. And you *enjoy* living in a beach hut, for crying out loud. No local would be caught dead doing that.' He waggled a long fore-finger at her. 'My dear, you and I are foreigners and we should stick together.'

Dry Martinis are marvellous for creating courage where there was once nothing but porridgey fear. 'Who do you think you are, ordering people to be your friend?' Stung by his assessment of her status in her bolthole, Billie turned snippy. 'Friendships develop. Perhaps I don't like you.'

'Perhaps you don't,' agreed Sam, disappointingly philosophical. 'Plenty of people don't.'

'No. Ah ha. Then.' Martinis, however, do not improve one's vocabulary. Particularly when sucked down like sherbet dabs.

'I'm not very nice. I'm loud. I'm rude. Apparently, I don't "recognise boundaries", whatever the fuck that means. Consequently, Billiver, I don't have that many friends. But,' he leaned forward, and that whiplash smile was inches from her face, 'the ones I do have, love me. And I look after them. And appreciate them.'

The kiss on her nose made Billie jump, but it also made her grin despite herself. 'So you'll be my "gay best friend" kind of thing? I'll tell you all about my emotional problems and we'll get drunk together and then you'll help me pick out new curtains?'

'Fuck off. I said I was gay, not Dale Winton. No curtains. Emotional problems only where appropriate. But lots of fun. And lots of Martinis. And lots of getting to know one another. Is it a deal?' he asked for the second time in their short acquaintance.

She looked at Sam for a long while. He attracted and repelled her in equal measure, as if she'd cuddled a kitten only to find out it was a crocodile in a fake fur all-in-one.

'You want to say yes,' he told her, like a stage hypnotist. 'But something's holding you back.'

A gay psychic with a powerful motorbike and rock-god dress sense. The old Billie resurfaced for a moment. The one who believed in yesses. 'It's a deal,' she laughed, aware she might regret it, and not caring a bit.

* * *

Sam was an artist, he told her, as his outline grew oddly blurred. Billie wondered if it was a party trick of his, not thinking to blame the Martinis she was massacring.

'That hut is my studio.'

'You don't look like an artisht.' What Billie meant was that he didn't look like Jake. He didn't smell like him either: this artist smelled of discreetly expensive cologne. 'Are you successful?' She knew that Jake had never sold one of his creations.

'Very,' said Sam, without pride. In fact, there was a noticeable curl to his full lip. 'I'm renting that big thatched cottage on the edge of the coast road for a few months. You know it?'

Billie knew it. 'Classy,' she slurred.

'Enough about me. I want to know about you, Billie-poos.'

'Oh. There's nothing to tell,' insisted Billie, not drawing breath until the staff diplomatically whispered that it was closing time.

Wobbling to the bike, Billie asked, 'Why the blackmail? That was horrid.'

'My twisted idea of a joke. I wanted to get your attention.' He pulled on his helmet, and helped Billie with hers. He was sober, having downed only one Martini in comparison to Billie's more impressive tally. 'Worked, didn't it?'

'Still horrid, though.' Her voice muffled, Billie poked her head into the helmet. 'You could have given me nightless sleeps. Er . . .'

'I know what you mean.' Sam picked her up and placed her on the pillion as if she was a dolly and not a connoisseur of the sausage roll and all its variants. 'I wouldn't have done it if I thought you'd be scared. I mean, nobody's dumb enough to take that kind of thing seriously, are they?'

Billie shook her head vigorously, and the helmet spun around her head, handily hiding her embarrassment.

It hadn't really been a date. So why was Billie unable to get Sam out of her head the next morning, as she watched a plasterer she couldn't afford smooth out the bumps in the shop walls? Her new – what? *friend?* – was rolling about in her thoughts. She smiled whenever she thought of him, and yet she shivered, too. His wildness appealed to her old self, the Billie still on the naughty stair back at her parents' house.

There was a mystery to Sam which intrigued her. How on earth had he landed at Sole Bay? He was like a deliberate mistake in a picture, a Sex Pistol who'd wandered on to a chocolate-box lid. He'd stonewalled her about his wealth, and about why he was going cold turkey on love. 'You're more interesting than me,' he'd insisted.

Over the next week, Sam popped in a couple of times. Not even pretending to be helpful, he tried to lure Billie away, whispering like Satan in her ear of vodka and tonic and all the crisps she could eat.

Resolute, Billie was faithful to the shop. She was chafing at the tight schedule and the tight budget, but she was determined to open on time. When she flagged, the thought of her brother's I-told-you-so's prodded her up the ladder again.

Debs visited, her ponytail so tight her feet should have been off the ground. 'Doesn't look like you'll be ready for the grand reopening on Saturday,' she said, noticeably unimpressed with the virgin cube.

Not daring to offer a sarky, 'Thanks for the encouragement,' to a girl whose aura bristled like a porcupine overcoat, Billie kept quiet, concentrating on screwing a new, plain mirror to the wall.

'We're having champagne!' gushed Dot, grabbing Debs' arm just as if she was a normal person. 'And canapé things. And there'll be special offers. And Jake is painting a new sign.' She stopped mid-gush, and looked anxiously at Billie: that information hadn't reached her boss yet.

That kind of decision wasn't in an assistant's job description. But, thought Billie, neither was staying late, listening to her boss whine, or getting baptised with Polyfilla. 'That sounds great,' she smiled, to Dot's obvious relief.

Like Nosferatu rising from his coffin, Jake sat up from where he'd been reclining on the floorboards. 'I can do it in emulsion . . .' His murky eyes narrowed. 'Or I can do it in soil mixed with menstrual blood. Very expressive. Very real.'

'But not awfully bridal,' suggested Billie.

'So you want me to stifle my creativity and toe the party line. You're asking a rebel genius to paint a stick-up-its-arse, common or garden sign that can only add to the sum of moribund banality in this stagnant world of ours?'

'Er, yes.' How Billie would have loved to bowl an orb of life at his head. 'There is another way you could help,' she realised, holding up a bulging carrier bag. 'We can't find the time to deliver these flyers. Could you possibly . . .' She didn't bother finishing the sentence. Jake had pulled his bowler hat over his eyes and lain down again, radiating an indignation so solid she could have stood on it to reach the higher shelves. 'Forget I spoke.'

'Give them here.' Debs picked up the heavy carrier bag as if it was a feather. 'I'll deliver them while I walk the pit bull.' She held out her hand. 'A tenner?'

'A tenner.' Billie fumbled for her purse. Debs was not the sort of girl you negotiated with. She even smiled.

'See you Saturday.' Debs headed for the door. 'Can't wait. I love champagne. Makes me fart, mind.'

'Until then,' said Billie, weakly.

Painting until they were cross-eyed, Billie and Dot smothered the dark old room in a tidal wave of brilliant white. Light bounced and played all around them, waking up dark corners that had been snoring for years.

Predictably vocal, Jake spat, 'White?!' as he lounged in the window, watching them work. 'That's not even a real colour. Not to an artist. Where's your imagination?'

'I'll settle for customers, thanks.' Billie quelled a strong urge to rearrange his beardy features with her trowel.

'If Picasso had this wonderful space he'd make it vibrant and irresistible,' lisped Jake.

'Maybe he would,' agreed Billie. 'But if I promise never to paint women with both eyes on the same side of their nose, perhaps Mr Picasso will promise never to open a provincial wedding-dress shop.' Billie was stung. She hated herself for being so snippy, but Jake's arrows had found their target: he was good at this.

The truth was that Billie had a secret vanity about her flair for interior design. Not that she'd ever had much outlet for it. Her house share with eight other girls had been a forest of Formica and yellow pine, and later the chrome and glass and leather of James's bachelor pad had contemptuously spat out her Cath Kidston oven gloves. Even so, she was an avid reader of all the interiors magazines, and liked to think she knew her decking from her laminates. All in theory, obviously, until she'd accepted the poisoned chalice of Barbara's Brides, but this talent was a bauble she liked to take out of the drawer and admire whenever life reminded her that she was single, practically homeless, and bobbing on the flotsam and jetsam of a great-aunt's life.

Friday was arduous, and never-ending. With the paint still tacky, Dot and Billie were still setting out the new stock at midnight. The dull months down the telesales saltmines had honed Billie's negotiating skills and she'd managed to fill the shop on credit. Thanks to this, the refurbishment had squeaked in on budget.

Pausing in the hanging of a simple satin strapless dress, Billie allowed herself a moment of pride. Just a moment – she wasn't built to preen. For the first time her head and her heart were hand in hand. Not only did she love the bricks and mortar of Barbara's Brides, but she could see the potential in it. Batty Billie had pulled on a business suit and lo and behold, it fitted. Her heart had a bad credit rating, but this time it wasn't in charge. This time things would work out.

Wouldn't they?

Eight

Even the most anticipated days finally roll around. Saturday came, and Billie woke early, due to a combination of bowel-loosening nerves and the booming of a furious sea. By the time she furtively left Herbert's Dream II, the waves had calmed and the town behind her was serene, yawning in the struggling sun of late spring.

Billie shooed a belligerent gull from her postage-stamp veranda. She'd never appreciated how *outsize* seagulls were: this one was big enough to saddle up and ride. And, God, they were bad-tempered. They were as mean as Billie herself just before her period, a time of the month when she could easily invade a small eastern European country.

Turning into Little Row, Billie saw a stork-like frame up a ladder outside the shop. Jake was finishing the sign. Billie approached him sideways, reluctant to look up at his handiwork in case it incorporated bodily fluids. She needn't have worried.

The new sign was sharp and clear and professional: Jake evidently had unpublicised traditional skills. There was only one thing wrong with the elegant black lettering on a clean white background.

'That's not the bloody name of the bloody shop!' Billie shrieked up at him, panic pulsing in her ears like the sea an hour earlier.

Emerging from the shop, Dot answered for him. 'Oh yes it is! I OK'ed it with Babs over the phone.'

Billie stared up at the words. 'Oh, Dot,' she said, trying to control the smile that was threatening to engulf her whole head.

'Billie's Brides,' read Dot. 'Has a ring to it, don't you think?'

'Billie's Brides' resembled a still life. The clean white walls sang. Dresses bristled with all the thrilling potential of unworn clothes.

69

The floorboards, repaying the girls' blood, sweat and swear-words, glowed.

The shop had woken up. Prodded by paintbrushes, it had shaken itself and stood up straight. A new energy beat through the wood that Billie liked to stroke when nobody was looking. She'd never related to any man so perfectly: this shop was her soulmate.

The upmarket savoury bites offered themselves selflessly, like lingerie models at a footballer's penthouse, and the plastic champagne flutes marched in orderly rows. The new pink tissue paper was piled in optimistic towers. A brand-new, and as yet blank, Gallery of Happiness stared down from above the new, computerised cash register. 'GOOD LUK MY DEERS!' shouted a postcard of a wallaby from Great Aunty Babs. In the absence of any message from her family, the card had warmed Billie when she'd plucked it from the new doormat. Even if it did remind her that the shop was only on loan.

In the centre of the still life, an unusual family portrait was arranged. Tense and upright, Billie wore her cleanest jeans and had chivvied her hair into an approximation of a bun. Dot, bullied into a plain navy dress that had neither a tassel nor an appliquéd butterfly to its name, was solemn. Debs had interpreted her new employer's request to 'dress classily' as an invitation to pull on a fluorescent-pink ruched tube dress, and stood with her docker's legs apart.

They were ready.

'Unlock the door, Miss Dot.' Billie nodded at her assistant, who was holding the key ready, like a high priestess in an arcane ritual.

'Hello Sole Bay!' sang Dot, as she flung open the door with a flourish.

Peter, the three-legged Yorkshire terrier looked in, sniffed, and stumbled on.

'Can we start on the booze?' asked Debs.

'We're serving it, not drinking it, remember?' said Billie, but gently, with due deference to the fact that Debs could (and possibly would) beat seven shades of shit out of her. 'Once the rush starts we won't have time to think about drinking.'

* * *

'Is she the rush?' asked Debs loudly, as Annie helped herself shamefacedly to a sausage on a stick.

'Sssh,' ordered Billie. (But gently.) 'Ask our customer if she'd like a glass of champagne.'

'Fancy it?' Debs waggled a chilled bottle in Annie's startled face.

'Oh. Oh dear.' Annie looked dismayed. 'I don't drink alcohol, dear.'

'I'll have one for you.' Debs could be very thoughtful.

'It's already midday.' Folding and unfolding her arms neurotically, Billie was fretting.

'Five and a half hours to go. Plenty of time for the crowd to build.' The glass was always half full to Dot.

To Billie it was half full of wee. It was humiliating, standing about with her staff in an empty shop. They were three prime 'Nobby No Mates', and she foresaw a week of living on mini quiches. At least she could drink herself into amnesia on the beach with the leftover champers.

The shop bell had them all standing to attention.

Then they all slumped. 'Jake,' snarled Billie by way of welcome.

'It's dead in here,' he noted, with open satisfaction.

'Have a breadstick,' suggested Billie, popping one in his mouth a little too vigorously.

The shop bell jangled again, and a young woman came shyly in. Dot, who had sneaked on an ethnic-y embroidered waistcoat over her dress, poured her some champagne.

A couple followed, full of questions about bridesmaid dresses. Then a handful of teenagers sloped in and laid waste to the ham pinwheels before Debs intervened with an authoritative, 'Sod off!'

The horror of throwing a party that nobody came to receded as a gentle wave of custom ebbed and flowed through the shop. From her mingling (Billie was a reluctant mingler and her small talk was atrocious – somehow it always turned gynaecological) the new proprietor learned that there was a lot of intrigued local interest in the revitalised business.

'It was a bit . . . eccentric before,' ventured one woman who looked as if she'd been born in Marks & Spencer's cardigan department.

'This is *tons* better,' gushed a chic twenty-something girl, slim and splendid in black. 'Even makes me consider getting married!'

'Oooh, don't get carried away!' laughed Billie, aware as soon as the words came out of her mouth that this was the wrong tack for somebody whose livelihood depended on weddings. She would have to crank round her attitude to happy ever afters by a full 180 degrees. Professionally, at least.

So, for the next few hours, she heard a voice – just like her own but perhaps slightly higher-pitched – saying things like, 'After all, it's the happiest day of your life,' or, 'We all dream of our big day, don't we?' and even, to a shrivelled fifty-something whose wrinkles had joined up to create a contour map of Ben Nevis, 'You look like a princess in that tiara.'

Men were heavily outnumbered by women, but some hapless blokes had been dragged in. They sensibly restricted themselves to nodding and smiling, lobbing the odd reckless compliment. 'Yes, love, you certainly do look like Julia Roberts in that white thing.'

The new stock was being whisked in and out of the revamped changing cubicles, as girls emerged from behind the new white velvet curtains, confident of raising squeals from their companions.

Ladling out champagne like an upmarket soup kitchen, Billie whispered, 'This is going fabulously!' to Dot.

'Of course.' Dot's smile was transcendent. A silver amulet or ten had wound their way around her neck.

A glass in each puffy hand, Zelda was impressed. 'The place looks like a palace,' she said. 'Much as I love Babs, you could never accuse her of having taste.'

'Well . . .' Slightly shocked by the older lady's frankness, Billie attempted an expression that both agreed and disagreed with the criticism of her great-aunt.

'Mind you, I don't either!' said Zelda, comfortably. Her tangerine trouser suit backed up this confession. 'I've never had taste. That's why I never married. I always chose wrong 'uns.' She sipped at each glass in turn. 'Besides, I was too busy to get married. Too busy making love, as we used to call it,' she confided to a woman in glasses who was trying on a white sheath that made her look like a knitting needle. 'Love 'em and leave 'em. Who wants to face the same old willy every morning?' She sounded as if she actually wanted an answer, but the knitting needle, now rather pink, stayed silent. 'Variety. That's the answer.' With this parting advice, perhaps slightly out of place among the white satin odes to commitment, Zelda shimmied off through the crowd, her corseted bulk jiggling in time to her a cappella 'Hit Me Baby One More Time'.

On the fringes, an area he evidently called home, Sam watched the scrum of brides over the rim of his champagne flute. He winked slyly at Billie and she giggled to herself. It felt reassuring to have his male bulkiness around, his creaking leather jacket contrasting starkly with the laces and silks of her new life. The embodiment of the wholesome cynicism that she wasn't allowed to express, Sam prowled the shop, raising his eyebrows at the gushing and gasping and emoting that a few white frocks could incite.

Raising those expressive eyebrows behind one buxom girl who cried with joy when she saw herself head to toe in lace in the mirror, he bent down to Billie to whisper, 'If she's going to shed tears, surely they should be for her thighs.'

'Shut up, you.' Billie delivered a smack and a vol-au-vent before mingling on. Ignoring overheard snippets of Debs' patter – 'I'll get you a size up. At least now we know who's been eating all the pies, eh?' – Billie asked Dot how much they'd taken. She lowered her voice. 'I suppose we can trust—' She jerked a nod towards Debs, who had awarded herself a drink for every one she gave out and was burping, 'I'm not being personal but that dress makes your arse look like a caravan,' at a customer.

'I told you. Debs is a diamond,' said Dot, emphatically.

'Very much in the rough,' sighed Billie, vowing for the umpteenth time to lecture Debs about her attitude. From a safe distance. And perhaps through a voice-disguising apparatus.

'Enjoying yourself, Annie?' Billie asked.

'It's a lovely party, thank you,' said Annie, like a well-tutored seven-year-old. Unaware of a quiche smear on her upper lip, she had homed in on the Ruby Wolff dresses. 'These are exquisite. Quite exquisite,' she said, softly. 'I used to be a seamstress, you see, so I appreciate quality.'

The unravelling had begun.

Beetling over to pour oil on the troubled waters left in Debs' considerable wake, Billie was stopped short by a firm hand on her wrist, a hand weighed down by a rock on the third finger that could be seen from space, and attached to a lanky blonde, obviously addicted to her hair straighteners. 'You're Billie.' It was more an accusation than a question.

'Yes.' Still that grip. Billie wondered what she was letting herself in for.

'I *love* your shop!' the blonde girl gasped, her horsey face lighting up. 'Don't we?' she went on, turning to a man at her side, built along the lines of a small block of flats.

'Yeah.' The big man seemed bored. 'How much for the whole wedding?'

This earned him a playful slap from his companion and a puzzled look from Billie. 'You don't ask straight out like that. You build up to it, Dean!' admonished the girl, whose face became even more Red Rum-esque when irritated. She turned back to Billie. 'Mind you, now he's brought it up, how much *is* it for the whole wedding?'

'Do you mean dresses for the bride and all the attendants?' Billie wasn't sure what constituted a 'whole wedding'. 'We don't do the groom or the male attendants, I'm afraid.' She un-prised the hand from her sleeve: she didn't like the way her arm hung there, like a small rodent in the grip of a peckish hawk. 'I'm sorry but could you just hang on for a moment? I'll be back in two ticks.'

It took rather more ticks than that to placate an ashen bride who'd just been advised by Debs that Sole Bay would laugh up its collective sleeve if she dared to walk up the aisle in white. Once ten per cent had been knocked off the price (and a cream version found) a deep voice behind Billie made her turn.

'I'm off.' Sam was propping his dark glasses on his straight nose. 'There's only so much oestrogen a guy can take.'

'Thanks for coming.' Billie meant it: she'd been surprised to see him. 'I know it's not your kind of thing.'

'Naw. But *you* are.' Sam held the back of Billie's neck and kissed her firmly on the forehead. 'You done good,' he whispered so that only she could hear.

Flustered, delighted, unused to unvarnished praise, Billie responded by pushing him out of the door. Tingling inside, she searched the crowd for the tall blonde, hoping she'd gone.

No, there she stood by the ransacked canapés, willowy in Next's take on Armani. 'Hey!' she hollered imperiously when she saw Billie hesitate. 'We were talking!'

It took a moment or two of conversation to discover that there had been a misunderstanding. 'Miss Dot. Cooee, MISS DOT!' called Billie, teeth set in an unconvincing grin.

Reluctantly, Dot left the side of a couple who had fiercely opposing views on jewelled hairbands. She had managed to accumulate a jangly bangle or eleven since opening time.

'Miss Dot,' began Billie, with synthetic calm, 'Dean and Heather here are telling me that we offer a comprehensive wedding package. Apparently we organise *everything*. Dresses, suits, venues, caterers, the lot. Apparently they discussed this with your good self.' *Apparently,* Billie tried to silently communicate, *you want to ruin what is left of my life.*

'Did they . . . ?' began Dot, vaguely.

Heather was not vague. Heather was every bit as pointy as her shoes. 'Yes, we did,' she said staunchly. 'You said this is a one-stop shop, and you arrange everything for the bride-to-be.' She pointed out to the street. 'The sign says Billie's Brides, not Billie's *wedding dresses*.' She stressed the distinction with an arch look, as if she was playing a lawyer in a Hollywood court-room drama and had just nailed the defendant.

The defendant wasn't going down without a fight. 'Sorry, but you're wasting your time. We really don't organise weddings.'

'But you must!' Heather's face folded in on itself. 'It's the biggest day of my life and I don't know where to start. I've left it all too late.' She was grasping Billie's arm again, clutching on as if she'd slipped overboard. 'This shop tells me that you have perfect taste, like myself,' she claimed, wildly. 'And I know you love weddings, just by listening to you. I need you. PLEASE HELP ME!'

That glimpse of hysteria, that resonating note of controlled feminine mania, was like a wormhole in the universe whisking Billie right back to her own wedding day. She wasn't revisiting that swamp of hormones and expectation. 'No. Sorry. Not at any price.'

'Dean. Get out your chequebook,' commanded Heather, regally. 'Write her a cheque right now for . . .' Heather thought, and one could practically hear the tiny calculators whirring inside her straightened head. 'Three thousand pounds.'

Well. Then again. Maybe for *that* price.

'Perhaps,' said Billie, 'if you really need me . . .' She was giddy on the smell of folding money (it would buy enough charity-shop furniture to fill a stately home) and the certain knowledge that she would regret this.

The 'Clossed' sign, a remnant of Great Aunty Babs that Billie couldn't bear to ditch, was turned over. On the counter was a pile of crisp cheques: beneath it, a pile of pissed shop assistants. Plus Zelda. Billie had accepted that Zelda would be a constant in her life: perhaps her Evil Eye would come in handy.

'Fudge, anyone?' muttered Zelda, almost asleep. She had been drinking all day, neglecting her shop, and the invalid Raven, for the lure of complementary Safeway own-brand champagne.

'You were ace, Mish Dot,' slurred Billie, chinking an empty glass with her colleague.

'Oh, you're a genius,' sobbed Dot. The champagne bubbles had scored a direct hit on her tear glands. 'We're going to make so many women so very happy.' She dried her tears on the tie-dye shawl that had snaked around her shoulders at some point.

Ugg boots pointing north, Debs had seemed to be asleep on the floor, but her snores stopped long enough for her to say, 'We'll take those silly cows for every penny they've got.'

In between them, literally and philosophically, Billie raised a toast. 'To Great Aunty Babs.'

'The mad old boot', added Debs.

Nine

Billie's naïve hope that champagne gave you a posher, and therefore less painful, hangover, was swept away on Sunday morning.
Sitting bolt upright and howling like a weregirl, Billie greeted
the East Anglian dawn with a head full of gruel that also
somehow accommodated a xylophone tumbling endlessly down
metal stairs. The accompanying mini-quiche indigestion put paid
to her Sunday, which was spent lying down and saying 'Ow'
occasionally.

Monday brought mixed feelings. There was relief that her
scraping days were done, but fear that she and Dot might sit
in their modern, pristine, white and down-lit Fresh Start all on
their ownio. Billie had stuck her head over the parapet and
now it was time to take the arrows: Billie's Brides' success or
failure was down to her.

Greeted by the new Gallery of Happiness, bare and blank,
Billie was glad to see the red light on the new answerphone
glowing when she got in. 'That's a good start!' she thought,
pressing the button. She jumped back when she heard Heather's
voice, loud and unamused.

'Oh. I see. You're not there. You shut on a Sunday, do you?
I need somebody to call me urgently. I'm having a crisis about
the pageboy. I think he might be ugly. And you're still on for
the meeting Monday afternoon, I hope?'

'Fancy calling on a Sunday . . .' Billie, who attended church
less than your average satanist, was shocked. It looked like
Heather was going to make sure Billie's Brides earned their
three thousand pounds.

Dot breezed in, all lovebeads and sandals, and while she put
the kettle on and chatted about the party, Jenkins's health and
other Dottish topics, Billie noticed the laptop sticking out from

behind the counter. Was it her imagination, or did it have a certain jaunty, even suggestive, air?

An image flashed through her mind. It was an unwelcome one, of her drunken self, tapping out an email to James with one hand while the other one kept a rigor mortis grip on a plastic glass of flat champagne.

Billie went hot, and then cold, which can be symptoms of pneumonia but in her case was a simple bout of sober regret. What, she wondered, had she written? She was loquacious when drunk, always ready to ring up some bloke she'd snogged a decade ago and deliver a detailed autopsy of his personality. Sometimes she would tell men she barely knew that she loved them, other times it would be all vitriol as she blamed a bloke who once took her to the pictures for all the pain of her existence.

Yes, that computer did have a smug air. It knew something she didn't. It knew whether or not she had made an absolute arse of herself in front of a man whose opinion still meant a lot.

That thought stopped her short. Even with thumbscrews, and possibly the threat of a *Hi-de-Hi!* compilation tape, Billie would never have admitted that she cared what James thought any more. Suddenly all action, she flew at the computer and manhandled it out of its case. As Dot poured tea and opened the post, Billie poked rapidly at keys, tutted through the interminable blinking and whirring of the awakening computer, and then fearfully read what she'd written, her fingers in her mouth.

Baffled, she read it twice. It didn't sound like the insane ramblings that usually followed a cuddle from the alcohol fairy. It was more like the musings of a fond aunt to a schoolboy nephew.

Lovely to hear from you.

—it began, as if The Story had never happened. Jauntily, it went on to exclaim:

I've moved! To the loveliest little town!

78

Billie's vile drunken alter ego could be relied upon to spread chaos, but this twittering, gushing new persona was somehow creepier. It was as if her tipsy self had decided to play along with James and beat him at his own game. The language used was every bit as airy as his.

Seen any good movies lately?

—it asked the man she'd last seen drunk in his boxers, dividing up their paperbacks as if he personally hated each book.

Even without the lure of free comestibles, the shop was pleasantly busy that first day. The crystal tinkle of the bell was music to Billie's ears, each note crooning, 'You haven't cocked up! Well, not yet!' to her bandaged self-esteem. She and Miss Dot listened to the needs and wants of the women who came in, with barely time to share a companionable biscuit.

Puzzled, Billie eyed a girl flicking through a rail. The thin, knock-kneed little scrap was surely a bridesmaid, not a bride. 'Need any help?' she asked.

'I need a dress,' the girl mumbled, her face resolutely turned away. 'A wedding dress.'

'For . . . you?'

'Yes.' The girl sighed, a real teenager's special that travelled all the way up from her trainers. 'Please don't you be horrible to me, too,' she murmured, staring down at the floor.

'Look at me,' ordered Billie, feeling quite grown-up next to this childish customer. 'Who's been horrible to you?'

'The big wedding shop in Neeveston shopping centre. The woman up the top of the town who makes dresses in her spare time. They just laughed at me.' She was operatically miserable as only the young can be.

'I won't laugh at you,' promised Billie. 'Are you old enough to get married?'

'Yeah. I'm sixteen. And my dad's given his consent.' The girl used the phrase carefully, as if she'd rehearsed it.

Wonder if she's pregnant, thought Billie.

As if the accusation had come out of the side of Billie's head on ticker tape, the girl said firmly, 'I'm not pregnant.

I'm not stupid. I love Moz and I want to marry him.'

'That's the best reason to get married,' said Billie, sobered.

'Tell me mum that. She thinks I'm throwing everything away. But I love him to bits!' the girl squealed, suddenly animated.

'One hundred and ten per cent?' asked Billie, who had seen enough *Trisha* to know the lingo. 'So much it hurts?'

'Oh, you understand!' A bubble of snot popped from the girl's nose.

Billie showed her the updated ready-to-wear range. Simple, unfussy dresses that needed no alterations, they were also cheaper, and better suited to a teenager's pocket.

It was hard to shake off the feeling that she was colluding in what might be the biggest mistake of the sixteen-year-old's life. At that age Billie had painted her room black and daydreamed about going ice skating with Phillip Schofield. She shook herself, and accepted the tenners the girl extracted from her Bratz purse. This was a business transaction, pure and simple.

Watching the girl leave with a bulky carrier bag, Billie hoped that loving Moz to bits would be enough.

Irreproachably tidy and respectable, the new housing estate sat primly on the edge of town, only the occasional belch of a seagull betraying its proximity to the raffish sea.

Heather Du Bois' house was square and neat, like its neighbours, except for the concrete Grecian columns that rose majestically either side of the double-glazed front door. *A very important person lives here*, they seemed to say, although Billie could also hear a whispered *Somebody with no bleeding idea lives here*.

Welcomed by Heather, enormous fluffy slippers complementing her sweatpant civvies, Billie was politely ordered to take her shoes off. 'New carpets,' explained Heather. 'Oatmeal wool/nylon mix. You understand?'

'I would never knowingly harm a wool/nylon mix.' Billie cursed her mismatched socks and padded after her hostess into a pale sitting room, all blond wood and white walls. With its plasma screen and careful arrangement of Buddhas, it was a room to pose in, rather than relax.

'Any chance of a guided tour?' Billie asked Heather, who had picked up and was beating a beige cushion as if it was a runaway slave. Congratulating herself on how professional it sounded, she enlarged, 'Your house tells me a lot about your personal style and preferences.'

'Like your thinking.' Heather pointed an approving acrylic nail at her.

Sounding professional was vital, because Billie felt distinctly amateur. She was in way over her head: the only other wedding she'd ever organised had ended with blood on the walls. Quite apart from the three-thousand-pound fee, Billie would be responsible for spending lots and lots and lots of Heather's money: it was a sobering prospect.

After the zen reception room, the country kitchen was a surprise. Herbs swayed like leafy hanged men from polystyrene beams above the Aga. In the bedroom an opulent four poster swathed in machine-washable silk changed the mood again. The modern, noodle-eating woman of the sitting room, who'd morphed into a Domestic Goddess in the kitchen was now Mata Hari.

It wasn't very useful. Heather liked props, and playing a part. Which of these characters was the flesh and blood woman? A stray hank of hair at the back of her head which had escaped the straighteners might be a clue: it curled exuberantly.

'Interesting,' Billie summed up as they seated themselves on the cream leather sofa, an instant coffee apiece.

Heather seemed to expect a fancier adjective.

'Impressive.' That did the trick. Heather's bony face relaxed. 'Let's have a chat,' said Billie.

'DON'T PUT THAT THERE!' shrieked Heather suddenly. She slung a coaster under the mug that Billie had been lowering towards the glass coffee table. 'Yeah, a nice chat,' she continued comfortably.

Recovering from the conversational emergency stop, Billie rescued a pad from the tangled entrails of her bag. 'First things first,' she said, as crisp and efficient as a girl who organises ten weddings before breakfast. 'What's the date of the wedding?'

'August the twenty-third.' Heather frowned. 'What's that look for?' she asked neurotically.

81

'Nothing,' coughed Billie. 'That's a lovely date.' So lovely she'd chosen it for her own wedding. 'Tell me a bit about yourself, Heather. Your likes and dislikes. It all helps,' said Billie. 'Shame Dean isn't here.'

'Why?' Heather seemed baffled.

'So I can find out what he wants from his wedding day.'

'Oh, he wants what I want.' Heather batted away such sentimental notions of democracy.

It transpired that Heather was in IT. This was a conversation stopper, as Billie understood alchemy better than she understood IT. Dean was a prison warder: 'Has all the top rapists and murderers,' Heather told her proudly. The bride-to-be was the adored elder daughter of parents who had given her a pony, an overbite and too much positive reaffirmation. Her mother had died some years ago, but, 'You'll love Granny,' prophesied Heather, with such confidence that Billie knew she wouldn't. 'A real character. Told me to tell you she'll watch you like a hawk and string you up in the church if everything isn't absolutely perfect!' In Heather's family this kind of threat apparently passed as humour. 'Shall I fetch the mood board?' she asked, suddenly.

'Oooh, yes please.' Billie had absolutely no idea what a mood board might be.

'Taaa-daah!' Heather leaned behind the sofa and yanked out a large cork noticeboard, studded with pictures and swatches and cuttings. 'This is like the inside of my head!'

A pang of sympathy for Dean shot through Billie. It couldn't be easy living with a woman whose head was full of white horses with feathered plumes, roast beef and calligraphy. 'Right. Hmmm. Let's see.' The mood board had an immediate effect on Billie's mood: it scared the offal out of her. 'Okaaaay,' she busked, floundering. She could feel Heather staring at her the way biblical personnel used to stare at Jesus. 'And you want all these things for your wedding?'

'Of course not!' The rush of relief brought on by Heather's reply was short-lived. 'But the plumed horses are non-negotiable.'

'Of course,' agreed Billie shakily, wondering where on earth she'd start to look for horses with feathers on their heads.

'This is just a starting point, to give you an idea of what I'm after.' Heather pointed excitedly from cutting to cutting, as familiar with her material as an Oxford don with an ancient parchment. '*That's* the feel I'm after.'

'The feel,' repeated Billie blankly, staring at a magazine photograph of a butterfly on a postbox.

'I'm thinking romantic but raunchy.' Heather stood up and paced the sacred carpet. 'Kylie Minogue meets Scarlett O'Hara. There have to be roses. Maybe orchids. Table diamonds. Candles.' She was shouting now. 'DOVES!'

Wondering what the hell a table diamond was when it was at home, Billie threw Heather a practical question. 'How many bridesmaids?'

'Just the dozen. The triplets dropped out.' Heather fell back on to the sofa.

Lucky, lucky triplets, thought Billie, scribbling 'twelve brides-sodding-maids'. 'Venues?' she asked, brightly, kicking the mood board covertly under the sofa.

'You'll think I'm mad.' Heather looked down at her lap, a pink, self-absorbed look on her face. 'My dream venue is the old bandstand, near the pier. Do you know it?'

'I do.' One of Billie's favourite spots in Sole Bay, the bandstand was loaded with charm, weather-beaten and peeling: not terribly Heather.

'When I was little, when Mum was still here, she used to take us there with sandwiches and Cokes every Saturday. It's my absolute favourite place in the world.' Heather sounded uncannily like the sixteen-year-old Billie had served earlier. 'I dragged Dean there as soon as he proposed. Kind of, you know, to let Mum know.' She smiled self-consciously. 'Mad.'

This was the kind of detail Billie needed to unlock her client. 'Well, I doubt that the bandstand has a licence for you to get married there, but we can include your mum's favourite hymn in the service, or the flowers she liked in your bouquet,' she said softly.

The suggestions seemed to warm Heather. 'I never thought of that.'

Thanks to a frantic Google, Billie had some venues to consider. She made a note of Heather's favourites and promised to make enquiries. 'We can go along and check out the rooms, taste the catering before we make a final decision.'

'What about the cake?' asked Heather. 'Dean wants fruit cake. He's such an old woman. Over my dead body, Dean Kelly, I said.'

'The *in* cake, the cake all the celebs are choosing,' began Billie, reciting parrot-fashion a paragraph from a catalogue, 'is a white chocolate mousse-based confection.' She was reeling Heather in like a canny angler with a prize trout. 'It's topped with crème anglaise and darling miniature truffles.' Forgiving herself for saying 'darling' she lied easily and shamelessly to close the deal. 'Catherine Zeta Jones had one.'

'Order it.'

Talk turned to themes, and Billie did her best to chart a course away from such aesthetically choppy waters.

'I've been toying with Cinderella.' Heather sent barbs of fear into Billie's heart. 'I could wear a big sparkly crinoline.'

This entailed casting Dean the prison warder as Prince Charming. This was challenging casting. Inspiration struck. 'That'll be a doddle to organise. *Everybody* is doing Disney at the moment.'

'Everybody?' Displeasure hovered in Heather's waxed eyebrows.

'Everybody,' repeated Billie, emphatically. Watching Heather out of the corner of her eye, she started, 'Since Jordan . . .'

'Nope. Gone off Disney,' announced Heather.

'Shame. Whatever you say.' Appealing to her pretensions was one way of handling this nervy racehorse of a woman. Feeling a need to say something real – so much of this meeting had been devoted to using a psychological cattle prod on Heather – Billie reached out to touch the girl's arm, thin in its velour sweatshirt. 'I'm going to do my very best to make this the most beautiful day of your life, Heather. I promise.'

'Aw,' purred Heather. 'Thanks.' She slapped her knees. 'For three grand I should bloody well think you are. More coffee?'

All talked out about headdresses and invitation fonts and the oldest bridesmaid's allergies, Billie stood up to go. Like the creeper around Sleeping Beauty's castle, her to-do list had grown and grown. 'Let's meet up again next week,' she suggested, quelling a yawn.

'Stay for dinner! We can discuss Granny's hat over a casserole.' Heather grinned encouragingly, obviously reluctant to let her wedding planner escape.

Temporarily blinded by Heather's impressive teeth, Billie edged towards the hall. 'Tempting though that is, I have to go.'

'And you still think macrobiotic sushi is wrong for the reception?'

'You are not Madonna. Your guests are not from LA. British people will feel short-changed if they roll up to a reception and somebody hands them a raw prawn.'

'You're right,' Heather caved in. 'I just want to stun everybody, you know? I want the wow factor.'

'The main thing is marrying the right bloke,' Billie laughed. 'The rest is just detail.' Billie's responses to Heather's wilder flights of fancy were growing braver. They might have been friends if they'd met another way. She admired Heather's energy in keeping up her front, even if that front was composed of borrowed stances. Billie suspected that Heather's heart was just as gooey as Dot's, it just wasn't worn on an eco-friendly sleeve.

Billie had managed to creep as far as the front door, and she leapt when it suddenly opened.

Heather's welcome for her husband-to-be was accusatory. 'You're early,' she said, suspiciously, as if this was proof of something evil in his character.

'I wanted to catch Billie.' Dean nodded an affable hello. 'Alright? Has she nobbled you about the fruit cake yet?'

''Fraid so,' smiled Billie.

'Did you get to the jazz band?' he asked, hopefully.

'Dean, for the last time, we are not having jazz bastards at my wedding. She turned to Billie. 'Can you get me a band that looks and sounds exactly like the Rolling Stones?'

'Hmm. Wouldn't that be the Rolling Stones?' Billie inched nearer the door and freedom and life before she'd discovered table diamonds. 'Let's discuss the music next week.'

Dean hung his jacket up on the banisters, not seeming to notice that his fiancée immediately rehung it on the coat stand with a loud tut. 'Pity you can't hang around for dinner. You could meet my best man.' He pointed to a framed holiday snap-shot by the coat stand. A crowd of lads, sunburned and peeling, were holding up pints to the camera. 'That's Ed. On the far right.'

Politely, Billie glanced at the photo. Then she stared, struck by something. 'Is he a fireman?' she asked.

'Yeah.' Dean looked dewy-eyed, his big round face soft. 'One in a million. Salt of the earth.'

'If I'd met Ed first . . .' Heather looked dreamily out at the distorted street through the dimpled glass of the front door. 'Poor old Ed,' she sighed, with a sympathy that seemed misplaced when discussing a physically perfect fireman.

'Poor? Old?' queried Billie, remembering the man who'd asked her name after the inferno of Little Row.

'He's so shy,' explained Heather. 'Goes red as a tomato when he speaks to girls he fancies.' Perhaps noting Billie's novel expression which encompassed both a raised eyebrow and a dropped jaw, she asked, 'Did I say something?'

'No,' lied Billie. Refraining from chanting NAH NAH NA NAH NAH THE HUNKY FIREMAN LIKES ME, she checked, 'He's single, then?' Ed's status shouldn't, and didn't, matter but she was window-shopping. It was her favourite kind of shopping. Those shoes might pinch if you took them home.

'Not for long,' said Heather, mysteriously.

'How come?' For a window-shopper, Billie was displaying a marked interest in the goods.

Pointing to another, larger, framed photograph, Heather said, 'Angela. My sister. Chief bridesmaid. She and Ed were meant for each other. I'm going to get them together at the wedding.'

With the look of a man who'd heard all this before, Dean snorted and went into the sitting room, where very soon men were chasing a ball around a pitch on the plasma screen.

Billie studied the formal studio portrait of Angela. Gauzy and flattering, the soft focus couldn't mask the essential person-ality of the subject. 'She looks nice,' ventured Billie, taking in the tonged flicks, the ruffled neckline and the general air of castrating menace.

'She's an angel. Clever. Witty. Has her own pest-control

business.' Heather gazed admiringly at her sibling. 'A real catch for any man.'

The question had to be asked. 'Does Ed go red when he talks to her?'

'All over. Even his hair.'

Ten

The summer had hit its stride early. Sweetie-coloured houses along the front dazzled in the sun's glare, and Sole Bay residents left their front doors cocking a snook at their cardies. Pale, shy shoulders met the outside world for the first time in months, and blue-white legs marched proudly about in last year's shorts.

Being the boss of a growing shop didn't just mean lounging about in luxury and drinking tea from bridal slippers. In fact, it didn't mean that at all. A distinct lack of minions meant that Billie did a little of everything, from cleaning to selling to putting on a funny voice to disrupt the East Coast FM phone-ins. Today she was delivering a boned bodice to an address near the front. Dot had offered the loan of her Reliant Robin, but Billie made it a rule only to drive cars with an even number of wheels.

'About time,' said the customer, closing the door in Billie's face.

'Not at all,' simpered Billie to the closed door. 'Any time.' She stomped off, and took a wrong turning, a frequent by-product of stomping off. 'Oh flip,' she muttered. Being new in town, she'd spent a lot of time exploring the byways and alleyways of Sole Bay, but this short, narrow street was new to her.

Too pragmatic to believe in fate – like fairies, fat-free biscuits and reliable boyfriends the basic premise was preposterous – Billie couldn't help humming *The Twilight Zone* music when she realised that this was Richmond Villas, the address on the Ruby Wolff invoice.

The other flat-fronted cottages could be forgiven for leaning away from mucky number twelve. A rotting tooth in a set of pristine gnashers, its net curtains were grubby and its front door peeling.

'Why not?' Billie dusted off one of her favourite sayings from the old days, before life had stepped in and shown her exactly why bloody not. Pressing the doorbell, she jumped back from the step, startled by the clamour the innocuous ding dong had set off in the house. A great huffing and puffing began, as if a steam train was coming up the hall, and she could hear things being pulled and dragged and kicked out of the way. It was a surprise when all this noise and fury delivered a tiny, scowling, gnome of a man on to the step. He pulled the door carefully behind him, as if to hide some glorious secret the dark, uninviting interior might hide. 'What?' he asked, with enough ill humour to power Sole Bay for a fortnight.

'Oh,' began Billie, with her customary élan. 'Is your wife in?'

'Don't have no wife,' growled the man. He wore an impeccably cut, and sensationally filthy, three-piece suit.

'I'm sorry.' So Ruby had passed on, as Billie's mother liked to delicately put it, as if death was part of some celestial relay race. Billie suddenly felt sorry for this dishevelled little man, who was finding it hard to cope alone, if the stink of whisky was anything to go by. 'I didn't know.'

'No need to be sorry,' snapped the gent, obviously insulted by her sympathy. 'Wives are nothing but trouble. One hand in your purse and the other on your manhood.' He shook his head vehemently. 'Give me a terrapin anyday.'

Privately thinking that a simple *God rest her soul* would suffice, Billie shrugged, taking slow steps backwards. 'Well,' she began, devising an escape route from this pungent little fellow, 'Ruby was certainly a talented lady. I run the wedding shop in town and I was going to ask her if she wanted to start making dresses again.' Until that moment, Billie had no idea that she'd been going to ask Ruby any such thing. 'But, sadly—'

Clipping her sentence rudely, Mr Wolff's face crumpled in disgust, as if Billie was officially the stupidest person he'd ever met, and he grunted, 'I'm Ruby, you halfwit.'

'You're Ruby.' Billie blinked, like Meg Ryan in a chick flick when she realises that Tom Hanks is the love of her life. 'But you're not . . .' She didn't finish the sentence. By his age Mr Wolff would know he wasn't a woman.

'Reuben.' He stabbed a nicotine-stained finger at her. 'Reuben Wolff. You silly chit.'

Irritated by his accusation of chittery, Billie didn't know how to reply. Why, she berated herself, had she summoned up this diminutive demon, his shoulders caked with dandruff and his breath a dangerous weapon. 'Sorry to disturb you.'

The door had slammed before she got to the full stop.

'I couldn't leave her at home,' reasoned Dot, looking down at the chicken scratching about on the newly painted boards. Lowering her voice to a whisper, she confided, 'She's been getting worse. Mood swings. Suicide attempts on the garden rake. Depression is one thing but this . . .' she waved a hand in the direction of the chicken, who was now pecking at a grosgrain shoe, 'is quite another.'

'I can see she's going through a tough time,' cooed Billie.

'Aw, can you really?' Dot seemed delighted with her boss's unexpected empathy.

'No, I can't.' Billie swerved back to normal service. 'It's a bloody chicken, Dot.'

Glaring at Billie, Dot bent down to say, 'Julia, ignore her. She doesn't know you like I do.'

The chicken scuttled across the shop floor in a crazy zigzag, as if a sniper was after her.

Considering a short homily appropriate to the occasion, centring on the incompatibility of neurotic chickens and wedding-dress shops, Billie decided against it. 'Try and keep her out of the way,' was all she said.

'I think you'll find that discretion is Julia's middle name.'

'And mine is Mug.'

It was actually a relief to see Heather bowl in. 'Can't stop,' was her greeting, as if they'd dragged her in off the street. 'Just wanted to say *think fuchsia*.'

'Right.' Billie nodded, getting used to this kind of thing by now. 'Guest list finalised yet?'

Not listening, Heather was peering in at the made-over changing room. 'There's a chicken in there looking at its reflection.'

'Yes, there is,' said Billie stoutly, leaving it at that.

'No, Julia!' yelped Dot, rushing to gather up the scrawny bird. 'You'll bring on one of your turns!'

Lowering her voice, Billie leaned towards Heather. 'Don't worry, she's not handling your wedding.'

Nodding, satisfied, Heather headed for the door at her customary speed. She halted, and checked. 'You're talking about the girl, right?'

'Right.'

Julia's middle name turned out to be Idiot. The bird got under customers' feet, sat on the tissue paper, stared critically at women in their underwear. When Sam dropped in at lunchtime, Julia was refusing to leave Billie's handbag, despite the encouraging offer of a Crunchie.

'Lunch, Billie-knickers?' he asked, when Julia had retired, huffily, to the bin. Glasses shaded his strobe eyes.

'Why not?' Leaving Dot in charge, Billie steered him past Dyke's ('Look! That old man in there! That's Sole Bay's answer to Russell Brand!') and towards the square. 'Let's have something in the Swan.'

'Oh God, more chintz.' Sam ruffled his hair so that it stood up even more. 'What I wouldn't give for a Pret A Manger.' He looked about him, crossly, like an angry baby sitting up in a pram. 'It's so damn clean here. They could learn something from London. Everywhere looks better with a bit of litter scattered about. Christ, I miss London.'

Billie was only half listening. She was weighing up a ploughman's against a pie. She'd heard Sam's spiel before.

'Dirt. Traffic. Casual sex.' Sam paused, savouring the idea. 'Horrid, nasty, gorgeous, casual sex,' he tapered off, dreamily.

A burglar alarm in a nearby house shattered the birdsong and gossip soundtrack of Sole Bay, making both Sam and Billie jump.

'Oh my God, is that a . . .' Billie ran her fingers through the blonde topiary of her hair and arranged her features to look pert and sexy and not bothered.

'No, it's not a fucking fire engine,' drawled Sam. 'You've been unbearable since that fireman gave you the eye. You think every vaguely bell-like sound is a big red machine.'

'I do not.' Pouting over, Billie stopped dead. 'Look!' She pointed across the road at the bookstore, which was housed in a drunkenly tilted half-timbered building. 'In the window. That poster looks like . . .'

'It is,' growled Sam, lowering his head.

Whooping, Billie dashed across the road, narrowly missing death by Hoppa. 'It's you!' she yowled, gesturing wildly at the window display of books and posters. 'You're *that* Sam Nolan!' She stopped, awestruck. 'You are the creator of Tiddlywinks the velvet rabbit.' She took a step back from him. 'Sam, you're famous.'

'If you happen to be four, I'm famous.'

'I know people who are four. So you're famous to me.' Billie's drawn-out, 'Awww,' was profoundly Dot-esque. 'You're Tiddlywinks' daddy.'

This didn't seem to please Sam, who was glaring in at the piles of books as if he wanted to break the window and ransack the shop. 'Look at the little shit,' he snapped, pointing at the adorable soft toy holding its little grey velvet paws wide. 'Oaf,' he spat.

Studying him, Billie reached up and took off his glasses. 'You're serious,' she realised. 'But Sam, he must have made you rich. Tiddlywinks is the world's favourite rabbit. It's been turned into a TV series. There are loads of different toy versions of him. I bought a Tiddlywinks painting set for my nephew.' She shrugged. 'You're probably like a millionaire, or something.'

'Yes,' sighed Sam, clamping his sunglasses back on. 'As well as destroying my credibility forever as an artist, the little git's made me a millionaire a few times over.'

'In that case,' Billie took his arm. 'The ploughman's is on you.'

Back at Billie's Brides, Billie left the hard graft of flogging a veil to Dot as she roamed the internet winkling out purveyors of horses with feathers on their heads. She dipped into her email for some distraction. Ah. James had replied. She twitched, but only slightly.

Hi Billie,

Thanks for replying. It can be daunting sending a message out into the ether after all this time. A lot of water has passed under our particular bridge, hasn't it?

You can say that again, thought Billie. She warily read on, ready to leap back, as if exploring a booby-trapped mansion with the *Scooby Doo* gang.

> Glad to hear you're living by the sea. You always wanted to.
> Well done!

Billie winced. James had always had a tendency to be patron-ising, and that 'well done' was a bit condescending. Or maybe, she reconsidered, *I am being paranoid and oversensitive and he is merely being nice.* Giving him the benefit of the doubt – never easy for Billie and particularly problematic with this man – she inched on through the email.

> The sea had a profound effect on us whenever we managed
> to escape London. Remember that weekend in Cornwall? So
> much ice cream, so much sand. The sky seemed huge over
> our heads, and there wasn't a single cloud. As we drove home
> we realised that we hadn't argued once, and we decided that
> the sea must have calmed us. Remember?

Relaxing slightly, Billie puzzled at the unmistakable note of yearning that ran through the email. She remembered that weekend as if it was yesterday. She could conjure up the slight sunburn on her nose and the sand in her sandals scratching at her toes. It had been great. Just great. And as James said, they hadn't argued once, not even over her map reading. Perhaps he missed her a little, teeny, tiny bit after all.

> By the way, did I mention my girlfriend?

And then again . . .

> She's great. You'd like her.

Billie took a moment or two to clench and unclench her fists. Suddenly she had the demeanour of a woman who had been sucking a lemon since puberty.

> She's a doctor, a real brainbox. (So *Hollyoaks* omnibuses
> are out!)

Those omnibuses had been the highlight of their week, recalled Billie, feeling unaccountably bruised by how easily her ex-fiancé had relinquished two and a half hours of quality television.

> She keeps me in line, I can tell you. It's early days yet, but we'll see how it goes. I thought it was about time I dipped my toe in the water again – ouch, crap analogy, but you know what I mean. She kind of reminds me of you in a way.

How? boggled Billie. Presumably they had the same number of heads, but there, surely, the comparison must end between herself and a telly-hating intellectual who saved lives during the day and kept James in line at night.

> But not as mad, obviously!

Obviously. *Nobody,* thought Billie bitterly, *is as mad as me, are they, James?* Harrumphing, she read on.

> And you? How's the love life?

There it was. The booby trap she'd been dreading. So casual, so conversational. It was like a hot brand on her skin. *My love life,* she told him silently, *has all the sensuality and promise of a dead cod.* Ed popped, unbidden, into her mind. He was very welcome, and he improved the dead cod no end, but he was just a daydream and no match for a sexy lady doctor.

> Tell me about Billie's Brides. I can't imagine you running a shop, but I bet you're good at it. Have you picked up any waifs and strays yet? That famous soft heart of yours always attracts them. What kind of customers come in?

Already composing her reply in her head, Billie thought of all the characters who would figure in it. There was Annie, and the indecisive mother, and the sixteen-year-old: so many stories already. She could imagine how he'd laugh at the serial killer's fiancée. She knew how to tickle James's funny bone. Smugly, Billie decided, on no evidence, that the lady doctor didn't make him laugh. She stopped short, warning herself to 'hold on'.

Why on earth was she competing with a woman she would never meet for a man she used to love? It was a knee-jerk reaction, and she pulled back from it.

Isn't it kind of strange, though – a wedding shop? I mean, after what happened.

There were a couple of blank lines then, presumably a kind of silence, before James resumed.

You know what? I'm not going to go there. Bad idea. Consider that part of the email cordoned off with yellow police tape, like the scene of a murder. You and I are the last two people on the planet who should discuss weddings. Sorry for even bringing it up. If I was within hitting distance you would be within your rights to give me a good wallop. (I know you can – I bear the scars.)

I'd better go now. Write back. I mean, if you want to. You don't have to. Oh God, I'm shit at emails. Look, it'd be nice to hear from you again but I'll understand if it's too, well, tricky, OK?

Emails. Hate 'em. Whatever happened to the good old quill and parchment?

J

Billie stood up and sat back down again. She coughed. She drummed her fingers on the table. Then she shouted very loudly, and quite unnecessarily, at Julia, who was optimistically squatting on a small handbag to see if it would hatch.

The days passed in an unfolding panorama of measuring women's bumpy bits, eating ice lollies, drinking with Sam and dreading the upcoming seminar with Sly. Billie hadn't rung her mother to tell her how well the shop was going, but she would, soon.

It was a sluggish Friday afternoon and Billie was still green enough to fret when the shop was quiet. Old hand Dot just made two more hot chocolates and turned up the radio. 'There'll be someone in soon,' she said.

And there was. What he lacked in hair, he made up for in belly. The pallid man in his sixties, dressed for the weather in a nylon short-sleeved shirt the colour of tea, circled the shop, obviously too intimidated to actually touch any of the dresses.

Secretly wishing he'd leave, the girls watched him over the rims of their mugs: they wanted to call *Chit-Chat with Charlie* on East Coast FM with a funny accent. Dot had pretended to be Dutch during yesterday's phone-in about fleas and they longed to repeat the prank. Taking pity on the man and his bafflement, Billie eventually approached him. 'How can I help?'

'It's Hayley,' said the man. 'She's getting married. I haven't got a clue.'

'You're Hayley's dad, are you?' prompted Billie.

'Yes.' He looked self-conscious. 'There's no mum. I mean, my wife . . .' He shrugged. 'Hayley's mother left us when she was a baby. So I'm Mum and all, I suppose.'

Another door had creaked ajar and offered Billie a peek into a life very different from her own. 'I bet you've done a great job,' she told him, hoping it didn't sound patronising.

The man didn't seem to take it that way. 'I've done my best.' He risked a smile. He was extraordinarily nervous, as if he expected the white dresses to gang up on him and give him a good kicking. 'I've just popped along in my lunch hour to get an idea of prices and . . .' he hesitated, before risking what he evidently suspected to be a deviant word. 'Styles.'

'Good idea.' Boosting this solo parent's confidence was Billie's aim, East Coast FM and her finely honed Welsh accent forgotten. She talked him through drop waists, sweetheart necklines, boned bodices and crinolines while he listened, wringing his hands and looking like a man who was hearing a list of war crimes. 'And there'll be shoes.'

'She does have a nice pair of white sandals. She got them for Tenerife last year.'

Hearing this level of ignorance, Billie exchanged a look with Dot, who joined them. 'Best to buy new,' advised Dot in her soft voice. 'It's a big day for Hayley.'

A crash course in weddings followed. They learned that he'd booked the church and the church hall, insisting on coronation chicken and trifle, just like at his own wedding.

'Vegetarian option?' queried Dot, and the man regarded her as if she'd quoted poetry in Venezuelan.

'Buttonholes?' said Billie.

'Car to the church?' asked Dot.

Mopping his brow, the man started to jot things down. 'Can't I take her in the sidecar?' he pleaded.

'No,' said Billie and Dot together.

They were joined by Zelda, who was canvassing opinion on some new fudge. 'Hello, stranger.' She addressed the customer as seductively as her rollered fringe under her hairnet would allow. 'Fudge?' She thrust a crinkly paper bag at him.

Reeling from the weight of information he was taking in, the man accepted the fudge absent-mindedly.

'It's not my best,' cawed Zelda, handing out sugary cubes to Dot and Billie, who were slavering like two Pavlovian poodles. 'It's not entrancing. It won't enslave you.' She regarded the man coquettishly under eyebrows that hadn't seen a tweezer since Victoria Beckham was a size twelve. 'I know how to make fudge that could bring you to your knees,' she told him.

Always on the lookout for a new way to accumulate calories, Billie said, 'Why don't you?'

Turning to her, Zelda hissed, 'I don't dare! I know the vital ingredient but I daren't use it.' Putting her hand on her heart, Zelda lowered her lids and whispered, 'Maybe one day.'

'I keep hoping my wife will hear about Hayley's wedding,' the man was saying, fudge crumbs down his shirt. 'And turn up. After twenty years.' He looked at the ladies, sheepishly. 'Old fool, aren't I?'

'Maybe she will,' breathed Dot. 'You'll be reunited after all these years.'

Zelda snapped, 'Why would he want her when she walked out, the hussy?' It didn't take much to bring out her territorial tendencies.

Out on the pavement, a male shape caught Billie's eye. She gave a little miaow of surprise. Although she'd been thinking about him, it was a surprise to see his face. ''Scuse me,' she whispered, and stepped out into Little Row.

'Mr Wolff. You look different.'

Reuben Wolff was clean, as if he'd been through the longest

97

cycle of a washing machine. His face, free of stubble, was arresting in an old-fashioned, biblical, large-featured way. Tamed and combed, his white hair sat in dated waves upon his head, and his elegantly cut suit was no longer a sanctuary for dandruff. Chest puffed out, he carried his five foot four frame as if he was an archduke.

Stiffly, he told her, 'I've come to talk to you about your business proposition.'

'Proposition?' Billie was puzzled, and wary. This tiny man was a steamroller, she could tell, and she didn't fancy being flattened.

'Unless I'm mistaken, you commissioned me to design and make wedding dresses for your establishment.' The tone conveyed that Reuben Wolff was rarely mistaken.

'Not exactly,' fudged Billie, uneasily. 'I only said—'

'My word is my bond. Is yours?' snapped the dapper little man like a Jack Russell denied his Pedigree Chum.

'Yes.' Billie was insulted by the old man's insinuation. 'A Baskerville's word is her bond,' she stammered, and instantly regretted it. Pomposity wasn't her forte. 'Come inside, and we'll talk about it.'

As they went in, Zelda was coming out, her arm hooked neatly through the male customer's. 'Come and try some of the stuff I keeps for my special friends,' she was whispering to him.

By the time Reuben Wolff left, Little Row was dark, and he had an order for five wedding dresses based on the designs in the trunk. He had haggled hard about the price, and had insisted that Billie find him an assistant, and had carped about the fudge he was offered. But he had also talked eloquently about his passion for making dresses that made women feel beautiful, and Billie decided she really rather liked him. In the same way she liked her grandmother's parrot, who hollered swearwords all day and pecked any kind hand proffering a peanut: they were both characters. Although presumably Mr Wolff didn't poo on the floor and shout, 'Show us your norks!' at the Queen on Christmas Day.

Watching his progress down the street, Dot said dreamily, 'Isn't Ruby lovely? What a gent.'

'You wouldn't have thought that if you'd seen him before,'

muttered Billie. 'He looked like a tramp, and he reeked of booze.'

'Loneliness is very corrosive.' Dot sounded thoughtful. She didn't seem to be speaking to Billie. 'Isolated people are never happy.' Then she did turn to her boss. 'Are they?'

'Why are you asking me?' frothed Billie, with the *sang froid* of a woman discovered at a murder scene with a bloodied axe. 'I suppose not. He's like a completely different person today.'

'You've given him something to live for,' said Dot, turning the key in the lock. 'You should be proud of yourself.'

'Oh shuddup.'

Eleven

Tall, broad and corn-fed handsome, Sly Baskerville posed with feet planted far apart and hands on hips, displaying the gold silk lining of his jacket. He exuded a confidence so palpable that it could have been his twin. The eyes and the nose and the jaw were vaguely reminiscent of his sister's, as if Billie's features had been fed into a Super Hero machine.

The shop was transformed into what Sly called his arena. A row of three chairs faced him, and behind him stood a massive flip chart, and an easel supporting a studio portrait of his lovely self. With an airbrushed cheesy smile, this laminated Sly pointed at them, both hands cocked like pistols. 'YES! YOU!' it said underneath.

Already cringing at the tinny strains of 'Things Can Only Get Better' from her brother's mini speakers, Billie squirmed. Other people were blessed with run-of-the-mill families, she thought. How come fate had drop-kicked her into the Baskervilles? She recalled James's parents, whose freakiest trait was breeding dachshunds. James's sister hadn't carried life-size portraits of herself everywhere: she was a chiropodist. Small wonder that Billie had turned out the way she did. She took a moment to gaze around her little empire: Billie's Brides was her stab at normality, where nobody quoted Noël Coward and, apart from today, nobody punched the air shouting, 'I wanna win!' It was her corner of the Earth, created in her own image. Until Great Aunty Babs came back. Disliking that unsettling detail, she turned her attention to Sly.

Slowly, he was studying the faces of his expectant audience, as if they fascinated him. 'Ladies, ladies, ladies,' he drawled, in an unexpected mid-Atlantic accent.

'Sly, Sly, Sly,' murmured Billie, whose stomach was starting to ask questions she couldn't answer: by now it was usually back at the hut getting to know a packet of Rich Tea.

'Here, in front of me, are three fine examples of twenty-first century womanhood.' Sly nodded approvingly.

Really? thought Billie, her natural cynicism sharpened by hunger. She peered sideways at Dot, whose organic hemp skirt was exuding a gentle hint of the cattle barn, and at Debs, who was scratching 'Baz' on to her forearm with a compass. Such raw material was unusual for Sly: most of his work was with besuited sales teams.

'I can see, just by looking at you,' began Sly, true to his word, looking at them, and flinching only momentarily when he saw that Debs was drawing blood, 'I can see that you all have an Inner Winner (trademark applied for).'

'We do?' Breathless, Dot was leaning forward.

'You do.' She was rewarded with a killer smile from Sly: his teeth were not standard-issue idiosyncratic Baskerville originals, and he liked to get value for money by blinding clients with them. 'I can smell originality and creativity and MAGIC in this room!'

'I think that's Dot's skirt,' mumbled Debs, whose compass had slipped at Sly's shout.

'A quick exercise.' Suddenly Sly was all movement and activity, ripping off his jacket as if preparing to box. 'Up!' He clapped his hands and only Debs ignored him, Dot jumping up as if her seat was electrified. 'Debs, isn't it?' Sly asked, bending down towards her.

'Yeah.'

'I know you want to succeed. I know you want to fulfil your potential.'

'After I've finished me tattoo.'

'I'm going to tattoo your soul.'

Debs looked up at him dubiously, pulling her shirt together.

'With one word,' Sly enunciated carefully. 'Success.'

'Naw.' Debs enunciated even more slowly, as if talking to a foolish foreigner. '*Baz.*'

'Oh Debs, the sooner you get up, the sooner you'll get home,' sighed Billie.

Up jumped Debs.

'We're going to work on trust. All organisations need trust,' Sly stated, emphatically.

'Lust?' queried Debs, who seemed to make it a point of honour to half listen.

'Sorry, ladies, I'm taken.' Winking at Debs and Dot, and ignoring Billie's cringe, Sly exhibited once again the porcelain assets he kept in his mouth. 'Seriously, though. You need absolute faith in each other to work together productively. Build the team, build the dream.'

'So true,' sighed Dot.

Sly split the seminar into pairs ('Debs and Billie, myself and Dot') and instructed them to catch each other as they fell backwards. 'You must fall backwards with your arms folded across your chest, fully confident that your partner will catch you.' Sly demonstrated with the aid of Dot, who looked like a very pretty eleventh-century martyr as she dropped, calm and trusting, into his arms.

'Now you two,' he said, encouragingly to Debs and Billie, as Dot righted herself, a little pink from the experience.

'I'll catch you, yeah?' Billie got this in quickly.

'No, no, no.' Sly waggled a long finger at Billie. 'That's not how it works. This is about trust, not leadership. *You* fall, and your assistant catches you.'

The unpleasant snigger from Debs didn't reassure her as Billie turned around and assumed the Joan of Arc position.

'You sure about this?' Debs frowned at Sly. 'She must be all of eleven stone.'

'I'm nine eight!' yelped Billie, who was ten two.

'Ladies.' Sly had brought his voice right down, as if he was dealing with two skittish chihuahuas. 'Begin.'

A long moment followed, where Billie conspicuously did not fall backwards.

'Begin,' said Sly again.

Another little while. Billie and Debs stood like waxworks. Billie just couldn't bring herself to drop into Debs' grasp. She didn't, she realised, trust or even know this girl at all.

'Begin.' A slight hint of irritation, surely inappropriate in a motivational speaker, was tickling the edges of Sly's delivery. It was a tone Billie recognised from the distant days when Sly had cast her as the rabbit in his favourite game, 'Kill the Rabbit'.

Billie gulped, shut her eyes and fell back.

Debs caught her.

Billie opened her eyes, looked up into Debs' upside-down features, and breathed a heartfelt, 'Thank you.'

And then Debs dropped her.

'You never said nothing about hanging on to her.' Debs, over the wails, was unrepentant. 'She's fucking heavy.'

They were all punching the air. It had to happen. Clichés are clichés because, on the whole, they're true. 'I WANNA WIN!' they were shouting.

Not shouting terribly loudly because of her headache (those floorboards were hard) Billie didn't really sound as if she wanted to win. Perhaps because she wasn't sure what she would win if she did win. Sly had lost her long ago, with his talk of 'individual personal empowerment' and 'self-enhancement advancement'.

'WHAT DO YOU WANT?' yelled Sly, pacing like a panther.

'I WANNA WIN!' Dot was surprisingly loud, and even Debs was getting into it, now that her iPod earpiece had been rumbled.

Suddenly, Sly turned his volume right down. 'What do we hate?' he whispered, fervently.

'NEGATIVITY!' shrieked Billie's fellow drones. She came in a little late and found herself shouting 'IVITY!' alone.

Sly upped his energy again. Punching the air, he bawled, 'WHERE ARE WE GOING?'

The answer wasn't 'STRAIGHT HOME TO BED!' as Billie would have preferred, but, 'TO THE TOP!'

'Time for the Ball of Blame (trademark applied for)!' Sly bounded amongst them like a *Playschool* presenter on heat. 'You throw this little ball to each other, and you have to say something you dislike about the person you're throwing it to.'

'Me first.' Debs grabbed the squashy little leather ball.

Putting up her hand, Billie queried, 'Isn't this a little . . . negative?'

'It's all within the protective framework of the seminar.' Sly traced a tent with his hands, but Billie couldn't see a framework. 'We accept and absorb, because we are *building*, not destroying.'

'Fat arse,' shouted Debs, tossing the ball, rather hard, at Billie.

Struggling to accept and absorb, Billie flung the ball back. 'Clock-watcher.'

A flicker of hurt, unmistakable and totally unexpected, showed in Debs' blank blue eyes. 'Too nice to animals,' she said, throwing the ball at Dot.

'Oh God, no no, I can't. I love Debs. I love Billie.' Dot accepted the ball as if it was a flying baked potato. 'Can I throw it to myself?'

'Throw,' commanded Sly, mercilessly.

'Ohhhhh,' squealed Dot, closing her eyes and slinging the ball in Billie's direction. 'Occasionally a bit rude, just a bit, not much, to my boyfriend.'

Over the next few minutes, Billie learned that Dot thought she was slightly, slightly, slightly not much but slightly impatient about the problems with the new till, and that Debs thought she was 'narky', 'snotty', 'up her own hole' and 'should wear jeans a size up'.

Absorbing this, even within a protective framework, was taking some doing, so Billie was relieved when Sly moved on.

'Remember, people, that you are the fuel that drives this company. Without fuel in the tank, ain't no money in the bank.'

Endeavouring to top that with a private rhyme incorporating 'wank', Billie almost missed the next gem.

'Winners never quit, quitters never win. Am I right?'

'YES!' shouted Dot, quite alone.

How Billie longed to quit. And if that meant she'd never be one of Sly's Inner Winners – heck, she could live with that.

Unimpressed, Sly shook his head. 'Mum was right. It's a shed, Bill.' His weighty presence shrank Herbert to the dimensions of a Wendy house.

'I like it,' said Billie, mulishly. She didn't, she *loved* it. Fear of ridicule prevented her sharing that with Sly: small, shabby, mod-con-free, it would never appeal to a status snob like her brother. 'Thanks for bringing more clothes.' Billie, gleeful as a spoiled child on Christmas morning, was unpacking dresses and jumpers and shoes and knickers and shirts from a flight bag.

'Please, love, come home.' Sly, possibly tired, was quite unlike the dynamic persona who had prowled Billie's Brides like a motivational big cat. 'Everyone's worried about you.'

Pulling a red V-neck on over a shirt, over a vest, Billie responded, 'There's no need. I'm . . . happy.'

'You sound surprised.' Evidently Sly never switched off his psychological searchlight.

'No, of course I'm not surprised. I'm always happy,' fibbed Billie, unwilling to expose any fleshy bits to his scrutiny. 'I meant, things are going well. I'm actually taking my job seriously for the first time and I like that feeling.' She threw him a bone: surely a business guru would like that titbit?

'And yet you think your customers are mugs?'

Ouch. 'It's not that I look down on them, or I don't want to do my best for them. I just mean that . . . I can't fathom why they want to buy what I'm selling.'

'You should be careful,' warned Sly, stretching and almost smashing the window. 'They'll catch on. And they'll stop buying.'

'Not a chance. I'm a lone voice in the wilderness. Everybody loves weddings. And the thought of a happy ever after. I'm out of step. Most people get married. Look at you and Sana.'

'Yes, we're very happy.' Sly snapped back into guru mode. 'Very very happy. A team. A partnership. Along with the kids we form a Trust Triangle.'

Disappearing into the sooty dark that began at the end of the veranda, Sly called, 'Goodnight, Billie. Don't forget next Sunday at Mum and Dad's. No excuses, now.' His voice receded as he got further away. 'You'll never regret locating your Inner Winner (trademark applied for).'

By the time he'd got to his Merc, Billie was locating her Inner Slob (no trademark necessary) with the aid of a kindly Wagon Wheel.

She couldn't sleep.

Billie sat up, rearranging her blankets bad-temperedly. Perhaps, she thought, seeing Sly had discombobulated her.

Something certainly had. She reached up and switched her transistor radio on.

It was dark. Not kind of dark, like in London, where street lights kept the night at arm's length. It was properly dark. Through the tiny window, Billie could make out the odd ruffle of cold white on the edge of a wave, highlighted by the moody moon.

The radio stuttered. The local station held her hand through the evenings now that she was estranged from her tarty friend, the TV. After initial amazement, Billie had grown addicted to East Coast FM's parochial world view – she suspected that a terrorist attack would have been bumped into second place on the news bulletins if a Sole Bay bike had been nicked. The 'cool' DJs were as dated as a feather cut. Right now, the traffic news was being seductively read out in a transatlantic-tinged local accent: 'A tractor has broken down at Groat's Corner. Hey, be careful out there, guys.'

The power wavered, and the DJ kept disappearing. 'My MP', she heard, then a static hiss, and 'all over the floor'. Remembering to buy batteries was a problem, as Billie's head was stuffed full of weddings and brides and taffeta and voile and where to find a company that would embroider 'Heather's Husband' on a pair of underpants.

'How ironic,' she thought, gazing up at her trademark jeans on their hanger against the white walls. 'Bloody weddings. Me, of all people.' Not prone to introspection – it was a slippery slope that led to crying along to Carpenters songs – she felt compelled to indulge in a little self-analysis for the first time since the rash of door slammings that had heralded James's exit from her life.

It was easy to think here, on her soft bed. Herbert's Dream II was a raft with a gingham sail drifting out to sea, and her thoughts drifted with it.

Billie had predicted feeling lonely in her Fresh Start. Back at her parents' she'd felt out of place, but there had been no room for luxuries like loneliness in their frantic world. With an almost sadomasochistic yearning, she had imagined being tragically, and photogenically, lonely in Sole Bay, far from home, in all senses of the phrase. The distance wasn't purely geographical: the isolation, she'd poetically believed, would suit her state of mind. Being a hermit was difficult in London, where her hair shirt had looked out of place among the bright plumage of her mates. Here, the gentler pace would suit her need to lick her wounds.

Now that she was here, the reality was rather different.

Nestled deep into the warp and weft of Sole Bay, Billie snuggled like a plump bug in a rug in her new way of life. She couldn't endorse the fluffy dreams of the women who came to the shop, but she could risk a hint of pride that she was offering them a valuable service. Along with her ragtag little team, she was adding to the sum of human happiness.

So, why did she feel strangely listless, as she fidgeted under Dot's crochet masterpiece? Was she lonely despite all these new experiences and new people and new emotions? It wasn't as poignant as she'd expected. It had no enjoyable undertones of silent-movie tragedy: it just hurt.

Perhaps it was just being alone. Billie, tired of this dangerous introspection, settled for that explanation. Yes, she decided, tucking a striped cushion behind her head and tickling the radio. I'm alone, not lonely.

The transistor fizzed, and a Carpenters song blared out.

'My subconscious has had a creative eruption,' Dot announced, balancing on a chair to dust the cornice.

'You mean you've had an idea.' Exposure to Sly made people sound as if they'd been fed into shoddy translation software. 'Spit it out.' Billie paused in her grooming of a mannequin's ash-blonde wig to point a tail comb at Dot. 'And before you ask, Julia may not have a managerial position.'

'Mock all you like,' said Dot comfortably. 'No, my idea is very definitely an H 'n' H.'

'A what?' asked Billie, before recognising, with sinking heart, yet another of Sly's gems. 'You mean it's a Heart and Head idea?'

'Yup,' beamed Dot. 'It's sensible *and* it's from my emotional core.'

'Enough, I understand.' Billie held up a hand. She'd travelled a long way to escape SlySpeak, and now her assistant was spouting it. 'What is this idea?'

From up on the chair, Dot said, delighted with herself, 'Henceforth you are the Billie's Brides wedding fairy.'

Billie frowned, a slight frown such as might greet the news that the specials are off. 'Fairy.'

'You'll wear wings.'

'Wings.' The frown deepened, possibly to the depth of one caused by a tension headache.

'And you'll carry a wand.'

The frown became more of a chilling leer.

'And you'll scatter glitter everywhere.'

Billie couldn't work up an expression that did the whole idea justice. 'Me?' she double-checked. 'Glitter? Wings?' She paused. 'Wand?'

'Don't be negative,' scolded Dot. 'Here.' She jumped lightly down from the chair and rifled the cloth bag covered in beads and tassels and shards of mirror that went everywhere with her. Billie stepped back: there was often a tiny animal with an unlikely name and an even more unlikely personal trait in that bag. 'I made these for you.' Dot produced wings and a wand that betrayed their humble genealogy of chicken wire, chopsticks and last year's Christmas decorations. 'Try them on.'

Glowering, Billie tied the ribbons of the wings under her bosom. She steeled herself to look in a changing-room mirror. 'Good grief,' she muttered. All this talk of glitter was having a terrible effect on her blood sugar. 'I draw the line at the wand,' she said, belligerently.

'Of course you don't,' protested Dot. 'How else can you work your magic?'

'There's no such thing as magic,' sighed Billie, sounding less like a fairy, more like the mayor of the town where all the stupid people live.

'Take the wand.' Dot pressed it into Billie's limp grasp. She stood back to admire her handiwork. 'Every inch a fairy.'

'I don't work magic. I sell wedding dresses. The magic is all in the eye of the beholder and it wears off pretty bloody quick, sometimes as soon as they hit the reception. If I wanted to be a fairy I'd call myself Rupert and hang around Old Compton Street.'

'Shush, now.' Dot put a finger to her lips. 'Only positivity, please, from those fairy lips.'

'I warn you, Dot—'

The threat would never be uttered. A girl of about twenty and her mother came in at that moment, and both women threw their hands to their mouths and squealed when they spotted Billie.

'A fairy!' shrieked the mother, who was old enough to know better.

'A wedding fairy!' screamed the younger one, who was on Dot's wavelength. 'Oh Mum, I love it. Don't you love it? Do you love it, Mum?'

'I do, darling. I love it.'

Standing up straight and holding her customised chopstick less like a weapon and more like a wand, Billie said, with the animation of one being forced at gunpoint. 'Hello. I'm the wedding fairy.'

A cascade of glitter, thrown by Dot's expert hand, fluttered down on them all. Only some of it went in Billie's eyes.

Twelve

Saturdays used to mean lie-ins and hangovers and mooching around Boots buying nail varnish she didn't need, but now they were the busiest day of Billie's week. Brides come out of the woodwork on Saturdays, and more and more of them were heading to Billie's shop.

Hopping from foot to foot on the tiled porch as Billie approached, Heather was the first customer. She'd chosen her frock some days before and it had been rushed to the alterations ladies with the kind of urgency reserved for donor hearts. 'Is my dress in? Is it altered? Is it ready? Is it here?' she gabbled, as Billie tried to get the door open without dribbling a melting Mivvi into her bag.

'Fetch!' As the door opened, Billie pointed to the gown that hung, swathed in plastic like a kinky backbencher, on the banisters.

Heather tore into a changing room, and pulled the curtain shut as Billie turned on East Coast FM and switched on the kettle, praying her client would be satisfied with the dress, a beautiful ivory velvet, with sheer sleeves.

Billie opened the post, put the float in the till, made a cup of tea. She was on her third Jammie Dodger before she remembered she wasn't alone. Perhaps Heather had gone through the back of the changing room into Narnia. 'Heather?' she asked, enquiringly, at the brocade curtain. 'Everything alright?'

'Mm hmm.' It didn't sound like Heather. It sounded like a lamb, with a blocked nose.

Gently, Billie pulled the curtain aside. Heather was gazing at her reflection as if mesmerised. The dress fitted and flattered her, translating her bony hips into curves. Even her face was transformed by the radiance of the fabric, and softened by the tears on the edge of her lashes.

110

'Damn. I promised myself I wouldn't be one of those stupid girls who cry,' she bleated. 'But my mum should be here . . .' She tapered off, pursing her lips to control her voice. 'It *is* alright, isn't it?'

'Your mum would love it,' said Billie softly to Heather's reflection.

A tear splashed on the forgiving velvet, sank in and disappeared.

The Gallery of Happiness was filling up. Resisting Billie's suggestion that they rename it the Gallery of Hapless Delusion, Dot pinned up snap after snap of Billie brides. 'What a pretty girl,' simpered Dot, at a fuzzy Polaroid of Bigfoot in a veil. Pinning up an airbrushed studio shot of a couple who looked to be in peachily lit shock, she breathed, 'Love changes lives, doesn't it?'

'Judging by that picture, it's given them matching strokes.'

Late again, Debs had the decency to explain. 'Man trouble,' she said, treating Billie to a view of her chewing gum looping the loop around her fillings.

'Right. Well, don't, you know, do it again. Or whatever.' Billie turned away, biting her knuckles and vowing to work on her telling-off technique. 'And tidy the changing rooms!' she ordered, when Debs was safely on the other side of the shop. She had to show Debs who was boss.

Shocked, Debs said, 'Gimme time to finish me nails,' effortlessly showing Billie exactly who was boss. 'Why are you all made up?'

'Am I?' asked Billie, through lips the colour of crushed roses. 'No reason.' She surreptitiously checked her hair in the mirror, and straightened her droopy wings.

Before Heather had left, she had turned out her handbag in a fruitless search for a vital photograph of a bridesmaid dress. Her casual, 'I'm seeing Ed later. I'll tell him to pop it into you,' had been received non-committally by Billie, who had leapt like a maddened gazelle to her make-up bag as soon as Heather left.

The mirror told Billie that her hair was behaving, but, like a grenade, it could go off at any minute. She hoped it would remain vaguely hair-shaped until Ed arrived. To drown her suspicious subconscious questions about why a random fireman's opinion of her was suddenly so important, she applied herself to a discussion about sashes with a permed woman. Billie had to raise her voice above the strains of 'Do Ya Think I'm Sexy?' from Zelda, who had come in to give them the latest bulletin on Raven's health. Apparently, he was 'on good form'.

Wondering if this meant that the mangy hearthrug was sitting on a bar stool relating witty anecdotes à la Peter Ustinov, Billie surmised that it probably meant he was awake: Raven liked to sleep twenty-three hours out of every twenty-four, farting louder than a sonic boom.

'Good old Raven,' cooed Dot. 'I love that cat. He's got real soul.'

In-depth contemplation of sashes was preferable to that kind of talk, but Billie's attempts to help her customer were disrupted by Jake's entrance.

Vinyl shorts squeaking, he sloped in and collapsed on to the chair meant for customers. 'I'm in Hell,' he groaned.

'Not quite yet,' whispered Zelda, who'd stopped singing.

Dot laid a hand on his forehead. 'Poor baby.' She appealed to the others for understanding. 'He's got a block. Can't paint. Just lies there. Can't do anything.'

He'd managed, Billie noticed, to put mascara on. Once more, she turned back to her client.

Hands on hips, Zelda approached Jake. 'Paint this little beauty,' she suggested, putting an arm around Dot. 'God knows, she does everything for you. Why don't you do something for her for once?' Her darting black eyes, quick as a bird's, were locked on him. She seemed to be daring him.

'Hmm.' Jake looked Dot up and down, as if he'd never seen her before. She was sucking her lips, staring at the floor, her discomfort obvious. 'Nah,' he said, finally. 'She's just not inspiring.'

Flinching just once, as if she'd been hit, Dot bounced over to Billie and brightly joined in with the sash symposium.

'You want to watch it,' said Zelda, quietly to Jake. Something about her posture reminded Billie of Raven watching the sparrows. 'One day you might have to answer for the way you treat that lass.'

About five o'clock the day bottomed out. Billie flicked her wand carelessly about. 'What's in that bin bag, Debs?' she asked dubiously.

'A job lot of these.' Debs pulled out a handful of L plates. 'Thought you could flog them for hen nights.'

It sounded like a good idea to Billie, but there was one detail she didn't like. 'A job lot?' As far as she was aware, Debs was not a DVLA executive. 'What does that mean?' She ventured a word she'd heard on *The Bill*. 'Are they hot?'

Debs said solemnly, 'I swear on little Monty's life that they're legit.'

Wondering who Monty was – a younger brother? – Billie doled out a couple of fivers, as a loud rumble, like a dragon trundling to a halt out in Little Row, drew them all to the window.

'Ooooh yessss!' Debs sounded husky. 'Firemen!'

Blocking the daylight through the bay windows was a red engine, every bit as big and shiny as any five-year-old boy could hope. Out jumped a smorgasbord of firemen, some tall, some taller, and all every bit as rugged as any twenty-eight-year-old girl could hope.

'They're coming in!' croaked Debs, whose 'whatever' demeanour crumbled at the sight of so many helmets.

'Oh my,' said Dot, rearranging her patchwork waistcoat needlessly.

Striding towards the door, Ed was tugging at the shiny buttons on his double-breasted navy jacket. Billie gulped, and tore her wings off: this was no job for a fairy.

The door opened, and an avalanche of testosterone swamped the tranquillity of the bridal shop. Men in bright-yellow waterproof dungarees filled all the available space. Their rough voices disturbed the frills on the dresses, and their gruff laughter tickled the tiaras.

Also tickled was Billie, who was pulling in her tummy, sticking out her chest and trying to rearrange her thoughts in a way that didn't involve Ed minus his waterproofs. 'Hello, boys,' she said, regretting it instantly: she sounded like Betty Boop. She looked round at them all, puzzled. 'Are we on fire?'

'I sodding am,' hissed Debs, who was twirling her ponytail between fingers bearing chipped evidence of a long-forgotten French manicure.

Billie said, feebly, 'So you're all from the fire station, then?'

'Nah,' Debs chipped in. 'They're from the florist's.'

'Debs, haven't you got something else to do?' Billie said meaningfully.

'Absolutely not.' Debs seemed sure of this. 'Nope.'

'When the lads heard where I was stopping off, they insisted on coming in.' Ed looked rueful. 'They're a bit like that. Sods, I mean.'

Sexy sods, though. 'The more the merrier.' Crikey. Where was this dialogue coming from? She seemed to be wired up to How To Embarrass Yourself In Front Of Hunks dot com. 'Do you have a picture for me?'

The clipping of a high-waisted peach horror was handed over, to a rowdy chorus of, 'Ooh, is that what you'll be wearing, Ed?' and, 'He's got the legs for it.' Perhaps that was why Ed was glowing like a nuclear tomato. Perhaps not, thought Billie, as their eyes met and his creased warmly.

'There's another reason why we came in.' Ed burrowed in a pocket, pulling out a small wad of paper. 'We're short of women for our disco next week, in aid of the local kids' charity.'

'We'll be there.' Debs moved purposefully, and snatched the tickets.

'Short of women? Really?' queried Billie. This seemed unlikely.

'Short of the right women.' Ed said this quietly. Only Billie could hear. And consequently only Billie's insidey bits pirouetted.

As quickly as the premises had filled up with firefighters, it emptied of them, but not before a small ginger one's personal space was invaded by Debs, saying, 'See you at the disco,' with a hint of threat.

In the lull that followed, Dot said, peering sideways at her boss, 'He's nice, isn't he?'

So Dot had twigged. 'Who?' Billie could be very stubborn.

'Him.' So could Dot.

114

'If you mean Ed,' and Billie couldn't suppress a twitch of her lips at his name, 'Yeah, he seems to be.' She turned to Dot, a floodgate opening. 'You can just tell, can't you? By his face. By the way he talks.'

'He's slightly shy. I like a shy man,' said Dot, dreamily, scrunching up a slip. 'And he seems honest. Straightforward.'

'*Normal*. Thoughtful.' Following a well-documented female tradition, Billie joined in with this instant appraisal of Ed's entire personality, based on his eyes, his smile and the way his mouth moved when he spoke. 'But he can't be.' Billie didn't sound happy. 'There has to be a catch.'

'Why?' Impatiently, Dot shook out the slip and started again. 'Some people are as good as they seem. You need to trust more. Just look at my Jake.'

It was an open goal. It was tempting. But Billie decided against it. 'No man is as good as he seems, Dot.' Moving briskly on before Dot could embark on more homespun wisdom, she said, shortly, 'And we've already spent far too much time talking about Ed. I mean, he's just some idle fancy. A bit of fun.' To change the subject, she asked, 'Who's Monty, by the way? Debs' little brother?'

Avoiding Billie's eye, Dot shook her head. 'Her long-haired hamster.' She paused. 'He's dead,' she said.

Thirteen

Having an email address, thought Billie, was a bit like living with your back door wide open. Anybody could barge in without warning, leaving mud on your floor and your emergency supply of Kahlua ransacked.

Two unexpected emails arrived that blistering Monday, while the Sole Bay sun melted daytrippers' 99s in record time. A colleague from her telesales days had included Billie's address (along with Rentokil and Ocado) in the round robin imparting the breathless news of her pregnancy. *'We can't believe it! Karl is going mental!!'*

'Congratulations,' Billie replied, politely. *'I'm really happy for you.'* Tea-break chat at double glazing HQ had pivoted on mortgages and fertility, two topics bound to hit Billie's 'mute' button. She had marvelled at how frank the girls were about their 'ovulation windows' – not something they flogged over the phone, but a much more personal matter involving thermometers, boyfriends armed with aromatic oils, and legs being held in the air for forty minutes afterwards. Billie knew so much about their baby-making efforts she could have picked out the receptionist's fallopian tubes in a line-up.

The other email was from her long-lost, much-mourned, old friend Jackie.

'Jacks!' gasped Billie, opening up the message with an anticipatory smile. 'She never changes,' thought Billie, settling herself more comfortably on the hard chair up in the stockroom and shaking her head as she read an account of Jackie's last few months.

While Billie had been selling double glazing and withstanding her mother, Jackie had fitted in a serious boyfriend, a not particularly serious boyfriend, and much random how's your father with barmen, not to mention a new job, being sacked

116

from her new job, and a much-regretted haircut that made her look like 'Carol Vorderman's evil twin'.

'It's time we met up,' wrote Jackie, baldly and plainly, just as she spoke. 'I miss you. We can't let a man spoil a friendship, can we? Just because James introduced us, it doesn't mean he gets to keep me after the break-up, I'm not a fucking futon!'

Jackie's defection after the break-up had been unexpected: the two girls had clicked instantly a couple of years earlier when James introduced them at one of his barbecues. Bonding over economy sausages, they were firm buddies by the time somebody thought it was a good idea to grill a banana.

This easy rapport had irked James, although he'd tried to hide it. James did his best to hide a lot of things: he needed to offer a composed exterior to the world. Billie was one of the few people who'd glimpsed the inner operetta of James's needs and fears: on some nights it was like the first day of the January sales in his head, even if outwardly he seemed to be meditating. 'Didn't Jackie want to speak to me?' he'd ask, hypercasual, after pretending to read the paper through a meandering, cackling phone call between Billie and his old friend.

There was always plenty to talk about with Jackie. Billie always reckoned it was a good thing she was so fond of Jackie or she'd be contractually obliged to hate her. Catnip to men, she was a brunette Amazon, with non-stop legs and curvy hips, who left a trail of destruction like a modern Helen of Troy: Helen of Battersea, perhaps. A trust-fund girl who didn't need to work, she did it anyway for the thrill of stealing office stationery.

A lone voice of dissent during the chorus of sentiment in the run-up to the wedding, Jackie had asked, coolly, 'Are you two quite sure about this?' When Billie had paraded in *the* dress, Jackie had murmured, 'Not really *you*, is it, darling?' Billie had laughed. She understood Jackie too well to take her seriously, but James had frowned.

But then, after the wedding had imploded, their friendship had suffocated under the weight of things unsaid. James loomed metaphorically over them, and Billie had been relieved when they'd both given up the pretence of being able to carry on.

And now here was Jackie, reaching out of the ether, like James had done. Billie missed the chaos, and knowing that her old mate wanted to see her was a welcome prop for her self-esteem. And yet . . . the snug rhythms of her new days were important to her, and Jackie had a habit of dynamiting her way into people's lives, rather than the more conventional door method.

A question drifted up from Dot holding the fort down in the shop. 'Can we get hold of a size twenty-two tutu?'

'Yes!' bawled Billie, neglecting to add that it was probably inadvisable. 'I'll come down.' Replying to Jackie would have to wait.

'She'll be over to see us in a minute,' prophesied Billie, peering past the empire-line dress in the window to spy on Annie, who was browsing the fifty-pee paperbacks outside the Nearly New shop opposite.

Over the death rattle of the kettle, Dot said, 'Sometimes I think we're all she's got.'

So Dot could smell it too. The solitude that mingled with Annie's lavender talc.

'I still haven't found out her story,' mused Billie. She sprang to the door. 'She's going into The Tasty Treat! This is my chance!' Billie dashed out, almost tripping over Raven who was being sick in the porch. 'Christ, Raven,' she muttered. 'What is it now? Mad Cow Disease? Post Traumatic Stress Disorder?'

Pausing in his leisurely chunder, Raven turned a glassy orange gaze on Billie that disquieted her so much that she found herself saying, 'Sorry. You carry on,' before stepping over his contorted body and skipping across the road.

Skidding to a halt outside the café, Billie composed herself to look surprised when she saw Annie. She wasn't much of an actress: like her deluded mother she tended to overemphasise and exaggerate.

Stepping inside, she breathed 'Annie!' like Maria Callas, and half the tea room swivelled to look. 'Fancy seeing you here!' she enunciated too carefully. 'Lets sit down and I'll order us a little something.'

Annie's, 'Honestly, no, there's no need,' seemed to go beyond politeness. She had the demeanour of a rabbit caught in car headlights.

118

'I insist. A nice cream tea?'

There was a pause. Annie, flustered, nodded and sat down abruptly. Congratulating herself, Billie positioned herself on the squeaky plastic banquette opposite. Annie's generation weren't comfortable talking about themselves. Unlike Billie's navel-gazing peers, they didn't spill their emotions readily. *But*, everyone has a price and it seemed that Annie's was a cream tea.

It was hard going at first. The old lady was as polite and reserved as a little girl allowed to sit with the grown-ups and her impeccable manners were an efficient shield to any intimacy. She couldn't meet Billie's eye, and replied very economically to attempts at conversation.

And then the scones arrived. Escorted by a bowl of thick cream and a silver bowl of rudely red strawberry jam, they sent a visible shudder through Annie's skinny frame.

'Help yourself.' Billie pushed the plate towards her guest.

'I shouldn't.' Anne shook her head.

'I insist.' Billie played her trump. 'I'll be offended if you don't.'

So Annie reached out a white hand. For such a modestly built woman she could put away a surprising amount of scone. The first one seemed to hit like heroin, and she slumped a little in her seat, turning a gooey smile on Billie.

'So, Annie, where do you live?' began Billie, starting with the innocuous, and oblivious of the hot-chocolate moustache she'd acquired.

Spilling nicely, Annie revealed that she'd lived in Sole Bay all her life. The furthest she'd ever travelled was Ipswich: she hadn't liked it, too many men with their tops off in the street, apparently. 'I'm widowed,' she said, simply. 'Twenty years I've been on my own now.'

A sadness the chocolate couldn't diffuse reached across the doilies to Billie. That was a long time to get up, and go about, and climb back into bed on your own. The information changed Billie's perception of Annie. The tidy coat and the carefully set hair were a triumph over the odds: if Billie had been alone for twenty years, she'd probably have floor-length fingernails and be speaking her own language of grunts by now.

'We love seeing you in the shop, you know,' said Billie, truthfully. Annie had become a mascot for Billie and Dot: 'Has our Annie been in?' they'd ask each other as the week wore on. The news that Annie was a widow made her Billie's Brides savings book even more intriguing. 'Do you mind telling me why you're saving for a wedding dress?'

Taking an emboldening bite of scone, Annie hesitated, then said, in a rush, 'I didn't have a wedding dress of my own. Too plain, you see.'

Not quite comprehending, Billie asked, 'Your dress was too plain?'

'No.' Annie shook her head. 'I was.' She looked down at the paper napkin on her lap. 'Mother said we shouldn't waste money on finery for me, so I just wore my Sunday coat.' She looked up, with a watery smile. 'I was never much to look at, dear.'

Billie quivered with indignation on Annie's behalf. The warm brown eyes, the delicate skin – how could a mother call that little face plain? Guessing that this refined woman wouldn't welcome a tirade against dead Mama, Billie said instead, 'I bet your husband thought you looked beautiful. You must miss him.'

'I wish I did,' sighed Annie. 'Oh, I mean, he was a good man. Hard, mind you. He had to be. He didn't have an easy life. But a very good man. Deep down. But no, dear, he didn't think I was beautiful. He settled for me. Nobody ever thought I was beautiful.'

Biting back a, '*Me*, I do,' in case the scene turned into some sort of across-the-years/same-sex/tea-shop drama, Billie was overcome by sympathy. 'So,' she asked, straining to understand a situation far more complex than her imaginings. 'You're searching for the wedding dress you never had?'

'Oh.' Annie seemed surprised by that interpretation. 'I suppose I am.' She became quite forceful for her. 'Yes, dear, I'm doing exactly that.' She risked an impish look at her hostess. 'Imagine! Me, at my age in one of those angelic white frocks!'

Billie imagined it. She liked the thought immensely. 'I bet you'd look wonderful.' There was more to say: Billie considered Annie to be a neglected treasure. It couldn't be said without embarrassing them both.

'I try and put more pennies by, but something always gets in the way. The roof needed doing last year. And now the cooker's gone all peculiar.' The scones were just crumbs, and a heavy curtain of inhibition dropped over Annie. Her back straightened again, and she retreated into politeness. 'Thank you so much for a splendid tea. I must be going.'

'Hold on a mo, Annie.' Billie had had an idea. It was obvious. It was genius. It was perfect.

Annie wasn't so sure. 'I haven't sewn in years, dear,' she said uncertainly.

'You admired his dresses yourself,' Billie reminded her, tenaciously. 'Ruby Wolff needs somebody to help. You'd be eligible for a staff discount.'

Sharply for such a meek woman, Annie said, 'I don't want charity.'

'And I wouldn't dream of offering it,' claimed Billie, who would gladly have given Annie a free dress. 'How about for— fifty per cent?' That discount wiped out any profit.

'I'll think about it.'

'Say yes, Annie.'

And Annie did.

Through the café window, Billie watched Annie cross the road, carefully looking right, left and right again, passing Jake who was wrapped – for reasons of his own – in a Nigerian flag.

'So that's your story,' whispered Billie, licking the last crumbs off her fingers. 'Well, Annie, it's not over yet.'

'I don't mean to be rude,' said Heather, a sure sign that she was about to be very rude indeed, 'but I was here first.' She elbowed her way in front of the small bespectacled woman holding up a basque, and reeled off a list of questions at Billie, ending with, 'Homestead Hall?'

'All booked for Wednesday. We're going to meet the owner, see the function room and have dinner.'

'Right.' Heather seemed disappointed: perhaps she was hoping for something to shriek about. She was as taut as a tightrope, and almost as thin.

'Are you eating properly?' Billie remembered her own pre-wedding nutritional plan: toast (occasionally), plus a bi-weekly, low-cal Cup-a-Soup. The pounds had dropped off, but she'd hallucinated in Waitrose and tried to climb into the frozen-food cabinets.

Ignoring her, Heather had another question. 'Hen night?'

'Getting there.' Hens are hard to round up. 'The limo's booked.' She handed Heather the hen guest list to check as Sam popped his slightly flattened shock of hair around the door.

'Liquid lunch?' he suggested.

'Busy,' mouthed Billie, pointing to Heather behind her back.

Heather turned, presumably to see Sam off, but instead she stopped and studied him intently. 'You're . . .' she said.

'Am I?' asked Sam, beaming archly. 'I am? Really? No!'

'You are, aren't you?'

'I am! Hang on. I've checked and I'm not.'

'He's Sam Nolan, if that's what you mean.' Billie spoiled Sam's caddish fun.

'OH MY GOD!' Heather turned to Billie. 'HE'S FAMOUS!' she yelped, adding less loudly, 'Kind of.' She pulled a disbelieving face at Billie to say, 'You know him?'

'Yeah.' Billie shrugged. 'It's easy.'

'Come to the wedding!' she blurted at Sam. Turning to Billie, she ordered, 'Invite him to the wedding.' She wrestled her mobile phone from her bag and rudely pushed past Sam to get out into the street. 'Wait till my god-daughter Tiffany Beulahbelle hears about this.'

Sam pointed at Billie. 'Are you? You are, aren't you?'

'Gasping for a drink? Yes.' She put on her jacket and shoved him out of the shop.

Post-ploughman's (Billie was partial to the Swan's cheese), Billie tried to shake Sam off. Despite the looming deadline for the twelfth Tiddlywinks book, he was a dedicated waster of time and once he'd realised that she wasn't heading back to the shop he was intrigued.

'Nowhere. I'm going nowhere,' insisted Billie, her temper fraying. 'And I'm doing nothing. Now sod off.'

'You don't want me to know what you're up to.' Sam had hit Billie's nail on the head.

A figure on the beach waved.

Waving back, Billie hissed at Sam, '*Please* go home. I don't quite know how I agreed to this, but Jake's taking photos of me to use in a collage depicting the history of the female delinquent.'

'Wild rent boys wouldn't keep me away now,' Sam assured her.

Resentfully, Billie dragged her feet towards Jake the way she'd used to walk to gym class. He was ready and waiting, squinting at her with his camera to his eye.

'Let your hair down!' he shouted.

So she let her hair down: literally, not metaphorically. Sam's presence on the steps of his hut was inhibiting.

'Move!' yelled Jake. 'Feel!'

Billie 'moved' like the Hunchback of Notre Dame and 'felt' like a twat.

'BE!' shrieked Jake, impatiently, whirling with the camera, crouching and leaping and pirouetting around his stiff, self-conscious model.

From the row of beach huts came a good natured shout. 'Give it to me, baby, come on! Come on!' His sunglasses at last appropriate for the lighting, Sam's Austin Powers was pretty good.

Billie laughed, but Jake didn't. Beefed up by his vindictive eyes and that Victorian preacher-man beard, his scowl was corrosive. When Sam stood up and started walking towards them, his pointy boots sinking into the pebbles, Jake roared, 'Back! I need space to tease substance from Billie's aura.'

'Easy, tiger. They can arrest you for that.' Sam, despite his lucrative talent for painting, didn't seem to share Jake's high-mindedness about creativity. 'Why don't you stand her with her back to the sun? Then that mad fluff on her head will look like a halo.'

'The word is hair, thanks very much,' Billie cut in. But they weren't listening. This was shaping up to be a personal grudge match.

With a nasty little affected laugh, Jake squinted into his camera and told Sam that he didn't welcome creative advice from a man who painted bunnies.

'Art's art, mate.' Sam was still Sarf London laconic, but Billie could tell he was wounded by the swipe.

'EMOTE!' commanded Jake in Billie's direction, before turning back to Sam. 'I do it for love. You're a prostitute.'

Without answering, Sole Bay's only hooker turned and staggered back up the stony incline in his unsuitable shoes. Billie was too busy being and feeling and trying to keep her hair out of her face to follow, but as soon as Jake declared himself satisfied, she scurried up to Sam's hut.

It was plainer than Herbert, and had no name. The inside was anonymously clean and tidy, as befitted a rental proposition. 'Don't mind Jake,' Billie told Sam gently. He was sitting on a canvas chair with his pad on his knees. 'He's made entirely of wasps. Go too near and you always get stung.'

Putting down his pencil, Sam looked levelly at Billie. 'Trouble is, I agree with him. Basically me and Jake are both artists, and we both know that Tiddlywinks is shit.'

'Wash your mouth out, Sam Nolan.' Billie was shocked. 'That rabbit has brought joy to millions of kiddies.' Her hand to her mouth, Billie gasped, 'Oh God. I've never called children kiddies before. Whatever Dot has is catching.'

'I didn't set out to be the hero of the under-sixes,' sighed Sam. 'I approached the publishers with a hard-hitting, gritty premise to revolutionise the soft, pappy kids' book market.' Sam looked dreamy, the way Billie looked when she passed a Dunkin' Donuts. 'Lucifer the Rat was a New York rodent. He lived in the sewers, making things from the rubbish he found down there.'

'Like the Wombles,' offered Billie, instantly regretting it when she saw Sam's expression darken.

'I'll ignore that,' he told her, hissing, 'Wombles!' before carrying on. 'I drew Lucifer in blacks and greys and reds. Very sketchy. Short jagged lines.' He scribbled a tiny rat on his pad for her, and Billie recoiled from the creature's claws. 'Lucifer made things for his little rat hole from the things he found: used syringes, condoms.'

It was hard for Billie to imagine her nephew enjoying the story of Lucifer at bedtime. The poor child would be climbing his Bob the Builder curtains.

'But after my editor got hold of it, and put it through a hundred layers of market research, the idea was refined down to a velvet rabbit who sits on the end of a little girl's bed.' Sam curled his lip, 'In Cheltenham.'

'Why didn't you say no?'

'The real reason?' Sam's mouth turned down at the corners. 'The advance was enough to clear my debts. Being a hard-drinking, hard-living gay-about-town doesn't come cheap. One book and I'll be free, I thought. But then the little bastard took off. More books. Spin-offs. I was invited on *Richard and Judy*!' Sam looked deeply insulted. 'And now I'm a hooker, as Jake pointed out. The money is too good to turn down.'

'At least you're a high-class hooker,' commiserated Billie.

'Darling Billie-poos, don't ever join the Samaritans, will you?'

Back at her portal to the electronic world, Billie was replying to James's latest email. It was about time, she reasoned. Her fingers took off on their own, borrowing James's breezy style.

> Hi, James. Just a few lines, it's pretty hectic here in Sole Bay!

Whittling off the exclamation mark – it was time to dump them, she reasoned – Billie glanced out of the shop window, to see Zelda sweeping her porch, with Raven yawning lazily at her feet. St Matthew's clock struck seven with slow bongs. A toddler coughed in its buggy.

You see, smiled Billie to herself. *Hectic*. She gritted her teeth.

> Glad to hear you've got yourself a girlfriend.

She gritted them harder.

> It's about time, after all.

Gritting so hard, it was a wonder her teeth didn't shatter and ricochet around the shop, she went further.

> She sounds

Slowly, painstakingly, she typed:

> lovely.

And took a deep breath. That hurdle negotiated, Billie thundered on.

> I've got my eye on a firefighter – insert your own joke about helmets here. He seems to be interested, but it's early days. For the moment I'm enjoying being young, free and single.

'So that's what I am,' thought Billie, taken unawares by the phrase. Young, free and single – it conjured up a laughing girl, dizzy from dancing all night, beating off eligible men with her stilettos. The only time Billie had danced since James left was when the telesales post boy had dropped drawing pins all over the floor.

> I'm too busy with Billie's Brides to think about lurve, to be honest. I've taken to shopkeeping like the proverbial duck to water. I love it, even the boring bits. I especially love helping women find that perfect dress, the one that makes them feel special, and beautiful, even if in their everyday life they feel dowdy and ordinary. You can sense their empowerment, they seem to grow a couple of inches in front of you. And then when they turn to you with tears in their eyes – I can't tell you how good that feels.

Rereading those lines, Billie almost erased them. It was too revealing. She'd never used that kind of language, even in her head, to describe the way she felt about her shop. *The* shop. Babs' shop.

But she didn't erase them.

> It goes without saying that I can't empathise with the 'happy ever after' aspect of it. I still think they're going up the aisle into an emotional black hole, but it's what they want, and I can't criticise them for being starry-eyed about love. I wish I still was . . .

No, thought Billie fiercely, that had to go. She backspaced the last five words. A change of tone was called for.

Maybe the best way to give you a taste of what life's like in a wedding shop in the middle of nowhere by the sea is to describe a few of our customers. Annie, you would love.

A brief, fond sketch of Annie was followed by a vaudeville version of Mrs Serial Killer. Grinning as she typed, Billie got into a riff, the way she'd used to at the end of the day when she lived with James. Telling him about her exploits as he sat, exhausted, on the sofa, his tie yanked undone and a glass of something in his hand, she'd known how to build a scene so that he'd eventually splutter Rioja all over the rug. Back then, Billie had often had the curious feeling that things hadn't really happened to her until she'd recounted them to James in the lamplight of their sitting room.

Billie stopped typing. That memory made her unbearably sad all of a sudden, as if a damp blanket had been dropped over her.

Things were happening to her now. She had no need, she reminded herself, to filter them through *anybody*. Her new life in Sole Bay was colourful and absorbing, without James. She typed:

Got to dash. Bye for now. Don't do anything I wouldn't do.

Like getting over us, for instance. Billie moved on, just like James had, to her next email. She'd been composing a friendly but arm's-length answer to Jackie all day in her head. Cosy in her Sole Bay niche, Billie couldn't risk a visit from her favourite 34DD anarchist. Soon. But not yet. The eco-system of Billie's Fresh Start was still fragile.

Fourteen

It was time for elevenses on Friday morning, but the Munchmallows preparing to meet their maker were enjoying a reprieve. Billie and Dot were waiting for a man.

'Mr Wolff is late,' pointed out Annie, whose concession to the heatwave was to wear a slightly less heavy coat.

'Only fifteen minutes.' Billie was lenient, aware that she didn't apply the same rules to Debs' timekeeping.

'Here he is!' Dot jumped up to let Ruby in.

Introductions were made, and then Dot and Billie moved discreetly away. Not so far away that they couldn't earwig. That would be silly.

'Are you any good?' asked Ruby, bluntly.

'Well. Dear me. What a question.' Annie did her twittering thing.

'Why can't a woman answer a straight question?' blustered the old man. His appearance may have been tidied, but his manners could do with a blow-dry. 'Are you any good, madam?'

'Mr Wolff,' quavered Annie. 'I am very good.'

'You'd better be.' Ruby handed over a carrier bag. 'Here's your first pattern pieces. I've put instructions in.' He turned to go, without a goodbye, but turned back when Billie called to him. 'What?'

By various gesticulations and wide-eyed, silent-movie gestures, Billie managed to convey that the carrier bag was far too heavy for Annie.

'Oh.' Ruby ran a stubby hand over his heavy features. 'Women!' he growled, snatching back the bag. 'Come on, what's-your-name, Annie. I'll walk you back with this.'

'There's no need,' protested Annie, who obviously didn't want this little oddball's company on her way home.

'I insist,' said Ruby sourly, ushering her out.

Watching them trundle down Little Row, Billie smiled to herself. 'Rather her than me.'

'Oh, he's alright.' Dot could find the silver lining in the most glowering cloud. 'Quick, get your wings on. Customer.'

The owner of Homestead Hall was posh. So posh that he had an arthritic Labrador stapled to his heels, and got away with wearing custard-yellow cords that would highlight him as an obvious homosexual in any context other than his crumbling mansion. The historic Tudor manor house was his courtesy of aggressive ancestors, who had ruthlessly fought off all comers over the centuries. These days Homestead Hall welcomed all comers, and Visa.

As the host showed Billie's little band of the bride and groom, Ed and Angela to some vacant sofas in the vast drawing room, Billie noticed that Heather's accent had scrambled up a few rungs of the social ladder. Suddenly, her client was a lot less Argos and a touch more Fortnum & Mason.

The owner ambled off to check on their table, his ancient dog dotted with tumours stumbling after him. Looking around her, Heather said approvingly in her new voice, 'Now, *this* is refained.'

She was right. Elegance and comfort cosied up to one another in the large room. The lighting was low, the hum of conversation from the other guests subtly exciting, and way up on the plasterwork ceiling, gilded cherubs winked down at them.

From the other end of the pleasingly tatty Chesterfield, Dean offered a morose, 'Bit poncey if you ask me.'

'But I didn't, did I?' bit Heather, her old tones surfacing. 'Ask you, I mean. Cos you'd probably say something unbelievably thick like *bit poncey if you ask me*.'

As a venerable grandfather clock struck disaster, Billie realised that she had inadvertently chosen exactly the wrong evening for the test-run wedding meal. She wasn't to know that the happy couple had had a ding-dong of a row minutes before leaving the house, but she would soon find out.

Before the alluring Martini on the low table got even half-way to Billie's eager lips, Heather dragged her off to the fussy splendour of the powder room and delivered an unexpurgated and slightly overlong account of the row. Like a diligent CNN war correspondent, she reported the build-up ('In he walks with a face like a slapped arse'), trotted through the preliminary skirmish ('So I sez, "What's eating you, Gilbert Grape?"'), described the heat of battle ('I threw the Marmite at him. Hard.'), and outlined the uneasy peace ('He started the Punto and said, "Get in if you're getting in, you dopey slag"').

Murmuring words of empathy as Heather applied even more make-up in the peachily lit mirror, Billie soon gave up. She wasn't being heard, so she accepted her role as silent sounding board and hustled Heather back to the drawing room as quickly as possible.

As they approached, Dean and Ed were laughing extravagantly, whacking the arms of their seats. Dean stopped suddenly when he saw Heather's affronted glare, and looked sheepishly into his lap as if he'd been caught browsing the underwear section of his mum's catalogue.

The other member of their party was looking a little left out. Angela was nothing like her sister. Where Heather was angles, Angela was curves. A marshmallowy blonde in a buttoned dress that was straining to do its job, her wide, pearly face was not improved by its burden of make-up.

'Angela,' snapped Heather. 'Sit beside Ed. He doesn't want to listen to Dean's so-called jokes all night.' She wasn't wasting any time embarking on her matchmaking duties.

The look of alarm that transformed Ed's face lasted a split second, but it wasn't lost on Billie. Nothing about Ed was lost on her: she'd been watching him like a private detective since they'd all met up on the steps.

Every word he'd uttered (and there hadn't been many) had been weighed and rated and valued. He was polite. He was eager to please – that smile was flashed often. He was perfect, easy company. But Ed was maddeningly difficult to work out. So far he'd said nothing surprising, nothing idiosyncratic, nothing that would make Dean turn to Heather and laugh, 'Oh that's *so* Ed!' He'd make a good poker player. But Billie didn't want to play poker with him: what did she want from him, she wondered, covertly eyeing him up as he discussed the weather with Angela. As Ed agreed that yes, it was nice to have a bit of sun, Billie studied his face.

It was rare to come across features so symmetrical, so ideal. Billie had scoured them for a defect, but had come up empty-handed. His nose was narrow, his bottom lip was full and slightly petulant, and his delicious colouring was the icing on his rather sexy cake. Billie was a fool for black-haired men with brown eyes.

Strange, then, that she should have found herself engaged to a blond guy with green eyes. Even as she entertained that thought, Billie knew she was being disloyal. She hadn't 'found herself engaged' to James: she'd jumped up and down like a Jerry Springer audience at his proposal. It wasn't often that Billie admitted, even to herself, how she'd once fallen victim to that very special dementia which addles the feminine brain when confronted with a diamond ring worth more than a month's salary.

Regret for the wasted hours spent planning an extravaganza that never was followed. This thought process was such a well-rehearsed one that Billie was able to trot through it, and dispense with it at speed.

As frosty arrows whizzed Dean's way from Heather ('Are those canapés alright for you, sweetheart, or should I ask if they do pork scratchings?'), Billie sadistically enjoyed Angela's assault on Ed.

Leaning towards her prey, Angela was employing techniques she may have learned at the Sledgehammer School of Flirting. She was directing her impressive – some might say terrifying – embonpoint at his nose, and baring her teeth, only some of which had lipstick on them, in a seductive smile. She seemed to find everything he said funny, even though he said so little.

Cowering on inherited cushions, Ed was a man valiantly trying to look calm. Billie could sense the disquiet seeping from him. She could also sense his thighs under the trousers of his charcoal suit.

She took a gulp of Martini so big she almost bit the glass. Fancying Ed was fine. Going any further was not. She had a plan for the next year, and it could be precised as work, more work, with a little work thrown in for fun. She had finally found something she could get serious about, and she was determined to apply herself.

And yet, it might be fun to apply herself to that hard chest . . . Billie put the Martini down. It wasn't helping. She was pro-romance only in her professional capacity as a Wedding Fairy. Personally, romance had shipwrecked her and left her clinging to the life raft of her parents' bungalow: she never wanted to be that sodden victim again. 'Look at him and see James,' she ordered herself. The James who had sworn to love her forever and who was now sending her gossipy emails about his new bird.

It was difficult to impose James on Ed's contours. Her ex was a strong character, whose aura, according to Sly, shouted 'success'. James was opinionated, forceful and funny. This man opposite, despite the gym-honed packaging, was a pushover, she could tell.

Despite the fact that Ed could carry grown adults out of burning buildings, he looked mildly alarmed by the world. Like a crab, he had a shell he retreated into. A damn attractive crab. A crab with thighs you could bounce coins on. Ed relaxed Billie: James had energised her. She liked Ed, she realised. And that made things a lot more difficult.

Contriving to puff out her chest like an inflatable dinghy, Angela was teasing her prey. 'You should wear a suit more often. *Suits* you.' She laboured the pun as if it was a gem.

'Don't really like them,' muttered Ed, his gaze flickering everywhere except Angela's beleaguered bra. He was, Billie noted with a stab of pleasure that shamed her, perfectly pale, with not a hint of a blush.

'Know what you mean,' simpered Angela. 'I prefer to be naked, too.'

Now Ed *was* red.

But, rationalised Billie, so am I. Even Dean turned pink. 'If God had meant us to eat naked, he wouldn't have invented soup,' chirruped Billie, hoping to rescue Ed from the swamp of sexual innuendo Angela was leading him into.

That got a laugh from Ed, and a giggle from Dean, but Angela's mouth turned down at the ends. She didn't seem to welcome another woman straying into her territory.

The dining room was stylish, and dimly lit. 'It's too dark,' complained Angela, as they took their seats. A button of her dress was undone: she was cranking it up a notch.

Opposite her, Ed still had vestiges of blush about his handsome face. At the head of the table, Dean sat stiff as a totem pole, radiating miffed-ness. Facing him, his bride was snapping breadsticks with a vigour and a concentration that suggested she might just do the same to one of his most precious body parts if given the opportunity.

Acting on strict instructions from Dot, Billie raised her glass. 'Here's to your happy ever after!' she toasted, toothily. There was a moribund echo from her fellow diners, and Billie was grateful for the distraction of the menu. So far, this evening had been like crossing a muddy field in stilettos. 'Ooh, yum. It all looks so good,' she chanted, before she'd even focused on the curly calligraphy.

'Steak.' Dean crossed his arms and didn't open the menu. 'Chips.'

'Oh shit, it's in French,' moaned Ed, shedding brownie points with Billie: she liked her men to have a sense of adventure.

'Oysters to start,' mouthed Angela, predictably. 'Although I won't be held responsible for what happens later.'

You'll smell of fish, predicted Billie comfortably. She could tell that Angela was flogging a dead fireman: Ed had zero interest in her opulent charms. With a jolt, it became clear to Billie that she had set herself and Angela up as rivals. That was all wrong, when Billie had only a rhetorical interest in the prize. It was hard to like the Billie who peeped out when there was a bloke at stake, the Billie who disparaged Angela's dress sense, conversation and breath. She was mean to dislike the girl, and even meaner to feel smug that poor Angela's Herculean efforts were doomed to failure.

As a penance, she said encouragingly to Angela, 'We'll need lots of input from you about the bridesmaid dresses.'

'Hmm.' Angela asked abruptly, 'Where are your wings?'

'Oh, I don't wear them everywhere,' said Billie brightly.

'For three grand you should wear them in the bath,' said Angela, with a smile as sour as the olive in her drink.

So, mused Billie, Angela thinks I'm overpaid. Well, so did

Billie, but it was really none of the woman's business. Perhaps she hadn't been so wrong to dislike her. 'A wet wand,' she said, 'is no good to anyone.'

'As the actress said, to, you know, the whatsit!' gabbled Angela, delighted with her double entendre.

'Ange,' said Heather, warningly, and waved a waiter over.

Offering up a silent prayer that the others would be ravenous and provide cover for her greed, Billie went first. Weeks of existing on canned things carefully burned over a camping stove meant that she was giddy with anticipation of proper food, at the appropriate temperature, lacking strange black bits. After her impressive list of wants, the waiter turned to Heather.

'Nothing for me,' said the bride-to-be decisively, handing the menu back. Gentle protests from the others were met with a raised hand and a shrill, 'I have to lose half my arse by August!'

'But Heather . . .' began Billie, genuinely troubled. This woman was already spare: a further ten pounds would render her dipstick-like. 'The whole point of this evening is to sample the food.'

'Have you any idea,' began Heather, viciously, 'of the damage one roast potato can do?'

Billie wouldn't have called it damage.

'I could turn your hair white with fat contents and carb ratings!' promised Heather. 'Food is full of evil. I have to drop a dress size for the wedding.'

'I'll eat for two, then.' Dean seemed accustomed to this kind of talk. He opened up the menu and chose some accompaniments for his disparaged steak. His order made Billie's look restrained, and she was grateful to him.

Conversation was stilted during the starters and the main course. Billie found it hard to disregard Heather's running commentary on each mouthful she took.

'Whoops. There goes twelve grams of fat right there! And three hundred and twenty-four kilojoules.'

Kilojoules were always welcome at Billie's house, as long as they were tasty. Slender hips were nice in theory, but she'd never fancied the cake-shunning tactics needed to attain them. She was glad when Angela perked up, and began to join in with the general conversation instead of murmuring sweet somethings at Ed.

Even if her opener was a baffling, 'I see holes.'

'Eh?' queried Billie, her mouth full of hot calories.

Heather whispered, 'Not now, Ange, I mean it.'

Sagely, Angela went on, 'Rattus Rattus. Our little Norwegian friend.'

Billie didn't have Nordic friends of any stature. 'I'm sorry, I don't . . .' She waved a fork to display confusion.

'Not here,' hissed Heather through her teeth.

'There are holes in that skirting board ple-e-nty big enough for rats,' Angela informed them all, calmly. 'And the patterned carpet would easily disguise droppings.'

'Ah. Of course. You're a pest-control, er, lady.' Billie caught her unpleasant drift.

'I am an operative in the pest-control arena,' Angela informed her. 'What I don't know about maggots isn't worth knowing.'

Throwing down his knife and fork with a clatter, Dean glared at Angela. 'Every dinner time. Like bloody clockwork. Out come the maggots.' He turned to Billie. 'It'll be regurgitative digestive juices next,' he said, loud enough to cause some discreet head-swivelling at neighbouring tables.

Stoutly defending herself, Angela said tetchily, 'Well, I can't help it if flies like to defecate on your food before eating it and vomiting it up.'

At this, even Billie put down her cutlery, and previously she had assumed that nothing short of a hail of bullets could achieve that. 'I'm sure we don't have to worry about hygiene in a place like this,' she said loud enough for the hovering waiters to hear.

'Oh, believe me, you wouldn't want to see inside the average restaurant kitchen.' Angela popped another button in her enthusiasm for her subject. Perhaps, thought Billie, this was all part of Angela's master plan: she would woo Ed into her boudoir with talk of fly poo. 'And don't get me started on cockroaches.'

'Nobody, but nobody, has any intention of getting you started on cockroaches.' Nerves sharpened by hunger, Heather had the look of a geyser ready to erupt.

'The German ones are great climbers,' Angela told Ed with an air of confidentiality, as if imparting priceless gossip. 'I've had customers wake up with them on their face.'

135

Standing up, Heather said commandingly, 'Take me home, Dean.'

Presumably, in Heather's vision of the next few moments, Dean would leap up and guide her tenderly out of the hotel. The reality was that he scowled, told her not to order him around and said, 'You're old enough to get home on your own. I want my pudding.'

At least, thought Billie, they were providing impromptu cabaret for the other guests. She tailed the furious Heather out of the room, flinging back a pleading glance at Ed as she went. It was time for his best-man duties to start with some groom pep talking.

Despite Billie's pleas, mouse-like even to her own ears, Heather marched off, down the gravel drive, leaving Billie on the steps. Her stiletto heels sank and wobbled, giving her aggrieved flight a lopsided lurch, as if the Elephant Man had somehow squeezed into a size ten, pale-blue trouser suit.

Tugging off his tie, Dean appeared and followed her, after the merest of pushes from Ed. The best man was evidently taking his position seriously. Watching Dean hurtle after his disappearing fiancée, Ed said to Billie, 'Don't worry. This is nothing.' They were the first direct words he'd spoken to her. 'They can argue over a frozen pea.'

'That I'd like to see.' She considered. 'Actually,' she grinned up at him (he really was thrillingly tall) 'I wouldn't.'

'No, you wouldn't,' confirmed Ed. He grinned back and wasn't there . . . yes, Billie could see a definite wash of red invade his face.

This close she could feel his breath on her face in the balmy night air. She shivered slightly, unsure if it was caused by the bareness of her shoulders or his proximity. There was no hiding out here in the glare of the moon: Billie wanted this man.

And to judge by his ketchup colouring, he wanted her. Ed was silent, but he didn't look shy. He looked uncannily like a man about to kiss a woman.

Billie leaned up. Ed leaned down. And Angela clattered out on her six-inch mules to join them, with an impatient, 'Can we please get back indoors and finish our dinner?'

'Yes! Yes!' Billie jumped back, coughing.

'Er, yeah.' Ed cleared his throat, and wriggled his shoulders.

They both looked supremely shifty, like shoplifters, but Angela either didn't notice their demeanour, or chose to ignore it. 'Come on.' She grabbed Ed's arm and span him efficiently back towards the entrance. 'That silly pair have made up already. Let's get back indoors and hit the liqueurs.'

Slightly deflated at seeing her very own fireman taken so abruptly off her hands, Billie turned to see her clients making their slow way up the crunchy gravel. Now Heather was leaning into Dean, a rueful smile softening her equine features. His head was bent, kissing her forehead, and Billie guessed he was whispering one of those secret incantations that couples concoct for making up.

'All better now?' she asked softly, as they approached her up the wide stone steps. The glimpse into the mechanics of their relationship had exposed their mutual reliance.

'All better,' said Dean, softly, before nudging Heather with a less tender, 'She's a stroppy mare.' He put his finger on his fiancée's lips before the tut could escape. 'But she's *my* stroppy mare.'

Fifteen

Uneasily watching Debs, who was dressing the windows, Billie didn't hear Dot's question.

'I said, how was Homestead Hall?'

'Not an undiluted success.' Billie jerked her gaze away from the window: when Debs bent down in her low-slung jeans Billie suddenly discovered far too much about her Saturday girl's tattoos.

'You've got a funny look on your face.' Dot peered at her boss.

Not liking the scrutiny, Billie swivelled her head. 'Blame it on Debs' buttock art.'

'No, no, it's something else. You've got a definite funny look!' Dot dipped and twisted like a cobra to get a good look at Billie.

'I haven't. See.' Billie faced her, presenting a serene expression.

'You have. Oh my God, something happened!'

'Nothing happened.' Billie was uneasy. She knew Dot had New Age leanings: could she be psychic?

'What happened?'

'What could happen?'

'Ed!' Dot almost shouted it. 'Ed happened!'

'God, you're good.' Billie capitulated. 'Did my face really look funny?'

'No,' answered Dot, smugly. 'I was fishing.'

'You conniving little . . .'

'Can you insult me later?' Dot pleaded. 'Tell me what happened with Ed.'

The facts were easy. Some loaded glances, a blush or two, an almost-kiss. The repercussions were harder. 'Thank God, nothing *really* happened,' finished Billie.

'I'm soooo disappointed,' mewed Dot. 'You need romance so desperately.'

'The way flowers need rain?' asked Billie, sweetly. 'The way heads need holes?'

'You're not as immune as you think,' Dot said, comfortably. 'You're like a hedgehog. All prickles on the outside, soft and cuddly in the centre. I reckon one look at him in his uniform would break you.'

'I am made of sterner stuff,' said Billie, who had sat down abruptly at the word 'uniform'. 'And hedgehogs are covered in fleas.'

'You are allowed, you know,' began Dot, hesitantly. 'To fall, I mean. You don't have to wave the flag for realists everywhere.'

'Customer, Miss Dot.'

The goth girl was taller than average, and wider than average, dripping an entire haberdashery of black lace and ribbons and feathers. Her face was a careful mask of white base and dramatic dark eyes. She was also shyer than average, and needed expert coaxing from Dot before she could describe what she was after.

'I don't want to be conventional,' she told them, through black lips. 'Not like all the other lemmings.'

A girl after her own heart at last. Billie slipped off her wings in deference to this customer's bracing cynicism. 'Something simple?' she suggested.

'Something black,' the girl insisted.

From the window, Debs, who was glueing a nose ring on the mannequin, sneered, 'It's a wedding, love, not a funeral. Everything in here is white.'

Billie and Dot looked at each other: their narky colleague was correct. Wedding-dress emporiums are pastel caverns. 'We can dye something,' said Dot. 'But you'll have to try them on in white.'

'Brace yourself,' advised Billie, as they ploughed a blizzard of dresses to the changing room. 'There's nothing quite so white as a white wedding dress.'

There was a clattering behind the curtains as heavy boots came off, followed by myriad chains and amulets, and the four-teen items of black outerwear that all self-respecting goths deem necessary. Eventually, a sheepish voice was heard. 'Do I have to come out?'

'Yes,' said Dot. 'Go on. We don't bite.' She gasped as the girl drew back the curtain. 'Oh, don't you look lovely!' she swooned.

The ghastly white face with black eye sockets and the back-combed dyed helmet of hair with a green streak weren't what you'd expect to stick out of a white ballerina number, but the goth girl had happened on a style that suited her.

There it was again. The Wedding Dress Effect. The acres of white fabric and the cunningly placed satin bows were working their cunning magic on the most unpromising raw material.

'Oh . . .' breathed the girl, staring at her reflection in open disbelief. There was a teary sparkle in her eye. 'Oh,' she said again, in a voice soft as talc. 'Is that really me?'

'It'll look even better in black.' Billie wasn't about to let her backslide.

For a second, the girl looked anguished, and her black finger-less gloves grasped at the frills of her dress. Then she relaxed. 'Yeah,' she agreed. 'It will.'

Dot pursed her lips.

'Don't do that, Miss Dot. Makes you look like a prune,' her boss said, smugly.

The finished window was fine, after the removal of the nose ring, the felt-tipped tattoo saying 'Dave 4eva' on the dummy's breast and the miniature bottle of vodka sticking out of the broderie anglaise bag.

'I was trying to make it look realistic,' moaned Debs.

'There's nothing realistic about weddings,' muttered Billie, pulling her wings back on. 'It's all smoke and mirrors.' She gave up trying to do up the dangling strings. 'Tie these for me, would you, Dot?'

'Have you run out of glitter?' asked Dot, solicitously, as she executed a pretty bow.

'No,' sighed Billie. 'I just can't bring myself to throw it. It goes against the grain. You wouldn't expect Paris Hilton to have a degree in biochemistry and you shouldn't expect me to throw glitter.'

'Negativity!' scolded Dot, as Annie came in.

140

'Nice dress, Annie,' said Billie, glad of an escape route from Dot's censure.

'It's not too showy?' Annie looked down uncertainly at the British Home Stores sundress as if it was a Jodie Marsh two-belts special. Picking up the silk thread she'd come in for, she allowed herself a contented smile as she told Billie that her work was coming along beautifully.

'Sorry about Reuben, by the way.' Billie wriggled her shoulders where the hated wings itched. 'He's a bit of a handful.'

From the changing room, where Debs was terrorising a size eight Filipina, came a mordant, 'He's a ratty old sod.'

'I've dealt with worse.' Annie pulled on some crochet gloves, pausing in her battle with a wonky thumb to reflect, '*Much* worse.'

Having sent Debs off with her wages and a sarky, 'Why not buy something nice for Monty?' Billie suggested adjourning to the Swan. 'Come on, Dot. You've been run off your recyclable espadrilles all afternoon.'

'Better not,' said Dot, reluctantly. 'I'd love a cider but, you know, Jake.'

Billie did know Jake, and he seemed an excellent reason not to go home. 'One drink, Dot. I'm sure he can manage not to play with matches or stick his finger in the light sockets long enough for you to have one drink.'

A patina of hurt washed over Dot's face: some days she was sensitive about Jake. 'By the way, I don't know whether I can come to that silly disco. Jakey would worry.'

Counting to ten didn't dampen Billie's urge to shout, 'HE'S A MANIPULATIVE, HAIRY-FACED SWINE!' So she counted to thirty-four before she reminded Dot how much they'd both been looking forward to the 'silly disco'. 'And why on earth would Jake worry?'

'He says I can't be trusted.' When this provoked a very loud snort of disbelief from Billie, Dot rushed to corroborate her boyfriend's strange take on her character. 'Well, after all, I don't know where I come from, do I? My real grandmother could have bad blood.' Dot pouted. 'Wish I knew who I really was.'

Locking the shop door and crossing the floor to cash up,

Billie detoured to give Dot a good squeeze. 'I know exactly who you are, and you are a woman who can be trusted to control her wild lusts at a church-hall disco, Dot.' The sums wouldn't add up properly, she kept arriving at a twenty-pound shortfall that couldn't be right. As she recounted the twenties and the tens and the strange out-of-date traveller's cheque that Dot had accepted in part payment for a feathered hairband, Billie felt eyes boring into her back. She realised that Dot was gazing upon her with the same exaggerated sympathy she lavished on small mammals with eczema. 'What?' asked Billie, then peevishly, '*What?*'

'I was just thinking that Saturday is the night for lovers to be together.' Dot made a wee sound, like a sparrow hiccupping. 'And you'll be sitting alone in that hut.'

'Me and Herbert like our Saturday nights in, thanks very much,' said Billie tartly, as a high-pitched and ragged chorus of 'Bat Out Of Hell' preceded Zelda's entrance.

'I thought I locked . . .' began Billie, frowning.

'Get a load of my new rig-out, girls!' Zelda twirled in a ruffled, tiered, beribboned gypsy number that should have been viewed through smoked glass for safety's sake. 'Babs lent it to me before she left.' The twirl ended badly, with one of Zelda's support socks slipping down. 'I'm swinging by the British Legion. They won't know what's hit them.'

That, thought Billie, was true enough.

'You never go out, do you, love?' Zelda asked suddenly. 'You're a sad little singleton, aren't you?'

'I wouldn't quite put it—'

'Could you babysit Raven? Only he's got another one of his colds.'

'I'd love to.' This was a lie of similar proportions to Stalin's, 'I promise to be a good boy.' Raven unsettled Billie, with his steady gaze and his twisted body and his hint of arcane knowledge. 'But I'm going round to see Sam tonight.'

Saving the day, Dot took Raven home in a basket, cooing down at his battered, phlegm-flecked face while flinging punitive looks at Billie.

Too relieved to be guilty, Billie dignified the fib by going to Sam's. 'Hi, honey, I'm home!' she yelled through the letter box of the pink thatched house, sedate in half an acre of sumptuous garden on the rim of Sole Bay.

Through the rectangle of letter box, Billie saw skinny bare legs stumble up the hall, tripping over themselves. Opening the door a crack, somebody who looked just like Sam but had spent the last twenty years in a skip peeped out. 'Christ, it's you, Billage.' He opened the door, and trotted, naked, down the hall ahead of her. 'Better slip some knickers on.'

When pants, jeans and a Clash tee shirt had all been slipped on, Billie and Sam settled down to the serious culinary business of ordering a fast-food delivery.

'What kind of beauty regime do you follow to look this good?' teased Billie, snuggling down on the luxurious sofa. Like the house, it was top quality and very attractive, but definitely not Sam's style. It was as if a surly teenage layabout had snaffled the keys to his rich grandma's.

Rubbing his eyes, which had shrunk to the size of Tiddlywinks' button ones, Sam said, 'I was up all night working.' He stole a look to see how that was going down, then admitted, 'Alright, I was up all night working at drinking. I'm good at it. If I drink about two bottles of Jack Daniel's I find I can get really drunk.'

Over the detritus of two extra-large pizzas, Billie, with one eye on the TV celebrity dog-grooming competition, asked, 'Got any drawings to show me?' She knew his deadline for book number twelve was weeks away, and had cast herself as his conscience.

'I don't show works in progress of Tiddlywanks to anybody,' sulked Sam. 'Let's not talk about him.'

'OK. Let's talk about why you're exiled in this chichi bolt-hole, then.' Billie was keen to know more about this man who had become such an important part of her days. Walks on the beach were more vivid with Sam: he pointed out the changing colours of the sky and picked up pieces of driftwood for Billie to look at, insisting that they looked like people they knew. His plush rental cottage had become a haven for her, fully stocked with Jack Daniel's, cynicism and the fond teasing that Sam specialised in. He made her feel unique, a work of art that only he fully appreciated.

And yet she didn't know enough about him. She gabbled on about herself, only noticing at the end of the evening that he'd been listening, lobbing grenades of dour insight, and keeping her glass topped up, without giving anything away about himself.

When Billie was fond of a person she was avid for detail: if Dot ever went missing Billie would be able to tell the police the colour of her pants, and which song was in her head.

'The usual reasons. The same as you,' winked Sam, bounding on to the sofa and laying his head on her lap. Even after a night on the booze and a day under the duvet, he smelled good. Sam was a perfect specimen and nothing could dent his rude health. In dog terms, he was best of breed. 'I'm not good at relation-whatsits.'

'Same as me.'

'I prefer lots of sex with the widest possible cross section of the male populace, some of it outdoors.' Sam pondered. 'Some of it on public transport.' He looked dreamy. 'Once in the John Lewis mirror department.'

'Eeeyurgh. Not the same as me.'

'No, you dull little straight.' Sam's eyes creased into slits as he grinned up at her. 'Thank God for poofs. We're the last people in Great Britain having fun. If you breeders had your way everyone would be upgrading their Ford Mondeos, shagging twice a month and pouring their repressed sexual energy into a *really good* weekly shop at Sainsbury's.' He composed his face again. 'Although there is such a thing as too much fun.'

'Did you burn out?'

'Rather OTT terminology, Billibles, but yes, I suppose I did.' He settled his cranium more comfortably in Billie's denim lap. 'All the things that are bad for me, i.e. all the things I enjoy best i.e. strong liquor and small blokes called Raoul, are too available in London. I had to escape before I ended up as a stain on the carpet.' He knitted his brows, looking almost serious: it didn't suit him. 'It got too much one morning and I jumped on a train as if a pack of dogs were after me. Can't really explain it.'

Billie could. Even sybarites like Sam have their limits, she reasoned. She risked a little probe. 'Are you searching for something, do you think? Something deeper?'

'Deeper than casual sex? Don't be bloody ridiculous.' He snorted. 'Can you really see me and some nice thirty something called Graham tootling off to the garden centre of a Sunday?' He threw her a soft look. 'But I know where you're coming from, hun. You can try and label me the pensive loner, drifting along, looking for meaning in his empty existence, but it ain't me.'

'If you say so.' Billie was almost over her fear of Sam, even though spending time with him was like travelling with a case of dodgy gelignite: he could go up at any moment. 'Is it evil to want another giant pizza?' she ventured.

'I'm so glad you said that.' Sam leaped up to grab the phone. 'That's why I knew you were the girl for me: matching weaknesses.'

Over the cheesecake that Sam accidentally ordered with the second pizza, Billie told Sam The Story. It was time.

As expected, he didn't turn dewy-eyed or offer a shoulder for weeping purposes. 'Good riddance,' he said, through a mouthful of New York Vanilla. 'James? An accountant? I know the type. All cold sheets and pinstriped knickers. He did you a favour by jilting you.' He mopped his mouth with one of the raspy paper napkins that had come with their feast. 'It would have blown apart sooner or later. All that happy-ever-after shit is a myth.'

Hearing bright, smart, strong Sam echo her theories scared Billie. 'Do you ever get lonely in this big house, Sam?'

Looking baffled at the question, he shook his head. 'Haven't you been listening, Billo? I'm not the tortured artist. I'm the slacker who came into money. I'm not lonely. I've got you.' He lifted his eyebrows at her. 'And perhaps, when I finish the book, I'll have that cute little guy in the post office who doesn't know he's gay yet.'

But Billie knew lonely when she saw it.

Bowing out when the tequila bowed in, Billie made for the sea. Tequila unleashed her inner traffic-cone-on-head wearer, and she didn't want to face her parents the next day with a hangover.

Or would it help? She slowed, but instead of retracing her

steps, she nipped down Little Row, for a moonlit tryst with the virtual world.

> James, it's late and you're probably canoodling with the lady doctor.

She typed, jacket still on and the mannequin snooty in the silvery half-light.

> Tried to explain to somebody tonight about why I'd rather eat my own spleen than have Sunday lunch at my parents' place, but he didn't get it.

Expecting Sam to be cynically sympathetic, Billie had treated him to a few of her meatier family anecdotes, but he'd surprised her by drawling, 'Sounds to me as if you're trying to replace your family with a new one down here without giving the originals a chance. Zelda, Dot, Sam – just add water. Instant Family!' He'd rolled his eyes when she hadn't laughed. 'Billie-willy, we've all got mad families. Mine think I can be cured of homosexuality by sitting me next to girls with large breasts. But I still visit the silly buggers. How bad can your lot be?'

James knew how bad they could be.

> *Chicago* is finished, and they're rehearsing a Noël Coward play. You understand what that means, don't you?

It was a risk to compose an email like this. There were no exclamation marks, no inanity, no Redcoat enthusiasm. She was just communicating with somebody who used to know her very well, and who could be trusted to understand. Perhaps James would shy away from this new honesty, but right now it was comforting to vent her frustrations.

James was a veteran of Baskerville get-togethers. He'd been there during the run of *Hamlet* when her father had strolled about the house in black forty-denier tights with a low-slung gusset; he'd endured being served Nancy Baskerville's 'famous hotpot' on every single visit because he'd manfully finished his first portion (Nancy's hotpot was a culinary Jade Goody –

146

famous for all the wrong reasons); he'd watched as Nancy's face stiffened with Botox over the years yet still managed a sneer for her daughter's progress through life.

> Sorry again. Get back to your snogging!!

Exclamation marks, like heroin, are a tricky habit to break completely.

Locking up the shop, trying to ignore the regretful reproaches of her subconscious – 'James will never get in touch again after that whinge!' – Billie yawned like a walrus. She hadn't realised how tired she was.

A rasping voice from the darkness of Little Row made her jump. 'You look knackered, girl.' Never big on compliments, Zelda peered into Billie's face.

'I am, Zelda.' Billie frowned. 'Aren't you supposed to be at the British Legion?'

'They don't deserve me,' growled Zelda, her expression suggesting there was a tale to tell. She held open the door to her shop. 'In you come.' It wasn't an invitation. It was a command. 'Through to the back.'

Traipsing through the spotless shop, disobedience didn't occur to Billie. She ogled the toffee and brittle and nougat as she passed.

'Keep going through the kitchen,' ordered Zelda, dawdling behind her in the shop. 'AND DON'T STICK YOUR NOSE IN!' She was paranoid about secrecy, never divulging her recipes to anybody.

Carefully keeping her eyes forward, sensing rather than seeing the vast copper pans and marble slabs, Billie ended up in a small square parlour, painted a rich, bloody red. She had never penetrated this far into Zelda's queendom before.

A stove, lit despite the hazy remains of the day's warmth, called to her. Without being invited, Billie sank into the welcoming cushions of a deep chintzy armchair that, although ancient and battered, was as comfortable as half-remembered childhood hours dozing on her mother's lap. Billie stretched languorously.

Switching off lamps, Zelda approached her, holding out a cube of fudge. The flames from the stove made the red walls move and dance. 'Oh, thank—' began Billie, before being silenced by Zelda's finger on her lips.

Zelda popped the fudge into Billie's mouth. It melted slowly, like a candle guttering out.

'That is so—' Billie couldn't find a word to describe the sweet taste of the fudge on her tongue.

'Tsk tsk.' Zelda silenced her again, popped another piece into her mouth, and left the room.

How long Billie slept for she couldn't tell, but she woke up feeling as if she'd had a languorous massage. From across the room Raven was staring at her, his glowing eyes suggesting an inner landscape far richer than a cat might be expected to have.

Sixteen

It's a long way from Suffolk to Surbiton. A Sunday paper lay in Billie's lap. She neglected its tear-stained lapdancer's tale of, 'I truly believed the famous soap star really loved me after shagging me once in a phone booth,' in favour of the scenery dashing past the train window.

She felt wide awake, and full of energy, like the streets of Sole Bay had looked that morning after their splash of rain overnight. Glittering and clean, the little town was difficult to leave behind. Billie licked her lips. She could still taste that fudge, the one that had sent her drifting off into the deepest, most delicious sleep she'd had in years. What the hell did Zelda put in the stuff?

Settling herself more comfortably, Billie recalled the unexpectedly speedy email reply from James. Just one line, but it had made her laugh out loud.

Shall I fetch Blankie?

Nobody else knew about Blankie. A tattered old tartan thing, James used to tuck it over Billie when she was assailed by period cramps and had self-prescribed lying on the sofa watching black and white films. Blankie's scope grew, and soon James flourished him like a matador whenever Billie had a hangover, an argument with her mother, or got the two-hundred-pound question wrong on *Who Wants to Be a Millionaire*: he was a busy Blankie.

'Hello, Aunty Billie. I thought you were dead.'

'So did I, Moto, so did I.' Bending down to kiss her four-year-old nephew at the front door of the Baskerville bungalow, she marvelled again at the poetry of his good looks. With caps of sleek black hair and tilted dark eyes, Moto and his sister were living proof that God wholeheartedly approved of the British and the Japanese getting it on. Reluctantly relinquishing the squirming Moto, Billie wished that her sister-in-law had been allowed to name both kids: an almond-eyed beauty called Deirdre was all wrong.

The kitchen door burst open at the other end of the long hall and a haughty beauty, straight from the roaring twenties, sprinted down the gaudy carpet, a cigarette holder between her perfect teeth. 'Dahhhling!' she squealed, the black feather on her sequinned headdress fluttering, 'It was too too splendid of you to come.' As she bent to kiss her guest she added, 'You're late,' in an undertone.

'I've come all the way from Suffolk, Mum.' Tussling to rid herself of her cord jacket, Billie did her duty. 'You look lovely.'

'Tish!' The volume was better suited to the stage than the narrow hall. 'Bless you, angelic one, for your kindness.' Tarantula false eyelashes fluttered in a face expressing constant lazy surprise, thanks to her doctor's heavy-handed way with the Botox. Nancy led the way to the kitchen. She was tall, and had the kind of looks that used to be called 'handsome'. Old black and white pictures revealed the strong-featured, long-limbed beauty that she was desperately trying to prolong. With the wind in the right direction she was still striking, with her full head of curling hair and her artfully arched brows. 'Be a poppet, darling girl, and stir the gravy, do.'

The chatter might be twenties, but the décor was pure seventies. Billie peered through the amber glass of the sliding doors to the sitting room as she stirred. She could make out the bulk of her father and Sly, side by side on the sofa, newspapers up like shields. They took no notice of the two blurred comets, Deirdre and Moto, racing about the room.

The doors juddered apart, and Sana joined the ladies. Hugging her sister-in-law warmly, Sana whispered, 'What play are we in today?'

'We're with Noël Coward and his chums.'

Making a small noise, possibly Japanese for, 'Oh cack,' Sana tweaked a fold in her taupe cashmere wrap and asked how the shop was going.

Enviously mesmerised for a moment by the sculptural perfection of the wrap – Billie looked like a cadaver in taupe, and any wrap she'd ever worn made her look as if she'd been hastily bandaged by a St John Ambulance novice – Billie said, 'Fine. Good, in fact.' It was always hard to find the puff to blow her own trumpet between these walls.

Sly joined them. 'Sis! You made it at last!' His hug was all-enveloping. 'So, the seminar helped, then?'

'Definitely.' Perhaps Sly doesn't mean to rob me of any credit, thought Billie. Perhaps Sam is right and I should give my family a break: he'd been right about that guy from *Holby City* winning *Celebrity Dog Grooming*.

A gong sounded. Her mother's talent for amassing props was formidable. 'Luncheon is served!' she trilled.

Like the Mad Hatter's tea party, they all fussed over where to sit. When Roger Baskerville spotted his daughter, he patted the seat next to him. 'Daughter! Sit next to your old pater.' He had the tones of Noël Coward off to a T, although his monocle kept falling off. 'What kept you?'

Crikey, thought Billie, kissing the top of her father's brilliantined head, did all the Baskervilles have digital clocks where their hearts should be? 'You look very dapper, sir.' The smoking jacket – last seen in a daring, foreign-language version of *Carry On Screaming* – had been resurrected from the costume trunk, and the room smelled of mothballs as a result.

'Splendid to see you.' Behind the monocle his eyes told her he meant it. 'Top hole.'

'How are things, Dad?'

'Super-duper.' And that, Billie knew, was as much detail as she would wring out of her father. Always a recessive presence, he was a smudgy blur at the back of family gatherings in old photos. Like the underwritten roles he took to help his wife shine, Billie's father had a bit part in family life. His quiet, rumbly voice was drowned out by his wife's shrillness and his son's butch confidence.

'Really, though, Dad, *how are things?*' Billie was feeling daring. Perhaps it was the sight of the gravy boat: gravy boats were high on Billie's list of Lovely Things.

Surprised, Roger laughed. 'Topping,' he enlarged. 'First rate.'

Billie lived in hope that one day her dad would speak, loudly and from the heart. In her daydreams his speech had the eloquence of Shakespeare, the technique of Olivier and the wisdom of Solomon: Nancy and Sly would gawp at him, silenced for once, and Billie would applaud with tears in her eyes.

Roger carried on. 'Tip top, in fact.'

'Good,' said Billie, with a sad smile. 'Good.'

The gravy was thin, but the beef was thick. It was a traditional, badly cooked roast dinner and Billie could feel it warming her right through. She smiled inwardly at her mother's attempts to twinkle *and* stop Deirdre anointing Moto with creamed horseradish.

'Now, now, my cherubs, my darling tots,' she tinkled, her feather bending backwards, lured by the extractor roaring away in the kitchen.

'KIDS!' boomed Sly, making the whole table jump. 'CUT IT OUT!'

Deirdre's head bent over her plate, and Moto slumped on to his mother for comfort. If Sly knew that everybody was looking at him, he didn't show it, shovelling the beef into his mouth as if it was his last meal.

Trying and failing to catch Sana's eye, Billie was puzzled. Sly prided himself on his patience with the younger axis of his Trust Triangle. Her mother's voice interrupted her thoughts.

'Billie, dahhhhling, even though you got Granny's legs, it would be nice to see you in a skirt once in a while.'

A safe conversational gambit was required, to draw friendly fire away from Billie's legs, hair, nose, teeth, work, lack of a man and lack of a proper home. 'How are rehearsals going?'

'Sublime!' Surgery had put paid to grins, but Nancy did her best, making Deirdre whimper in fright. 'You will attend our first night, won't you, babycakes?' Nancy was attempting to twinkle and threaten simultaneously. 'You know how your mama needs your support.'

Before Billie could answer, Deirde, whose milk teeth weren't up to her grandmother's cooking, put down her knife and fork to ask, 'Will you sell your own wedding dress in your shop, Aunty Billie?'

'Deirdre!' Sana had always trod very carefully around the

subject of Billie's non-wedding. 'That's none of our business.'

'I think your grandma cut it up for dusters,' Billie told her niece. 'Antique white lace is just the job for getting into all her nooks and crannies.'

'There was precious little point keeping it.' Nancy sawed away at her beef. 'She's hardly likely to risk another wedding after *that* debacle.'

Deirdre wasn't finished. Perhaps she'd been on a course: How To Mortify Your Aunty. 'Why haven't you got a boyfriend, Aunty Billie?'

Seizing the opportunity for some evangelical feminism at her mother's staunchly pro-marriage table, Billie said, 'You don't *have* to have a boyfriend, Deirdre.'

'So brave.' Nancy wiped a tear from a carefully kohled eye. 'You're among family, my angel. No need to pretend with us.' Leaning over the table to Deirdre, and employing a strange sing-song voice that she evidently assumed Jazz-age women used when speaking to children, she said, 'You know Barbie and Ken, my precious? Well, Aunty Billie used to have a Ken, but he ran away, and left her all on her own.' She sighed, hand on heart, before raising her head sharply and adding to her daughter in a very modern tone, 'You do know I'd pay to have your nose done, don't you?'

'MUM!' It was Billie's turn to raise her voice.

'Heavens above, such temperament!' Nancy flounced back to the twenties.

Roger Baskerville coughed, and harrumphed, then was silent. That, Billie knew, was as far as he'd go. Her father's cap gun was no match for her mother's cannon.

Holding his cutlery like a caveman, Sly used his best sane and reasonable voice to say, 'Mum's only worried about you, Billie.'

A hanky, lace trimmed and dainty, was flourished. In a wilting tone that didn't suit her robust frame, Nancy breathed, 'Nobody knows how I worry about my little gel.'

Your little gel knows, thought Billie, spearing a cauliflower floret as hard as a conker. *You're always bloody telling her.* Conversation drifted on, touching on ticket sales for the play, before moving on to Sly's problems with his people carrier and

Sana's belief that Moto was destined to be a hairdresser. Billie wasn't listening.

The knowledge that she was quick to anger around the other Baskervilles, that she was partly to blame for the descent of family meals into bloodbaths, didn't help with the knowledge that she was mired at the bottom of the bungalow's rigid pecking order.

Her folks' constant worry manifested as constant criticism. What if I were to stand up now, she thought, thump the table and announce that things are going right for a change? That I'm enjoying my work, that I'm making a success of it, that I'm spreading some happiness while I'm at it? (She didn't dwell on whether that happiness was fleeting – she just sold the dresses, she didn't force anybody to get married in them, after all.) I could tell them I'm sleeping well, that I'm making friends, that I'm carving a little Billie-shaped space in a strange town. I could even amaze my mother with the stop-press news that somebody, a *male* somebody, is interested in me. Despite my hair, my nose and Granny's legs, a Blokeus Normallus fancies me.

Tuning back in briefly to hear Sly refuse, uncharacteristically, to talk about his latest seminars, Billie took her daydream further. She stole a look at her mother.

Nancy's beauty was undeniable, despite Harley Street's intervention, but Billie felt unable to offer her mum a sincere compliment because the older woman expected fulsome praise at all times, and just gobbled it up without listening. Billie would have liked to tell her mother how she'd loved the shape of her pre-surgery eyes, and the way they used to crinkle up with sympathy when Billie told her about her latest disaster at school.

What if she was to be completely honest with her mother, now, at this late stage? To say, 'Mum, things aren't going wrong, but I do need your help? I need you to help me straighten out my frazzled feelings. I need you to advise me, like a woman, not a character from a play, about whether I'm ready to fall again. Whether I deserve another chance. Or whether I should stay in the shadows until I'm stronger.' Wishing she could say it out loud, she said gently, 'I need you, Mum,' with the tender voice in her head that was never heard at this reproduction dining table.

'A little smidgin of something for dessert?' Nancy was still tinkling, but her feather was feeling the strain. She turned to Billie, and didn't seem to notice the plea in her daughter's eyes. 'Billie?' She paused. 'Better not, my cherub. We don't want to be at home to Mr Double Chin.'

Billie caught Sana's eye, but embarrassment stopped her acknowledging the sympathy there. 'I'd better catch my train,' she said, standing up abruptly among the post-lunch debris. Her mother walked her to the door, brandishing her cigarette holder and sashaying like a woman half her age.

'Goodbye dah-ling,' she said, in a swooping voice, air-kissing her daughter. The feather on her headdress had completely given up, and dangled down her nose like a hanged man. 'Darling,' she suddenly said, in her usual voice, as Billie stepped on to the crazy paving. 'Darling . . .'

'Yes, Mum?' Billie looked hungrily at her.

'Nothing. Just, you know.' She ground to a halt. Nancy was no good at speeches unless somebody else had written them. 'I do worry, you know,' she finished in a small voice. 'Do you have to go so soon?'

'Mum, it's a long way from Surbiton to Suffolk.'

Thank God.

Seventeen

A brief 'thank you' was necessary. After all, James had cheered her up on her way to her date with doom (and roast beef).

> Thanks. I miss Blankie.

Oops. That was a little intimate for their fledgeling correspondence. A little revealing. Billie shrugged – missing Blankie didn't mean she missed James – and pressed 'send'. She was far too busy flogging white frocks to spend much time on emails to an ex.

The alteration ladies were busy these days. One complained, as she handed over a bustier covered in tiny pearls, that she hardly had time to smoke.

The week crawled, dragging its feet through the mud of paperwork that had been piling up in the stockroom. Staring dumbly at pro forma invoices and carriage notes, Billie shouted down to Dot to check that she was definitely coming to the fire service disco.

'We-ell . . .' Dot's answer, drifting up the stairs, wasn't encouraging. 'It's not really fair to Jakey. It's not his kind of thing. I should stay home with him.' She shouted for corroboration. 'Shouldn't I?'

'You might as well be married,' yelled Billie, in distaste. 'Love isn't about binding yourself together with ropes and padlocks. Does he love you?' she asked, baldly.

'Of course he does.'

'Well, then.' Billie stalked to the top of the stairs and squatted there, talking down to Dot. 'Where's the harm in dancing around your handbag for an hour or two, while he sits at home and makes portraits out of unlikely ingredients?'

'Jake's not like other men,' said Dot, an observation Billie had often made for herself. 'If you knew him better, if you'd heard about his childhood, you might understand him. Like I do.' Dot sounded apologetic, presumably accustomed to disbelief when she discussed Jake's hidden virtues. 'I'm precious to him, and he doesn't trust the universe to let him keep me.' With a gentle shrug that barely lifted her patchwork waistcoat, she summed him up. 'He just holds on a bit too tight sometimes, that's all.'

Billie was wrong-footed. Her customary stance on Jake was disapproving, ironic, arch. She'd made no effort to understand him, had assumed that what she saw was what she got. 'You really love him, don't you, Dot?'

The enthusiastic nod from the bottom of the stairs made Billie feel even worse. She didn't know what to say about Jake when forced to consider him in 3D: she preferred rolling her eyes at the pantomime baddie. 'Even taking all that into account,' she began carefully, trying to be fair, 'you're still entitled to do things you want to do, if they don't hurt him. Do you want to go to the firemen's disco?' asked Billie, as impartially as she could.

'Yes,' admitted Dot, with a guilty grimace.

'Well then.'

'When you put it like that . . .' This capitulation was very sudden. Almost as if Dot had only needed a gentle nudge to abandon Jake to his gloomy fireside and pull on her disco pants. 'What are you wearing?' Evidently, Dot was as shallow as her boss in some departments. 'I have some gorgeous hemp dungarees in the wardrobe.'

'And that's where they'll stay,' decreed Billie. She was relieved. Dot was her posse. She needed Dot to provide cover for her stalking of Ed. She wasn't committed to pouncing, but a little light stalking can do wonders for a girl's frame of mind.

Even Billie didn't quite believe those claims of 'a little light stalking': doing things behind her own back was second nature to her. Blinded by perfect pecs or a deep voice, she'd sleep-walked into love affairs with unsuitable men many times before. 'Just looking,' she'd say, minutes before joining some panther-eyed beauty on a table top for a quick fandango. Back then, she'd enjoyed the fallout of her fast-track romances, but now she was battle-scarred and wary.

The new Billie was cautious and careful, and she worried that she might be joining up the dots to create a personality for Ed, based on the few sentences she'd heard him utter and the tingling in her lingerie.

Later, when Billie thought back to that quiet Saturday afternoon in the shop, she couldn't remember any warning signs. No, the sedate conversation with the last customer of the day hadn't been disturbed by anything unusual in the air, no birds flapping hysterically, no mention of a twister sighting on Chit-Chat Charlie's weather report.

Sam had arrived to escort them to the disco, not in the silver chaps he'd threatened but a sharp black suit, cut lean to show off his ink-drip limbs. 'Debs,' he breathed, taking in her strapless, backless, tasteless Lycra. 'You're a goddess.' He had a soft spot for his friend's unruly Saturday girl, considering her to be a work of art every bit as relevant as any old tent Tracey Emin ran up on her Singer. 'You just don't care, do you, sweetheart?'

Unaware of her status as post-modern icon, Debs told Sam, 'Your roots need doing.'

'God, I love her,' smiled Sam.

Discarding her wings, Billie clattered up the bare wooden stairs. 'I'm just popping up to the stockroom to get changed,' she shouted over her shoulder. 'Then how about a little glass of something to get us in the mood?'

'Maybe,' sighed Dot. Billie didn't know if Dot was angsting over deserting Jake for the evening, or angsting over the eighteen-pound shortfall in the till, or angsting over some challenged mammal, but angsting she was. It wasn't the first time the takings had been out by that kind of amount, but Billie had decided to defer her own angsting until after tonight. She couldn't count with sequins in her eyes: tonight was all about Ed.

'I don't need nothing to get me in the mood,' Debs announced. 'I've been in the mood since I clapped eyes on that ginger fireman.' She jiggled the acres of chest only loosely reined in by her dress. 'He hasn't got a chance.'

'By the way,' said Billie, halfway up the stairs and therefore a safe-ish distance from her Saturday girl. 'You were half an hour late again this morning, Debs. What was all that about?'

'Oh.' Debs' voice lost all its previous animation. 'Yeah. Couldn't help it.'

Leaving a decent pause for the 'sorry' that would never come, Billie gave up and carried on up the stairs to where her new black trousers and a silky wrap top were waiting. One day she'd tackle Debs about her timekeeping, but it would have to wait until she had the time. And the muscles. She'd already composed the ad she'd place in the *Sole Bay Gazette* to replace the unpunctual, rude and scary Debs.

Hopping on one foot as she cajoled her toes into a strappy silver sandal, Billie leaned over her laptop and opened an email from James.

So, how was lunch? As bad as you feared? Or only as bad as being torn apart by stampeding elephants?

Billie giggled. He understood.

Thanks for being nice about the new girlfriend. I kicked myself for telling you about her. Even she reckoned it was 'a tad sadistic'. I didn't mean it that way, I wouldn't. So I was relieved when I got your reply.

I keep thinking about your customers and smiling to myself. The way you described Annie makes me feel as if I know her. Look after her, won't you? But try and avoid the serial killer newlyweds, for God's sake. Do you think the Death Row groom will wear new white shackles for the occasion? Imagine the vows – 'till death by lethal injection us do part'.

Reading on, the giggles were switched off abruptly, as if they were controlled by a coin meter.

When I told my Significant Other about Blankie, she demanded one too. Have I found the secret way to the modern woman's heart?

Significant other. Billie harrumphed. Significant bloody other, I ask you. James had been reluctant to award her the anaemic title 'girlfriend' until they'd been going out for a year and Billie had pointed out that either she was his girlfriend or a very unusual poltergeist was leaving tampons in his bathroom cabinet.

Outlining her lips in the sliver of cracked mirror available to her, Billie harrumphed again. Why did James have to go and tell his significant other about Blankie? The little tartan rag was part of their shared past, too special to be bandied about with highbrow medical women. She squinted down at the rest of the message.

Work's busy, but I'm enjoying it. I keep meaning to book a week away somewhere. Can't decide if I want to lie on the sand somewhere hot or dash around looking at ruins. I'd better get on with it – the summer will be over before we know it.

There was a page of this vanilla fluff. Billie could read the invisible ink between the lines. James was laying boundaries, glaring enough for even her short sight. He didn't want intimacy, or nostalgia, or her cutesy whines about missing Blankie, just an olive branch, after months of discord, from one friend to another.

Fine, thought Billie. She put the matt peachy lipstick back in her bag. *That's fine*, she thought, filling in her pout in scarlet. *Absolutely bloody fine by bloody me.*

The to-do list for Heather's wedding curled out of her bag. Billie tucked it back in. Blushing firemen notwithstanding, for Billie romance had atrophied to a list of facts and figures.

Somebody was banging energetically on the door down in the shop. 'Tell them we're closed,' Billie hollered down the stairs. Tutting at Dot's soft-heartedness, she heard the shop bell clang. This set off an explosion of chatter downstairs, followed by loud hoots of laughter. Billie stopped dead. She knew that voice. 'Jackie?' she yelled.

'Billie!' the voice shouted back.

'Oh my God, Jackie.' Half falling down the stairs, Billie threw her arms around her old friend. 'Where did you spring from?'

Tall and curvaceous, the statuesque brunette had lips like a bouncy castle. 'All the way from London, darling.' Jackie's accent was pure Belgravia, but her vocabulary could stray to the fishmarket. 'What an arse of a place this is. No fucking taxis at the station.' She regally handed Debs her linen coat, and Debs was so surprised she took it. 'I jumped on a bus that took the scenic route past every trading estate and bingo hall, and here I am!'

Billie had forgotten how exhausting just listening to Jackie could be. Exhausting, but worth the effort; like sex; unlike hiking. 'But . . .' she stammered. 'You didn't warn me, you didn't—'

'Thought I'd surprise you. I'm unemployed now, and bored.' Jackie's background allowed her to work when she felt like it without having to resort to packet stuffing on toast for dinner during jobless patches. 'You always loved surprises,' beamed Jackie, her eyes lighting on the bottle of wine that Debs had been wrestling the cork from. 'Ooh, I've arrived in the nick of time. No doubt you'll be needing some help with that booze, folks.'

Out came the plastic glasses and the home team, even Sam, were silent as Jackie held court. They heard the stirring tale of her latest amour. 'Said he'd leave his wife when the time was right yada yada yada. I fell for it, hook line and hotel room. It's my fault, I just can't resist a man who's spoken for. You know?' Jackie raised a waxed eyebrow at Dot, who shrugged nervously and took another gulp of wine.

'Not everybody likes to break the rules,' Billie reminded her old mate, whose bosom and personality seemed to have swelled in the months they'd been apart: Jackie's persona effortlessly filled the shop. 'Which hotel are you at?'

'I thought . . .' Jackie threw a questioning glance Billie's way. 'I thought wrong, obviously,' she laughed, looking a little flustered.

'Oh, you want to stay with me?' Floundering, Billie said, 'Of course, yes, it's just that . . .' She took a breath. 'I know people say their places are small, Jack, but mine is minuscule. There isn't room.' She threw a desperate glance Sam's way: his cottage had empty bedrooms to spare. He was looking away. And down. And up. Billie got the message: there would be no help from that quarter. Perhaps he didn't want a lodger whose charisma rivalled his own. Billie relented. 'But we'll make do somehow.'

'Perhaps we won't need to,' said Jackie, musingly. 'You slappers are off out somewhere, aren't you?' She listened to the details of the disco. 'Firemen! Oh, for fuck's sake,' she roared. 'As if I'll need a bed tonight. I'll be rolling around some fire-station bunk.' She knocked back the dregs of her cheap wine. 'Lead me to the firefighters!'

Typhoon Jackie had hit Sole Bay.

Fairy lights had magically transformed the village hall into a village hall with a few fairy lights slung around it. The music throbbing through the small wooden building had to compete with the gobby seagulls and the dull whump of the night sea.

'I hope Jake will be alright on his own,' fretted Dot, as their little group approached the bar. She pulled at the form-fitting dress Billie had foisted on her.

'Oh, he'll be fine.' Billie was short on sympathy. The butter-flies in her tummy were making like rhinos.

A round of drinks was plonked down on the chipped Formica bar. Sam stared at the small, dark barman for a moment too long, earning him a, 'Careful – you're in redneck country now, Soho boy,' from Billie.

'Is your funky firefighter here?' Sam asked Billie, handing Jackie a drink without looking at her.

'Who?'

'Oh, don't annoy me.' Sam dropped the subject.

'Be honest,' asked Jackie, who had roughed up her hair and hitched up her skirt. 'Do I look like an easy lay?'

'Oh, I wouldn't say that,' said Dot, shocked.

Billie nodded.

'Excellent!' Jackie scanned the crowd. Only a few brave pioneers were dancing, and everybody had the furtive look common to the sober, early part of a British night out.

Tugging at Sam's elbow, Billie whispered, 'You don't like her.'

'Of course I don't.' Sam looked down at Billie as if she was mad. 'Jackie's a bosom-shaped battering ram.' He looked appraisingly over to where Jackie was preening herself, preparing for the chase and the kill. 'The way you tell it, she dropped poison in James's ears all through your engagement and then walked away backwards when everything went pear-shaped.'

'Nah.' Billie was adamant. It hadn't been like that. 'You've got her wrong. She's wild, not bad.'

'Whatever. So long as you remember,' he bent to whisper, his breath hot in her ear, 'I'm your gay best friend and I trump your slaggy blast from the past, OK?'

'OK.' Billie dead-legged him, flattered that he could find the energy to be jealous.

Then it was Jackie's turn to tug at Billie's elbow. 'Gay, right?' she nodded in Sam's direction. 'Shame.'

The DJ, betraying a quiet desperation, said in a thick local accent, 'Everybody on your feet for this classic, boys and girls!' As a Bucks Fizz song that even Bucks Fizz's mothers had forgotten blared out, Debs' teetering mules took her off across the sort of sticky lino that only village halls still offer.

'There he is!' she hissed, heading for her marmalade-headed prey in a smokey corner. 'OI GINGERNUT!' she bawled. 'Get your hose, you've pulled!'

'Enjoy yourself!' called Dot, indulgently, as if Debs had scampered off to play nicely with the other children, instead of press-ganging an innocent man on a tour of her tattoos.

Bemused at the lack of champagne – 'Are you quite sure? Could you look again, darling?' – Jackie was buying the second round. As she turned to dole out the Lambrusco, her eyes narrowed and she reminded Billie suddenly of Raven. 'Oh my,' she drawled huskily, looking across the room. '*He* is so mine.'

'No, you don't, sister.' Alarmed by her own vehemence, Billie watched Ed push his way through the crowd. Her breathing stumbled. 'That one's spoken for.'

Eighteen

'Hi,' said Ed.

'Hi,' said Billie.

'Are you alright?' asked Dot, sweetly. 'You look a bit red.'

Billie put her mind at rest. 'It's the lighting. He's fine.' She threw a questioning glance at Ed. 'Aren't you?'

'I am now.'

Something primeval and dark was tugging at Billie. A fluttering of panic made her shiver. Tonight was the test drive, she told herself. She would discover more about this man. Sod all the primeval stuff, the riot in her loins, she had to be confident that Ed was nice before she jumped him.

Nice. She smiled inwardly at the banal word. What did it mean?

Jackie had already introduced herself. 'Can't hang around, I'm afraid,' she sang. 'Other fish to fry.' She leaned in to say smokily near Ed's ear, 'And you're off limits. Unfortunately.' With a slow wink at Billie, she sauntered away, as confident as a huntsman off to shoot fish in a barrel.

Winching Ed's attention back from the departing jelly on springs that was Jackie's backside, Billie made a mental note to thwack her with a wet newspaper later. 'Dance?' she asked.

'If I must,' he gulped, and came quietly.

Somehow, Ed's dancing was both sexy and funny, two attributes that usually cancel each other out. James had certainly been funny. He had hardly ever danced, though, waving Billie away when she tried to drag him up at weddings.

Valiantly mincing to the Scissor Sisters, Ed was doing his best to get down with his bad self. Possibly of the small percentage of the male population that tries to get on, and not just off, with girls, he was racking up impressive points with Billie. The way his trousers hugged his buttocks wasn't entirely lost on her either: how she envied them their job.

Ed's treatment of Dot was another plus. Sam had gracefully retreated, aware that something was brewing, but Dot had no such instincts. Chatting above the music about llamas and recycling, she was a gooseberry so large and green she was visible from France. Patiently, Ed listened, and bought her drinks, and danced alongside her as she swayed like a Thai temple dancer with eccentric little moves of her own.

Working it into her impressive routine, Billie danced over to Sam, who stood with a bottle in his hand, his look of ennui more convincing than usual.

'Not what you're used to?' teased Billie.

'Bit wholesome,' he winced. 'Like the school hop in *Grease*.' He looked at his watch, a chunky thing that cost more than the land the village hall stood on. 'Might creep home soon. Now that you've bagged the best-looking bloke in the room, there's not much point staying.'

'Is he really?' burbled Billie.

'You've got taste, Billie-bolly.' Sam lifted his bottle in salute. 'Go get him.'

Making her way back around the fringes of the dance floor, Billie watched Ed. He looked great. He smelled better. He glanced up from talking to Dot and his eyes found hers immediately, across the acres of chewing gum-pitted floor: the thread between them was taut. But was Ed a good bet for a love affair? After years of buccaneering, Billie wanted a decent man. She'd got one in James, and, give or take a devastating heartbreak, she'd rather liked it.

'The Birdie Song' finally broke Ed. 'I can't. The lads would never let me live it down.' He gestured to a mob of blokes, all fairly wobbly of leg and sweaty of face, who had been shouting a running commentary on his dancing.

'Let's have a drink.' Billie looked around for Dot, but she was being chatted up by a man at least eighteen times as attractive as Jake. Billie bit her lip: could tonight be the start of something for Dot? The girl didn't seem to grasp how attractive she was. Could Dot's horizons be broadened until Jake was just a grubby sail in the distance?

Billie's own horizons had shrunk to the space between her and Ed. She reasoned that only he could answer the big question. 'Ed,' she began, 'are you nice?'

'This is girl speak,' he said immediately, leaning back as if she'd pulled a knife on him.

'Aw, Ed, come on. Level with me. Are you nice?' persisted Billie, laughing.

He wasn't laughing. He seemed uncomfortable, his chocolate-drop eyes flitting here and there. 'I'm not the right person to ask, am I?'

'Are you nice?' she almost shouted.

'Well, I wouldn't murder anyone,' he admitted, finally. His mouth relaxed into a smile. 'Yes, Billie, I'm nice.'

'Knew it!' Billie was triumphant. And intrigued. And riddled with lust. She smiled up at him, dancing on the spot, wriggling her hips.

'Don't do that. It does funny things to me.'

Looking away to hide her excitement and confusion, Billie finally faced facts. This man was hers if she wanted him. 'Do what?' she asked, wide-eyed. 'This?' And she shimmied again.

Groaning slightly, Ed pulled her to his side with one arm. 'Don't. I won't be responsible for my actions.'

His arm was like a red-hot wire across her skin. She tensed. An hour in, and already the end of the evening seemed a fore-gone conclusion. 'I should find Sam. And Jackie,' she muttered. She flicked her hair. 'Don't you want to spend some time with your mates?' she asked, almost aggressively.

'Trying to get rid of me?' Ed was trying to smile.

Evasively, Billie replied, 'No, no. I don't want to monopolise you.' She looked down into her drink. Why was she sending away the best looking, *nicest* man in the room? 'They'll think something's going on.' Perhaps because her home-made chastity belt was chafing.

'Something *is* going on.' Was there a hint of temper in the downward curve of Ed's lip as he put his pint down with a thud on the bar? 'Or maybe I'm getting it all wrong.' He turned and shouldered his way through the tipsy mob, his dark, close-cut head a foot above most of them.

Cutting off her companion mid-lousy-chat-up-line, Dot burrowed through the crowd. 'What did you say to Ed?' she accused, slamming down her dandelion and burdock, and bundling Billie into a quieter corner. She was a formidable bundler, despite her size. 'He looks upset.'

'I just said I should look after Sam and Jackie and maybe he should find his mates.' Billie had felt like this at school, when pressed on exactly how the dog had got hold of her homework and why an elderly King Charles spaniel should suddenly develop a taste for geography.

'That's the same as telling him you're bored with him!' Dot put a hand to her head. She was close to exasperated, a novel look for such a placid girl. 'Sam went home ages ago, and Jackie's sitting on the bar.' She looked horrified. 'Ed's been so brilliant, buying us drinks, putting up with me, dancing . . .' She petered to a stop. 'He'll think you don't like him.'

'Well, I don't. Particularly.' Billie shrugged.

'You're scared.' Dot was scornful and Billie was startled, as if a Teletubby had sworn.

'I am not,' she laughed.

'I don't get it.' Dot shook her head and her dangly silver earrings leapt. 'You have the guts to turn a dying business around, to live in a shed, but you can't face your own feelings.'

'I told you, Dot, I'm not scared. I'm just not that into him.' This new, opinionated Dot was fearsome, like a soft toy that had developed kick-boxing skills.

'You are into him.' Dot sounded sad. 'And he's into you. You are allowed to have fun, you know. You can have a romance. You can even fall in love if you want.' Dot's mouth fell open, a perfect circle. 'That's it! You think you might fall in love with Ed. *That's* what's scaring you!'

It was like being hit on the head with a dead pigeon. (And, yes, Billie knew what that was like: don't ask.) Dot was right. Billie didn't deny it. A quick roll in the hay was scary enough, but loving a man – that was too much of a risk. That would make her human again.

It would replace James once and for all.

'Alright,' whispered Billie, enervated by the rush of self-awareness. 'I'm scared.'

Hugging Billie, Dot came over philosophical. 'We're all scared,' she breathed against Billie's hair. 'But we do it anyway.'

She broke away and held Billie at arm's length. 'He's over by the fire exit, looking all Heathcliff. Go and tell him.'

'Tell him what?' How the hell did Dot start calling the shots?

'I don't know.' Dot gave Billie a shove. 'Tell him . . . tell him you like him!' she laughed.

The impetus of the shove sent Billie stumbling through the herd. Knocking into people like a drunk, she kept going until she reached the fire exit. Ed gazed moodily out through the half-open door, with its bar across it, ignoring her.

'Ed . . .' she began. He didn't turn, but gazed resolutely out. 'I like you.' She gulped with surprise, as if the words had come out by remote control. She put her hand to her mouth.

That got his attention. Ed turned quickly to her, and reached up to pull her hand away from her lips. Grabbing her by the waist, he lifted her out on to the gravel, the fire door swinging heavily shut behind them. 'And I like you, Billie's Brides,' he murmured, before overwhelming her mouth with his.

The scratch of his stubble and the velvety feel of his lips were sensory overload after Billie's long drought. She responded with a whole-body shudder of pleasure. It was the first kiss since James. And one of her best kisses ever. She was in the hands of a natural.

'I've been dying to—' Ed tilted his head to whisper, but Billie pulled it firmly back with a patrician, 'No talking!'

'Ohh,' she gasped, eventually, when they really had to stop or die.

'Christ.' Ed ran a hand through his hair. He was looking urgently into her eyes. 'You're—'

'And you're—'

Whatever they both were would have to wait, because Ed pounced again, a broad hand on either side of her face. Superglued together, they lingered, delighting in all the spooky sexiness of their first embrace, until a rogue band of wandering, beer-sodden firemen happened upon them and launched into a medley of rugby songs that would probably have killed Annie.

Polishing up his credentials as an A1, tip-top, twenty-four-carat prospective boyfriend, Ed insisted on walking Dot home.

Watching her let herself into the cottage, Billie said, 'You're very gallant. I heard tell of a lock-in.'

'Hmm.' Ed wrinkled his nose. 'Thirty hairy firefighters and an endless supply of booze. Didn't fancy it.'

Billie knew who would fancy it. 'Jackie will be crowned queen of Sole Bay before the night is out.' She'd noticed her friend getting very cosy with Debs' red-haired victim, and could imagine the girls fighting over him, like King Kong and Godzilla in heels. She knew who she would bet on: Jackie had an unbroken record. 'I hope that ginger bloke can stand the pace.'

'Chugger can look after himself,' Ed assured her.

'Chugger? Is that his surname?'

'Nickname,' Ed explained. 'All our watch have them.' Ed screwed up his eyes. 'There's Humpty. Moggsy. Fried Egg. Oh, and Ronnie the Pig.'

'And you?' Billie leaned into him, slightly surprised at how natural this felt. Distracted by his sharp, gorgeous, hormone-rousing smell, she recovered to ask, 'What's your nickname?'

'Unfortunately, I'm Treacle.'

Girls, thought Billie, would come up with endearing nick-names. If they bothered at all. 'Boys are funny, aren't they?' she pondered, neatly encapsulating centuries of female thought.

'Never mind bloody Chugger,' said Ed, in a voice thick with meaning as he snaked his arms around Billie in the lamplight.

Slipping away from him, Billie raced down the quiet street.

'OI!' Ed's guttural voice echoed around the sleeping houses as he took off after her.

A good runner, even in heels, Billie stayed in front until they reached the steps leading to the beach. 'Thought you'd never catch me,' she panted, as Ed's scent surrounded her.

'You'd have to run an awful lot faster than that.' His hands delved into her hair and pulled her face towards his.

Kissing dreamily, they edged towards Herbert.

Perhaps Ed was impressed, but he could also have been dismayed. 'This is really where you live?'

'It's snug,' conceded Billie, still grasping the bulk of Ed as if she was drowning and he was a novel lifebelt.

'Do you think I'd fit?' Ed pressed himself lasciviously against her.

169

Without warning, Billie disentangled herself and took one rapid step back. Ed had moved things on, and suddenly she saw herself as if viewed from above. The girl down there by Herbert's verandah, with her hair all messed up and her cheeks flushed, looked defenceless.

'I'm sorry,' she started.

'No, I am.' Ed surprised her by backing off, hands in the air as if Billie was flammable and could go up at any moment. 'I'm rushing things.'

'No, you're not . . .' spluttered Billie, floundering. Seeing Ed recede panicked her. She'd expected to fight him off and now she felt herself missing his warmth. 'But it's been a while and—'

'I understand.' Well, that made one of them. 'I'll drop by the shop in the week. See how you're doing.'

'I'd like that.' Billie smiled at Ed, suddenly shy. He was trying so hard. He was being so *nice*. 'Do I get a goodnight kiss?'

'Oh, you get that alright.'

All kissed out, Billie fell into her narrow bed alone, sighing with pleasure and happy exhaustion. The sea answered her, sigh for sigh.

The knocking seemed to have been going on for hours. Billie surfaced through sticky layers of sleep, wondering if the seagulls had turned nasty and were beating down her door to demand protection money. Shaking herself awake, she tugged on her dressing gown and dragged Jackie inside.

'Bloody hell,' she hissed. 'You'll wake the whole town. I'm not supposed to be living here, remember.'

'Oh. Yeah. Sorry.' Jackie didn't look sorry. Jackie looked as if she'd been dragged through a hedge backwards, forwards, then backwards again, before being diligently sandpapered. 'Forgot.' Billie knew that the dishevelment meant that Jackie had been bouncing up and down for most of the night with a gentleman caller.

'Good night?'

'Oh, not good,' leered Jackie, who had all the attributes of a male philanderer bar the willy. 'Great.' She threw her arms in the air and arched into a long stretch, thrusting out her unmissable bosom. 'These firemen are *fit*, girl!'

'I wouldn't know,' simpered Billie, hoping to elicit questions.

She was disappointed. Jackie had moved to the mirror. 'Christ. Did I really walk through the town with mascara down to my chin? What do I look like?'

'Shagged, Jackie, is how you look,' laughed Billie. 'At least, that's the technical term. Is Chugger still alive?'

'Ah, Chugger!' Jackie threw her head back in nostalgia. 'A man every bit as intoxicating as his name suggests.' She picked up a comb from the shelf and made a start on detangling her sex-dreadlocks. 'What a conversationalist. I now know everything I'll ever need to about smoke alarms.'

'He saved you the price of a hotel room,' Billie reminded her, wincing as her friend tugged at her hair.

Grimacing at her reflection, Jackie conceded defeat and put down the comb. 'Maybe I'll just cut it all off. Have some human decency and give me cotton wool and make-up remover, would you?' she pleaded. 'And stick the kettle on. Can I smoke in here?'

'No, you slattern, you can't.' Billie tried to look disapproving, but she loved the bustle that Jackie brought with her. 'Only two minutes in the door and I'm slaving for you already. Would you like a croissant with your tea, Your Majesty?'

'Ooh yeah. And jam.' Jackie seemed to distrust the word 'please'. 'Alright if I lie on that bed? I haven't had a wink of sleep.'

For the rest of that Sunday morning, Billie catered to her hung-over guest, bringing her treats and fancies on demand. They caught up efficiently: Billie's year had been pretty samey, consisting of work/parents/mental turmoil, whereas Jackie had a complex tale to tell.

'Richard was a sod. A real player. Jeremy was short. *Short* short. Wore school trousers. I rather liked Jean-Pierre, but his wife didn't care for me, not after I'd put my foot through her best sheets. Simeon wanted to marry me. Can you imagine?'

Billie couldn't. Listening to the litany of lovers, she felt the familiar mixture of amusement, admiration and repulsion. She didn't aspire to Jackie's score card, but hearing the details, told with such relish and such complete lack of remorse, always made her laugh. Mention of wives and girlfriends dampened the fun: Billie hated the emotional carnage Jackie wreaked so carelessly. 'Do you have *any* conscience at all?' she asked, after a hair-raising tale of a wife who turned up at Jackie's door to return her cap and deliver a right hook.

'I did have one, but it died of malnutrition years ago.' Recumbent on the bed, Jackie pulled her knees up to her chest: as Billie had suspected, Jackie looked better in her dressing gown than she did. 'Admit it. You wouldn't like me half as much if I was a polite little smudge like your assistant.'

Bridling, Billie took away the tray to cover her discomfort. 'Dot's lovely,' she said quietly.

'Not a barrel of laughs, though.'

'She is, actually. We have a lot of fun,' said Billie truthfully. She frowned at Jackie. 'You don't know her.'

Holding her gaze for a moment, Jackie seemed to realise something. 'No,' she said, in quite a meek tone for her. 'I don't. Sorry. She's your new me, is she?' The throwaway tone didn't quite ring true. 'Or is that Sam's job?'

'No, of course not, but they're good mates.' Billie raised her eyebrows. 'Trust me, Jack, nobody could ever replace you.'

'What's with Sam and the "rock star stance"? Bit eighties, isn't it?'

Hmm, thought Billie. So the dislike was mutual. 'I think he looks cool,' she giggled. 'He created Tiddlywinks the velvet rabbit, you know.'

'Tiddly-who?' When Jackie wasn't interested, she didn't delve: children's books did not cross her radar. She swung her legs out of bed. 'I saw James and his new bird the other night,' she began casually, before stopping dead. 'Should I be careful about this stuff, or are you OK with it?'

What a huge question, thought Billie. Assuring Jackie that she was 'OK with it', Billie did her best to be. Suddenly unwanted details were flying at her like bats in a Hammer horror movie. She now knew that James's new girlfriend was called Antonia, had long blonde hair, long brown legs, great dress sense, and pots of money. Perhaps sensing that none of this was what an ex would want to hear, Jackie added, 'No balls, though. Nothing like you. She's a big step down.'

Archly, Billie said, 'James reckons she reminds him of me.'

Looking flabbergasted, Jackie queried, 'You're in touch? You and James? Christ.'

'It's not that amazing.' Billie reconsidered. 'Is it?'

'After what happened . . .' Jackie began to refurbish her face in the mirror. 'I'm amazed you're talking. Glad, but amazed.' She stopped, blusher brush suspended in mid-air. 'It's time some forgiveness was trotted out. It's all water under the bridge. You were a good pair. Maybe you can be better friends than lovers.'

'That's the idea,' said Billie. Watching Jackie bring out her cheekbones with a subtle flick of the brush, she asked, hesitantly, 'Do you think it's possible to forgive that kind of thing?' It was a question that had kept her awake at night.

With her usual honesty, and a bracing lack of diplomacy, Jackie said absently, 'For James's sake, darling, we must hope so.' She rooted around for her mascara. 'Anyway, you're moving on. There are plenty more fish in the sea. And, handily, the sea is right outside your window.'

'Well, I already have somebody. Remember?' Billie felt sure that Jackie couldn't have forgotten Ed: Ed was not forgettable.

'Oh. You mean what's-his-name, Ed.' Jackie waved the mascara wand about. 'Yeah, him, but I mean somebody special. Not just some pretty boy.'

'He's special.' Billie was wounded: this, too, was familiar territory around Jackie.

'But you haven't . . . have you?'

'No, but that's not the be-all and end-all.' Properly riled, Billie went waspish. 'They're not all in it for the sex, you know.'

'Hmmm.' Pouting at her reflection, Jackie left that opinion hanging in the air. 'You sure about that?'

'You're annoying me, Jackie,' warned Billie, darkly. 'May we change the subject?'

'Sure, darling.' Jackie's good humour was unperturbable. 'Why don't you perform a short mime for me about how on earth one pisses in this hovel. I'm *bursting*.'

Nineteen

'Dot, why are you hovering?' grouched Billie. 'You know I'm dangerous when I'm working out VAT.' She lifted her head from the pile of invoices she had brought up to the stockroom to stare at in mute horror. 'Was Jake alright when you got home? Didn't have a go at you?'

'He never has a go at me.' Dot corrected her boss mildly. 'He was already in bed. Had a terrible stomach ache apparently. Thought it was peritonitis.'

Tosser-itis, diagnosed Billie, meanly. 'Poor him,' she said, acidly, certain that it had been a strategic pain designed to make poor Dot feel guilty. 'He didn't die, I take it?'

'Oh, you can be horrid,' said Dot, reprovingly. 'Of course he didn't.' She fingered her embroidered hem idly, and asked, 'Did your friend leave town alright? Jackie, wasn't it?'

'Yes, thanks.' Billie looked up, intrigued. A note of distaste had coloured Dot's innocuous question. 'What did you think of her?'

'Oh, nice. Very nice. Very very nice.' Dot nodded briskly to supply the certainty her tone lacked. 'Coming back, is she?'

'Probably. You never know with Jackie.'

'Right.' Dot sniffed, and scrumpled up her hem. 'Nice for you to have a friend about.'

'Oh, I'm well off for those.' Billie wasn't too involved with the VAT to know when reassurance was called for. 'Now, if you don't mind, Dot, I have so much to do . . .'

'Sure. Sure.' But Dot's Jesus boots were stapled to the spot. 'Seeing Ed soon?'

Throwing down her pen, Billie sighed, 'You'll have to work on your casual questions, you know. Yes, Dot, I *am* seeing him again. And before you ask, I don't know when. OK?'

'Bet he comes in today.' Dot's freckles reshuffled themselves as she smiled. 'Bet you anything.'

'Some time this week is all he said.' Billie stared down at the papers in front of her, all of which now had Ed's face in the watermark. 'So it might even be next week.' She didn't want to expect too much: as Jackie had pointed out, they hadn't even you-know-whatted.

'Today, I reckon.' Dot clambered down the stairs, in answer to a hopeful shout of, 'Yoo hoo! I'm desperate for a crinoline!' from the shop floor.

After successfully evading thoughts of Ed all morning, Billie was ambushed. She could accurately conjure up the gentle sand-paper of his chin, the curve of his lips in the moonlight. VAT paled into insignificance as her skin's memory reproduced the pressure of his hands on her back.

'What does *this week* mean?' Billie was plunged back into the dating girl's universe of second-guessing and motive evalu-ation. Did Ed mean literally a week? Therefore, should she worry if he didn't drop in by the time the shop closed on the coming Saturday? Or was it a looser version of a week? A man-time week, perhaps?

Billie knew from what felt like centuries of experience that man-time runs to a very loose-knit, nebulous calendar. 'I'll call you soon' could be translated as 'I'll call you long after your teeth have dropped out and you've started forgetting people's names'. 'See you around' could simply mean 'See you around' but in man-time it also meant 'Now that I have achieved sexual congress with you I will avoid you as if you are leprous'.

The perils of trying to mix and match man-time with her own more straightforward diary had been one of the reasons Billie had always avoided commitment, scorching blokes before they'd had the opportunity to do the same to her.

Until James, that is, and his refreshing approach to time. 'I'll call you later,' meant that she'd hear from him later that day, and, 'Let's go for a drink this week,' had always resulted in clinking glasses before seven days were up. She had been spoiled, relying on his calls the way Italian fascists relied on Mussolini's fabled trains.

'He's not James,' she reminded herself. It was self-evident, but it needed saying. Mind you, Billie realised that she'd been saying it a lot. Everything Ed had said and done so far had been compared to James: his score was good, but it worried her that she was keeping score.

Standing up to pace the tiny stockroom, she told herself off, in a voice uncannily like her old headmistress's. It was unhealthy to compare the two men. And unhelpful. It could only get in the way of that Holy Grail of all battered hearts: moving on.

Billie could never move on while she was comparing other men, favourably or unfavourably, to the big, floodlit ex. It had to stop.

Proud of her sensible self-counsel, Billie reapplied herself to the VAT. Down in the shop, the bell over the door sang. Freezing like the family spaniel used to when it heard the fridge door, Billie only relaxed when she heard a female voice ask for a refund on a bolero. This anticipation was *horrible*. Billie hated the way she watched the door, scanned the street, mistook every red Ford Fiesta for a fire engine. Why couldn't she be calm? Why couldn't she be cool?

Because she cared about Ed. Already, after a few salty seafront kisses, she was bovvered.

There was somebody she wanted to tell. Before she had the opportunity to examine this impulse, she had bashed out James's email address.

Guess what?

She asked her ethereal ex, floating out there on the worldwide web like a stray astronaut.

I've found somebody, too.

This had to be carefully judged. James had set very clear guidelines for their new correspondence. She must keep her touch light.

The fireman finally came across. But, he doesn't remind me of you at all. Who knows what will come of it? Nothing, perhaps. But for now, it feels good. Right, enough hearts and flowers. Can you help me with a VAT problem?

That was the plain unvarnished truth: James had been so important to her once that it seemed right to be telling him how she felt. It was cleansing, like an emotional power shower. And the VAT query would make him laugh. If she still held that power.

The bell jangled again. This time Billie shot up so fast she had to snatch up her computer before it hit the stockroom floor. Ed's voice was asking, 'You on your own, Dottie?'

'No, no, she's not.' At the bottom of the stairs before Ed had finished his question, Billie smiled, broad and soppy. 'How are you?' she asked, for want of something better, or intelligent, to say.

'Recovering.' Ed was smiling too, almost as broad, almost as soppy. 'I wasn't a pretty sight yesterday. Hangovers get worse as you get older, don't they?'

Nodding, Billie hid her puzzlement. She hadn't realised that Ed had drunk enough to merit a punishing hangover. A warty gremlin, the sort who hangs around vulnerable girls embarking on new relationships with sexy firefighters, whispered that perhaps he'd been sozzled when he kissed her? That perhaps he regretted it?

Casting a furtive look at Dot, who wasn't making a very good job of pretending to be interested in a bridal underwear catalogue, Ed held up a small bunch of white flowers.

The gremlin disappeared in a puff of green smoke. Regretful men tend not to buy flowers, reasoned Billie. 'Are they for me?' she asked, in a small voice.

'Well,' Ed looked teasingly around the room. 'Unless Dot wants them.'

The bell jangled again, and suddenly Heather materialised between them, like a panto witch. 'God, it's hot,' she moaned, demonstrating her mood to be somewhat panto witch-like, too. 'Oh.' She stopped mopping her brow and took in Ed's presence. 'What are you doing here?' she asked, seemingly cross that parts of the universe were cross-pollenating without her permission. 'Did I ask you to pop in?' She looked from Ed to Billie and then back to Ed again. 'Flowers, Ed?' she queried, rather like a policeman might query, 'Heroin, sir?'

A number of thoughts flashed across Billie's consciousness like text messages from her psyche. HTHR MST NOT KNOW OR

MY LIFE OVR, one read, recalling her client's plans for Ed and Angela. Then, in even bigger letters, PLSE DNT TELL HR!!!

'Yeah,' conceded Ed, looking down at the freesias. 'Flowers.' He looked at Heather for a long while. 'For my mum,' he finally said, in a dubious voice that suggested he didn't even believe himself. 'She's not been well.'

'Oh, isn't he nice?' Heather grabbed the tall man and chucked his chin as if he was an adorable two-year-old. 'Dean only buys me flowers if they're reduced.' With a sly look, she said, 'Angela is a sucker for flowers. She'd do anything for a gerbera.'

'I'll keep that in mind,' promised Ed, who seemed to be purposefully not looking at Billie.

'Anyway, run along,' ordered Heather, who seemed to automatically assume that all humans were in her employ. 'I have a million and one things to talk to Billie about.'

'See you around,' said Ed. Behind Heather's back, and hopefully out of range of those eyes Dean swore were in the back of her head, Ed shrugged exaggeratedly at Billie, and pulled a sad face over the flowers.

'See you!' said Billie, casually, attempting to imply by subtext that when she did see him she would snog him until he begged for mercy.

'Horses,' proclaimed Heather, undoing a low-carb chocolate bar as if it contained the antidote to a fatal snake bite.

'Booked. Two. White. Gorgeous.'

'Plumes?'

'Fuchsia.'

'Carriage?'

'Silver.' On a gasp from Heather that coincided with ingestion of low-carb chocolate and turned into a violent cough, Billie added, 'But will be sprayed lilac for the big day.'

'Oh, I love you!' gabbled Heather, as her throat seized up.

So you should, thought Billie wryly. She had made more phone calls about those horses and their sodding feathers than President Bush had made about foreign policy. 'No problem,' she said. Now that she was settling into her role as Billie Baskerville Ace Wedding Planner, Billie prided herself on keeping the ugly mechanics of her work away from the prospective bride. Like a veal calf, Heather had to be kept in the dark, protected, humoured. 'Don't worry, Heather, everything is under control.'

'Of course I'm worried!' snapped Heather. 'According to my schedule, it's almost time to panic.'

This was familiar territory. Billie remembered her own sweaty palms and thudding heart every time her mother opened the wedding folder that had lain on the coffee table for months. Fear of her dress going out of fashion had kept her awake at night, and she had almost punched a second cousin who turned vegetarian after the menu was finalised.

There was no time for a cup of something reviving after Heather had left. A new customer took her place. The accent was eastern European. The voice was a throaty growl. The lipstick was bright. And the breasts were not as God made them. 'Is best quality, yes?' asked the prospective bride, snatching up a tulle skirt between silicon talons that could pluck nails out of walls.

'Is best quality,' mimicked Billie, unwittingly. She was keeping a safe distance from this woman, who had the unpredictable feel of a lioness with piles.

'And this?' The customer snatched up a posy, delicately fashioned from silk flowers. 'Will rot?' She rolled her Rs like a circus master.

'Will not.' It was a novel feeling, but Billie wished that Debs was there.

'Why you wear those wings?'

The lazy question insinuated all kinds of things about Billie's mental health, so Billie ignored it and asked, 'When's the big day?'

The insignificant man trailing the statuesque foreigner answered merrily, 'As soon as possible!' His myopic eyes twinkled, and his sandy moustache quivered as he daringly reached out a hand the size of a child's to take his fiancée's claw. 'We can't wait, can we, my passionflower?' His milky face gazed up adoringly.

'God, always you paw me, Clifford,' snapped his passionflower, shrugging him off. 'I need quick dress, so we can get married before his mother stops us. What is most dearest dress?' she asked, peremptorily.

'Err, that would be the Angelica.' Motioning to a raw-silk extravaganza in the window, Billie added, 'But it's over three thousand pounds.' She looked apologetically at Clifford, who was looking down at his hand as if it had blistered. Billie didn't really expect to sell the Angelica, it was merely there to inspire customers.

'I try on.' Heading for the changing room, the bride-to-be was already undoing her top.

'Bloody hell,' gasped Billie, before she remembered who and where she was. 'I mean, of course.' It was vital to act as if she sold three-thousand-pound wedding dresses every other day.

The gown looked wonderful, despite the sour look on the customer's haughty face. 'Is not worth the money,' she stated, baldly.

Why not say what you think, thought Billie, doing up the last tiny button. 'The lace is handmade, and the silk is French. Look at this stitching.' But the woman was busy checking her teeth in the mirror.

'You think these front teeth too big?' she demanded, leaning towards Billie. 'Clifford buy me crowns. I think they are too big, like mouth of camel.'

From outside the curtain, her generous groom insisted, 'No, no, Ivanka, my love. Your teeth look wonderful.'

Lowering her voice, the woman confided, 'He think I look wonderful if I have sanitary towel on head. He know nothing about woman.' She eyed Billie properly for the first time, and growled, in a desperate whisper, 'Is like making sex with an oven glove.' She dragged the dress off, and thrust it at Billie. 'I take this one,' she declared, loudly.

'Really, my love?' Clifford's voice sounded weak from the shop floor. 'Wouldn't you like to try on some others? Some not so, um, I mean, less extravagant ones?'

'You mean cheap?' roared the woman, tearing the curtain aside and striding out into the shop in her scarlet underwear. 'OK, bring me the cheap rubbish. I will wear nastiest dress in shop on most special day in life!' she howled. 'I am not worth three thousand pounds! Clifford would rather keep it in the bank!'

'No, no, not at all.' The little man's translucent pallor was compromised by two throbbing dots of red on his alarmed face.

'Perhaps you do not wish to marry your Ivanka?' Hands on hips, his Ivanka glared at him, her rock-hard breasts of unlikely proportions roughly at the height of his watery eyes.

Across the shop, Dot retreated into the tiny loo and locked the door. Billie envied her, but she couldn't leave her post. 'We have beautiful designs for about five hundred pounds,' she suggested, meekly.

'No, he does not want to marry me!' Ivanka was struggling with her glittering knuckleduster of an engagement ring.

'Don't say that, kitten!' whimpered Clifford, hunched with anxiety. 'Please!'

'You can go to your mother and say *old woman, you were right. I should stay at home with you and spend life savings on static caravan.*' She paused, and was calm again. In an austere voice, she sneered, 'I suppose you want your tits back.'

'Don't talk like that, Ivanka.' Clifford seemed close to tears. 'Have the dress. I insist. And shoes to match. And a tiara. And a veil to cover your beautiful face. Only, please, my love, don't shout at your Clifford like that.'

'OK.' The storm had passed. As insouciant as a teenager who's just got their own way and had their Big Mac super-sized, Ivanka turned to Billie. 'Show me best shoes in shop.'

Lounging companionably against the counter with Zelda, idly snaffling fudge from her bag, Billie watched Dot fling glitter over the window display. Her aim was a little shaky, thanks to the muttered running commentary from Jake, sprawled like a daddy-long-legs on the floorboards.

'I shouldn't be surprised, really, when you behave like a Jezebel,' he was saying, in a disappointed voice. 'Who knows what blood is in your veins?'

A quiet growl sounded from Zelda at Billie's side. Billie knew what she meant: it was torture watching Jake try to strip Dot down to her chassis like this.

'Your grandmother could have been a lunatic. Or a sex

maniac,' Jake carried on, sadly. 'After all, what kind of woman abandons a baby? She can't have loved your mum much to do that to her.'

Dot kept flinging the glitter. Silent and unresponsive, she was like a sleepwalker.

Chewing, Zelda pointed out, 'You shouldn't talk about a lady you don't know nothing about.' She skewered Jake with a narrow-eyed gaze.

Lazily Jake told her, 'It's none of your business.'

Billie shifted uneasily from foot to foot, her gaze on Dot's defeated back. The knowledge that Dot would suffer after any interference stilled her tongue.

Zelda had no such scruples. Defiantly, she said, 'If Dot's grandmother were here she'd love her, just like we all do. Everybody loves that girl.'

As if Zelda hadn't spoken, Jake carried dreamily on, almost under his breath, 'If Dot wants to kick our relationship to death there's nothing I can do about it.'

Now Dot was galvanised into action. Not the sort of action Billie would have taken, involving Jake's beard and a box of matches, but a gentle, reproving, 'Oh Jakey, don't.'

'Perhaps we're not meant to be.' Jake assumed a look of mock misery, perhaps copied from Renaissance paintings of Christ on the cross. 'Perhaps you can't cope with my genius.' He unbent his limbs and made for the door.

Jake left the shop, but not before Billie had seen Zelda throw Jake a look so venomous, so vengeful, so – there was only one word for it – so *murderous* that Billie gasped.

'I've chosen,' said Annie, looking amazed at her own effrontery. '*That*,' she pointed to a dress hanging near the stairs, 'is the one for me.'

'Ooh, Annie,' cooed Billie. 'That's my favourite, too.'

The Ruby Wolff design was regal, grown-up. Cream velvet, with an austere high-buttoned collar and a gently puddling train, the dress had a purity and simplicity that drew Billie to it. She was constantly tweaking it, rehanging it, nuzzling her face against its luxurious fabric. 'I'll put it away for you.'

Annie, pink and delighted, trotted out to meet Ruby in the

street, but he darted back to the shop, leaving her on the pavement.

'Mum's the word,' he croaked, surreptitiously passing Billie a fiver.

'Oh.' Billie looked down at the crumpled note. 'That's so sweet of you, Ruby.' Billie asked, smug, 'So how is your new seamstress coming along?'

'I've never seen such exquisite work,' enthused Ruby, waving his gnarled hands for emphasis. 'The woman has a wonderful touch.' He shuffled out hurriedly to join Annie on the pavement.

'Aww, look,' simpered Dot, seemingly recovered from Jake's psychological assault. 'He's taken her arm.'

There was no time to dwell on Ruby's rehabilitation: the VAT beckoned. 'I want calories. Now. In this hole in my face,' insisted Billie, shuddering at the thought of the pile of papers upstairs. 'Fudge, Dot. Fetch fudge.'

'Noooo,' whined Dot. 'Please don't make me. I can't bear to see Raven at the moment. He looks ill. I'm so worried about him.'

Not quite so concerned about the devilish, dreadlocked little moggy, Billie joined the queue in Zelda's sunlit shop. Somebody joined the queue behind her and she budged up slightly. Then she realised who it was. 'Ed!' she quacked.

'Billie.'

'What are you doing here?'

He bit his lip. His lovely, fleshy, slightly moist lip. 'Buying fudge?'

'Of course you are, it's a fudge shop.' For some reason Billie was shouting. Then she laughed. Much too loudly, as if fudge shops were intrinsically funny. Ed's charms short-circuited her conversation wiring. Perhaps she should give up trying to sound coherent and communicate with him by means of diagrams. Or mime.

'Sorry about the flowers.' As usual, it was left to Ed to steer them to saner conversational waters. 'I guessed you wouldn't want Heather to know.' He swallowed. 'About us.' He swallowed again. 'If there is an us.' Ed looked directly at Billie, but his lickable face was expressionless.

Quietly, Billie said, 'I hope there is.' And that was it. She'd chosen. There was going to be an us. A smile broke out and ran riot all over her face.

An answering grin rendered Ed even more handsome. 'When can I see you again?' he whispered, perhaps aware that a Sole Bay queue is avid for kicks, and could be listening in.

'Dinner at my place?' It came out before Billie had time to think. Her place was a bad place for dinner, but it was too late. Ed had nodded happily and she was committed to cooking and serving a romantic meal in a space smaller than the average lift. 'Saturday?'

Crinkling up his eyes, Ed said slowly, 'Ye-es, I'm off Saturday night.' He gazed into the chilled cabinet behind them. 'Think I'll go for the vanilla,' he said.

God, he's sexy when he talks fudge, thought Billie.

She was a lost cause.

Twenty

It had first struck Billie halfway through cashing up one evening: the till had been short only on Saturdays. Once she'd realised that, she realised that the amounts had all been similar. From there it was a hop, skip and a jump to Debs.

It *had* to be Debs. Only the three of them had access to the till; unless Billie had had some kind of amnesia, she could rule herself out; the world would topple from its axis if Dot ever stole; which left Debs. Surly, rude, work-shy, aggressive Debs. In any of Billie's beloved TV cop shows, she would be *too* obvious.

Two things stopped Billie from confronting her Saturday girl. One was the lack of hard evidence, the second was the aforementioned Saturday girl's demeanour, which was generally that of a grizzly bear immediately after a clumsy rectal examination.

'I have to tell her she can't use the till,' Billie resolved, as she opened up the shop. 'Simple as that. Nice and easy. No need for bad feeling.' She groaned gently.

'Nice day,' sang Zelda, interrupting her own rendition of 'SexyBack' as she put out her 'FRESH FUDGE HERE' sign.

'Lovely!' The weather was mentioned every day on Little Row, even though scorching days were commonplace, the summer's success anointed with a hosepipe ban. As if Billie had summoned Debs up by thinking bad thoughts about her, her Saturday girl sauntered to the door.

Trying not to stare at the web of white strap marks across the irradiating sunburn on Debs' chest, Billie preceded her in. 'You're early.' She was surprised.

'Yeah.' Debs never explained anything. 'There's bird cack all down the window.' She paused. 'I ain't cleaning it up,' she added, lest there be any doubt.

'Of course not.' Billie strode out back for a bucket. 'The very idea.'

Wondering idly just what birds ate to achieve that chalky texture, Billie scrubbed at the poop Rorschach, as Debs dealt with the first customer of the day.

'Boss!' yelled Debs raucously from inside. 'Get in here! The till's stuck!'

Not stuck, but locked. It was time to tell Debs that she couldn't use the cash register. Bracing herself, Billie picked up her bucket and strode back in.

'This one 'ere needs a refund.' Debs jerked a thumb in the direction of a pale, pained woman in her thirties, who was clutching a Billie's Brides bag between reddened fingers. 'She's been dumped.'

The woman's self-possession cracked, and she started to sob. Slipping an arm around the distressed jiltee, Billie suggested putting the kettle on to Debs.

'Bloody hell, I've only just got in!' yelled Debs, dragging herself out to the back of the shop. She stopped in front of the woman to ask, in a kinder voice, 'It was for someone younger, prettier, yeah?' Her only answer was harder sobbing. 'Thought so.'

Luckily Dot arrived, and took over on the 'there, there' front so Billie could process the refund.

'You're late, Miss Dot,' Billie told her over the distraught woman's head. 'Not like you.'

'No.' Dot seemed reluctant to go any further. Her eyes, Billie suddenly realised, were as red-rimmed as their lachrymose customer's.

Jake. Billie knew it. The sod. She didn't say anything more, just hoped that it was the end of his campaign.

The day was a blur of white fabric and veils. Billie's wings buckled at some point, but she had no time to straighten them out. Lunch was a snatched sandwich made by Dot ('I call it my mung-bean extravaganza!') and Billie barely had time to take Debs to one side and ask her to please wipe off the hair-removal cream on her upper lip.

'But I'm going out tonight!' moaned Debs.

'I don't care!' answered Billie, emboldened by her suspicions.

A brief face-off ensued, but Debs lost the cream. The show-down over the till had been an anticlimax too: 'Not bothered,' she'd shrugged, when told she would no longer take payments.

Billie was a powerhouse that Saturday. Those promised few hours with Ed at the end of the day shimmered like light at the end of the tunnel. In fact, like Las Vegas at the end of the tunnel. Getting to know him better, getting to kiss him again, would be her reward for this demanding day.

One of the demands it made on Billie was twenty minutes alone with Jake. She'd never had one-on-one time with him before, and the prospect was prickly. 'Dot's not here,' she told him, as soon as he sloped into the shop, his floral kilt a touch too short for her liking. 'She's delivering some shoes to a bride on the estate.'

Jake uttered the terrible words, 'I'll wait,' and settled himself on the chair reserved for customers.

It was Debs' lunch break, so Billie found herself trying to make conversation. 'Been painting, have you?' she tried. When that was met with silence she said, in a small voice, 'I can't draw. All my heads come out too big.'

'You don't like me, do you?' whispered Jake.

'God. What? I mean, God,' began Billie, shocked. She didn't like Jake one bit. She liked him less than ironing, than exercising, than being asked if she wanted to take out a store card every time she bought a skirt. But there was no way she could baldly tell him so. 'Don't say that,' was her lame concession to both politeness and honesty.

'Do you want to know what I think of you?'

'No.' Billie was sure about this.

Apparently, Jake's question had been rhetorical. He leaned forward, skinny hands on skinny knees, and told her, 'You're a bad influence. You unsettle Dot.'

'I'm Dot's friend.' Billie stressed that last word. Slowly, she was mentally peeling her gloves off.

'You lead her astray.'

'You sound like a puritan papa.' Billie frowned in incomprehension. 'Why are you so hard on her?'

'Haven't you noticed by now?' Jake was doing one of his abrupt gear changes. Suddenly he was all passion. 'She's the moon and stars to me. She's my night and day. I can't breathe when she's not near me. It's like being trapped in an abyss.' He slumped, spent.

Billie stared at him. Where had all that come from? By the look of Jake it had come from deep, deep down and the effort of releasing it had left him exhausted.

'Do you tell her that?' asked Billie, quietly.

'She knows.'

And now Billie knew, too. Perhaps, she thought, fidgeting with the till and straightening the Gallery of Happiness, Jake's childhood had left him tongue-tied, a foreigner to the language of affection. That outburst had been the only positive thing he'd ever said about his girlfriend. Heartfelt, eloquent, loving, the speech had been profoundly non-Jake.

The old Jake returned soon enough. 'From the back,' he told Billie, 'you could be a man.'

The 'Clossed' sign was finally slapped over. The last woman claiming to be a size twelve had left. They were alone. Dot collapsed like Dali's melting clock over the counter, and Debs croaked a heartfelt, 'I 'ate fucking work.'

A peek at her watch told Billie she had an hour to wash, change, civilise her hair and make-up her face: it was do-able, if she postponed cashing up. She paid her little team and shooed them out like geese, just as her unpredictable mobile phone buzzed.

'Sam,' she said warmly, and slightly breathlessly, speed-walking in the direction of Herbert's Dream II.

'Drink?' he asked, with the confidence of one who knows the answer will be yes.

'No.' Billie tried not to sound as if she'd won the lottery. 'Date!'

'Oh, I forgot. The fireman.' Sam tutted. 'Have fun, I suppose, you little turncoat. Where are you cooking for him?'

Billie cut Sam off and walked into a lamp post. How could she have forgotten she'd promised Ed dinner? She'd been fanta-sising solidly for twenty-four hours about this date and the most important detail had slipped her (admittedly slippery) mind. She broke into a run.

Small towns don't stay open late. By twenty-five to six, Sole

Bay High Street was shuttered and dark, all the buckets and spades whisked inside and all the doors resolutely shut, as if a gunslinger had ridden into town. But Billie wasn't downhearted. She was headed for Tesco Metro, which kept urban hours and could be relied upon to dispense dinner-party-style titbits until at least nine p.m.

Racing along, Billie tried to compose a menu in her head. She was no cook, although she was a champion eater. Asparagus? She wondered wildly what one does to it. Toast it? Roast it? How about a nice chicken? That was easy. She'd watched her mother countless times. All she'd have to do was beg its pardon, introduce a lemon to its cavity and pop it in the oven. The oven she didn't have. Oh God. Bacon and eggs?

Skidding to a halt outside the small supermarket, she pushed her way through the small crowd gathered there for some reason. With a twitch of foreboding she recognised them as staff. 'What's going on?' she asked, fearful of the answer.

A chain-smoking lady garlanded with gold chains who was a chum of Zelda's said, 'Them fool Saturday boys larking about. They've only flooded the place.'

'But you're not ... shut?' Billie grasped the lady's flabby arm, which yielded like marshmallow.

'Ow,' said the woman mildly, then, 'of course we're shut, love. It's like *The Poseidon Adventure* in there.'

Her reaction drew stares from the rest of the little huddle, so Billie stopped whimpering and beetled off in the direction of the only other establishment that would be open at this hour.

Garage forecourt shops are cornucopias of plenty if you want a *Daily Mirror* and a squeegee, but Billie suspected that celebrated socialites don't rely on them when entertaining. 'Oh Lord,' she sighed, dancing from foot to foot, wildly grabbing at the limited selection of foodstuffs on the shelves. 'I can't offer him biscuits for a main course,' she muttered, suddenly loathing the Jaffa Cakes and the Digestives and the Jammie Dodgers that she usually greeted like long-lost chums. 'Ah ha!' A break at last. 'Pringles. That's the starter sorted,' she muttered.

Pre-plastic surgery, Nancy Baskerville had eschewed electric light in the evenings, labelling bulbs 'cruel'. Struggling to find the rude bits of her D. H. Lawrence GCSE set book in a flickering interior reminiscent of the caves of early man, teenage Billie hadn't appreciated the romance of the candle.

Tonight, looking around at the dusty pastels of her tiny home, softened and polished by countless tealights, Billie got the point at last. 'Dreamy,' she murmured, approvingly. Admittedly, the beach hut now constituted a serious fire hazard, but at least her guest would know what to do if the gingham curtains went up.

The faithful black trousers understood about Billie's bum, and the strappy top showed off her fashionably pale shoulders nicely. Even her hair was cooperating, acquiescing meekly when introduced to a large clip.

The fly in the evening's ointment was the food. James had always cooked when they'd invited mates around. Billie had been in charge of taking coats, passing around nibbles and getting tipsy. And she had been damn good at all three. Coats had been carefully thrown on the spare-room floor, mini pretzels had spread round the room quicker than the clap in a Student Union, and she had usually managed to embarrass/insult at least one diner before they'd sat down to something involving prawns.

Tonight, flying solo, she arranged Pringles on a melamine picnic plate with the confidence of one who has handled nibbles before. The surly teenager behind the garage counter, his attention wrenched from a particularly engrossing article in *Knave*, had answered, 'Tarama-wot?' when quizzed about dips. She might as well have asked him for a haunch of venison, or a quail within a duck within a goose. The Pringles would have to fly solo as well.

The scrape of male feet on Herbert's veranda startled her. *He's early!* she squealed to herself, running in all directions yet getting nowhere, like a scalded cartoon moggy. *He's early! He's fucking early!* The rap at the door was loud. Billie slapped herself suddenly round the face, and breathed in so hard the candle flames wavered. 'Coming!' she sang.

'I'm early.' Ed's even, stolid voice was apologetic.

'Are you?' Billie managed to look amazed. 'No problem.' She accepted the bottle of wine and the supermarket flowers with exaggerated delight, as if he'd handed her the Koh-i-noor diamond. 'So beautiful!' she breathed over the drooping heads of carnations that would all be dead by dessert.

Looking around him as he took off his jacket, Ed said, 'It's bigger than I thought.'

Hoping he wasn't referring to her arse, Billie invited him to sit down. Or perhaps she ordered him to: nerves brought out the dominatrix in her.

By the time Ed's grade A bottom hit the deckchair Billie had uncorked the wine. 'Cheers!' she said toothily, dismayed at just how twitchy his proximity made her. There was an intimacy to having this long-legged, broad-shouldered man in her home that she hadn't anticipated. Outside these weather-beaten walls they were just two more people in the crowd, held apart by social boundaries and etiquette. In here, they were alone. A couple. In the sensuous candlelight he could pounce at any moment.

Almost horizontal in the deckchair, Ed didn't look like a man primed to pounce. He seemed relaxed and content, even when a plastic platter of Pringles was thrust under his nose. 'No, ta,' he said mildly. 'I've never liked them.'

Shit. They're the best bit, panicked Billie, as she paced with her wine glass. Pacing in such a small space, around such long outstretched legs, wasn't easy, but she managed it. Her body was hot-wired, and wouldn't agree to sit still. 'So,' she began, a little too loudly, a little too assertively, 'how's work?'

'You look very sexy tonight, Ms Baskerville.'

'Me? No! Shuddup.' Billie was bad at accepting compliments but good at forgetting: when James had told her she looked nice, she had been prone to bark, 'And what does bloody *nice* mean? Have you even looked at me? Is my hair funny at the back? Is this skirt too short? Can you see the hole in my tights? Should I cover up the tops of my arms? Nice is not enough information, man!' She returned to her question. 'So, how *is* work?'

'I like your hair up like that.'

'Nah, it's too fluffy.' Ed's comment had pleased her more than he could possibly know. Billie's hair was a natural phenomenon that only James had admired. His fascination with it – 'You've got the best hair' – contrasted nicely with her mother's 'Dear God, you could keep owls in that. GET IT CUT!' Billie gulped at her wine. 'My hair's always a mess,' she insisted confidently, as the gluey red hit her empty tum.

Slicing through the nerves, the cheap wine and that carping inner voice, Billie rapped herself over the knuckles: James wasn't here. He hadn't touched her hair for a long time, and, thankfully, never would again. This tall, fit, *keen* chap endeavouring to make adult conversation with her was not a replacement: Ed was fresh, clean and new, like the salty breeze that pinched her cheeks each morning.

No more comparisons.

But perhaps some more wine. 'You were going to tell me about work.'

'Was I?'

'Rescued anybody from certain death this week?'

'Not really.' Ed drew his legs in.

Oblivious to the eloquent body language, and somehow missing the neon signs saying *Stop! Don't go there!* Billie rambled on. 'Your job fascinates me.'

'Does it.' Less a question, more a blank statement.

'I mean,' gabbled Billie, perching on the bed like a jumpy bird, 'everybody runs from a fire. But you run *towards* it.'

'Hmmm.' Ed's face was set like granite in the candlelight.

'I mean,' Billie repeated, 'you're a hero!'

'Not what I'd call myself.' Ed stood up and crossed the room to tower over her. 'Look,' he said gravely, before another gauche compliment could fly his way. 'Can we talk about something else?'

'Of course. Anything you like.' His nearness and his sudden seriousness threw Billie again. 'Politics? Religion?' She scrabbled. 'Fruit?'

Taking her hands in his, Ed kept his voice low, as if she was a volatile chimp who would baulk at sudden noises, baring her teeth and throwing things.

'I don't give a toss what we talk about. I'm with the best-looking girl I've met in a long time, and I want to get to know her. OK?'

'OK.' Her hands felt small in his. The little homily calmed her, although his next utterance kicked the trainer wheels off her rediscovered self-possession.

'Let's eat. I'm starving.'

It was Billie's turn to go grave as she 'served' dinner. She produced a selection of processed cheese triangles, a Pop Tart, and a stick of Peperami, cut into varying lengths. 'Bon appétit,' she sighed.

Hot, sated, they lay back on her little iron bed, in a kind of swoon, swapping stupefied looks of delight.

'That was . . . so good,' groaned Billie, a satisfied sigh travelling the length of her body.

'No, Bill, that was the best.' Ed had melted into the mattress. Not post-coital bliss, but the eerily similar post-chip bliss.

Licking his fingers, Ed suddenly turned to her, and kissed Billie full on the mouth. 'You taste of salt and vinegar,' he whispered.

She couldn't whisper anything, although if pressed she might have been able to come up with 'blaargh aaargh yaaargh' or similar. 'I never thought I'd say this, but that kiss was better than chips,' she eventually told him.

'You're full of compliments,' he said, his voice dry, as he leaned in to do it again.

The chip paper got in the way, and the charity-shop cushions got in the way, but these obstacles were soon dispensed with. Greedily kissing, Billie and Ed held each other close, their bodies joined from lip to toe.

'You're lovely,' he muttered, with a huskiness that prompted her to press herself even harder against him. He put his fingers to her trouser zip, while his tongue explored her mouth with explicit desire.

Suddenly something else got in the way.

Billie.

Lurching upright, she gasped, 'We can't!' like an Edwardian convent girl.

'We can't?' Ed's voice was high now, in marked contrast to his recent Barry White impression. 'Sweetheart . . .'

'It's too quick.' Billie was scrambling off the bed, her bare feet cold on the boards. She put a hand to her forehead. 'It's not right. It doesn't feel right.'

'It does.' Ed reached out to her. 'You know it does.' He was seductive again, although his face was clouded. 'Come on,' he added, anxiously, as if he could see something wonderful slipping away.

'No, I'm sorry.' Billie suddenly wished he'd go. She'd been daydreaming about the contents of his underpants since the day they'd met, but now she wished he'd walk out and evaporate into the mist. 'It's me, not you.' She paused, to look wryly at him. 'I know everybody says that, but it's true.'

It was Ed's turn to hear The Story.

Over the last of the wine, Ed listened, with far more patience than a man with an erection might be expected to. He nodded in the right places, said, 'Aww,' when he should, and even threw in a, 'If I could get my hands on him . . .'

The sea rumbled and roared in the silence when she'd finished. Billie felt like a fool. Why tell the man who wanted her that she was bad at relationships, that they ended with people running screaming in all directions, their hair on fire?

Because she wanted him right back, and her jitters had to be explained. 'It's too soon, Ed. I mean, I was just about to be *married*. I'm still raw. Do you understand?' She studied his handsome features, indistinct in the candle glow. He couldn't guess how badly she needed him to understand.

Smiling regretfully, Ed nodded. 'Of course I do. Only a fool wouldn't.' He let out a heartfelt sigh. 'Shame, though.' He shrugged his shoulders. 'Looks like it's cold showers for me for a while.' He looked intently at her. 'Not forever, though, eh?'

'Not forever, Ed,' she promised, to herself as much as him. 'Is cuddling forbidden?'

'It's mandatory.' Billie held out her arms, and he filled them beautifully. Some of the candles had guttered out, and the hut was darker, its corners secret again. Lying on the bed, with Ed snuggled into her embrace, Billie ruffled his hair. She'd been aching to ruffle his short, puppyish hair, and it was every bit as enjoyable as she'd imagined.

'OK?' she asked, gently.

'Mmmm,' he assented, sleepily, from the level of her chest.

'Good.' Billie was relieved that he was still here. His big male presence was a bulwark against the scope of the sea, and the scope of her memories. She could have been a crying heap here on her second-hand cushions if he'd walked out. She squeezed him a little, and he pretended to choke. 'How come you're so nice?' she whispered.

His voice was loud, too loud for the moment. 'Don't say that.'

'But you are,' she insisted, in the same gentle tone.

'Don't start.' The traditional male plea was muffled by the headlock.

'Alright. I won't,' Billie humoured him, and relinquished her hold.

Shifting uncomfortably, Ed fished about in the tangle of bedclothes. 'Something's digging into me,' he complained, dragging out a perspex box of gold-wrapped chocolates. 'Christ. I didn't know they still made these!' he laughed.

'Gimme!' shrieked Billie, forgetting her manners at encountering the dessert she'd bought at the garage. It was no substitute for a wild night of twiddling and nuzzling but . . . 'Oh, ambassador,' she grinned at Ed. 'You are really spoiling us.'

Twenty-one

All the signs were there. Billie was humming to herself, bestowing extravagant welcomes on the trickle of Monday customers, pausing to gaze into the middle distance, drifting off in the middle of sentences, refusing a white Malteser.

'If you ask me you're in love,' Dot opined over a past-its-sell-by-date slimline soup.

'As if.' Billie knew exactly where she was on the Everest of her new relationship. She was in the foothills. She'd left base camp, but she was still on the relatively easy slopes. No snow yet. No crevasses. Smarting slightly at how thinly she could stretch a metaphor, she vowed that this time she wouldn't be reduced to eating the Sherpa. 'It's brand new. I couldn't possibly have deep feelings for Ed yet.' She couldn't admit, even to Dot, the effect he'd had on her. Ed was on her mind: the feel of his mouth was on her lips.

'I knew Jakey was the one straightaway.' Dot spoke wistfully, for all the world as if Jake was a normal human and not a pubic-chinned sadist. 'I was at a fancy-dress party. I'd gone as a badger. What?' she asked solicitously, as Billie choked on her soup.

'Nothing, nothing, go on.' Billie waved her concern away.

'It was a bit boring, to be honest. I got stuck talking to an Oompa Loompa about house prices. Then I noticed Jake. Over by the trifle. And that was it.' Dot smiled at the memory. 'He won first prize that night. He was wearing a blanket with a hole cut in it to make a poncho, a top hat, and trousers that only came down to his knees.'

Intrigued, Billie had to ask. 'What on earth had he come as?'

'Oh, he didn't know it was fancy dress,' explained Dot. 'He just came as he was.' Sucking her lower lip, she asked casually, 'So, did Ed stay late?'

'If dawn is late.'

'Oh.' Dot studied her fingernails. 'Did you talk a lot?'

'Loads. When we weren't kissing.'

'Kissing?' Dot reacted as if this was a novel first-date activity. 'Right. Just . . . kissing?'

Feigning ignorance of the question Dot was too decorous to ask, Billie tortured her with, 'Oh, kissing and stuff.'

'Stuff?'

'Stuff.'

'Big stuff?' Dot asked idly.

'Medium stuff.' Billie frowned in thought. 'You know, biggish.'

Just then the shop door opened enough for Sam to insert his artfully dishevelled head. 'Shag 'im?'

'No.'

Sam withdrew his head and Dot drank on in silence.

It was like one of those dreams where you know you're dreaming and you long to wake up. You struggle and strain but you remain in an absurd other world. That was how Billie felt when she realised that Zelda had been sitting on the chair meant for customers talking about her troubles with her feet for three-quarters of an hour.

The phone rang and Zelda's feet receded when Billie heard Ed's voice. This man didn't run on man-time: he ran on demigod-time. He made a date for Wednesday, simply and straightforwardly.

See? Nice.

'Dating', with no promise of sex at the end of the evening, was quite liberating: for a start, Billie didn't bother to shave above her knees. She felt like Doris Day as she buttoned up her striped sundress in Herbert on Wednesday evening. Although Doris Day never had to beat her hair with the hairbrush to calm it down.

For a reason locked in the vaults of Billie's psyche, she was sticking to her newfound celibacy. Perhaps it was because she didn't want to be unfaithful to the shop, but it wasn't because she didn't fancy Ed: she would have gnawed through a dungeon door to get a glimpse of his gluteus maximus. It wasn't for reasons of morality: she'd once had carnal knowledge of a boy she knew only as 'him from the swimming baths'. It was hard to pin down and name her motives, but they had something to do with self-preservation. Perfect though he was – and as a non-believer she didn't bandy that word about lightly – Ed was still a man, and as a man he held the power to disrupt her carefully ordered new life.

If Ed could wait, perhaps he would be worth risking it all for. If he couldn't wait – well, then it would be better to discover that he wasn't perfect before it got to the stage where she *was* forced to eat the Sherpa. As it were.

Sole Bay had a selection of pubs, and, as Sam had pointed out, they were all big on horse brasses. And fishing nets. And witches' balls. And pewter tankards. Billie, who had never liked pubs, preferring their loucher cousin, the wine bar, had never been in the Sailor's Lament before and she looked round nervously.

There he was by the bar. Still beautiful, despite being framed by a cornucopia of sea-themed car boot sale fodder. 'Hello, sir,' she said, eyes twinkling overtime: Ed made her feel giddy.

'Matron,' he responded, in a very poor attempt at a Kenneth Williams.

Perhaps it was nerves, but that was the first of a handful of impressions that peppered their evening. Billie dutifully smiled, and even laughed (albeit for the wrong reasons) at his Frank Spencer, his Billy Connolly, his John Wayne and his Sean Connery: 'I'm going to the little boysh room. Shtay there.' It wasn't the first time she'd endured boyfriends' impressions. It seemed to be a bloke thing, like being able to take your drink: you just weren't a real man until you could yodel a perfect Jimmy Savile.

It didn't make any difference to her feelings. Something told her that when they eventually got down to rude and dirty business, it would be all Ed, and no Frankie Howerd. Missus.

'I can't wait for you to get to know Sam. And my friend Jackie.' She loved this part of the process, the light and airy bit with the stabilisers still on. 'You'll love them,' she said confidently.

'I'm sure I will,' agreed Ed, in marked contrast to Sam's sour attitude.

'What are you doing tomorrow night?' she asked, the three vodka and tonics she'd rescued from a life of misery behind the bar emboldening her. 'You could meet my folks if you want.' She heard herself and, straightening up, backtracked hurriedly. 'Oh, I don't mean it like that. It's just that they're in a play, this amateur crap, and I'm going, so you could come, but I didn't mean, you know, inverted commas, *meet the folks*.'

'Don't panic,' smiled Ed, holding his beer in that loving way men have. 'I know what you meant. You're the one putting the brakes on, not me.' His other hand moved to her knee, and stroked it firmly.

Billie liked a firm stroke. She detested men who came at her all fluttery and limp, like novice aromatherapists. 'We'd have to set off in the afternoon. They live on the outskirts of London.'

'I'm working tomorrow night. You're going to learn to hate my bloody shifts,' prophesied Ed. 'A fireman's girlfriend always does.'

'Fireman's girlfriend.' Again, the vodka was in charge. Billie giggled. 'Ooer.'

Across the bar somebody was raising a glass to them. It was Mr Dyke. He winked, and Billie winked back. She was safe from Mr Dyke: she was a fireman's girlfriend now.

'You'll hate it. You shouldn't have come. You'll just laugh at everything. Why did you come, Sam?'

'Because you invited me.' Sam, lounging on the first-class train seat like a broken toy, lifted his sunglasses to add, 'Because I'm the only layabout who could leave town this early to go to a play.'

Layabouts don't have eleven books to their name. Billie prodded him with her toe. 'I've never gone first class on the train before.'

'We stupidly rich sad sods travel everywhere first class,' said Sam evenly. 'Easy come, easy go.'

'I wish you'd try and be proud of Tiddlywinks,' Billie chided. 'The whole world loves him.'

'They don't have to live with him,' said Sam, bitterly.

The careful facade of bored cynicism that Sam had built, and now polished daily, dismayed Billie. A seasoned cynic herself, she was chilled by Sam's more extreme wing of the church. 'When did you last fall in love?' she asked suddenly.

'Who says I ever have?' The arms were resolutely folded.

'So you never, ever have?'

'Once.' He looked out of the window, at the sprinting countryside. 'Long time ago.' He turned to Billie and took his sunglasses off. 'It wasn't love at all, it turns out. Similar, an easy mistake to make, like picking up cherry Coke instead of the classic variety. It ended, as these things tend to. And I'm not yearning, or pining, or turning to casual sex to blot out the pain, OK?'

'You're soooo scared that somebody will work you out,' laughed Billie, prodding him again. 'Sam Nolan, international git of mystery.'

Billie was a veteran of West End opening nights: west end of Surbiton. Looking around her in the over-lit foyer of the community centre Billie saw all the usual first-nighters, a veritable who's who of Surbiton, from the man who used to run the minimart to the Collett family, proud owners of the area's first hot tub and Surbiton royalty. The only face missing was Sly's. He had to work, he'd told Billie on the phone. It was the first opening night he'd ever missed. Hitching Sam to a Jack Daniel's and Coke, Billie ventured backstage.

Following the trail of the loud 'LALALALALALALALALA!' of her mother's vocal exercises, Billie opened a scuffed door, adorned with a sign ordering 'Check with janitor if damp'. She took a deep breath before peeping in. Her mother was super-volatile on opening nights.

Nancy Baskerville sat at an improvised dressing table. A desk lamp shone on a mirror leaning against the centre's cleaning rota. She had stopped caterwauling and was staring at her face as if she'd never seen it before, with an expression so unusual that her daughter almost didn't recognise her. Nancy jumped and looked around. 'My lucky charm! You made it, you utter angel!'

Now Billie recognised her.

The first act was long and, as played by the am-dram troupe, confusing. 'Who's that?' Billie whispered to Sam in the dark.

'Is he her husband?' A little later, she hissed, 'Where did they come from?'

During the interval, in the cupboard-sized bar, Billie asked what he thought of her parents' endlessly rehearsed posh accents.

'Oh, it's in English?' Sam seemed surprised.

After a challenging second act when the nervous man playing Nancy's lover forgot every single one of his lines, and improvised with all the easy confidence of a coma victim, the curtain fell to rapturous applause. There were cheers, whistles and bravos. Sam, catching the mood, jumped up and hollered, 'NANCY I LOVE YOU!'

Back in the bar, the cast trickled out to join their friends, looking different and diminished in everyday clothes. The man who'd forgotten his lines appeared to have been crying. Last to emerge, of course, were the Baskervilles, who milked the spontaneous applause until Billie's palms were sore.

'How was I?' Scurrying over to Billie, this was Nancy's first question. She was clutching a glamorous silk wrap around her, and still wore her heavy stage make-up. 'Was I too much? Or too little? Was it awful?'

Before Billie could speak, Sam, glasses firmly off, leaned over and took Nancy's hand to kiss it. 'You were magnificent,' he said, throatily.

Laughing artificially like a trunk full of bone china dropped from a skyscraper, Nancy, whose appetite for praise was similar to Billie's for pasties, pretended to be overwhelmed. 'How kind,' she simpered. 'You are . . . ?'

Lying, thought Billie disloyally. She introduced them, and Nancy leapt like a mountain goat to the wrong conclusion, saying, 'I always hoped she'd meet a creative type one day.'

'No, Mum, no, Sam's not my boyfriend.' She wondered whether or not to tell all: she risked it. 'Although I *am* seeing someone. A fireman. He couldn't come tonight.'

'A fireman?' Nancy examined the idea and evidently found it wanting. 'Each to their own. I've always preferred an artistic man.'

'Is that why you married a newsagent?'

Ignoring her, Nancy swept the room with her dramatically painted eyes. 'Where's that bitch from the *Surbiton Enquirer*?'

she whispered. 'She'll have her knives out, I suppose. You know how it is for we artists, Sam. We give and we give and we give until there is nothing left.' She leaned her head to one side like a fragile bird. A great, big, scary, fragile bird.

When Billie had told Dot that living in Herbert without a television would give her time to think she hadn't meant it. But balanced between sleep and wakefulness that night, Billie was thinking about her mother. As the waves chased each other outside, she recalled her mother's expression in the mirror.

It came to her – that look was fear. Outspoken, ball-breaking Nancy had been terrified of her own face. In that little snapshot Nancy was a woman, not a mum. What's more, she was a woman who had always been judged on her looks and who could now see them changing, morphing, disappearing, leaving her an old lady with no currency left.

This was strange territory for a daughter. Although obvious, it had never registered with Billie that Nancy had been a woman long before she was a mother. A woman whose life hadn't turned out the way she'd planned: the young Nancy had dreamed of the professional stage, not the local community centre.

They had something in common. Disappointment squatted like a stone in both their hearts. 'Oh, Mum,' thought Billie, feeling sorry for her for the first time ever.

Putting down the phone to Heather, Billie felt as exhausted as if she'd been to the gym. Not that she knew what going to the gym was like. 'I am *dreading* this bleeding hen night,' she told Dot.

'I meant to say. I can't go.' Dot bustled straight up to the stockroom. Her eyes were that giveaway red again.

'What's he done to you now?' shouted Billie up the stairs.

'Nothing,' Dot replied, with a sniff. She looked down from the top of the stairs, hands on the hips of her flared jeans. 'You don't understand, Billie. I wish you'd give Jake a chance. He's insecure.'

'So he should be,' scoffed Billie.

A warning light in Dot's expression made her back off. 'Sorry. I don't understand, you're right. I'll keep schtum. Friends?'

'Of course.' Dot pulled out her hanky. 'I'll be down in a sec.'

Leaving her to have a little weep, Billie dealt with a small Scottish lady who didn't seem to understand the theory behind garters. 'No, they don't go round your head,' she began gently.

Passing the market cross on her way back from delivering a strapless gown, Billie stopped short. Sole Bay had short-circuited; a detail was wrong.

'Jackie?'

Jackie also stopped short. 'Billie,' she said, 'there you are.'

'What are you doing here?' said Billie rudely.

'Aren't you glad to see me?' teased her friend, who was, as usual, a technicolour, slightly larger than life, sight for sore eyes in a clingy red sundress and platform sandals. 'I thought you could take the day off and sit on the beach with me.'

'I can't,' protested Billie, still computing Jackie's presence. 'But I can do an early lunch.' She amended this to, 'An early, long lunch,' to stem Jackie's pout.

Thanks to Dot's understanding nature (or doormat tendencies, depending on your point of view) Billie was down on the pebbles at noon, decanting loot from the organic delicatessen on to a blanket filched from Herbert's Dream II. 'How's things? You look tired,' she said.

'I am.' Jackie's vivacity was stilled, as if she was a glass of champagne abandoned at a buffet.

'Anything wrong?' Billie opened some juice. 'Can't be man trouble.'

'You'd be surprised.' Jackie was looking out to sea. 'It would be nice, wouldn't it, Billie, if just occasionally one of them proved us wrong?'

'How do you mean?' Billie held out a tumbler of juice but Jackie didn't notice it.

'We know they're sods, they know they're sods, but once in a while one comes along and you think *please please don't be a sod*. But they can't help it.'

'That's fine talk for a heartbreaker.' Billie decided to jolly her friend along. 'You haven't been whiter than white yourself.'

'I knew you'd say that.' Jackie sounded bitter.

This was not the picnic banter Billie had anticipated. 'Jackie, are you annoyed at me? Have I done something?'

'You? No.' It should have been reassuring, but the way Jackie spoke was verging on aggressive.

'You're doing my head in, if I may lapse into the vernacular. What is it, Jackie?'

'Nothing. I'm sorry.' Jackie made a visible effort and took the juice. 'Cheers!' she said, her old self once again.

Putting a hand to the shop door, Billie frowned. It was locked. This didn't compute either, it was only four thirty. Recalling Dot's rabbity eyes of earlier, she felt alarmed.

Billie looked left and right down Little Row, baking in the summer heat. Zelda would know where Dot was: she seemed to know what the whole town was up to.

The fudge shop was jam-packed with customers, Billie noticed enviously. The summer staff were taking care of the customers, so Billie went through to the kitchen, eyes carefully blinkered so as not to clock any top-secret ingredients, and knocked on Zelda's parlour. The door swung silently open, to reveal Dot on the very same armchair that Billie had once occupied. Her eyes were half closed, her head fallen back to one side. On a footstool beside her, Zelda was feeding Dot fudge, while Raven watched them from beside the stove, now cold.

'Ssssh.' Zelda put a finger to her mouth, and motioned Billie away.

Twenty-two

The D-Day landings were a doddle compared with coordinating twelve girls for a hen night. Counting heads outside the shop, Billie raised her voice, 'We're one short, ladies! Who's not here yet?'

Dot, despite Jake's misgivings, was present, tie-dye smock tucked into tie-dye skirt (Billie couldn't rule out the possibility of tie-dye knickers). Debs was there, sullen and sexually available in a brief denim skirt and a tee shirt with a misspelled diamanté slogan ('BICTH' it screamed). Heather was there, already bedecked with L plates, cheap veil and scowl.

'Angela's not here. Anybody know where Angela is?' Even to her own ears, Billie sounded like an exasperated Geography teacher on a field trip, and she wasn't surprised that the hens were more interested in each other's PVC shorts and body glitter than they were in listening to her. 'Ah. Here she is.'

Turning the corner of Little Row, Angela's lateness was explained by the tightness of her plastic nurse's outfit: low cut and two sizes too small, it made a walk any faster than a purposeful mince impossible, her patent black platforms further impeding her progress.

'Ange, you look *gorgeous*,' Heather shrieked, as her posse caterwauled around her.

'Bloody hell,' murmured Debs, into Billie's ear. 'There's less meat in Mr Dyke's window.'

Pots. Kettles. The colour black. There was no time to discuss these, as a white stretch limo was negotiating the corner. Its arrival on Little Row set off the kind of whooping and shamanic dancing that Billie would have expected only from women who had been kept in a darkened room all their lives and had never heard tell of the combustion engine.

Hands clasped together, Heather squealed, 'Oh, it's so glam!

I love it!' The scowl was banished in the excitement, and she led the gang into the vehicle.

It was like a little white nightclub, with leather seats all round, fluffy carpet on the floor, music blaring and a minibar. 'Oh God, I could live here!' gasped Angela, trying to sit down without tearing her skirt.

Champagne was opened, champagne was spilled. Legs were kicked in the air, and every comment was greeted with guffaws. A massive vibrator, a thoughtful gift from one of Heather's friends, was passed around. When Dot asked if it was a gardening tool, they all hooted at her wit: Billie knew she was serious. 'Seen better,' commented Debs, handing it on.

'Lucky you!' Angela's bon mot set off more shrieks. She nudged Billie in the ribs. Hard. 'Cheer up, it's a hen night.' The tone was light-hearted and accusatory.

'Something the matter?' snapped Heather. 'What's up? What are you worried about? The table's booked, isn't it?'

Suspecting that that was exactly the reaction Angela had wanted, Billie calmed Heather down. 'I'm not worried about a thing, I'm just staying focused so that I can make sure everything's perfect.' She inched away from Angela, her intuition prickling with certainty that this particular pest-control operative did not have her best interests at heart. It was a good thing, Billie thought smugly, that Madame Ratcatcher didn't know who her favourite fireman was kissing on a regular basis.

To find a venue that pandered to the whims of hens, Billie had cast her net outside Sole Bay, the Sailor's Lament being short on oiled bar staff. The flashing neon scribble of the Shady Ladies sign in Neeveston encouraged the girls' communal blood pressure even higher as they all piled out of the limo.

'Ooooh!' and 'Yesssss!' and 'Wahey!' they hooted, clattering to the entrance. Waved through by the bouncer, they were led through the bar, giggling and neighing. It was an ordinary sort of bar, enlivened by winking lights and swags of silver fabric. At the back was a row of booths, leatherette horseshoe banquettes around circular tables. The VIP booth, which differed from the bog-standard booths by virtue of the thin chain across its opening, was theirs.

'COCKTAILS!' chanted one of the girls, whose top half was

dressed as a nun, and whose bottom half had forgotten to get dressed at all. 'I WANT A LONG SLOW SCREW AGAINST THE WALL!'

A waiter who had dispensed with his top, but hung on to his bow tie, took their order. Rolling his eyes good-naturedly at the hilarity involved in asking him for a Screaming Orgasm or a Slippery Nipple he was only genuinely taken aback by Dot's request for a dandelion and burdock.

'OK?' Billie checked her client's emotional temperature.

'This is perfect,' said Heather, patting Billie's hand. 'Ta.'

The music cranked up a few decibels and conversation from then on had to be shouted as if they were communicating on the deck of a sinking ship. After the first round of cocktails, the shots began. Billie, who needed to be sober to keep the evening on course, passed hers to Debs, who knocked them back with the calm efficiency of an expert.

The bar filled up, and the place throbbed with sweaty energy. It was a long, long time since Billie had set foot in a pulling palace such as Shady Ladies and she wasn't immune to the tug of cheap music and overpriced drinks.

'I love these girls,' Dot confided to Billie, over the din. 'Such lovely, sweet people. Especially Angela,' she said, gazing up fondly at the lumpen nurse high-kicking on their table.

'How many shots have you had?' asked Billie, taking in Dot's eyes, which were neatly crossed.

'Hmm? Dunno.' Dot peered into her empty glass. 'Are they alcoholic?'

'Oh dear.' Billie did another headcount. 'Where's Debs?'

'I saw her leave half an hour ago,' said Dot. 'She didn't look like a bunny happy. A bappy hunny.' Dot hiccupped. 'She looked shad.'

'Charming.' There was no time to focus on Debs' customary rudeness: Billie had to help Angela down from the table when her stethoscope caught in the glitter ball and she almost garrotted herself. As designated grown-up, quite a few tasks fell to Billie over the evening. It was she who had to convince the half nun not to punch the slag staring her out across the bar: 'That's your reflection,' Billie yelled. It fell to Billie to dissuade Dot from treating them all to some lovely Morris dancing. And it was Billie who frogmarched Heather to the Ladies when the inevitable happened and her hysterical laughter segued into hysterical tears.

'Come on, come on, you're alright,' soothed Billie, taking the crumpled girl into her arms by the cruelly lit mirrors. 'It's overwhelming, I know.' And she did know. She mopped Heather's streaked and smeared face, remembering how her own hen night had ended in a bare-knuckle fight between her and Jackie over an Opal Fruit.

'I don't want to do it,' wailed Heather. Other punters were washing their hands a tad too slowly, one eye on this unexpected sideshow.

'Do what? We can go home if that's what you mean.' Billie was having trouble supporting the taller, bonier girl's melting frame, and was manhandling her like a trainee ventriloquist.

'The wedding!' shouted Heather, impatiently. 'I'm not ready. I'm too young! I've got too much life to live!'

The Ladies was filling up: evidently word had got round Shady Ladies that a shady lady was going bonkers by the sink. 'No, no,' cooed Billie. 'You love Dean. It's a match made in Heaven.' Running the shop meant that such gooey phrases were second nature to her now, and she could utter them without her sphincter constricting.

'But I don't know if I really love him!' Heather's words were delivered with full side orders of snot as the tears cascaded down her face. 'I can't go through with it. Don't make me!' she begged Billie.

'Let me through, I'm a porno nurse.' Angela barged through the rubberneckers, and wrested Heather from Billie. 'There, there,' she said, breathing one hundred per cent proof fumes over her sister. 'Angie's here now.'

'An affair!' Heather yelped, twisting in her sister's embrace to avoid her dragon breath. 'I could have an affair! A last fling.'

The drink was talking, and as usual it was talking crap. 'Think about that tomorrow,' advised Billie, a Geography teacher once more. 'Let's get back to the table. You've still got a surprise to come tonight.'

'It's perfect! A fling!' Heather raised her head from Angela's sticky PVC bosom as if she'd had a vision. She fell back on to Billie. 'And I know just the man. Don't tell *her*,' she hissed, pointing at Angela who was now adjusting her nurse's hat and recalibrating her breasts in a mirror. 'She'd kill me, but he fancies me and he's gorgeous and he's decent and he's good and he's got to be better in bed than Dean.' She hiccupped, and spoke again at her normal volume. 'Mind you, Sooty's probably better in bed than Dean.'

'Too much information,' said Billie decisively, and propelled Heather back towards their VIP booth. The girls greeted them with an onslaught of drunken concern, manifesting itself in repeated, 'Wassamatter babe?'s and exhortations to have 'a nice little shot'.

Checking her watch, Billie scanned the crowd. It was past midnight. Spartakiss was late: perhaps it was misguided to expect punctuality from a man who called himself Spartakiss but she felt she deserved some professionalism for her seventy pounds. 'You can't miss him,' the agent had promised. 'Six foot two and dressed as a roman slave.' Then, obviously reading from a card, she'd continued, in an uninterested voice, 'This untamed beast from ancient Rome will definitely light your fire.'

Darting back to the loos, Billie pecked out the agency's number on her mobile, only to reach an answerphone. Tutting, she made her way back to the booth, cheered by the noises coming from it like parrots being massacred. From the leering bellows of 'GET 'EM OFF!' and 'WHAT A PACKET!' she guessed that her strippergram had arrived.

Oiled and gyrating, Spartakiss towered over the delirious hens, who were clapping and stamping as he removed a tiny suede loincloth to reveal an even tinier thong.

'Excellent bum,' thought Billie admiringly, as she inched through the crowd towards his back view. The excellent bum was wiggling plenty hard enough for seventy pounds of any woman's money, and the front view had evidently rehabilitated Heather's mood completely: the bride-to-be was being restrained from clambering up beside Spartakiss.

The bored agent had asked Billie if this was an 'all the way' booking. Billie had given this some thought: personally she had no need to see the regenerative organs of a complete stranger, but she'd guessed that a dozen drink-fuddled hens would feel cheated without a genital grand finale. 'Yes,' she'd said.

Inching on to the banquette beside Dot, Billie almost choked on the fog of drunken female desire. Dot, who was clapping out of time to Spartakiss's routine, shouted above the howls of 'SHOW US YOUR WILLY!', 'He sheems like a lovely man.'

The lovely man was inviting Heather to pull off his thong, grinding his crotch at her face as if trying to whittle her nose to a point. Heather, evidently torn between really not wanting to and really, *really* wanting to, was being pushed towards Spartakiss's oily nether regions by her friends, like peasants pushing an aristocrat towards the guillotine.

A hand over her mouth, Billie watched the whole scene torn between raucous laughter and baffled disbelief. It was impossible not to be affected by the high spirits of the hens, but to a sober woman a male stripper always seems faintly ridiculous. She wondered how Spartakiss's girlfriend felt about his job.

Heather reached out a shaking hand, yelling delightedly, 'No, no, I can't, I can't!' but getting closer and closer to the stripper's undulating thong all the same.

'OFF! OFF! OFF! OFF!' The pagan hens chanted. Even Dot was chanting, albeit quietly and with her head on the table. Billie, now a Geography teacher desperate to be liked by the fifth form, chanted too.

'OFF! OFF!' she shouted, then, more wildly, 'ON! ON!' She'd dragged her eyes up from Spartakiss's hard-working loins and taken a proper look at the grotesquely sexual gurn on his face in the fractured glare of the glitter ball. 'SLY!' she yelped, and batted Heather's hand away from him: she hadn't seen her brother's machinery since they'd been bathed together twenty-seven years ago and now was not the time to discover how much he'd grown.

'OI!' Heather shoved Billie away, and grabbed for Sly's equipment.

Paralysed at hearing his name, Sly stopped in mid-grind as if somebody had pulled out his plug and stood, eyes locked on Billie's.

'What the hell is going on?' shouted Billie.

'YESSSSS!' A communal hiss of triumph went up as Heather whipped off the thong. Sly cupped his manhood in his hands and leaped from the table without a shred of his former cocky rhythm. Hunched over, he darted through the throng.

'Get back here!' cried Billie, taking off after him.

'That one's a dark horse,' belched Angela, knowingly.

Sly careered through the door of the Gents toilets, hotly pursued by Billie. An arm barred her way when she tried to follow him.

'I don't fink so,' said a bouncer.

'Please. I've got to talk to Spartakiss,' gabbled Billie.

'Yeah. Talk. We've got a licence to keep, darling.' He turned Billie around by her shoulders. 'You hen nights are a liability. We're still getting the stains off the seats from last week.'

'But . . .' Billie could think of no Buts that would get her into the Gents, so she waited. She waited until it occurred to her to ask the bouncer if there was a way out through the loos.

'Yeah. You can get out to the car park.'

Surmising that Sly had stashed his clothes in the toilets, Billie realised she'd lost him. Dazed, she dragged her feet back to the table. They were still discussing her brother, in frank terms no sister wants to hear.

'The size of it!' Angela was marvelling. With the air of an expert, she slurred, 'You only normally see that kind of thing abroad.'

Head bursting with uncomfortable questions, Billie sought out Heather's face in the melee. It was pale, with two livid spots on her cheeks. She looked as if she might cry, throw up, burst into song, or a mixture of all three. Leaning over, Billie whispered, 'Do you want me to get you home?'

Nodding sadly, Heather let herself be extracted from the cackling circle of hens, who now seemed to be moving with many limbs but just the one brain, an amoeba on the pull. Gathering up Dot, who could only walk in the style of an orangutang, she herded her two charges into a minicab that smelled of air freshener and vintage vomit.

'I'm gonna do it,' promised Heather, settling her head on Billie's tense shoulder. 'I'm gonna have 'im.'

'Who?' asked Billie, manoeuvring Heather into a less precarious position.

'You know who,' leered Heather, her sentence clipped by a snore.

And suddenly Billie did. The only good-looking, decent man that appeared in the Venn diagram of Heather and Billie and Angela was Ed. 'My boyfriend,' thought Billie, peering down at her client. Heather had seemed very confident that Ed would take her up on her offer of a last fling.

'Are we in Kansas?' asked Dot.

Twenty-three

And it was only bloody Sly! Up there on the table! Shaking what I can only call his unmentionables at me!

For once the exclamation marks were forgivable.

Nobody here really knows Sly, so I just had to share it with you, James. You can appreciate how much of a shock it was. Now, of course, he won't answer my calls.

The messages that Billie left for her brother were increasingly forceful. She'd progressed from, 'Please call me when you get this message,' to, 'SLY, YOU WERE WAVING YOUR COCK IN PUBLIC! I'D LIKE AN EXPLANATION PLEASE!' Being angry with Sly didn't come easily. He was her big bro, the yardstick against which she'd been measured all her life. He was the Baskervilles' pride and joy, and he was probably worshipped as a god on some remote Tahitian island.

When Nancy had called on Sunday, Billie had planned some discreet probing, in case her mother knew anything, but had spent most of the time defending her refusal to try the Atkins diet. 'But I love bread, Mum. And spaghetti. And potatoes.'

'One day your bottom will sue you,' her mother had warned.

Nothing revealing about Sly had been gleaned: Nancy just reiterated her pride in him, her admiration for him, her maternal satisfaction with him. At no point did she suggest he limit his intake of carbs, or avoid horizontal stripes.

'Mum,' started Billie, urgently, as the conversation wound down.

'Yes, my darling cherub?' Nancy was back in character.

'Look after yourself.' It was a feeble precis of her concerns for her mum, but Billie felt unable to go any further. The vision

213

of her mother's troubled face in the dressing-room mirror swam in front of Billie, but that vulnerable woman was nothing like the iron lady on the end of the phone.

Ed's prophecy was coming true. Billie hated his shift schedule. She hadn't reckoned on the fact that when he came off a night shift he would sleep the whole day. Monday rolled around and she still hadn't had a chance to tell him about her brother, or kiss him insensible.

Leaving a penitent Dot in the shop – 'Was I a total embarrassment at Shady Ladies? I didn't swear, did I?' – Billie called round to Ruby's house to drop in some stiffened organza.

Waiting for Ruby to answer the door, Billie couldn't help noting that his net curtains were dazzlingly clean and hung in self-righteous folds.

'This is a surprise,' said Ruby, without a growl or a snuffle. He was as spotless as his curtains, and he surprised Billie by inviting her in.

The house looked bright and inviting, not at all the dank pit she'd glimpsed the first time she'd knocked on the door. 'In here. We're just having afternoon tea.' Ruby preceded her into the dated kitchen, where Annie was setting out thin sandwiches on patterned china plates.

'Hello,' said Annie, looking coyly up from the magnificent spread that boasted a teapot with steam curling from its spout, and a tiered cake plate displaying iced sponge.

'Oh.' Billie couldn't keep the insinuation out of her voice. This didn't look like two tailors hard at work. She looked from one to the other: Ruby and Annie both seemed to be trying not to giggle. Suddenly Billie was the oldest in the room and she had two naughty children on her hands. 'Ruby,' she began, 'do you want to explain that smudge of lipstick on your cheek?'

Ruby's hand flew to his face and he stared, startled, at Annie. They shared a wide-eyed moment before he said, in his gravelly baritone, 'You can be the first to know. After all, you brought us together. Annie has agreed to be my wife.'

Annie flinched at the scream Billie unleashed, but she allowed herself to be kissed and hugged and then kissed again as Billie scattered congratulations. 'This is the best news ever!' she gasped.

'It's all down to you, young lady.' Ruby took her hand. 'Will you do us the honour of being a witness?'

'I'd be proud to.' Billie was trying to get away with wiping her eyes surreptitiously. 'When's the big day?'

Her voice like running water, thanks to its new note of excitement, Annie laughed, 'As soon as possible. We've booked the registry office for the fourteenth of August. There'll be no frills, no fuss. We can't afford them. But there's no sense in waiting.'

'I want her here. With me.' Ruby gazed across the fondant fancies at his fiancée, and she looked demurely down. He reached into his pocket and withdrew his wallet. 'Here's another twenty towards the dress.'

Taking it, Billie wanted to throw the notes in the air and yell, 'HAVE THE DRESS FOR NOTHING!' but she knew that that wouldn't be acceptable to these pensionable lovebirds. She toasted their good health with tea and left them as soon as she could. Any fool could tell they wanted to be alone.

Revived slightly by the news, Dot used the opportunity to further her case. 'See. You approve of *their* wedding. You're softening up. You're in touch with your romantic side.'

'Never. Ruby and Annie are a one-off.' Billie was vehement. 'They're the perfect antidote for each other's loneliness. Ruby doesn't need to pickle himself with whisky any more, and the next time Annie's cooker goes funny there'll be somebody to share the burden. See?' Billie finished triumphantly. 'Not romantic at all. Practical.'

There was no time to argue the toss. An archetypal mother and daughter combo were already through the door.

The mother was saying, 'But we have to invite your dad's brother, Lucy love. We still owe him three grand for the time-share.' She smiled at Dot and Billie. 'You're our last hope!' she laughed.

The bride-to-be was an orange colour that flatters citrus fruit but works less well on humans. Her thick make-up was drag-queen subtle, and her hair extensions seemed to have been put in by monkeys. 'Not trendy enough,' she damned the shop, looking around.

Good-natured Dot showed her a few funkier designs. 'Nah. Nah.' The girl's Jaffa face scoffed. 'You kidding?' She sighed. 'Have you got anything a bit more revealing?'

'For the hundredth time,' wailed her mother. 'The wedding is at Saint Hilda's, not Spearmint Rhino.' She turned to Billie, seeking an ally. 'She wants to show off her back, her boobs, her legs. Can you tell her? Tell her that marriage is an institution and she should show it some respect?'

Aware that she was very much the wrong tree for this dog to bark up, Billie sidestepped by pointing to a design she particularly liked that Dot had prophesied would never sell. 'How about this white satin trouser suit?'

'Oh.' Jaffa girl forgot to be scornful. She picked the hanger up. 'I'll try it on.'

Mouthing, 'Thank you,' the mother put her hands together in a praying position outside the changing cubicle. In a confiding tone, she said, 'She's put years on me since she got engaged. I thought this would be some quality mother and daughter time, but we've fought like cat and dog.' She sagged. 'Maybe it's me.'

Watching the woman's introspection, Billie wondered sharply if her own mother had had similar epiphanies in wedding shops back when they'd been searching for Billie's bridal gown. She and Nancy had disagreed about everything, too.

The girl's voice said grudgingly, 'I like it,' before she stepped out, the jacket gaping to her navel. 'Especially if I get a really bling bra.'

Breaking it to her gently, Billie said, 'It's designed to be worn with a top under it.'

'Nah,' said the girl, admiring her cleavage in the mirror. 'Mum,' she asked, sounding like a greedy eight-year-old. 'Have I got time to get implants?'

By Friday there was still no response from Sly. Telling Ed how she encountered her brother naked on a table top made a good story as they strolled, entwined, along the front in the kind dusk. Slathering on the detail, listening to Ed hoot, Billie felt

216

hollow. She needed to know what the hell was going on: Sly was a pompous ass and a hard family act to follow, but he had always been a fixed point in her universe and she wanted him to stay that way.

'Anyway,' she said, lightly and without emphasis as they approached the Sailor's Lament, 'what have you been up to?'

Maybe it wasn't as light as she thought, because Ed's dark face clouded and he asked, uneasily, 'What do you mean? Up to? How, up to?'

'Calm down!' laughed Billie. 'I'm not the FBI. How has work been?'

'Fine. Quiet. The usual.' He shook off her grasp and held her at arm's length. 'The boys were right.'

The boys, Billie knew, were seldom right when it came to their mates' girlfriends. 'What have they been saying?' she asked dubiously.

'That I've got to watch myself,' smirked Ed. 'Going out with a bird who runs a wedding shop.' He puffed out his cheeks. 'Gotta be careful. You sound like a wife, checking up on me.'

Perhaps he hadn't been listening properly when she'd told him The Story. Perhaps her morbid fear of long white dresses had gone over his head. She frowned. Ed had misunderstood a fundamental detail about her. 'Now, listen,' she began, all lightness of touch forgotten. 'I don't want—'

'Oh shush, I'm only teasing.' Ed smothered her with a hug, cutting off her defence. He kissed her ear, and whispered, 'Although, remember, you did try to introduce me to your folks the other night.'

That wasn't fair. 'No, I—' Billie protested, feeling that this was important stuff to get right while still in those relationship foothills she'd been talking about. When Ed kissed her neck, he accidentally located her amnesia zone, and she gave up defending herself and got on with some serious canoodling.

'Karaoke!' promised the blackboard outside the pub.

'I love karaoke!' squealed Billie.

Ed didn't. 'You're not getting me up there,' he vowed. 'I can't sing.'

217

There was beer, there was vodka, there was a certain amount of hand-holding across the sticky table, there was crisp-sharing, then there was singing.

'Stand By Your Man', belted Billie Wynette, eyes closed, thoroughly in the moment. Swaying slightly on her heels, she gave it her all. Spent, she bowed from the waist, and swayed there a moment.

Then it was Ed's turn. His persuasive chum Stella Artois had bolstered his courage. Even listening through ears of lust, Billie had to resort to some strange expressions not to laugh at her boyfriend's touching rendition of 'My Way'. The barmaid could be heard handing in her notice during the final chorus, but Ed punched the air as he hit the last note and bounded from the stage to wrap Billie in a big, sweaty hug.

'Let's come here every karaoke night!' he suggested, letting her go.

'Maybe.' Billie put his arms back where they'd been. 'Up for a bit of slap and tickle in the bandstand?'

A rhetorical question when aimed at a drunk male in his early thirties. Ed practically dragged her out of the pub. They slapped and they tickled and Billie fell for him all over again. 'How come our lips are such a perfect fit?' she asked, during a break in proceedings, when Ed was leaning back on the peeling bench, looking like he'd gone ten rounds with Muhammad Ali.

He smiled at that, and his smile was so gooey and so boundless, the way babies smile before they take delivery of teeth, that Billie started with the kissing again.

Walking home along the dark, breezy front, sharing freshly made chips, Billie squeezed Ed's broad back. 'We're having the archetypal seaside romance. Just like couples did back in the fifties.'

'Right down to the last detail.' Ed lifted an eyebrow down at her in the yellowy umbrella of a flickering street lamp.

Billie knew what he meant. 'Soon,' she heard herself say. Not, 'Now!' Not, 'Get your kecks off, mister!' But, 'Soon.' Lunging for and securing a particularly big chip, she asked fearfully, 'Are you sick of waiting for me?'

'We're only getting to know each other,' said Ed, reassuringly.

'Don't be daft.' And then they got to know each other some more on a bench.

Her epidermis tingling as if she'd been massaged by hundreds of ants who really knew what they were doing, Billie let herself into the starlit shop. Pulling away from Ed's embrace was getting more difficult. Soon, she thought happily, she wouldn't have the willpower.

Until then Billie could kid herself that she wasn't an adulteress: the shop was still her main squeeze. She liked to nip in at night, to check the computer and quail at the schedule for Heather's wedding: Billie's Brides felt as if it was all hers at these times, and not on loan. Expecting to find an email reply from a company that had let her down over a delivery of stockings, she 'Oh'ed in surprise as she opened up a message from James. 'Blimey.' It was *long*. Billie hesitated. Was James stepping over the boundaries he'd set? This email had to be more than their habitual chatter. Trepidatiously, she scanned the first few lines. With a half tut, half laugh, she shook her head. 'That,' she said, 'is *so* James.'

After expressing astonishment at Sly, James told her:

I'll have to rethink everything now. I mean, if Sly Baskerville can have a secret life as an oiled strippergram, then *anything's* possible. Perhaps the Earth isn't round. Perhaps I *do* like anchovies.

James got down to business.

Re: your VAT problem. I think I know the answer. Let me begin by explaining the basic premise of Value Added Tax.

And that's what he did. At length.
'Thank God,' breathed Billie, 'for firemen.'

Twenty-four

The first phone call of Saturday was, predictably, Heather. 'You're sure the bridesmaids' satin pumps are light lilac and not medium mauve?'

'Every bit as sure as when you called me last night,' said Billie patiently. 'Try and chill out.'

'Chill!' yelped Heather. 'Out! I still have eight pounds to lose!'

'The dress will look awful if you're too thin,' warned Billie, realising that a straightforward *eat something you skinny fool* wouldn't work.

'Thanks,' snapped Heather. 'Thanks a lot for the support.' A stifled sob could be heard as the phone slammed down.

'Gee, ain't weddings just magical,' grimaced Billie to the empty shop. She stiffened as Debs arrived. Partly because the till had still been twenty-two pounds down last Saturday despite the precaution of keeping Debs away from it. And partly because Debs had a head full of hair extensions.

'Your hair's nice,' Billie managed to say, examining the back of Debs' head covertly. It looked like it hurt.

'Ta.' Debs did not seem to need Billie's approval. She shook her head and Billie copped a mouthful of nylon hair.

'What happened at Shady Ladies?' coughed Billie. 'You just disappeared.'

'Yeah, I did.' Debs chewed an extension and leaned against a shelf that needed dusting. A middle-aged woman wandered in, and Debs asked loudly, 'Do you want me to do 'er?' then dragged her feet across the shop floor to enquire, 'You the bride? Or the mother? Or what?'

Watching her, Billie's dilemma sharpened. Money was disappearing. If it wasn't Debs then it had to be Dot.

It. Was. Not. Dot.

Some things are constant: the temperature at which water boils; the speed of light; male reaction to the word 'threesome'. Billie would have staked her life on Dot's honesty. But she would make no such bet on Debs'. Some kind of showdown was inevitable. Even if Billie discounted the (possible) thieving, there was the timekeeping, the belligerence, the sensational rudeness.

A hair extension had detached itself from Debs' head, and lay across the counter. Billie prodded it gingerly. How, she wondered, could Debs afford such luxuries? Great Aunty Babs' exhortation to 'keep an eye on Debs' was taking on a very different hue.

As Billie was trying Sly's number yet again, Dot turned up. A slightly subdued Dot, whose bangles weren't jangling. Knowing better than to ask if Jake was still torturing her, Billie asked instead, 'Is that a gun in your pocket or are you just pleased to see me?'

'It's a hedgehog.' Dot tickled a tiny pink nose that appeared over her embroidered pocket top. 'He keeps having fits.'

'Nice.' Billie backed away.

'He just needs some love,' said Dot, looking down at the spiny creature but looking as if she saw past him.

'Dot,' began Billie uncertainly, guiding her out to the kitchenette by the elbow. 'I think Debs might be stealing from the till,' she whispered. 'Did Great Aunty Babs ever mention anything about having suspicions?'

'Babs loves Debs,' said Dot, missing the point. She was thin-lipped and resolute. 'Debs is part of this place.'

'And I suspect she takes part of this place home with her at night,' hissed Billie, crossly.

'She has a lot on her plate,' said Dot, quietly.

'Knowing Debs, it's actually somebody else's plate.'

A familiar face disrupted this lopsided character analysis. 'Hello there!' Billie recognised one of 'her' brides. 'How's married life?'

The sixteen-year-old's face looked different without her scowl. She was a rosy, sunny girl today, slightly tongue-tied as she said, 'It's great. Really great. And I wanted to, you know, thank you and that.' She shrugged, uneasy but evidently determined to stumble on with her heartfelt, clunky little speech. 'You made me feel special, and then the wedding was brilliant, and, you know, I just wanted to say thanks. So thanks. It was the best day of my life.'

'You've made my day,' beamed Billie. 'No, my week.'

'It's mad, but I can't bear to put away my dress and my headdress,' giggled the girl. 'It feels funny to put them in the loft when they've only been worn once. They were such a big part of my day.'

'S'pose so,' said Billie sympathetically, remembering that she had drop-kicked her tiara into the hotel swimming pool. She sat up, animated by sudden inspiration. 'I've just thought of a way they could be a part of somebody else's big day as well.'

After the teen bride had left, Billie dug out the customers' address book. Maybe Annie was going to get a few frills after all.

A queue, excitable, lively, and on the whole no taller than three feet, snaked down the street from the door of the bookshop. Inside, the book-cluttered room, with its crazily sloping mediaeval walls, was dominated by large posters of Sam. Avuncular, kindly, oozing kiddy-friendly charm, the poster didn't resemble the Sam Billie knew.

Beneath this poster sat the hero of the massed abbreviated humans. His hair a jagged white pineapple above their curls and ponytails and Alice bands, Sam was signing book after book. The dim interior of the cosy shop hadn't moved him to ditch the dark glasses, and the leather collar of his jacket was turned defiantly, moodily, Fonzily up.

Plucking a hardback of *Tiddlywinks and the Naughty Ragdoll* from a teetering pile, Billie joined the queue, looking around for Heather and her grandiosely named – Fifi Boo? Betsy Bobbins? – godchild. Billie had made a loose arrangement to meet them. Perhaps, she thought, they'd already been. Without a tiny hand to hold she felt exposed, and slightly daft, waiting to have a picture book signed. All the other adults were attached to bouncing, squealing, hyperventilating children. Even Ed's hand would have done, but he was working. A wall of sound, worthy of a miniaturised Wembley football crowd, was being emitted. 'Is it really him, Mummy?' breathless voices asked, as they spotted the stony-faced would-be punk scribbling morosely at the table. 'Is it really truly him?'

Another reason for the kids to pogo and yelp was the presence of Tiddlywinks himself. Six foot of grey velvet, with buttons for eyes and a nose of hard black plastic, Billie passed the time watching Tiddlywinks interact with his weeny fans, once she'd conquered her fear that Sly might be under the velvet.

Tiddlywinks waddled around, happily hugging tiny stockbrokers-in-waiting and letting them launch themselves at his padded tummy. Even Billie was hugged: she caught a whiff of Hugo Boss.

Nearing the top of the queue, which never seemed to shorten, as if there was a Hyperactive Child Machine in the back room, Billie witnessed Sam's technique with his diminutive worshippers.

'Name?' he'd bark, like an eastern European border guard. Having scribbled rapidly in his incomprehensible hand, Sam held out the book between two fingers as if it was diseased. 'Enjoy. Next.' Heart-warming it wasn't, but his public found it thrilling.

'He spoke to me, Mummy,' gabbled one tiny innocent as she was led away, clutching twelve ninety-nine's worth of Sam's integrity to her chest.

Finally at the head of the queue, Billie laid her book down.

'Name?' Defeated, Sam didn't even lift his head.

'Wilhelmina Baskerville. Aged four.'

The glasses were snatched off. Sam lifted tired eyes to hers, suddenly full of gratitude and hope. 'A person!' he gasped, like a starving man who's just spotted a KFC. 'At last.'

'Come on, sign, book slut,' chided Billie.

Having scratched a few words on the title page, Sam swivelled *Tiddlywinks and the Naughty Ragdoll* around for her to read, *Create diversion (poss set fire Tiddlywinks) & regroup in pub.* 'There's a tenner in it for you,' he hissed.

'Grow up,' she advised, aware of her shaky qualifications in this area.

'Alright, a hundred.'

'Try and be brave,' laughed Billie. 'I'd do anything to have this kind of adoration in my life.'

'Short-arsed groupies,' sneered the kiddies' fave. 'I sold my soul for this.'

'Take a leaf out of Tiddlywinks' book.' Billie gestured at the man-sized soft toy bounding about the room, a crocodile of happy children tailing him.

'OI! TIDDLYWINKS!' Sam beckoned him over. In a low voice that only Billie and the 'resting' actor imprisoned in eight metres of furnishing fabric could hear, he menaced, 'You are a toy rabbit, not a clubber mashed on E. You're making me look bad. Tone it down, OK?'

Off sloped Tiddlywinks, looking very like a gigantic rabbit whose self-esteem has been trampled.

'You weren't kidding when you warned me you were hard to like,' murmured Billie, picking up her book and turning away.

'You love me, though,' said Sam, taking the next eagerly proffered book. Ignoring the shiny-faced tot grinning up at him he asked Billie's back, 'Don't you?'

Without turning round, Billie admitted with a regretful smile, 'For some reason I can't fathom, yes, Sam, I do.'

The fire station was an ugly, angular shed of a building on the road that led to Heather's housing estate. A couple of hours after having her book signed and now AWOL once more from the Saturday crush of Billie's Brides, Billie felt guilt pluck at her Capri pants as she approached it. She'd hastily pinched her cheeks and pulled the straps of her camisole down to achieve a wanton look: her plan was to ask to see Ed and then kidnap him for a brief but sexy snog down an alleyway before scuttling back to her dream-peddling duties. She saw it as a taster, an aperitif, for the injuries she would inflict on him after his shift.

The territory was against her: Billie could see no alleyway. There was a skip, but that didn't strike the right note. Perhaps she would have to content herself with smouldering at him in the reception area.

Except there was no reception area. Discouraged, Billie was on the verge of retracing her steps into town, when two firefighters stepped outside in their navy-blue basics. 'Alright?' shouted one of them across the primly clipped front lawn.

'Chugger!' Billie was glad to see Debs' paramour. 'Can you tell Ed I'm here? I want a quick word.'

'Ed? He finished as I came on,' said Chugger. 'A good hour ago.'

'You sure?' Nothing about this saucy visit was going right. 'I thought . . .' Then she realised: book signings were probably low on Ed's agenda. 'Thanks anyway.'

So Ed fibbed to get out of meeting her friends. That wasn't so nice. Disappointed, and feeling mug-like, Billie headed back to the shop, a sneaky serpent-hiss in her ear directly from dating Hell: *wasn't it odd that both Ed and Heather were missing?*

There were no customers, but the ranks had been swelled by Zelda, who had thoughtfully brought Raven for a visit. The ugly black cat sat licking the hardened ringlets around his bum. Billie averted her eyes: she so didn't want to know. 'I'll be upstairs, tackling the VAT,' she lied.

Shop-floor chatter drifted up and disturbed Billie as she tried Sly's number again without success. She was privy to Dot's anxieties about Raven's health, Zelda's ramblings about her new octogenarian boyfriend's inability to 'satisfy' her 'as a woman', and her obsessive quest for the ultimate fudge. Debs was quiet, until she joined in with the general hubbub when a reduced handbag toppled off a high shelf and landed with a thwack on Raven's head.

When, Billie wondered, peering out of the tiny stockroom window over the back gardens, does kooky become surreal? She tried to block out the screams of, 'Raven! RAVEN! NO! DON'T KILL THE HANDBAG! BAD CAT!' and focused on Ed. It was absurd to suspect him and Heather. He wasn't that sort of man. But perhaps Billie was driving him to it, with her Doris Day born-again virgin routine.

Flicking open her laptop, Billie typed James's email address. She needed a diversion from the rut her thoughts were running down.

Thanks for the VAT advice. I've filled in my forms exactly how you suggested so hopefully I won't get thrown in prison anytime soon. How come I understand VAT when you describe it, but go all cross-eyed when I read the leaflets? You have a knack. If only you could deal with other aspects of my life so succinctly. Like whether or not my Saturday girl is nibbling at the profits. And whether my brother has lost his marbles along with his undies. And whether or not I'm ready to get serious with the fireman. It feels right, but I'm out of practice. And a bit scared. Well, very scared. Oh, ignore me, James, like you used to do when I talked about soap characters as if they were real people. Remember the time I drove you to violence by wondering what kind of career Dirty Den might have had if he hadn't run a pub? I think you snapped and threw Blankie at the wall when I theorised that he might have made a good driving instructor.

Calm had broken out downstairs. Billie ventured down to discreetly check the till. It was twenty-one pounds short. In response to the eloquent plea in Dot's eyes, Billie paid Debs at home time and said nothing.

Once Debs had gone, with a cheery, 'This place does my head in,' Billie warned her assistant, 'Dot, I *have* to tackle Debs soon.' She sounded braver than she felt.

Due to meet Ed at nine, Billie decided to waste the hours in between teasing Sam over a bottle of something cold in the Sailor's Lament.

The bookshop was closing up as she reached the door. The dishevelled manager let her in. 'Never again!' he croaked, surveying the carpet which was barely visible under a stratum of sweet wrappers, juice cartons and wet wipes. 'I'd rather hold a hoodie convention.' Groaning at the sticky fingermarks on a Martin Amis signed copy, he gestured over to a door marked 'Private'. 'Go through to the back. Mr Nolan's just freshening up.'

Skirting the self-help section, Billie pushed open the 'Private' door, feeling vaguely naughty to be trespassing. Less brightly lit than the public areas, this part of the shop was a confusing muddle of flimsy partition walls and unmarked doors.

Following her nose past pinned-up tea-break rotas and piles of books lounging about like street people, Billie made for the end of the long dim corridor, towards light spilling through a partly opened door.

Drawing nearer, she slowed. What was that rhythmic noise? A soft, insistent thwack, it kept perfect time, like a metronome hitting meat. Oddly familiar, recognition loitered just around the corner of her mind. She heard a voice mutter urgently.

'Sam?' she called out, mildly alarmed for reasons she couldn't place. The rhythm sped up, and Billie's footsteps matched it. She pushed the door at the end of the corridor and peeked in.

Sam, glasses firmly on but trousers a puddle around his boots, was grunting, 'Take it, Tiddlywinks. Take it!' as the man-sized rabbit, minus his cotton-wool tail, leaned forward over an untidy desk. Long velvet ears bobbed in time to Sam's thrusts, and muffled gasps of what Billie assumed was rabbitty pleasure escaped through his plastic snout.

Stumbling back out to the shop, barging into piles of marked-down celebrity biogs as she went, Billie stuttered, 'They're just, erm, finishing off,' to the manager and escaped into Sole Bay's blameless, certificate U high street for a gulp of fresh air.

She suspected she might never feel quite well again.

Twenty-five

A man who can look sexy playing crazy golf is a man worth hanging on to.

Ed was just such a man. He even bought the ice creams afterwards. His post-tutti-frutti lips planted strange but thrilling cold kisses on Billie's neck, and she wriggled ecstatically. It was a good Sunday.

Saturday night had been clouded by her dark imaginings, gradually chased away by Ed's behaviour. He was so attentive and fond that she felt ashamed of her suspicions, and had relaxed again. But not *that* relaxed: she'd gone to sleep untinkered-with.

As the sun drowned in the bay, Ed, snuggled up to Billie on Herbert's verandah, confessed, 'I used to think Sam was your boyfriend, you know.'

'I've got entirely the wrong equipment for him.' A flashback of the rogered Tiddlywinks made her pull a rather unattractive face.

'I was well chuffed when I found out he was a bender.' Ed paused, then said, as if risking it, 'And a twat.'

Billie elbowed him hard in the ribs. 'Oi. He's one of my very best friends and he's not a twat.' She rose to his teasing every time, and felt vaguely daft every time. Wanting to add that she didn't think 'bender' was the right word to apply to a beautiful and manly man like Sam, she took the coward's way out and absolved Ed on the grounds of working with men all day: his vocabulary was bound to be a bit crude.

Besides, she was perversely glad that he'd admitted his dislike of Sam: now she had a credible motive for his fib about his shift.

'You'll grow to love him,' she said, confidently, snuggling deeper into his arms.

* * *

228

Hi Billie,

I'm flattered that you think I have potential as an Agony Uncle, but I can't agree with you. I'm not the right person to advise you about getting 'serious' with your fireman. Sorry! If it feels right, do it – that's the best I can come up with.

Hope you're well. Me and the significant other have just booked a short trip to Marrakesh.

Love,

James

He'd upgraded his sign-off to 'love', Billie noticed. Perhaps it was to soften the blow that the rest of his email could be paraphrased as ARE YOU MAD, WOMAN? DON'T INVOLVE ME IN YOUR LOVE LIFE: IT'S LIKE ASKING YOUR MURDERER TO SAY A FEW WORDS AT YOUR FUNERAL! Now that the haze of suspicion had melted, her impulse to canvass James seemed absurd. Kicking herself wouldn't cover it. Maybe she should go down to the Sole Bay museum and lock herself into the old set of stocks they had on display. Then the local kids could throw tomatoes at her, their overqualified village idiot.

'Marra-bloody-kesh,' she muttered to herself as she bounded down the stairs in response to Dot's, 'Your mobile's ringing!'

At long last. Grabbing the phone greedily, Billie couldn't keep the irritation out of her voice. 'About time, bro. Are you going to tell me what's going on?'

'I can't believe you were there,' he began. 'The booking was in the bride's name, you see.'

'*You* can't believe *I* was there!' echoed Billie unhelpfully.

'I thought you never ventured out of Sole Bay these days.'

'I get let out occasionally, Spartakiss.' Billie was surprised at her own annoyance. She'd been envious of her big brother since she could make a Lego house, and now fear that he had feet of clay was making her spiky. 'Why are you dancing on tables?'

'If you must know,' Sly sounded peevish as if he'd hoped she could be fobbed off. 'I'm broke. Bust. Kaput.'

'Pardon?' For the first time in many years Billie used one of her mother's preferred words.

'Inner Winner Incorporated collapsed weeks ago.'

'No!' Billie put a melodramatic hand to her throat.

229

'Nobody knows. Except you. And my bank manager.'

'And Sana, obviously.'

'Well, no,' Sly admitted. 'I've been protecting her.'

'Lying to her, you mean.' It felt wrong to be browbeating Sly: beating brows was his job. 'Please don't tell me you pretend to go to work every day?'

'As far as she's concerned I've still got the office and I still travel to organise seminars.'

Trying to take in this new world view – it was as if she'd just heard that the Queen organised Ann Summers parties – Billie asked, 'Where were you on Mum's first night?'

'I was at a twenty-first birthday party in Brighton.'

'As Spartakiss?'

'No,' admitted Sly uneasily. 'That night I was the Horny Highwayman.'

'Sly, you can't keep this up. Stripping can't be nearly as well paid as, er, guru-ing.' Billie had never known how to describe her brother's career.

'Billie, I'm going to lose everything. The house. The private schools. The holidays.' Sly didn't sound hysterical, he sounded defeated. He had located his Inner Loser. 'I've failed. I'm going to lose the whole fabulous lifestyle I've built up.'

'Success isn't just about money.' Billie had never noticed anything 'fabulous' about the lifestyle Sly promoted: a better car, a bigger house, a longer job title. 'There's more than one way to be fabulous,' she reminded him.

'Sana will leave me the moment she finds out.'

'That's not true.' Defending her sister-in-law, Billie urged him to do the decent thing. 'Tell her, Sly. Tell her today. She deserves to know. I bet you any amount of money you like that she surprises you. Sana is made of stern stuff.'

'You think so?' Sly was asking her opinion. On an important issue.

Billie waggled the phone and looked at it, hoping that she'd heard right. 'I honestly think so.' Common sense was on her side, so she marshalled it. 'Besides, you can't go on like this forever, leading the silliest double life in the history of double lives.'

'You're right.'

Another first. 'You'll tell her?'

'I'll tell her,' said Sly with his beautifully modulated motivating voice.

'You promise?'

'I promise.'

'Attaboy, Spartakiss.'

'Have you got one like this only with sleeves?' asked the girl. 'I hate my arms, see.'

The girl also hated her knees, her neck, her calves and her back. Billie couldn't see anything wrong with the customer's figure, indeed would have gladly traded body parts with her, but the girl was adamant. 'I wish I was like Posh. Or Kate Moss.'

'I think you're a bit like Scarlett Johansson,' Billie told her.

'Yeah. Right,' jabbered the girl. 'If she had a huge nose and one boob bigger than the other.' Immune to praise, she finally left with a cream velvet design that Billie picked out for her. The dress flattered its wearer, just as Billie knew it would. She was starting to enjoy being a matchmaker between women and clothes, but there was no tearful happiness from this customer, just a prolonged huffing and puffing about how it made her tummy look big.

'*That* is what glossy magazines have reduced us to,' thundered Billie self-righteously as if she read only Chekhov. 'Dot, are you listening? I thought we could have a debate about the female self-image in a time of mass consumerism and conformity? Before the East Coast FM *Chit-Chat with Charlie* about flatulence?' She prodded her assistant, who was chewing a fingernail and looking unseeingly past the dummy in the window. 'Earth to Miss Dot.'

'Eh? Sorry. I was thinking.'

'About . . . ?'

'Oh nothing.'

'Jake, you mean.' Billie sighed, managing to inject disapproval into it. 'Has he been giving you hell over the hen night?'

'I shouldn't have gone.'

'Don't start that!' Billie had had enough. One self-flagellating female per morning was enough. 'So you went out and got tipsy with some girls. It's not a crime.'

Dot had tears in her eyes. 'Jake said I disgusted him.'

That made Billie seethe. 'Tell him *he* disgusts *me*.'

With a small snort, Dot turned away. Billie shut up: she wasn't helping.

The door slammed back on its hinges. Heather made an entrance worthy of Dracula, eyes blazing and satanic vibes bouncing off the shelves. 'I want to die!' she announced. 'LOOK at this.' Heather jabbed a finger at her chin.

'It's a chin.' Dot got out of the way quickly when Heather's unamused gaze scorched her.

'IT'S A SPOT!'

'It'll have gone by the wedding.' Billie was having no mole-hills promoted to mountains in her current mood.

'I have porcelain skin,' spat Heather. 'It will MARK!'

Wondering why she was being yelled at as if the pimple was her fault, Billie could only say, 'Please don't worry too much. I'm sure it will fade,' adding an, 'at least it won't kill you, will it?'

Glaring hard at Billie, as if deciding whether or not to whip out a handgun, Heather started to spew questions. Was Homestead Hall booked? Had the chef been warned about her uncle's liquorice intolerance? Had the bridesmaids' marabou boleros arrived?

'Yes. Yes. And yes.' Longing to say, '*Please* have a cream cake and put us all out of your misery,' Billie chose to fish instead. 'Still planning on having that fling?' she asked, innocently.

The expression on Heather's face transformed instantly, from a kind of equine crossness to equine secrecy. 'I was drunk.' She looked around her, as if Dean might have bugged the satin drawstring bags. 'We all say silly things when we've had a few.'

'So you won't be approaching a certain dashing young stud of our acquaintance with a view to naughtiness?' laughed Billie, without much in the way of humour.

'I didn't say that.' Heather now assumed a look of equine mystery, as if Mata Hari had been crossed with Black Beauty.

When she'd gone, Billie stared at the spot where she'd been for quite a while. Her rediscovered peace of mind was ruffled again.

Dot reappeared. 'By the way, Ivanka rang,' she said. 'Reckons you can have her veil for Annie.'

'Good.' Billie snapped out of her morbid daydream. 'When is she bringing it in?'

'We have to collect it,' reported Dot placidly. 'Said she's on honeymoon in the Swan, and she's not leaving room service for anything.'

'That sounds like our Ivanka.' Billie picked up her trusty fake Gucci bag and headed out, pausing to take Dot's pointed little chin in her hand. 'You feeling better, Miss Dot?' she asked, gently.

'I'll be alright,' smiled Dot, with her trademark sweetness.

The receptionist at the Swan, Sole Bay's celebrated old coaching inn which sat, sure of itself, on one side of the main square, rolled her eyes when Billie asked for Ivanka. The newlywed had evidently made an impression.

Announcing herself with a surly, 'You! Lady at desk! Please to change the bed in my suite. It is hard, like bloody coffin,' the new Mrs Clifford Larkin appeared. Wearing a cantilevered feather-trimmed negligee, she approached Billie, holding out an exquisite veil. 'This is for penniless bat you speak of,' she said, bored already.

'I'm so grateful, Ivanka.' Billie folded the veil carefully. 'How's married life treating you?'

Instead of an answer, Ivanka lowered her voice to ask, 'Tell me. Is possible to die from sex? If you are oldish man?' She sighed, and whined, 'Oh don't bother. I know answer. *Nothing* will kill him. Is just my luck.' She peered out through the undulating, ancient glass in the front window of the Swan. 'Vot is happening out there? Everyone running about like blue-arse fly.'

A giddily excited boy stuck his head around the main door. 'The Galleon's on fire! It's brilliant!' he yelled, before dodging out again.

'A ship on fire?' Ivanka was puzzled.

'A tea shop,' Billie clarified. Sole Bay was the world capital of tea shops. 'The old timbered one across the square.'

Reception emptied as everybody dashed out into the sunshine. Tea-shop customers, some still clutching Pyrex cups of sugary tea, stood about dazed, gazing back into the sedate little tea room which was now the centre of attention. Before today its main claim to fame had been the staleness of its macaroons, but now the whole town was rolling up to see it destroyed.

Like a pagan version of a celeb personal appearance, the fire was pulling in the crowds. Billie saw Dot near the front of the semicircle keeping a respectful distance from the Galleon, and pushed through the onlookers to reach her. Ivanka, bouncing along behind in her negligee was nearly as fascinating as the fire to gentlemen in the crowd of a certain age.

Billie had never been so close to a real conflagration. From halfway across the cobbles, she felt as if her nose was melting. Flames quivered and jumped in the heart of the building, occasionally visible through the tiny leaded panes. A searing orange, they appeared and retreated like teasing ghosts, enjoying the 'Oooh!'s they drew from their audience.

Her hand to her mouth, Dot was white despite the heat. 'Jakey sometimes has a reviving doughnut in the Galleon,' she whispered. 'What if he . . .'

On the far side of Dot, Zelda's expression could be translated by any casual observer as, 'Would that be so bad?' Frowning at her, Billie put an arm around Dot. 'He'll be safe somewhere,' she said, confident of Jake's self-preservation skills: like cockroaches, Jake would saunter on, flat-footed, after a nuclear holocaust. In fact . . . 'There he is!' Billie pointed him out on the other side of the square, sketching the fire, a doughnut clenched between his teeth. Beside him stood Debs, arms folded in contentment as she watched the unfolding excitement.

'Oh thank you, Lord!' breathed Dot, while Zeida sighed, as if disappointed.

Behind Jake and Debs, Sam, shades firmly clamped on, was watching the free show, too. He waved breezily over at Billie, as if they were at a carnival, but she shuddered and didn't wave back. This close, the fire was awe-inspiring. She could sense its power as it doubled and redoubled, like a mythical beast that had suddenly appeared in their midst.

Thinking hard, she trotted through Ed's schedule in her mind's eye. She was almost certain he was on duty. Almost. The fire, more visible now, showing off by pushing out a window

here and spitting out a jet of sparks there, seemed too formidable for mere men to tackle. She hoped she was wrong about
Ed's shift. Wryly she recalled that she'd been wrong before.

A banshee wail announced the arrival of the fire engine. It
braked on the cobbles and spat out a handful of fireman. Their
sudden furious activity added to the tumult and townspeople
backed away to make space, fear and fascination luridly
expressed on every upturned face.

Searching the faces of the firefighters as they shooed onlookers
back like sheep, Billie couldn't see Ed. Relief flooded her,
followed by a tickle of something like disappointment. That
didn't fit with any of Billie's ideas about herself, so she booted
it away hurriedly: she was *not* the sort of girl to glean sexual
excitement from watching men put themselves in danger.

Strong men. Brave men. Fit men.

She booted the thought away again: it was a persistent little
bugger.

Appearing behind them, Mr Dyke, still in his stained apron,
whispered, 'Hot stuff, eh?' in Zelda's ear.

'You behave yourself,' scolded Zelda, unequal to the task of
disguising her delight.

A figure strode around the engine, his face obscured by
breathing apparatus. Billie would know that bottom anywhere,
even swathed in yellow waterproofs. 'ED!' she shouted, rather
pointlessly. All at once, the drama was very real. Not just a
show for Sole Bay to chatter about over the next few days, it
was a fire, and her boyfriend was about to walk towards it.
This was no saucy fantasy, but a flesh and blood man in unequal
combat with an inferno.

'Is your boyfriend?' queried Ivanka, squinting over at Ed,
who was consulting an older, heavier man. They were nodding
and jabbing at the direction of the fire with their hands, using
their professional shorthand.

'Yeah,' whimpered Billie, who was suffering torments of guilt
about her earlier base thoughts.

'Can I interest you in swap for Clifford?' Ivanka showed all
her pricey crowns in an operatic laugh. 'Only joking!' she
howled, then again, quieter and slightly bitterly, 'Only bloody
hell joking.'

Over on the other side of the cobbles, Sam had evidently picked out Ed, too, because he had assumed a serious look that didn't entirely suit him. Flicking nervous glances at Billie, he threw her a thumbs up that almost undid her.

Ed's trained. He'll be fine, she assured herself. After all, he raced into holocausts every other day without her being there to witness it. There was a fresh purpose to the way he and two of his colleagues were double-checking their breathing apparatus: she could sense that this was it.

A lump in Billie's throat stopped her shouting something along the lines of, 'DON'T DO IT! IT'S REALLY HOT IN THERE!' so she just stuck her knuckles in her mouth. Now it was Dot's turn to do the arm around shoulders routine, but Billie could feel her thin frame shaking against her.

Suddenly, all three firefighters made for the Galleon's narrow doorway. All chatter stilled, as if by decree. Every eye stayed on that dark slit as the crowd waited for the men to reappear.

Standing alongside time, Billie's next few minutes seemed to take a year, ticking off on some slow, cold clock of their own. The fire belched and gulped and carried on, gleefully devouring the dry old bones of the poor tea shop. Every now and then a loud thump sounded, as the red and gold flames, insolently leaping out of the windows, ate away at a framework that had survived Henry VIII, two World Wars and the advent of reality television. Sole Bay held its breath but the doorway remained empty, and the fire staggered drunkenly on.

And suddenly there they were. The three firemen trotted out into the square, tearing off their masks. 'CLEAR!' shouted Ed.

A burst of applause competed thunderously with the flames. A bubble of relief and pride broke in Billie's throat and she could breathe again. Beside her, Dot was, of course, sobbing. Even Zelda dabbed her eyes, and popped some fudge.

Milling around the fire engine, firefighters unfurled a giant hose, and yelled incomprehensible instructions to each other. Busy, focused, they seemed unfazed by the danger.

Now that he was out, Billie could concentrate on her boyfriend without fearing for his life: a new sensation she hadn't much liked. She was accustomed to fearing that blokes would show her up, would dump her, or would suggest something rude with a mango that would put her off fruit salad for life, but she'd never before worried that they'd walk into a fire and never return.

Watching him talk animatedly to the crew, pointing back at the Galleon, Billie cooed gruffly to herself, 'He's so manly.' Before long those hands, currently making choppy gestures as he debriefed his colleagues, would be on her. Reprimanding herself, Billie was horrified by how shallow she was. How base. How one-dimensional.

How turned on . . .

A shrill cry made the crowd turn. 'PETER!' Bobbing up and down on her invalid vehicle, old Mrs Davis was pointing up at the stricken building. 'MY PETER!'

All eyes followed her arthritic finger up to where Mrs Davis's terrier was framed in a jagged window opening. Barking loudly, Peter's eyes were maddened, and he was matching his mistress bob for frantic bob. He looked as if he might jump.

Shielding Dot's eyes – it would take years of hot chocolate and whale music to rehabilitate her if she witnessed a canine suicide – Billie looked up at Peter, horrified at his predicament. She'd grown quite fond of the three-legged creature, despite his habit of weeing on her porch.

Billie's gaze clicked to Ed. Like everybody else in Sole Bay, he knew how Mrs Davis felt about Peter. The dog was her constant companion: losing his leg in a dishwasher incident had only brought them closer together. Ed was staring over at Mrs Davis, hyperventilating on her trike.

Under her breath, Billie was already whispering, '*Don't*,' as Ed pushed the breathing gear back over his face. She knew him, and there was a horrible sense of inevitability as he ignored the shouts from his mates and raced back through the coffin-shaped door of the tea shop.

Twenty-six

A cheer, louder than the fire, louder than the blood beating in Billie's ears, went up. It was a cheer worthy of England winning the 1966 World Cup, but it was all for a tall, staggering figure clutching a sooty three-legged dog in his arms.

'HE'S A HERO!' burbled Dot, jumping up and down, while Zelda took the opportunity to smother Mr Dyke in a fleshy embrace. The whole of Sole Bay seemed to be dancing, but Billie stood very still as Ed delivered Peter safely to a weeping Mrs Davis.

Tearing the safety mask from his face, Ed crossed the square in a handful of strides. The sea of people parted as if he was a modern-day Moses, and Ed made straight for Billie. Without speaking, he took her face in both his blackened hands and kissed her full and hard on the lips. Then, he turned and marched back to his crew.

Staring dumbly after him, her face smudged with black, Billie supposed that she might as well die right now, as she would never top this.

A couple of candles lit the darkness of Herbert's Dream II. Hugging her knees on the iron bed, Billie lost herself in their flickering prettiness. Her thoughts were formless and flirty, like the shadows thrown around the boarded walls. Neither happy nor sad, she felt *right*. She was the right temperature, in the right place, waiting for the right man. There was no thinking to be done now. Ed would come, and she would be waiting. She was ready.

Sketchy fears about Heather seemed ludicrous now, like the worried machinations of a schoolgirl. Ed had kissed her, and only her, when he'd emerged from the fire.

The night deepened and melted around the beach hut. She

could hear the sea stretching and falling but it might have been on a distant planet: Billie's world had shrunk to this small, wooden room and the expectations in her heart.

A tap sounded at the window. Her face lit up. He'd come, just as she'd known he would.

Framed by the door, Ed had cleaned up. She could smell his shampoo. It excited her more than any expensive cologne. 'For once, you've got to let me say it. My hero,' she whispered. She reached out her arms and he bent into her hug.

The expected tearing-off of her (deliberately) flimsy clothes didn't happen. Ed freed himself and sat at the little picnic table. 'Got any beer?' he asked.

This was deviating from the script. 'Well, no,' said Billie. She bent over him from behind, wrapping her arms around him. 'I thought we'd . . .'

Coldly, Ed shrugged her off. 'What is all this?' he snapped, bursting her candlelit bubble.

'Don't you want to . . .' Billie blushed, as vulnerable as if she was naked in a shopping centre. 'After today, I thought we could . . .' Shy suddenly, in the face of his stoniness, she couldn't say the words. She looked over at the bed, meaningfully.

'You want to shag a hero, is that it?' Ed stood up, and seemed to fill the hut.

'It wouldn't be a shag,' Billie suddenly hated that word. 'I want us to make love, yes. Don't you?'

'I want to have sex with you. *You*.' Ed stabbed his finger at her viciously. 'Not some fucking fairy tale.' He rubbed his hands over his eyes as if he wanted to gouge them out. 'I was doing my job. I'm not a hero. It was a dog.' He paused, took his hands away from his eyes and added, as if he couldn't quite believe it, 'A dog with three sodding legs. And I got bollocked for going in on my own, and putting the guys in danger.' He looked at Billie, almost pleading. 'If you say I'm nice or a hero once more, Billie, I swear I'll . . .'

'I won't, I won't!' promised Billie placatingly. She could sense this historic evening drifting off on the tide over Sole Bay and she wanted to drag it back. 'I don't think you're a hero. Or nice. In fact,' she freewheeled, 'I think you're horrible. Awful. And such a coward.' She smiled, hopefully.

Ed's Adam's apple bobbed as he threw his head back and exhaled exhaustedly. 'I'm being a bastard, Billie, I know. Days like today . . .' He closed his eyes. 'I don't have the right words. All I can tell you is that they make me feel funny. Not proud. Not happy. Kind of hollow.' He looked at her. 'Sad, if I'm honest.'

This, Billie felt, was a breakthrough. He was opening up to her. 'I think I understand,' she said, carefully. 'We can just sit and chat. We don't have to do anything saucy.'

For the first time that evening, Ed smiled. He looked devilish. 'Come here,' he said.

'Are you sure?'

'Ermm . . .' Mock thinking for a moment, Ed asked, in a low voice, 'Are you going to come here or do I have to come and get you?'

'I rather suspect you're going to have to come and get me.'

Billie slung herself back on to the bed. She was swiftly followed by Ed, and for the next few hours the little iron bed proved itself to be the bargain of a lifetime.

It was just a short, four-minute walk to work but in Billie's head it was a fully choreographed technicolour Hollywood musical with lights, music and extras. She could have danced through the bandstand, swung from the lamp posts, pirouetted past the shops, with a special tap solo for the gutted tea shop, before running, leaping and jumping down Little Row to the front door of Billie's Brides. The song in her head had limited lyrics, and they scanned and rhymed abominably, but to Billie's ears they were sweeter than anything *The Sound of Music* had to offer: 'My boyfriend is Ed/and at last we went to bed/and he's even sexier than I thought/and I thought he was very sexy indeeeeeeeeeeeed!'

As she unlocked the door, snapshots of the previous evening flashed in her head. The kissing, the nuzzling, the delicious lingering had been worth the wait. Ed had brought life and light and a strange screaming that she'd eventually recognised as her own voice. Ed put out fires for a living, but even he'd been surprised by the one he'd started in the beach hut last night.

'Don't do that with anybody else but me for the rest of your life,' he'd told her, as he kissed her goodbye.

'Careful,' Billie had chided him. 'Don't go all silly on me.'

Now, picking up the post, Billie felt a bit silly herself. She would allow herself one morning's mooning about, one morning's membership of the girlie club that insisted on drawing hearts with arrows through them and looking up his star sign but that was all. Her soul was still ring-fenced.

Remembering she'd given Dot the morning off to take Jenkins to the fair, Billie tackled all the little tasks that brought the shop to life. She washed mugs, she tidied stock, she tweaked the window display, she put on her wings. But she might as well have been milking yaks: all Billie saw and thought about was Ed.

She was glad she'd waited, and even gladder she'd stopped waiting. Making love with Ed had brought them closer together, she could feel it.

James would want to know the latest, she told herself. He'd be glad that she'd decided to 'get serious': there was no need to be more specific. James wanted her to be happy, and no, of course she wasn't typing out a long, detailed description of Ed's daring rescue just to rub in how gorgeous, brave, sexy and – she could use the word when Ed wasn't around – *heroic* her boyfriend was. She just wanted to put him in context. He wasn't a doctor; he was tons better than a dull old doctor.

One pair of white elbow-length gloves had already been sold before Billie remembered to check the answerphone. Bracing herself for a slew of Heatheresque demands, she pressed 'play'. The voice she heard was quite unlike Heather's assertive lowing. 'Ah. You're not there.' The deep, hoarse, evidently elderly man sounded dismayed. 'Can you hear me? Damn these machines. If I speak, will you get this?' She recognised Ruby's signature mix of rudeness and politeness. 'Billie, dear, I can't deliver the finished dress today. I'm afraid we've had some bad news. I'll be spending the day at the hospital with Annie. Now what do I do? Does one say goodbye? Or over and out, or some—'

The merciless machine cut Ruby off, leaving Billie staring at it.

Shoulders sagging in his bespoke suit fashionable forty years ago, Ruby asked, 'How did she look to you?'

They were on a bench outside the hospital. A few feet away traffic thundered along the main road, belching fumes over the demoralised flower beds. Neeveston felt a million miles away from Sole Bay.

'Small,' said Billie, truthfully. Annie's head had been a little apostrophe on the pillow, barely denting it. She'd lain with her eyes closed, as if unwilling to take in what was happening to her. 'Where is the tumour?' That word felt clunky and angular in her mouth.

'Her stomach.' Ruby sounded angry. 'Those fools can't even tell me if it's benign or the other thing.'

'They're doing their best.' Billie decided never to use the word 'malignant' in Ruby's hearing: if he couldn't face it, she wouldn't force him to.

'Apparently, they open her up,' he grimaced at the phrase. 'Once she's strong enough. My poor girl's anaemic, you see. And they remove the . . . the thing, and do a biop-whatchamacallit. The damn results won't be in until the next day.'

'We've got to think positive, Ruby.' Billie was adamant. She even risked slipping her bare arm through his.

'Positive?' scoffed the old man. 'I wait seventy-eight years for something good and when it comes along – pssssssssfft!' Ruby threw his hands in the air.

'We'll get through it.'

'I tell you this right here and now.' Ruby's gnarled old face was shaking with emotion. 'If that lady has to suffer, I'll never set foot in a synagogue again. And if she goes,' he looked Billie defiantly in the eye. 'I go.'

'It won't come to that.' This was that mushy, flabby talk that Billie railed against, but she didn't know what else to offer in the face of Ruby's fears. 'You're getting married. You have plans. We won't let a silly old tumour mess that up.'

'Didn't you hear the date of the operation?' Ruby sounded almost triumphant, as if long-held suspicions about God's sarcasm were being proved. 'That's right. The day of the wedding.'

Groaning inwardly, Billie just clutched his arm tighter. 'You and Annie are getting married. It'll just be a little later than planned. Hang on to that.'

The first wedding that Billie had felt genuinely passionate about was off.

It was hard telling Dot the news about Annie because they had to keep breaking off for her to sniffle, or gasp, or squeak, 'No, not Annie!' When all the details had been aired, she said, 'What if she shuffles off her mortal coil?'

'Dies, you mean?' Billie was weary of pussyfooting around.

'Oh, don't say that!'

'She's not going to die,' declared Billie, wilting. Her lost sleep was catching up with her. 'I won't let her. She's going to be alright and she's going to get married and that's that.'

'Yes.' Billie's certainty seemed to be catching. 'Annie is not *allowed* to die!'

'Exactly.' Billie paused. 'She still owes us for that wedding dress.' She flicked Dot with a veil. 'Don't look at me as if I just ate Julia. I have to be cynical, it's how I am.' Billie knew it would help her get through. She looked at her watch. 'Nip off and see Annie, if you like. Give Ruby a break.' She kept the tone light, as she said, 'We're going to have to be Annie's family, Dot.'

Dot nodded. She didn't speak. She didn't have to. As she was leaving, tucking Jenkins into the pocket of her gingham sundress, she reminded Billie to ring Heather. 'She sounded agitated.'

'She probably sounded like a woman on a diet.' Billie dialled Heather's mobile.

Confusingly, Dean picked up. Even more confusingly, he said, 'Heather?'

'Dean?'

'Darling?'

'No, no, Dean, it's Billie.' An alarm wailed at the back of Billie's consciousness, way back past the accumulated debris of Annie's sudden illness and her own multi-orgasmic evening class in fireman-pleasuring. 'What's going on?'

'She's gone.' Dean sounded stunned. 'She's left me.' He gulped. 'The wedding's off.'

Twenty-seven

Perhaps Billie's mother was right to worry constantly. The last few hours had certainly borne out the perils of being too happy. The post-coital glow had been chased from Billie's cheeks, and she looked back to that morning as a golden era of carefree joy when the only concern she'd had was whether to straddle Ed on the floor or the bed. That reminded her: she needed a new picnic table. There had been casualties in among the yelps of pleasure.

Speed-walking on wedge sandals is tricky, but Billie was heading for the sea as fast as she could. She knew exactly where to find the Missing Presumed Bonkers bride, and as she neared the neglected bandstand she could make out a lanky shape in the shadows.

Out of the sun, the bandstand was cool and dim. Leaning back against the central pillar, a cut-price French Lieutenant's Woman, was Heather. She'd lost all her angles and sharp edges, and had wrapped her long arms around herself like the sleeves of a straitjacket. 'Go away,' she murmured, as Billie climbed the rotting wooden steps.

'And good afternoon to you, too.' Billie put her hands on her hips and looked at Heather. She'd known a girl just like her once: herself. Except Billie had kept all the angst and fear and disillusionment inside her, whereas Heather was externalising it nicely. 'Got to you, then, all this nonsense?'

'It's a real shame, the way they've let this bandstand go.' Heather looked around her, shaking her head. 'Graffiti. Peeling paint. This town is so prissy about appearances, but it's forgotten this little place.' In a quieter voice, she added, 'It was lovely when I used to come here with my mum.'

'Heather, *everything* was lovely then: you were a little girl.' Billie put her hand on her arm. 'And you had your mum,' she said, gently.

Shaking her off, Heather sharpened up a bit. With a flash of her customary arrogance, she said, 'I know what you're here for. I'm not going back. The wedding's off.'

'I'm not here to persuade you. That's not in my job description.'

'Good. Cos I've made my mind up.'

'Dean deserves to know why.'

'He knows. Deep down.'

There was a question Billie needed to ask. The answer would help with her own recent calculations, but there was a danger it could stamp on the fragile new happiness she'd allowed herself. 'Is it to do with the fling you were threatening to have?' Billie couldn't forget that Ed's mysterious absence from his shift had coincided with Heather's no-show at the book signing. 'Have you fallen for somebody else?' She considered sticking her fingers in her ears rather than hear the reply: Billie needed Ed to be a hero for a bit longer.

Heather snorted. 'I got turned down, didn't I? In front of quite an audience. Surprised you haven't heard all about it from that stinky boyfriend of Dot's.'

So Billie's calculations were wrong, thank God. She should have known. She'd always been a dunce at maths.

'It's nothing to do with another man,' said Heather, impatiently, as if nobody would try and understand. 'It's about me. I want to see the world. I want to sow my wild whatsits. Wheat?'

'Oats,' Billie corrected her, admirably managing not to smile.

'And I don't want my kids to have Dean's nose,' ended Heather, bitterly.

Billie took a deep breath. The gloves were coming off. This girl may have handed her three thousand pounds to do a job, but Heather needed a talking-to. To be specific, she needed the talking-to that nobody had given Billie and James. 'Go on, then.' Billie folded her arms. 'Cancel it. I'll do it all for you. You don't have to lift a finger.'

'Good.' Heather was looking at Billie out of the corner of her eye, as if trying to gauge what was coming next.

'The world won't end. Tall buildings won't crumble. Sole Bay won't fall into the sea. Life does not stop at the end of your nose, Heather.'

'Hang on,' began Heather, straightening up a little.

Ignoring her, Billie trundled on. 'This wedding has been your life for the past few months, but for most people it's just an invite perched on their mantelpiece and a last-minute panic about whether or not to dry-clean their matching dress and jacket. You need to get things in perspective.' Billie's tone heated up a little. 'I just left a sick woman in Neeveston hospital. She's planning to get married. If she lives. That'll be a wedding of love and devotion, and it won't matter a bit whether the bride's bouquet matches the bridesmaid's eczema.'

Looking defiantly out to sea, Heather's unconcerned expression was unconvincing.

'So go on, break Dean's heart. Destroy something, if you feel the need. He'll survive. I know that from experience. But he'll be changed forever.' She swallowed. This was harder than she'd thought. 'And so will you.'

Achieving quite a stomp on the bandstand steps, Billie left her client alone. Slowing past the shrimping nets and lilos lolling like good-time girls outside the high street shops, Billie hoped that Heather had recognised the pompous, ill-thought-out speech as coming directly from her heart.

There was no time to dwell on Heather, or Annie, or Ed's outline in the dark, when Billie got back to the shop. She barely had time to shrug on her wings before asking, with a wide smile that was a triumph in the circumstances, 'How can I help you?'

The tall, fair woman, with hair set hard as rock and real pearls at her throat, had a bray loud enough to be heard by the trawlers out on Sole Bay. 'This gel,' she gestured to a small brunette who was looking at the floor, 'is marrying my son.' The upper-crust accent had been refined through centuries of the highest quality inbreeding. 'My only son. My precious infant. My darling Alexander. I am not – obviously – Lisa's mother, but I'm helping out with all the arrangements as we're paying for the wedding.'

'I see.' Billie was surprised to hear this much personal and unnecessary information.

The woman wasn't finished yet. 'Dear Lisa's parents are suffering some financial embarrassment. For some reason her poor father cannot find work. I'm here to make sure that Lisa doesn't show herself up at the church. She's not really used to big occasions and I'd hate her to feel out of place.'

'I can see that.' Billie smiled to sheathe the double edge. She turned to Lisa, and asked her what she was looking for, but she really wanted to ask if she was sure she wanted to cement her relationship to this woman with the skintight bonds of matrimony.

'I thought,' interrupted the mother-in-law-in-waiting, 'we could find her something like the dress I got married in. Full length. High neck.'

'Yes, lots of neck, I imagine,' Billie smiled. 'Perhaps, Lisa, you'd like a dress like *your* mum's?'

Butting in again, the tall woman asked, '*Are* your parents married, Lisa dear?'

Lisa's cheeks blazed. 'Yes, they are.'

'Bless them,' simpered the woman. As the bride-to-be crossed the shop to look at the window display, she confided in Billie, 'They live in a council house, but it's spotless.'

Billie threw an appalled look at Lisa, hoping to signal DON'T DO IT! but the girl's head was down. And it remained down as she tried on a succession of plain, elegant dresses, cunningly chosen by Billie to fulfil the harridan mother-in-law's requirements *and* flatter Lisa's neat shape. The reception was shaping up to be hellish, but at least the bride would look fantastic in the photographs.

The day had started with an orgasm and ended with a runaway bride, with a gravely ill dear friend tucked in the middle for some variety.

'I need . . . Sam,' Billie realised, with a dart of happy surprise. Just the thought of him cheered her: Sam would have a bracing, realistic approach to the complicated mosaic her life had become.

'Bloody hell,' said Sam from the depths of the sofa in his conservatory. 'I feel like I've missed a few episodes of my favourite serial and everything's changed.' He asked a very un-Sam question. 'How are you feeling?'

'No, no, no emotional analysis please.' Billie waggled her Jack Daniel's for emphasis. 'Just cynicism and jokes.'

Sam's face didn't flicker, but his voice sounded slightly flat. 'I can be sympathetic if I really try, you know.'

'I don't want sympathy. Sympathy will make me cry.' Billie couldn't get Annie's white face out of her mind.

Springing up to sit on the edge of the seat, he asked, eyes gleaming, 'Was the sex good?'

'Shut up!' squeaked Billie, Annie's face chased away by her embarrassment. 'Get off!' she added, for good measure.

'I bet he's athletic,' mused Sam, his full mouth pouting lasciviously. 'Hung like King Kong, goes without saying.'

Choking, Billie gasped, 'I'm hardly going to tell you stuff like that.' She recovered, and looked down at the ice in her drink. 'You're not wrong, though.'

They both guffawed, and Sam continued to pester Billie with questions that outraged her. He wanted every gory detail, and had an uncanny knack of guessing the truth.

'Well, yes, actually.' Billie squirmed as intimate details were wrung out of her. 'How did you know?'

'If I was on *Mastermind*, sex would be my specialist subject,' said Sam, matter-of-factly. 'I've had it all ways. Back. Front. Sideways. In a gondola.' He looked up at the ceiling, smiling to himself as if there was a small air steward up on the chandelier. 'I'd like to report that it was empty and meaningless and taught me that true love is the answer, but it didn't.' He looked at Billie again. 'For me, Billie-boos, casual shags with the nearest chap in leather shorts are the answer.'

'Really?' pressed Billie. 'Really, though?' Sam's extremism made her question her own attitudes. 'Wouldn't it be nice to have sex *and* love?'

'Like you and your fireman?' Sam pulled a sour face. 'Sorry, doll. Not for me.'

'I didn't say I loved him.' Billie was punctilious on this point: should she be sued in the court of relationships she could swear on the Bible that she had never said that. 'Yet,' she added, with a girlish giggle that made Sam roll his eyes.

'You've got to be careful around heroes,' he warned her, slipping down on to the rug like he always did at some point in the evening. 'They can't always live up to what it says on the box.'

'He already has,' Billie reminded him.

'Oh, anybody can rescue a fucking three-legged mongrel,' scoffed Sam, as if he did it every day before lunch.

That wasn't what Billie had meant. Her boyfriend was a hero because, she now knew, he'd spurned the advances of a volatile bride-to-be. She'd doubted him, on purely circumstantial evidence, and she would make it up to him. She checked her watch. Why not make it up to him right now? In a very raunchy way, possibly involving stockings.

'Got to go, Sam.'

'Stay a bit longer.'

'No. Rudery calls.'

'Ah. Off you pop. I never stand between a girl and her orgasm.'

'Poo,' said Billie. It helped, even if it wasn't elegant English. Ed's mobile was on voicemail. A plump plop of rain hit her squarely in the middle of her forehead. She was dashing towards Billie's Brides, to appropriate some of the stock: it had been a long time since she'd felt the need for fishnets. White ones would have to do.

The trees along the side of the recreation ground were trembling, and the sign outside the Sailor's Lament creaked to and fro. More raindrops followed the advance party which had already fluffed up Billie's hair to Ronald McDonald proportions. She scurried to the shop, and let herself in.

Having successfully rifled the stockings drawer, and put the right money in the till, Billie's shoulders slumped as she gathered up her bag. It looked as if a disaster movie was being filmed in Little Row. The rain lashed viciously down, bouncing high off the pavement. With no umbrella, Billie was forced to sit in the dimly lit shop and gaze out at the deluge, trying Ed every couple of minutes to no avail.

For the want of something better to do she tried Sly, not at all confident that he'd pick up.

'Hello, sis.'

'Oh. You're there. Told her yet?' Billie cut to the chase.

'Not exactly.' Sly paused. When Billie didn't fill the silence, he sighed, 'I can't find the right time.'

'That's cos there isn't one,' said Billie. She begged him, again, to come clean. 'It will be OK. I swear,' she promised, recklessly, as they said goodbye.

Outside the rain was redoubling its efforts to wash away Sole Bay.

Bored, Billie remembered her laptop. As she'd expected, there was an email from James. It made her smile. He was highly impressed with Ed's valour:

> That kind of physical bravery is a mystery to me. I'm not sure if I could rescue my own mother. Hang on to this guy. He sounds like one in a million. We've moved on, haven't we, Billie? That's a good thing, isn't it?

The beep of her mobile phone made her jump, and the sight of the word 'ED' in caller ID made her slam shut her laptop and forget all about James. 'Hello,' she said seductively, sounding a little like Zelda gargling.

'You've been calling?' Utterly unseductive, Ed was surrounded by the telltale noises of the fire station.

'You're at work,' pouted Billie, her plans scuppered. She changed tack, lowering her voice to a sultry purr. 'Here I am, all alone and thinking about you, and about what I'd like to do to you, and you're at work.' She felt foolish, but she'd always wanted to be one of those girls who give good phone.

'Ye-es.' Ed seemed to have caught her drift. 'So behave yourself.'

'But I want to be a naughty girl,' she growled, trying not to laugh. Countless magazine articles were adamant that men loved this play-acting stuff. 'I want to be verrrrrry naughty.' Oh Gawd. Were those trilled Rs too much?

'Do you now?' Apparently not, if the hoarse interest in Ed's voice was anything to go by.

'Yes, incredibly, erm, naughty.' Billie was running out of steam. In a low voice, Ed pleaded, 'Don't.'

Billie could practically hear his erection. Evidently originality was unimportant. 'Will you punish me if I'm a bad, bad girl?' To her own ears she sounded educationally subnormal, but it had the desired effect on her firefighter.

'Just you wait,' he warned.

Better buy a new picnic table, thought Billie smugly as she snapped her phone shut. She dared to hope that now that Ed was opening up to her, she could share her worries about Annie. But then again . . . Billie pictured the bored face he would pull. Handsome, but bored.

The storm outside was flexing its muscles. The heavy clouds bullying each other above Sole Bay darkened the streets, even though it was only seven o'clock. Not ready to go home and face the strange churning stew in her head that married sexual frustration to anxiety about Heather, Sly and Annie, Billie couldn't face the long walk back to Sam's in the pounding rain.

Instead, she turned up, bedraggled and wet, at Dot's door. 'I could do with some company,' she explained apologetically when Dot finally managed to drag the warped door fully open.

'I know what you mean,' said Dot with a wide, sympathetic smile. She always understood, or tried to. 'Come in and get dry. Jake's just made some delicious soup.'

That, thought Billie, could take her mind off the imminent destruction of the planet by scheming aliens: she'd come to the right place. Soup à la Jake had the consistency of wet cement, but rather less flavour. Luckily, Billie couldn't really see it, as the electricity had flickered and died just as she walked through the door. Jake was of the opinion that it was somehow connected to Billie's arrival, and the electromagnetism of female eroticism, but she preferred the more prosaic probability that the bad weather had caused problems with the supply.

The kitchen defied Billie's theory about candles: it was *not* improved by their influence. The dark corners grew and shrank boisterously, offering glimpses of the jagged junk that Jake accumulated. His shadow on the peeling wall bobbed and morphed, leering over Billie like a phantom, then shrinking to Mickey Mouse proportions. Despite Dot's angelic presence, it was not the best place for soothing the nerves.

Even Dot seemed affected. She was quiet, and her face had a sewn-up look to it. She was making no attempt to big up the dismal soup, and she kept her head down as Jake approached a subject Billie would rather protect from his sticky, paint-stained fingers.

'So how's the big love affair?' he asked, leaning back on his chair to survey Billie through half-closed eyes. 'Wonderful? Marvellous? Phantasmagorical?'

'I wouldn't use any of those words,' said Billie, as pleasantly as she could. 'It's fine, thanks. I'm enjoying getting to know him.' Every taut, toned, naughty inch of him, she added to herself.

'Good. I'm happy for you.' This sounded as likely as if Jake had said, 'I am a part-time model for Calvin Klein.'

'Thank you.' Billie minded her manners. It was best not to provoke Jake. As she took another slurp of her muddy main course, she learned she didn't have to.

'He might surprise you, you know.' Jake's tone implied that this surprise wouldn't be a nice one, in a Tiffany bag, with a helium balloon saying 'I love you' attached to it. 'I've seen him with somebody that might surprise you.' He grinned, a proper happy grin. Breaking people's hearts cheered him up, apparently. 'Getting very cosy.'

'I know all about it.' Billie, acting her part with more conviction than her mother had ever managed, stayed calm. She felt furious at this man's need to drag her down, but his tepid revelations about Ed and Heather couldn't hurt her: she thanked God that Heather had confessed. 'Sorry to disappoint you,' she couldn't help adding. She glanced at Dot, knowing how much this kind of exchange perturbed her.

Still, Dot stared down at her soup. She was concentrating on it hard, as if she was trying to make it move.

'Oh.' Jake was no actor: his dismay showed. Even his beard drooped. He pushed his plate away, and retreated to an only partly eviscerated soft chair on the fringes of the candles' reach.

A tile slipped off the roof, and landed in the garden with a splashy crash.

Dot jerked her head upright, and Billie was alarmed to see real fright in her eyes.

'It's only a tile,' said Billie, soothingly.

'I hate rain like this,' said Dot through gritted teeth.

'It's just water.' Jake's sulky voice drifted over from his shadowy chair.

'I do know what rain is,' said Dot, veering closer to irritation than Billie had ever witnessed. 'My mum always told us it was a night like this, a really filthy night, when she was abandoned.' She bit a nail. 'Bad things happen on nights like this.' The shadows behind her were as lively as the fire in the town square had been.

Shivering slightly, Billie frowned. 'Stop it, Dot,' she laughed. 'I'm getting spooked.'

'Sorry.' Dot's face mellowed, and she laid a hand on Billie's arm. 'I think the whole Annie and Ruby thing is getting to me. I don't know whether to hope for the best or . . .' She left the alternative unsaid.

'Me too. I'm so ignorant about cancer. I know that we want it to be benign, but I have no idea what the chances are.'

From the armchair, came a flat voice, 'We all die. We must all face death alone.'

Making a mental note never to book him for children's parties, Billie ignored Jake. 'She looked so weak. So much older.' She shook her head, as if that might dislodge the memory.

'I know,' said Dot, sympathetically. 'I had a chat with the nurse. Ever such a nice girl, has a goat, you know.' Dot veered back to the subject in hand. 'She told me that the operation itself is quite an ordeal for somebody like Annie.'

'You mean there's a chance she might never wake up?' Billie wanted to run from that much-too-real thought. 'That would kill Ruby.'

'They wouldn't even be married.' Dot sighed.

Like a spider, Jake unbent his body to lean forward, into the circle of light. 'You can gas on about this as much as you like, but if she dies, she dies.'

'We love Annie,' protested Billie, hearing the tiny cry that Dot made. 'We need to talk about her.'

'Love love love,' Jake sneered. 'You don't love her. You hardly know her.'

Galvanised, Dot said in a shaky voice, 'We're all she's got. Our little shop gave her something to hope for and plan for.

253

And we introduced her to Ruby. Maybe we do hardly know her but I know how I feel and I love her, in my own way.'

Face unreadable in the gloom, Jake was silent.

So was Billie. She'd never witnessed Dot standing up to him like that.

Turning to Billie with glassy eyes, Dot changed the subject. 'I saw Dean on my way home. He was very pale. Looked all confused, as if he'd just woken up from a long sleep.' She shook her head. 'Jilting is a terrible thing to do to anybody.' Jumping, she bit her lip. 'Oh, Billie. I forgot . . .'

'It's OK.' Stagnant waters were being stirred. 'I gave Heather the benefit of my experience. She wasn't thrilled with me.'

'I hope they get back together,' said Dot, fervently.

'Hmm.' Billie tried not to sound as if she agreed or disagreed. Perhaps the pain Heather was spreading around was preferable to years of a bad marriage. Look at her and James: they both knew they'd had a close escape. She was at last believing there was life after jilt. But then she thought of Dean and what he'd be going through. There were no easy answers.

'Why should you care?' asked Jake sourly. 'Or do you love them, too?'

Just at that moment, a loud clap of thunder boomed over the cottage, as if trying to jump down the chimney. Dot leapt to her feet, her hands over her ears, and the back door crashed open.

In ran Julia, clucking as if her tail feathers were on fire. She criss-crossed the kitchen, bumping into table legs and brushing Billie's shins.

'Julia!' shrieked Dot, trying to catch her feathery friend. 'She hates storms, they bring back terrible memories of her youth!'

'Right.' Billie, unsure quite how Dot would know this, tried to help round up Julia. Another clap of thunder seemed to rock the whole house, driving Julia behind a basket of dolls' heads and Jake to his feet.

'IT'S YOU!' he screeched, his face gaunt and terrible in the candlelight. A bony finger pointed at Dot, who had bent to gather Julia to her chest. 'YOU'VE CAUSED THIS STORM WITH YOUR NEGATIVE FEMININE MENSTRUAL ENERGIES! STOP IT! STOP THE STORM, YOU WITCH!'

Looking fearfully at Dot, Billie was ready to scoop her up in her arms and steady her. But Dot didn't need any such help. Another clap of thunder rattled the cutlery on the old table, as she shouted back, 'GET OUT! GET OUT OF MY LIFE, YOU MEAN LITTLE MAN!'

Jake couldn't have looked more astonished if Julia had answered him. 'This is my house,' he said feebly. 'You can't throw me out.'

'WATCH ME!' yelled Dot, who was getting out of her pram in an epic manner. 'OUT!' She rushed Jake, as if shooing a belligerent sheep. 'OUT YOU GO! OUT!'

All Jake's cocky self-assurance dissolved in the face of this new, all-shouting, all-ranting Dot. He scuttled for the front door and paused at the threshold, looking back hopefully.

'AND TAKE YOUR FUCKING STUPID HAT WITH YOU!' Dot bowled a top hat towards him.

'Good shot,' murmured Billie, who had so far stood stock still throughout this scene.

Finding his voice, Jake spat, 'This is *her* fault,' gesturing at Billie. 'I said no good would come of your having friends.'

'GET. OUT.'

And out Jake got.

Twenty-eight

The effort of finally standing up to her persecutor drained Dot. After a contemplative hour, Billie left her to get to bed and await Jake's return. And to talk Julia down from the top of the wardrobe.

Fighting the wind that seemed determined to deliver her to the wrong end of Sole Bay, Billie trudged through the storm. The thunder was becoming more insistent, its complaints closer together. The lightning was flexing its muscles, lighting up Sole Bay for a second or two at a time. Head down, Billie made for Herbert and hoped that he was intact.

Her route took her down Little Row. Squinting at the spitting insults of the weather, Billie saw lights gleaming foggily from the back of Zelda's shop. In her mind's eye she imagined the little blood-red room with its stove and its paintings and its inviting chair and its never-ending supply of soporific, soothing fudge.

Perhaps Zelda would take her in, like she had before. Zelda, despite her bizarre ways and her weakness for elderly gents, had a nose for unhappiness. Tonight Billie could do with some of her special treatment. She knocked boldly on the fudge-shop door.

Inside, the light flickered and moved. Billie could hear sounds of upheaval, but Zelda didn't appear. Billie knocked again, louder. Perhaps Zelda couldn't hear her over the rain, or over whatever grossly inappropriate pop song she was singing.

Bangs, crashes, a sudden bright light through the crackled glazing of the door to the parlour. Billie peered into the shop. She could see a shape moving about, hunched, as if dragging something heavy. 'ZELDA!' she shouted, over the fury of the storm.

256

Heavy-footed in her wide-fit sandals, Zelda at last plodded towards the door. She opened it an inch, and poked her nose through. 'Who's that?'

'Me, Billie,' said Billie. 'Is everything alright?' Those loud noises had disturbed her, and Zelda didn't seem her usual self. She was tossed, and twitchy.

'Everything's fantastic!' Zelda grinned, and despite the dentures that seemed to have been made for a bigger mouth, she looked years younger. 'Tonight's the night, child. I'm inspired. I can feel the fudge in my veins.'

'Oh. That's nice.' Billie nodded, as if she understood.

'I feel like Doctor Frankenstein.' The lightning obligingly flashed at this point, illuminating Zelda's lined, gleeful face. 'Out of tragedy comes forth sweetness.'

'Like I always say,' laughed Billie. Mad as she was, Zelda would be company so she tried a casual, 'Fancy a cup of tea?'

'Tea?' Zelda was shocked. 'I can't stop now. I'm possessed.' And she looked it as she shook her flopping, unnaturally black hair out of her eyes.

'Maybe tomorrow,' said Billie, bravely, feeling the red parlour and its magical fudge slipping away.

'Goodnight, petal.' Zelda put up one hand to push an unruly cowlick back from her forehead: her arm was stained a dark, gooey red all the way to her elbow. 'You can be the first to taste my new recipe in the morning.'

'Goodnight,' said Billie to the slammed door. Thunder crashed above her head. In the confused lighting of the storm, that red on Zelda's arms had looked like gore. 'Must be the famous secret ingredient,' mused Billie, heading for the shelter of Billie's Brides' porch. 'Strawberries? Plums?' Neither seemed all that groundbreaking.

Drenched and defeated by the angry rain, Billie decided she could go no further and let herself into the shop. Looking murderously out at the monsoon she decided she'd sit it out in the dry, safe interior until this Old Testament God had got whatever was eating him off his chest.

The light switches were impotent, as was the radio. Billie lit a fat candle she found in the kitchenette, and trailed shimmering shadows in her wake back to the counter. Sole Bay was cracking under the strain of the storm: a handful of other houses out in Little Row were blackly dark as well. She settled down in the candlelight, the plush upholstery of her bottom meeting the plush upholstery of the refurbished 'customers only' chair, and plonked her feet on the counter.

Her only company, apart from the monotonous music of the driving rain, was her unsettling thoughts. So much was crumbling around her. She wanted to cling harder to the things she valued in case they went haywire, too. Ed. This shop.

Somewhere out in that rain, Jake was lurching around in his top hat; Sly was oiled up and waggling the family jewels in a stranger's face; Annie was trying to get to sleep between the starchy sheets of her hospital bed; Dot was crying into Julia's feathers.

Billie wondered if she could read her emails despite the blackout. She had an uncertain grasp on how the internet worked. If asked she would have muttered something about frequencies and wavelengths, and kept the bit about web elves to herself.

Happily charged up, her laptop glowed and purred, and displayed three messages she hadn't had the time to open when they'd arrived. Those elves were on overtime, apparently.

The first, from her mother, contained a link to a website offering 'pre-emptive plastic surgery for the twenty something'. The second was a price list from a company specialising in 'unusual cake toppers'; Billie was surprised to note that an unconvincing marzipan portrait of the happy couple was a mere one hundred and twenty pounds. Third in the queue was James. He was, typically, in advice-giving mode.

> Try not to panic about Annie. Don't assume the worst until you have to. Talk to doctors, get the 'big picture'. Think positive. If I know you, you'll be chewing your fingernails down to the knuckle. You always get so involved. Annie sounds like such a sweetie, I hope the prognosis is good. It all makes you feel so helpless, doesn't it?

That was true. Billie braced herself for mention of the doctor bird. It came soon enough.

My girlfriend might be able to answer some of your queries. I could let you have her email address if you like.

And this man has the cheek to call me mad, thought Billie, her eyebrows somewhere up in the stockroom.

Marrakesh is cancelled. Well, the holiday is. I feel confident that the place is still there. I can't get the time off work. Sound familiar?
It's very late, and it's raining hard.

Spooky, thought Billie.

As you often said, rain doesn't suit a minimalist loft apartment. Rain feels reassuring when it falls on a thatch roof, but it's intimidating drumming on my metal balcony. I've had a whisky, and I've had a shower, and I'm feeling very mellow. And a bit sad. Perhaps it's your little Annie getting to me.

With all the dark thoughts of the past few months, Billie had forgotten how caramel-soft James could be underneath the accountant's carapace. There was a PS.

I've been taping the *Hollyoaks* omnibus to watch when my girlfriend is working nights. Does this make me a bad person?

BANG.

Billie tensed. The noise was the infuriatingly indefinable sort that only happens in the dark. During the day, noises always sound like something. 'Oh, the mini fridge fell off the shelf,' she could say, confidently. Or, 'That'll be upstairs' au pair doing her dancercise again.' Only at night did bangs sound like burglars. Or worse.

Not sure what was worse than a burglar but unable to rule out vampires despite her advanced years, Billie picked up the candle and climbed the stairs up to the stockroom.

BANG.

Billie stopped halfway up, hastily analysing the sound as the hair on the back of her neck stood on end. It had unmistakable vampire overtones, but could just as easily be one of Dot's animal chums bumping into something. An invalid cat can sound very like the bloodsucking undead if conditions are favourable. Slowly she carried on, bemoaning the lack of a blunt instrument.

When the noise sounded a third time, all became clear, and Billie sagged with relief. The tiny, square window that looked out on to the yard had been blown open by the stroppy wind, and was now banging listlessly, its latch broken.

Billie balanced the candle on the nearest shelf, pushing aside a small nest made from old veils that Dot had fashioned for Jenkins's naps. Straining, she pulled at the rotting window, which had come away from the frame and now refused to shut.

A movement outside in the long rectangles of yard caught her eye. Somebody was in Zelda's garden, a much nicer and better kept plot than Billie's Brides' bin colony. Pushing her hair out of her eyes, Billie strained to see through the teeming rain. Zelda wouldn't be gardening at this hour in this weather: whoever it was had to be up to no good.

Her heart banging louder than the window had been, Billie peered anxiously down at the grainy figure, moving amongst the rhubarb plants and the wolfsbane. A loud clap of thunder growled over Sole Bay, shadowed by a long bolt of lightning so powerful that for a long moment the whole of Little Row was floodlit with a mercurial glow.

Down in next door's garden, Zelda stood by a narrow, deep hole she had evidently just dug. A lumpy bundle, covered with blankets and indistinct in the dark, lolled at her feet. As Billie watched, mesmerised, the old woman, her hair streaming like a banner, threw back her head, brandished the shovel and unleashed a banshee howl up into the tempest, her eyes tightly shut.

The window chose that moment to have an encore bang. Like a cat sensing a mouse, Zelda's eyes flew open and locked on to the window. Flattening herself back against the wall, Billie blew out the candle with stuttering breath. Not daring to move, she stayed stuck to the wall in the darkness until she heard Zelda's back door lock.

She hoped that Zelda hadn't seen her. Wedging the window shut, she examined that thought. Why was she suddenly scared of a woman she knew well? Was it the shallow ditch? The shallow, *grave-like* ditch? The suspicious bundle? Maybe the werewolf howl?

All of these things, decided Billie, setting off for Herbert's salty embrace at quite a clip. All of these things.

'You're no bloody help.'

The Gallery of Happiness was, like Miss World, pretty to look at but poor company. Appealing to it for help, in the absence of any walking, talking humans, Billie received fourteen inane, almost imbecilic, grins in reply. The brides' preoccupations were clearly stamped across their foreheads: 'This dress is too tight!'; 'Do I look like a mobile home from the back?'; 'That chuffing photographer is taking his time!'; 'I should have married Phil.'

They were too busy to help Billie with her peculiar stew of anxieties. Her list of worries, already healthy, had grown to include Zelda. Zelda, who made fudge in the dead of night pausing only to dig shallow graves and howl like the undead into a thunderstorm. Zelda of the evil eye and the droopy drawers.

'So, to precis, my favourite old lady is mortally ill, my most lucrative client has gone nuts, my assistant is depressed, my brother's living a double life worthy of the most unfeasible TV movie, and my neighbour's a witch.' A witch who had possibly finally crossed the line and committed murder. That bundle in the mud could have been Mrs Davis. Or Mr Dyke. Billie chewed her lip, unsure whether her suspicions were credible.

Outside, Sole Bay was righting itself after the storm, like a respectable middle-aged lady who had somehow found herself embroiled in a break-dancing contest. Bins had blown over, trees had shed their leaves, the striped awning that stood to attention outside Dyke's was ragged and ripped. Billie felt as crumpled as the town, but the Gallery of Happiness grinned gormlessly on: nothing could dent their manic good humour. Billie tucked her hair up into a clip and greeted a robust woman keen to discuss corsets.

As she'd been ordered, Dot had taken the morning off. By now, her drenched and hopefully penitent boyfriend would have shuffled home and there would be a lot to talk about. Before last night's outburst, Billie would have expected Dot to melt at the sight of a bedraggled Jake, but now she wasn't so sure. The Dottish worm had turned.

The bell above the door chimed and in bounced a beaming girl with the looks of a milkmaid, all creamy curves.

'I'm mad, me,' said the customer, three times in ten minutes. 'Totally bonkers. Crazy.'

'Are you?' asked Billie, conversationally. The girl didn't look mad: she was wearing a pleated skirt.

'Me and Tony's both nutters,' said the girl. 'Everybody says so. "They're mad, they are," they say.'

Feeling that the customer's lunatic credentials had been sufficiently stressed, Billie showed her a few dresses.

'No. No.' The jolliness of the expression didn't change. 'Do you know where he proposed? On stage at Butlins. I wet my knickers, I was laughing that much. Mum was laughing. Dad was laughing. And as for Tony—'

'Laughing, was he?' ventured Billie.

'He was.' Ignoring the pretty off-white empire-line number Billie was holding up, she rattled on. 'We met at the Benny Hill Appreciation Society. Tony knows everything about Benny Hill. Everything. I always wanted a man with brains.' She seemed to remember why she was there, and waved away the dress. 'Too expensive. It's got to be cheap,' she explained. 'We're planning a food fight at the reception.'

When Dot appeared just before lunch, she was idly chewing, and wearing a hessian sundress that Billie had never seen before. No tear ruts down her face. No dishevelled misery hair.

'What time did he crawl back?' asked Billie, wryly. 'I hope you didn't let him off the hook too easily.'

'Oh, he didn't come back,' said Dot, easily. 'Fudge?' She held out a creased bag of pinkish fudge. 'Zelda's new recipe. It's . . . indescribably good.'

'No, ta.' Billie was perturbed. 'He didn't come home? So, where is he?'

'I have no idea.' Dot, who worried about everything up to and including the welfare of passing flies, didn't sound worried.

'Dot, have you been taking drugs? How can you calmly tell me that you don't know where Jake, the love of your life, is?'

'He can look after himself.' Dot sounded ever so slightly bitter. 'Sure you won't have some fudge?'

For some reason, Billie backed away from the outstretched bag. 'It's a funny colour.'

'Pink,' smiled Dot.

'More . . . flesh colour.' Billie shuddered.

'Don't say that!' Dot pulled a face. 'It's delicious. Very very moreish.' She was licking her fingers, and for some reason Billie was repulsed. 'I cleaned the cottage from top to bottom this morning. You wouldn't recognise it. I slung all the junk out into the garden, put flowers everywhere. I even used the Hoover. I never get the chance normally, because Jake says the noise reminds him of the tormented souls in Hell.' She paused. 'Dickhead.'

'Dot!' Billie was disoriented.

'Oh, that was awful of me.' Dot was blushing. 'I'm sorry. But it helps. With the anger. But he's not a dickhead.'

'No,' said Billie with dignity, adding, 'he's a twat.'

Going out with Ed had morphed into staying in with Ed. Tearing off your boyfriend's kecks is frowned upon in public houses and cinemas, so Billie and Ed generally decided to stay in, after a token discussion of the alternatives.

'It's jazz night at the Sailor's,' she'd say. 'But it'll be packed.'

'Too many daytrippers on the front to enjoy a walk,' he'd muse.

Pretending to consider it, she'd suggest, 'We could always go into Neeveston and catch a film.'

'Nothing I fancy seeing, really.' Ed would wrinkle his nose.

'I suppose,' Billie would say slowly, dropping the strap of her top. 'We could just stay in.'

'Seems rude not to,' Ed would agree, suddenly closer than her skin.

Their nights in were all spent in Herbert, as Ed's all-male house share was not relationship-friendly. 'If these walls could talk, they'd be X-rated,' giggled Billie on Wednesday night as she rearranged her clothing. She curled one arm and then the other into the air, like a cat after a bowl of the best farmhouse cream. 'You are damn good, Edward.'

'All part of the service.' Ed jumped up, with the kind of springiness that was beyond Billie, and stalked over to the wash-basin to splash his face.

Billie watched him, like an antiques expert evaluating a Georgian commode. The width of his shoulders and the way his torso narrowed down to his buttocks thrilled and delighted her. It was like owning a never-ending bag of sweets. Or fudge.

Startling her, Ed asked, 'Have you tasted your mad neighbour's new fudge?'

'No. You haven't, have you?'

'You sound worried. Of course I have. The lads are all nuts about it.' He licked his lips. 'It's unusual. I love it.'

'It's bad for you,' she said.

'Since when do you turn something down because it's bad for you?' He grinned, towelling his face. 'Like me, for instance.'

'You're good for me,' said Billie. 'You are the fat-free biscuit I've been searching for.'

'You reckon?' Ed's face was obscured by her favourite polka-dot towel.

'Yes, I do.' Billie didn't like this talk. Ed always shied away from being told how she felt about him. Her programming was different from the women who came into her shop: Billie didn't fast forward to a happy ever after. She'd had that beaten out of her and she appreciated a happy right now. But part of that happiness was the luxury of believing that Ed belonged to her in some small, non-freedom-threatening way, that they were experiencing something real and worthwhile. 'Why, don't you?'

'Hang on. This is girl speak. I don't do girl speak. I'll get sucked into a situation where I can't say anything right.' Ed chucked the towel at her with a masculine bark of laughter. 'This is dangerous stuff. You talk about weddings in your shop all day and that's scary for a bloke. I could fall asleep a bachelor and wake up married.'

Billie didn't answer, too busy computing the fact that Ed, who could recognise her clitoris blindfolded, had misjudged something as integral to her personality as her attitude to marriage, didn't realise that she would rather join a leper colony. 'You're quite safe,' she said, not entirely successful in keeping the acid out of her voice. 'This particular bird doesn't want to marry anybody.'

'See. I've cocked up already.' Ed knelt in front of her. 'Men and women shouldn't talk about anything important. It always ends in plates being thrown.' His chest was within touching distance.

So she touched it. 'No you haven't cocked up, silly. Just let me tell you how I feel about you once in a while. You don't have to respond.'

Ed seemed stilled by that. He took Billie's face in his hands and stared into it for a delicious while. 'You're no ordinary woman, Billie Baskerville. What are you doing with me? I'm not as nice as you think, girl.'

'That started well,' smiled Billie, 'but frankly you've got to work on your endings.'

'Come on,' laughed Ed, bounding up. 'Let's get dressed and go out.'

'No,' laughed Billie, laying back. 'Let's not.'

It wasn't a hard argument to win. Later, as they lay entwined in the mess of blankets, Billie remembered a phone call she'd had that afternoon. 'Jackie's coming up on Saturday,' she told him in the darkness.

'Right.'

'Well, sound pleased. She's one of my best friends.'

'Hurray,' said Ed, limply.

Somehow Billie had amassed a little group of people who couldn't stand the sight of each other. 'Do you want me to see her on my own?'

'Definitely.'

Disappointed, Billie changed the subject. 'Jake's still not back. Dot's taking it all very well.' She chose to interpret his silence as fascination, 'And we've started a rota for visiting Annie.'

If the continuing silence was anything to go by, Ed was *really* fascinated.

'Well?' Nudging him a little too enthusiastically, Billie got her reaction.

'Ooof. Yes. Your sick old lady, lovely,' muttered Ed, sleepily.

'They're important to me,' grumbled Billie.

'Yes, darling.' Ed was cruising away, over the horizon.

It was difficult for Billie to find sleep, sharing a narrow bed with a wide man. Ed was never going to work up interest in Annie's health, or Sly's cowardice, but maybe it was wrong to expect him to. After all, she was safe in her niche, the little Billie-shaped crevice she'd dug for herself in Sole Bay. Back in the land of the living, with a functioning relationship, and friends to rely on and worry about.

Setting off on Saturday for the hospital, Dot asked blandly, 'Shall I take Annie some fudge?'

'No,' said Billie sharply, adding, 'she doesn't like rich things.'

Lurking by the door, ignoring a customer peering needily at her over a rack of dresses, Debs commented, 'That fudge is fucking wicked.' She was wearing a pair of denim shorts that didn't even begin to control the wild frontier of her bottom. 'Alright, love, keep your hair on,' she advised the customer, who had coughed politely.

The queue for Zelda's new recipe stretched past the door of Billie's Brides. Looking out at it, Billie felt her wings begin to itch. 'Dot,' she asked carefully, 'have you been in touch with Jake's family?'

'They haven't seen him.' Dot was using the carefully non-committal expression she'd cultivated since Jake loped off into the storm. 'Nobody's seen him.' She pulled on a cotton cardigan, home-made, possibly in the dark. 'He'll come back when he's ready. He's doing this to worry me.'

'Is he succeeding?' Billie didn't buy this new, disengaged Dot.

'No,' Dot insisted. 'I'm not alone. I've got Julia. And Jenkins has been a tower of strength.'

'So you don't think anything bad's happened to him?'

'Like what?' asked Dot innocently.

Like being murdered, dismembered and buried by the over-protective sorceress who lives next door. Like being the secret ingredient in Zelda's best-selling fudge. Billie couldn't dismiss the gore on Zelda's hands that night, or that lumpy bundle on the ground. 'Oh, I don't know. I'm sure you're right. He's licking his wounds somewhere.' Her murder/fudge scenario seemed ludicrous but still it nibbled at her peace of mind. Perhaps it wasn't ludicrous: perhaps it was NFSB.

'I don't have time to worry.' Dot was determined to make the best of things. This steel spine was a revelation to Billie, who had supposed her friend to be composed of much floppier materials. 'I'll get myself some fudge. That'll cheer me up.'

Not knowing how to phrase, 'NO! IT'S WRONG TO EAT YOUR BOYFRIEND!' in an acceptable way, Billie opened the door to let her out.

In the lull that descended round about Cornetto time that afternoon, Debs talked smugly of her one hundred per cent pulling success. 'I put it down to me high self-esteem. Men go for that.'

Billie put it down to many things, including Debs' blink-and-you'll-miss-them skirts, and a soupçon of naked fear. She smiled inwardly at Debs' claims, knowing that her record wasn't quite one hundred per cent: Chugger had got away.

After Debs went home, as night follows day, as regret follows a whole Mars Bar, the till was short.

Twenty-nine

According to the rota, it was Billie's turn to visit Annie. Meeting Ruby in the car park, Billie sniffed whisky on his breath. 'You look after yourself,' she urged him.

'It's her I'm worried about,' replied Ruby, gruffly. 'How much do we still owe on the dress? I want the wedding as soon as she comes out. So we can live together, and I can make her comfortable.'

'The dress is paid for.'

'It can't be.' Realisation crept over Ruby's face. 'Oh. Thank you, my dear,' he coughed, and walked abruptly away.

Over the initial shock, Annie had rallied. Sitting up in a crisp nightie, her hair carefully swept up into a white bun, she was reading *The Lady* when Billie slumped on to the uncomfortable plastic chair at the side of the bed.

'You shouldn't waste your time on me,' protested Annie, taking off her glasses.

'We go through this every visit,' laughed Billie. 'If you're trying to shake me off, it won't work.'

Smiling wanly, Annie admitted. 'I look forward to seeing you. Breaks up the day. I'm accustomed to being so busy.' She tucked a stray hair behind her ear. 'I get so tired, even though I'm doing nothing.'

During their game of Scrabble, Annie firmly disallowed 'grunty', and put down the dictionary. 'I want you to promise me something,' she said, timidly.

Not liking the sound of this at all, Billie held a Scrabble tile in mid-air. She had never liked morbid conversations, and when mortally ill people start asking you to make promises, it just *has* to be morbid. 'What?' she asked, warily.

'Please tell Reuben not to visit again.'

'Annie, that's madness.' She dropped the Scrabble letter and sat back. 'Have you two had a row?'

'Of course not. I want you to convince him that he should stay away. He doesn't need a burden at his time of life. I don't know what lies ahead for me,' quavered Annie, struggling to collect herself. 'But it might be difficult. He's free. Tell him I set him free from his obligations. Will you do that for me?'

'No.' Billie was straightforward. 'I won't.' Talking over Annie's complaints, she said, 'I wouldn't be so cruel.' Leaning over the tidy bed, she said adamantly, 'Try and be selfish for once in your life. Ruby wants to look after you. Let him.' She was doling out tough love again. 'If you really want to help Ruby, then get home to him as quickly as you can. He's drinking again.'

'I know.' Annie flinched. 'He's not up to this. He's better off without me.'

'He's nothing without you.'

Annie and Billie gazed at each other. An impasse had been reached. Annie shut her eyes, always the cue for visitors to go. Billie squeezed her elderly friend's hand, and walked quickly away, but not before she'd spelled out 'ANNIE FOR RUBY' on the Scrabble board.

In the car park, a blank concrete plain that Billie had come to hate because it was always the spot where she collected herself after visiting Annie, Billie paused beside a Ford Mondeo, her shoulders drooping. Cheesy declarations, overblown expensive gestures: Billie heard about them every day in the shop. But real love, selfless and muscular, still held the power to stop her in her tracks.

'What are you doing here?'

As welcomes for riotously handsome lovers go, this was lukewarm, and Ed looked dismayed. 'Nothing,' he muttered.

Rolling her eyes, Dot retreated diplomatically to the kitchenette. At least one member of staff at Billie's Brides knew how to nurture romance.

'Shall we start again?' asked Billie, sheepishly. It took a while to shrug off the long hand of the hospital. 'I meant to say—' She reached up and kissed him slowly on the lips, like a novice at mouth Braille.

'That's more like it.' Ed seemed compensated. 'Where you been?'

'Umm,' Billie thought better of telling him the truth: she didn't want to see his eyes glaze over. 'Out. Doing stuff. You know. Wedding stuff.'

Laughing, Ed put his fingers together to make a cross and brandished them as if to ward her off. 'Only joking,' he said apologetically when his girlfriend didn't laugh. 'I came in to . . .' He looked at her, as if considering what to say. 'There's no other way to put it. I came in to look at you.'

'Oh, Ed.' Billie's smile was soppy. There she stood, with her wayward hair and her tired eyes and her droopy wings, and Ed had made a detour to look at her. This scrumptious man was her anchor to the real world. 'Thank goodness for you,' she whispered.

The face was familiar. 'Cheryl!' Billie clicked her fingers as she nailed the customer's identity. 'How was the wedding?'

The new Mrs Mississippi Mutilator glowed as she shared her memories of the big day. 'The wedding was perfection. Every girl's dream. The whole of Death Row cheered. And now . . .' Cheryl lowered her lashes and patted her tummy. 'I think I'm expecting a happy event.'

'Aw,' said Dot. 'A little Mutilator Junior!'

'I didn't realise they allowed you to . . .' Billie regretted starting that sentence. 'Erm, have conjugal, erm . . .' she faltered.

Luckily, Cheryl cottoned on. 'Oh, they don't. Physical contact is strictly forbidden,' she said, breathily. 'But,' she continued, her face ablaze with the memory, 'the way he *looked* at me through the high-security plexiglas, the way his eyes *burned* into my body, I could feel our union deep within me.'

Wondering if Mr Dyke's OAP Special Discount customers felt the same, Billie trod carefully. 'Have I got this right? You're pregnant?'

Lowering her voice and half closing her eyes, Cheryl intoned movingly, 'I feel his babe quicken within me.'

Taken aback, Billie asked, 'When are you seeing Len again?'

'Oh, he's dead,' said Cheryl airily. 'He went to the chair right after the wedding.' She plonked a pair of white shoes on the counter, seemingly unaware of the horrified looks passing between Billie and Dot. 'Sorry it's taken me so long to get back to you, I've just got home from the States. Do you still need my shoes for your friend's wedding?'

'Not any more, I'm afraid,' said Billie regretfully, picking up the shoes to hand them back. Then she stopped, mules in mid-air. 'Although, then again . . . Thanks, Cheryl, we'll accept them. I'll give you a ring when you can have them back.'

As soon as the perky bride/widow/expectant mother left, Billie rang the hospital. 'Is it possible,' she asked an administrator, 'to carry out wedding ceremonies in your hospital?'

It was unavoidable. Billie had to nip next door to Zelda's to ask for change. A bullish woman had insisted on paying cash for her satin two-piece and Billie had to break a twenty-pound note to give her the correct change.

'I'll serve this one!' Zelda elbowed her assistant out of the way to grin over the glass counter at Billie. 'What'll it be, my lovely?' she asked indulgently.

Billie couldn't answer. She was mesmerised by the battered top hat sitting at an angle on Zelda's exuberant, coal-black bouffant.

James,

I felt you should know the latest about one of your favourite customers. Mrs Serial Killer is back from America and is expecting. Don't start knitting any bootees, because it appears to be an immaculate conception, caused purely by the ardour of The Mississippi Mutilator's gaze. Poor woman.

Annie is much the same. We're doing our best. I bought her a new nightie, a pink one with a frill around the neck.

Crikey, thought Billie. *James will be fascinated.* She needed an outlet for this kind of talk. Dot was too involved, and too prone to tears. Ed was prone to looking into the middle distance. And as for sharing it with Jackie when she arrived . . . the very notion made Billie roll her eyes. No, James would have to listen. He was good at that.

* * *

Sprawled on Billie's renovated deckchair out on Herbert's veranda, vodka in mitt, Jackie said, 'Seriously, though, when are you coming back to the action, babe?'

'I couldn't take any more action, thanks very much,' laughed Billie. She'd spent the last two hours of her working day ringing round the various companies she'd wheedled deals out of for Heather's wedding cancelling everything. Phone silence from Heather had confirmed that the jilt was going ahead. 'It might look peaceful, but Sole Bay is more eventful than your sex life.' Sitting on the boards, her knees to her chin, she looked up at Jackie mischievously. 'For one thing, Ed's been unfaithful, so I hear.' She would enjoy sharing the tale of Heather's doomed attempt to board the good ship *Fireman*.

'Oh.' Jackie sounded only vaguely interested.

'Jake told me Ed has been doing something I'd be surprised at.'

'Yeah?' Still Jackie wasn't intrigued.

Billie ploughed on, determined to hook her audience. 'With *somebody* I'd be surprised at,' she said archly. Surely Jackie, who had heard many tales of Heather's arrogant high-handedness would guess. 'But I already knew all about it! Can you take a wild guess at who the someone is?'

'Christ, you bore me.'

It wasn't a joke, and Billie reacted as if she'd been slapped. 'You what?' she frowned.

'Listen to you.' Jackie mimicked her vindictively. 'Ed's been unfaithful, who with, ooooch!' She stood up, hands on hips, and looked down at Billie, still on the floor. 'Why not just have it out with me? Be straight about it? The bearded weirdo snitched on us, so why not say so?'

From far away, a skinny idea suddenly piled on the pounds. 'Jackie . . .' was all Billie said, too unhappy to continue.

'Yes, I shagged him,' declared Jackie, as if the confession had been wrung out of her with hours of merciless interrogation. 'OK? Got it? I shagged him the night I met him and I've been shagging him, train schedules permitting, ever since. As if you don't bloody know.'

'I didn't,' said Billie quietly, standing to face her. 'Bloody know, I mean.'

'You did.' For the first time, Jackie blushed. 'What was all that about, then? You were torturing me.'

'I thought Jake was referring to Heather. She told me she chased him.' Billie folded her arms, a mutinous look on her face. 'But she obviously can't run as fast as you.' It was as if Jackie had mutated before her eyes into another creature altogether. The bouncy hair looked overdone, and the full lips looked ravenous. 'I thought you were my friend.' She couldn't trust herself to think about Ed yet: at the moment he was still an abstract. Her breath came in short spurts, as if she'd just run for the bus.

'Shit.' Jackie sank back into the deckchair. She looked up at Billie, and incredibly she was biting her tongue, trying not to laugh. 'You mean, I just confessed all for no reason?' She shook her head in disbelief. 'You weren't supposed to find out, ever. We didn't want to hurt you.'

'Spare me the fucking clichés,' growled Billie, in a deeper voice than she'd ever used before. The sunny world of moments before had turned on its head, and she felt sick. 'You're boring *me* now.'

'It's true.' Disconcertingly, Jackie didn't look like a woman who'd just been caught cheating on one of her greatest friends. She looked relaxed, blameless, with her legs stretched out in front of her. 'It's not like Ed and I have been having some wonderful love affair behind your back. It's just sex. We don't discuss you. Honest. And we don't talk about our feelings or any of that crap.'

'Gosh, I feel so much better now.'

'Listen, Billie, listen properly. This doesn't have to mean the end of you and me. Or you and Ed. Can't we put it behind us? You know I'm a greedy cow.' She hesitated. 'And you went and found yourself a greedy guy, too.'

'I can't get my head around this.' Billie needed some details. 'You've been coming here without me knowing?'

'A handful of times.' Jackie was able to hold Billie's gaze. 'That time we bumped into each other and had a picnic, I was heading for the cab office after spending the night with Ed.'

'Where?' Billie's mind raced. Then she knew. 'At his place?'

'Yeah. What a dump. Lad Central.'

A new arrow struck Billie. 'Oh God, you were with him last night, weren't you?'

'If you must know, yes.'

'Oh *God*,' groaned Billie, wringing extra syllables out of the word. The precious interlude in the shop yesterday afternoon had been about Ed's guilt, not his need to look at her. 'I've never even been to his flat.'

'You're the girlfriend, I'm just the bit on the side. His flat's not good enough for you.'

'Are you, *you*, trying to make me feel better?' scoffed Billie.

'Wouldn't dare. You've got the moral high ground, and you're galloping about on it on your high horse.' There was silence as the dusk knitted itself tighter to the beach. Jackie broke it. 'You needn't believe this, but I really wanted to tell you after the first time. Looking back I wish I had. You wouldn't have gone out with him at all.'

'When was the first time?' said Billie, sounding as if she was falling asleep. She was weary of this evening and its tacky revelations.

'The first time I met him. The night you kissed him.' Jackie seemed to be willing herself to be as plain as possible. 'The night of the disco.'

'But he came back here . . .' Billie woke up.

'And you sent him packing.'

'You stayed with Chugger that night.'

'Nope. Your chavvy assistant did. You never really asked me, so I never really told you.'

So, Debs' one hundred per cent success rate was safe. This news also explained Ed's mysterious hangover the day after the disco. The implications for Billie's feelings for Ed, for her peace of mind, for her faith in her own judgement were looming and taking shape in the lilac evening. He was another Mr Wrong, after all. That million pounds she'd have to hand over to Dot if she ever tied the knot was safer than ever. 'Go, will you, Jack?'

Standing up, hauling her oversized bag up from the boards, Jackie said, 'It's only a man. It's only sex. It's not important. I wouldn't have done it if I thought it would split you and me up.'

Shrugging her shoulders, Billie could only offer, 'You did do it. And you'd do it again. I'm just one of your anecdotes now, a casualty of your quest to have fun.'

Angry now, Jackie stamped down on to the concrete. 'I hate that tone you use. You want everything to be just so, like that fucking dreadful, perfect wedding you tried to organise for yourself. Billie, life is a mess. I make messes because I live. I cry over it then I carry on. I don't bury myself in a backstreet shop that doesn't even belong to me, reaching out a virtual hand every so often to a man who shouldn't matter any more. I don't eulogise some common-or-garden bloke with a hard-on as The One. I'm a real person. I'm a whole person. And I choose life, every time. I don't say "no", I don't say "maybe", I grab it with both hands. And if you don't like real life and its messes, well, that's your fucking problem.'

Fuming, Billie watched Jackie clatter off in shoes she'd thought fabulous a few hours ago but now considered ridiculously inappropriate. 'Apology accepted!' she yelled, before going back inside Herbert for a really good, really long sob.

Thirty

There's only so much crying a girl can do before she wants to buy a hatchet. Luckily for Ed, there were no hatchet shops in Sole Bay, so Billie resorted to phoning him. And phoning him. And phoning him.

Ed was not picking up. He'd been forewarned, or 'got at', as Billie preferred to call it. His partner in crime had warned him that the unwitting filling in their sex sandwich had rumbled them.

Replaying recent history in her head had made for a troubled night. First she'd re-examined the times she'd spent with Ed to discern if his feelings for her were real. Then she'd looked sadistically for clues that he had no feelings for her at all. Ashamed, but unable to stop herself, she then tried to prove that he preferred her to Jackie. 'As if that matters,' she thought miserably.

As a subject, Jackie was closed. As closed as Billie's copy of *King Lear* the day after her English Literature GCSE. Billie vowed never to mention her, or talk to her, ever again (perhaps she had inherited some of her mother's dramatic tendencies after all). The shadow cast by Jackie's betrayal polluted their history: Jackie's vocal scepticism before Billie's non-wedding was starting to look malevolent rather than playful. Perhaps if Billie examined the past she'd discover that Jackie had been instrumental in the horrific, historic jilt. Best not examine the past in that case, decided Billie, who had enough to deal with just now.

Dumped squarely in the middle of no-man's-land without a map, Billie flailed about. If only she'd been faithful to the shop, she wouldn't be in this stew. It made no sense to call Ed. He had deceived her, used her and turned his high-pressure hose on her self-confidence. There was nothing he could say that would get him off the hook. But not seeing him was unthinkable, even if all she could do was repeat the word 'GIT' over and over into his face.

Filtering all her varied wants and needs, one thing was plain: she *had* to meet up with him. Billie needed to hear in his own words what had gone on between him and Jackie. Perhaps there was some consolation to be found, some reasoning that she couldn't fathom.

But, apparently, Ed did not need to meet up with her. At first she assumed he was at work, out on a call, asleep, pinned down by pygmies. Slowly it became obvious that he simply wasn't answering. Hating herself, she withheld her number. Hating herself even more, she began pressing redial every fifteen minutes.

Ed didn't crack. He didn't pick up. Perhaps, she hoped, he too was being stirred into a vat of fudge.

With both their swains AWOL, Billie and Dot devoted much of the next week to deep bemusement. 'So I'm single, then?' Billie asked herself, on tiptoe to measure a tall girl's bust. She hadn't dumped Ed, and he hadn't dumped her: there had been no specific dumpage. She was marooned in the fog of a dissolving relationship, and that is a dispiriting, confusing place to be. Billie might never see Ed again, or he might saunter in tomorrow and suggest a kebab.

With one hand on the tape measure and the other on her phone, Billie redialled yet again: she needed to see Ed in order to tell him she never wanted to see him again.

Standing patiently in line, waiting for Mr Dyke to finish flirting with a woman bent over on two sticks and sporting a pre-war, microwave-sized hearing aid, Billie had high hopes for the Scotch egg in her sights. Lolling on its chaise longue of cress, that egg didn't know it yet, but it was going to make her Feel Better: a task beyond the brisk sales in the shop, the sun splitting the trees outside, and Dot's call to East Coast FM's *Chit-chat With Charlie* posing as a Zambian cross-dresser.

A talon dug into her shoulder. Billie span round to meet Zelda, eyeball to evil eyeball.

'Haven't seen you for a while, love.' Zelda raised her drawn-on brows. 'You avoiding old Zelda?' She tittered hoarsely, as if this was a ludicrous premise.

'No, no,' Billie tittered back. 'Just been busy with the shop.'

'You haven't had a nibble of my special fudge.' Zelda slowly tweaked open the small paper bag, and insinuated it under Billie's nose. 'Everybody's mad about it. The whole town's under its spell.' She waggled the bag.

It might have been Billie's imagination, but Zelda seemed to be watching her more closely than one human offering another human a sweet might be expected to. Close up her eyes were bright, and youthful, with clear whites and a steady focus.

'I'm on a diet.' Billie had her fib ready.

'Really?' Zelda looked down at Billie's jeans. 'Might be for the best.' She folded over the bag, and said, 'Another time.'

'Still no sign of Jake,' said Billie, boldly.

'Wouldn't be the end of the world if he never came back.' Zelda didn't take her eyes from Billie's as she put the fudge back in her apron pocket. 'Would it?'

A shout of 'Next!' from the counter saved Billie from answering. Her saviour wasn't Mr Dyke, but a peachy-looking boy of about nineteen with a cap of indie curls.

'My grandson, Darius,' explained Mr Dyke. 'He was born into meat. He'll look after you.'

Darius dissuaded Billie from the Scotch egg she had her eye on, pointing to the one behind it. 'Much fuller shape. The bread-crumbs are crispier.'

Liking a boy who gave snacks the attention they deserved, Billie warmed to Darius.

'That Dot,' he said abruptly as he was tenderly wrapping her Scotch egg. 'She got a boyfriend or what?'

Unsure how to answer – possibly with a 'Yes, but he's in this lady's pocket' – Billie narrowed her eyes. 'Why?'

''Cos she's the prettiest thing in Sole Bay, that's why.' Darius was as forthright about romance as he was about meat products.

Pushing rudely past Billie, and almost knocking the other customer off her walking sticks, Zelda rapped on the high glass

278

counter, and hissed, 'You keep that pup of yours away from our Dot, Dyke.'

'Ah, Zelda,' said Mr Dyke indulgently. 'Boys will be boys.'

'You have,' Billie teased Dot, wiping crumbs off her wand. 'You've got an admirer. And he stands to inherit the Dyke meat millions.'

'Oh shush,' said Dot, teasing her hair in front of her face. 'He's only a kid.'

'He's a bloody big kid.' Billie recalled the large hands dealing so gently with her comestible. 'You could do worse.'

'I'm spoken for.' Dot grimaced. 'Or am I?'

'Look at the two of us.' Billie managed a hollow laugh. 'Neither of us knows where we stand with our men, and here we are, flogging wedding dresses.'

'I thought Jake was the one.' Dot pursed her lips. 'Now I don't even know where he is.' Dot had dropped the nonchalance and now looked more or less anxious at all times. She turned to Billie, as if she'd just had a eureka moment. 'You do, though! You know exactly where your runaway is. There's no need for you to suffer like me. Go to the fire station. You have a right to speak to him. And I bet he has an explanation.' Seeing Billie's doubtful expression, she backtracked. 'Well, OK, not an explanation. But he might make you feel a bit better.'

The Scotch egg certainly hadn't managed it. 'You're right.' Billie stood up, and kissed Dot on the top of her head. 'I'm off to nab me a fireman.'

Déjà vu of an unpleasant kind assailed Billie as she crossed the neurotically neat lawn in front of the ugly modern fire station. The last time she'd visited Ed here, he'd been across town, busy between her friend's legs. Loitering outside, she looked up at the tall windows of the recreation room. Ed had pointed them out to her, describing how the watch spent their time there, waiting for emergencies.

The door in the side of the building clanged open, spitting out two men in the navy-blue firefighting basics. Chatting animatedly, they took a short cut along the lawn. One of them was patting his pockets in search of cigarettes. He found them just as Billie, swallowing hard, approached them.

Shyly, she asked, 'Excuse me. Do you know Ed? Is he on duty?'

'Treacle?' laughed the bloke putting a cigarette to his lips. 'Everyone knows Treacle. Yeah. He's on.' He stopped suddenly. 'At least, I think he's on.' He turned to the man beside him, who had found something of great interest down on the grass. 'Is Treacle in there?'

'No idea,' snapped his colleague without looking up.

'Could you do me a big favour?' asked Billie nervously, aware that her face and demeanour simply screamed 'chucked bird'. 'Could you tell him Billie's here to see him?' This eggy conversation was already embarrassing but it held the potential to become memorably humiliating: like chucked birds all through history she helped it on its way.

'Course.' Putting his unlit cigarette regretfully back in the packet, the man hurried back into the fire station, leaving Billie with his colleague, who seemed intent on a forensic analysis of his toes.

In no time at all the door swung open again, and Billie, hopeful despite her fears, suppressed a groan when her messenger reappeared alone.

'I was wrong,' he said, too loudly. 'No sign of him. Sorry, love.' He looked sorry. He looked sympathetic.

Instead of helping, his sympathy made Billie feel like a tinker begging for coins. 'Never mind, I'll catch him later,' she said, as brightly as she could manage, even adding a cheery, if trembling, 'Thanks!' before she sauntered off, delivering an unconvincing portrait of a girl who didn't care.

Bruised shins, a battered heart, and a brain stuffed with clamouring problems like a nest full of starving chicks, Billie lugged her laptop along the lane to Sam's cottage. His computer had 'gone apeshit' and Billie had offered him the use of her little machine.

Opening the gate to the manicured front garden, Billie spotted Sam sunbathing on the emerald-green grass, its glossy perfection suspiciously unaffected by the hose-pipe ban which caused Dot guilty torments about brushing Jenkins's teeth.

'How do,' he called, in a terrible northern accent.

'Where do they sell knickers that small?' Billie couldn't tear her eyes away from the tiny black strip that was somehow containing Sam's machinery. 'Are they made by elves?'

'These are not knickers, thank you very much.' Sam sounded affronted. 'I'm wearing two hundred quid's worth of Versace swimwear.' He sat up, his brown torso glistening with tanning lotion. 'Any word from Ed?'

'Ed who?' said Billie, passing him and letting herself into the cottage.

The interior was dim after the brightness of the late afternoon outside. Billie made for the kitchen, and hoisted the computer on to a granite island bigger than her first flat. 'I went to the fire station,' she told Sam sheepishly, as he padded in after her, flip-flops slapping on the ceramic tiles.

'Oh dear. Something tells me he didn't run out and smother you in a thousand tiny kisses.' Sam took a bottle of sparkling water from the huge fridge and glugged it straight from the bottle.

'His mates pretended he wasn't there.' Billie's body executed a kind of Mexican wave of shame. 'It was one of the worst moments of my life, right up there with a vaginal scrape.' She ostentatiously looked away from Sam. '*Please* cover yourself up. Those Versaces are a little too graphic for my taste.'

'A bit of willy never hurt anybody,' grumbled Sam, reaching for a waffle dressing gown slung over a designer kitchen stool. The dream cottage was as messy as a stripper's dressing room. 'It's time to give up with the calls, and the turning up at his work, Billie-dillie.' His eyes fixed hers. 'It's dangerous out there. We've got to roll with the punches. You'll drive yourself mad if you keep looking for answers and reasons and explanations.'

Pretending to concentrate on the computer screen, Billie said, 'I can't just walk away. It's unfinished business.'

'Life is full of unfinished business,' argued Sam. He relished debate, and would never let Billie have the last word. 'My God, Ed comes out of this looking like the perfect gent compared to the way I've chucked blokes in the past.' He leaned against the costly worktop, remembering. 'One guy fell asleep in a cab and

281

I just got out at the lights. Poor little Manolito turned up at my flat to discover I'd sublet to Mormons. The Greek guy I shagged for a fortnight in the nineties couldn't track me down because he thought my name was Cedric Tattybye.' A smile played on his lips. 'Do you hate me yet?'

'No, Cedric, I don't,' laughed Billie. 'But I should. Those are people's hearts you're playing with.'

'Nah.' Sam shook his white-blond head. 'I only play with other parts of their anatomy. I've heard some of your stories, young lady. Don't come on like Mother Teresa in lippy. I know you've trampled on feelings before and never looked back.'

'And karma got me, fair and square.' Billie's face crumpled. 'I was enjoying being normal again. Being part of the human race. And now it's all been whisked away.'

'All?' Sam sounded testy. 'I'm here. Dot, God bless her irritating little hen-loving ways is still here. The shop is here. You're down one fireman who couldn't keep his cock in his underpants: good riddance.'

'But having a boyfriend again was reassuring, as if I was a fully paid-up Earthling again, after months of living as a freak,' whined Billie. She could hear the wheedling note in her voice but was powerless to do anything about it.

'Listen to you,' snapped Sam, evidently unmoved by his friend's desolate expression. 'You sound just like one of those needy, self-deluding women you rant on about.'

'Don't expect me to make sense right now,' whinged Billie, 'I'm going through emotional trauma.'

'Your pride is hurt. Your libido is disappointed. But your heart isn't broken, so don't come the emotional trauma bit with me.'

'Where are the hugs? The *you're too good for him*?' Billie was almost shouting. 'What kind of a gay best friend are you?'

'The real kind, Billious,' laughed Sam, his face all good humour again. 'What are you typing?'

'Just a quick email before I hand this over to you.' Billie had planned to bash out a refusal to pay a cancellation fee to the man who owned the plumed horses, but talking about Ed had changed her mind. Instead she'd composed a few angry lines to James.

The fireman has shat on me from a great height with your lovely friend, Jackie. Thank you sooooo much for introducing us. Not.

'There. All yours.'

'Ta. I've got to scan my latest drawings and send them to my editor.'

'Can I see them?' asked Billie, hopefully.

'No,' said Sam flatly. 'It's bad enough drawing the little sod without watching people go all gaga over him.'

'And you and Tiddlywinks were getting on *so* well in the bookshop the other day.'

If she was trying to provoke a response from Sam, Billie was disappointed: Sam was beyond shame, had left it behind some years ago, along with his morals. 'Look, Billie.' Sam was suddenly serious, draping an arm around her shoulders. 'I know what it's like to miss things. I don't mean my exes, and I certainly don't mean my family, who all made the sign of the cross and backed away brandishing garlic when I came out. I miss my life back in London, the pace of it, the excitement of it, the down and dirty flavour of it. And you've helped me with those feelings.'

'How?' asked Billie, leaning against Sam and liking the solid feel of his body.

'By being your delightful, awful, contradictory, soft-as-butter self. You've made this whole hideous rural idyll bearable. And if it's hugs you want—' Sam folded her into his dressing gown and squeezed tightly. 'How's that?'

'Nice,' smiled Billie. 'Got any food?' She longed to be the sort of girl who can't face a bite during times of stress, but adversity made her hungry. As did happiness. As did boredom. As did being awake.

Over a supper of crisps and a Chocolate Orange in the conservatory, Billie outlined her fears about Jake's sugary fate.

'This is less realistic than *Murder She Wrote*,' scoffed Sam. 'Don't be such a fucking moron,' he advised, robustly.

'You explain the shallow grave and the bundle on the ground,' challenged Billie, 'and the mysterious secret ingredient. She's corrupting Sole Bay, turning us all into cannibals.'

Deadpan, Sam mused, 'From anybody else that might sound far-fetched.' He tapped and unwrapped a second chocolate fruit. 'Does this count as one of our five a day, by the way? I love the detail about the blood dripping down her arms. That'll look fabulous on the *Crimewatch* reconstruction. Oooh.' A thought struck him. 'Who will play you when they make the movie? And don't say Kate Winslet.'

'As if.' Billie had been just about to suggest Kate Winslet.

'Don't lose any sleep over this, doll. If you're going to lose sleep, do it over something worthwhile, like the probability of dying alone, your bones gnawed by cats.'

'I do love our little chats.'

'For you,' Billie heard a deep voice saying down in the shop, and got to the bottom step just in time to see Darius Dyke handing a bouquet to Dot.

It was a lovely tableau, the strapping young lad offering a love token to the dainty young woman. But then Dot recoiled with a heartfelt 'Oh yuk!'

The bouquet was a wrapped selection of meats. A scarlet lamb chop nestled among a sausage or two, and a turkey drumstick, all tied up in a red bow.

Intervening, Billie told the puzzled Darius, 'Dot's a vegetarian. A committed one.'

'Oh.' Darius seemed lost for words, as if he'd never encountered such eccentricity.

Still looking away, Dot managed to say, 'It was a kind thought.'

As Darius left, his chop drooping, Billie advised quietly, 'Why not go the conventional route next time, and try a bunch of roses?'

'What kind of woman prefers a rose to a sausage?' marvelled Darius, heading back next door.

'Virtually every kind of woman,' Billie called after him. Coming back in, she dissolved into giggles with Dot. 'Lucky you, though. Another gentleman caller already.'

Her giggles braked when she saw the distress on Dot's face. 'I don't want any other man, I want my man. Oh Billie, I'm starting to worry now. It's been so long.'

'He'll be back,' said Billie, hoping she sounded convincing. Dot's pining face, so woebegone when she let her guard down, haunted her. When should Billie speak up? When should she tell the police about the cigar-shaped hump in Zelda's yard, now sprouting a fine crop of tall weeds?

Thirty-one

'You probably recognise me,' said the plump man hopefully, edging in front of his bride-to-be. They were the first customers of the day.

Ever helpful, Dot asked, 'Weren't you once in charge of recycling at Tesco?'

With a look of consternation, the bride-to-be, the victim of an inept lip-plumping technician, snorted, 'I don't think so, love! He's Charlie Little.'

This had the desired effect. Both Dot and Billie, who had been lost in separate, miserable worlds all morning, perked up at the name. '*Chit-Chat with Charlie*!' squealed Dot, clapping her hands for euphoric punctuation.

'Your servant, ladies.' Charlie bowed low, showing his bald patch. His Hawaiian shirt was tucked into his lemon leather shorts, and his small, clever eyes were disguised behind the smoky lenses of glasses as big as two television sets. 'Signed pics?'

The girls took one each, strangely excited to own a 10 x 4 black and white shot of Charlie with a bare chest and what looked like a squirrel skin stretched over it.

'You get us through the day,' Billie told him, admiringly.

'Oh be still my beating heart.' Charlie staggered backwards. 'That's music to my ears, ladies. We all wanna spread happiness, don't we?'

'Can we get on?' His fiancée had evidently spread enough happiness and now preferred to spread a little tension. 'I've a seaweed wrap at eleven.'

'Of course, my love.' Charlie turned to Billie and Dot. 'I heard you were the best, so Kiki and I made a beeline for Billie's Brides.' Charlie leaned in, and so did Billie and Dot. 'There's a mention in it for you if you look after us,' he promised with a wink.

'Thank you.' Billie sized up Kiki, who could give Sam a masterclass in looking insultingly bored. Crushed velvet, she guessed. Low cut. She'll say she's a fourteen and we'll have to let all the seams out.

'Look after her, girls,' begged Charlie. 'She's my diamond. She's my rock. She's my harbour in the storm. When this crazy world of fame gets too much, she keeps my feet on the ground.'

Compulsively, Billie looked down at Charlie's feet in scuffed Scholls. He had a hammer toe, she noted. 'We all need a rock,' she said, sagely. It surprised Billie to hear that Charlie's fame as a DJ on a small provincial radio station could be a burden. 'Will it be a big wedding?'

Gravely, Charlie told her, 'It'll be the hottest celebrity shindig since the reopening of Shady Ladies in 2006. And they had three *Big Brother* contestants at that, you know.' He tapped his nose, and said, in a mysterious way, 'I'm not promising anything, but if I say Les and Dennis, do you get my drift?'

'Yes,' said Billie, adding a, 'wow,' as it seemed called for.

'Ah now,' said Dot thoughtfully, evidently glad to be able to re-enter the conversation with her idol. 'He *did* run the re-cycling at Tesco, didn't he?'

Dot was biting her nails as Billie put down the phone. 'Did he say yes?' she asked, tight with fear.

'Finally,' said Billie. Her shoulders sagged. The consultant had taken some convincing that Annie's situation merited a hospital wedding, and without his say-so it couldn't happen.

Dot sagged with relief. 'You're a genius!' she told Billie.

Billie picked up the phone again. All her calls today were daunting ones. Now she had to negotiate a way out of the hefty cancellation fee that the owner of the white horses she'd booked for Heather's wedding was demanding. She didn't dial his number, though. On impulse she dialled Heather's, knowing that she'd get the answerphone as she had the countless other times she'd tried. She had a special invite for the runaway bride.

Very few of Debs' hair extensions were still in. From the back she looked a little like Raven, during an attack of the mange. Tired of belittling customers, she was out in the kitchenette making tea. Billie could hear her nattering to Dot, and risked a hearty, 'Where's my cuppa?'

Emerging from the back of the shop with a mug in her hands, Debs said, loudly and quite slowly, 'What on earth is that up the tree outside?'

Crossing to the window, Billie peered up into the tree, an overgrown specimen outside Dyke's. 'I can't see anything.'

'Oh my God!' gasped Dot, coming up behind Debs. 'It's Raven. Poor Raven. He's stuck up the tree!'

Next door's arthritic old cat hadn't been around for a while, and Billie doubted that he could make it up a tree. 'I still can't see him.'

'Look!' persisted Dot, waggling a finger. 'There!'

'Yes!' Debs nudged her, and Billie went flying into the window display. 'There.'

'You're not pointing at the same spot,' puzzled Billie.

'I'll get the ladder,' said Debs, very decisively for a girl who usually shirked lifting anything heavier than her eyebrows.

The three of them stepped out into Little Row, which was in shade at this time of the day. 'Still can't see him,' complained Billie.

Plonking the ladder against the trunk, Dot motioned to her to step on it.

'Why me?' asked Billie. She distrusted Raven. The spitting, cursing, malodorous frightwig would probably sink a claw in her jugular if she tried to manhandle him down from a tree.

'I'm having my period,' confided Dot, as if this devastating physical condition excused her anything more demanding than walking upright.

'And I'm scared of heights.' Debs wasn't scared of pit bull terriers, chlamydia or stealing from under her boss's nose, but she couldn't face climbing a ladder.

'Oh alright.' Billie, weakened by the thumps life had doled out over the past few days, couldn't be bothered to fight. She clambered awkwardly up the ladder, her wings waggling. 'Where is the little sod?' she asked, squinting into the mass of greenery.

'Go to the top of the ladder,' shouted Dot. 'And then he's on the end of that thick branch. Yes!' she encouraged. 'That one. Just ease yourself on to it.'

That was easier said than done. The ladder wobbled as Billie reached out for the bumpy branch, sticking out from the tree's carcass. 'Ohhhhh God,' she muttered, swinging a leg inelegantly over the rough extended arm. Straddling it, she looked down and mewled. The tops of Debs and Dot's heads were a long way away. 'I still can't see him,' she said, but shakily this time. With a shriek, she squealed, 'What are you doing?'

'Nothing,' said Dot innocently, as she and Debs grappled the ladder away.

'I need that to get down!' Billie pointed out the obvious, holding on to her branch as if it was a runaway stallion. 'Debs!' she yelled, as she saw her Saturday girl stab the same digit three times on her phone, and a penny dropped loud enough to be heard at sea. 'Don't!'

'Fire brigade,' Debs was saying into her phone. 'Could you come quickly please? There's a cat stuck up a tree on Little Row.' She looked up at Billie, her eyes full of wicked pleasure. 'And hurry. Poor dumb pussy's in a right state.'

'Your shout, Treacle!' yelled Chugger, who leapt off the fire engine before the others and had the first look up the tree.

Up among the leaves, Billie straddled her branch, her bum now familiar with every knot and bump. Back straight, lips thin, she was attempting to hold on for dear life while appearing carefree, relaxed: as if she preferred to spend part of every afternoon high up in a tree.

There was the thud of a ladder against the trunk, and the yobbish laughter of Ed's delighted mates. Then her branch swayed in rhythm to Ed's feet as he climbed the rungs. Billie shook her hair (which was unwashed) and licked her lips (which were unglossed) and steeled herself. They were about to have her long-awaited little chat.

Refusing to look at him, preferring to be mesmerised by a distant leaf, Billie only faced Ed when he said flatly, 'You're not a cat.'

Slowly turning to meet his gaze, she was reminded just how brown his eyes were. 'You're a hound, though,' she said. More sad than satirical, she sighed. 'This wasn't my idea.'

'Really?' Ed seemed sceptical.

'Yes, really.' Affronted, Billie shifted on the knotty bark. 'I'm not desperate, Ed. I mean, I know I turned up at the fire station and everything, but—'

Cutting her short, Ed said, 'I'm sorry about that. That was low of me.'

'Yeah.' Billie readily agreed with him. 'It was.' She paused. 'Did you care about me at all, Ed?' The question shocked her: she'd planned to lead up to it with subtlety and finesse. Perhaps the splinters in her behind had travelled to her brain.

Feet firmly planted on the ladder in his heavy steel-toe-capped boots, Ed gave a tiny sigh, and leaned on her branch, resigned. His arm, brown and taut, rested inches from her. Billie tried not to stare at it. It looked as good as cream horns do during a diet: a few days ago she could have reached out and bitten it, or stroked it, or written her name on it (a favourite trick of hers); but today it was out of bounds.

'Well, did you?' she asked again.

'Don't start,' said Ed, morosely.

'Eh?' Flabbergasted, Billie became shrill. 'What did you expect? That I'd just shrug? Say *oh well, never mind*? You're going to have to put up with some "girl speak", mate. I slept with you, I trusted you and you lied to me, over and over again.' In her agitation, Billie wobbled on the branch and had to reach out to steady herself.

'You make it sound so dramatic.' Ed was as still as if he was made of stone.

Had he changed personality in the days since she'd seen him? Billie was amazed by his detachment: Ed looked bored, as if he was watching a documentary about the EU. Maybe lust had deceived her and he'd always been this cold. 'I happen to think it *is* dramatic.' Billie hated the way she turned snooty in an argument. 'What you did was unforgivable. Don't you realise how hurt I am?'

Ed didn't answer. 'Keep your voice down. My mates are lapping all this up.'

'Ed!' It was like talking to a small boy about a broken window. 'I need some answers. Why did you—' Billie stopped short of accusing him of breaking her heart: he wasn't guilty of that. 'Make a fool of me?'

Simmering, Ed spoke impatiently, as if the truth was so obvious that she was daft to ask. 'Because it was there. It was on a plate. I didn't have to lift a finger.' Eyes down, examining the gnarls on the tree, Ed let the story out in a rush. 'After the disco, when you weren't coming across, I looked in at the lock-in, and Jackie came over like a guided missile. She was all over me.'

Until that moment Billie wouldn't have believed that she would stick up for Jackie. 'So it's all her fault. You couldn't say no?'

'I'm a man,' he said, simply.

'Not every man would have taken her up.'

'You sure about that?' asked Ed, cynically. 'She's a persuasive girl.'

'I'm sure.' There and then, Billie decided to hunt down Bonnie Tyler, and have a quiet word with her about her strategy. Billie had Held Out For A Hero and she'd got a goat. 'My hero,' she snorted.

'I told you I wasn't one of them,' said Ed, impatiently. 'You wouldn't listen.'

'Oh. Of course. Now it's my fault.' With mock gravity, Billie hung her head. 'I'm so sorry.' She jerked her head up and met those gorgeous eyes again. 'Remember that word?'

Biting his lip for a moment, Ed said evenly, 'I *am* sorry. I wish I'd done things differently. But I didn't.'

'Did you enjoy it, two girls at once?' Billie couldn't stop herself. 'Was she better than me?'

'Billie, don't talk like that.' Ed looked as if he had a pain in just about every soft bit of himself. 'Look, does it have to be over?'

'Which script are you reading from?' spluttered Billie. Despite her heartache, despite being further off the ground than she would like, she wanted to laugh. He'd told more lies than Billie had at Weight Watchers, he'd trashed an important friendship, and he'd avoided her as if *she* was the villain of the piece. 'Does it have to be over?' she repeated incredulously, running out of steam even as she said it.

'OK. Dumb question.' Ed held out his arms and the gesture brought tears to Billie's eyes: it no longer meant what it used to. 'Ready? We're wasting the guys' time.'

Once upon a time, Billie would have placed a fireman's lift in her top three ways to travel. Now, she tensed as Ed gave her clear, professional instructions on how to inch along the branch towards him.

Into his arms she slid, tucking herself over his shoulder. A small cheer went up from Debs and Dot at the foot of the ladder. Billie blinked a hot tear from her lashes. Those strong hands were touching her for the last time.

Back in the shop, Dot watched Billie like a researcher studying a child recently returned from living amongst wolves. Even Debs was silent, sullenly picking diamanté from one of the more expensive handbags.

There were many phone calls still to make about Heather and Dean's wedding, and Billie made them mechanically. She was shipwrecked again, her cynicism vindicated. Batty Billie was an outsider once more. She caressed the silky mahogany of the counter while another supplier spoke darkly of deposits on the other end of the line. She should have stayed true to her first Sole Bay love: the shop hadn't let her down.

The bag of fish and chips was pleasingly warm against the crook of her arm as she passed the burned-out tea shop on her way home. It was boarded up now, smutty and ruined. Billie walked determinedly past. She wouldn't think about him. It was over now. She could achieve closure.

Closure schmlosure. She'd never even heard the bloody word until about ten years ago. How did people cope before closure? Victorians hadn't had closure, Henry VIII hadn't sought it. It was highly elusive, even when your ex had admitted to you, up a tree, that he'd been introducing his rude bits to your friend's rude bits on a regular basis.

Instead of closure, she had sought chips. Even chips had their painful memories, reminding her of the many bags she'd shared with the man Debs now referred to as the Sole Bay Shagger. Chips, she felt sure, wouldn't let her down.

As she approached Herbert, she saw somebody tall and man-shaped nip up on to the veranda, round the far side facing the sea. Speeding up, she concocted a short speech designed to see off Ed. Yesterday his sudden appearance would have thrilled her, but now it fanned the flames of her indignation.

'Sly!' The bulky stranger was her brother.

'I took your advice.' Sly dispensed with hello's. 'And here I am.'

'You don't mean Sana threw you out?' Shock brought Billie's hand to her mouth.

'As soon as she took the call from the bank, I was history.'

'Hang on.' Billie cocked her head. 'So she found out from the bank?'

'Well,' Sly's look of discomfort was so rare that he was unrecognisable until he reinstated his smug expression. 'As soon as the bank told her it was withdrawing credit and calling in the overdraft, I sat her down and told her everything.'

'As soon as you had no choice, in other words.' Shaking her head, she opened the door. 'Get in, you big lummox.'

It became clear that Sly was properly broke: not the half-fat version that still allows one to cavort through Top Shop with a credit card. Sly had no money at all, and owed plenty.

Swiftly thinking this through, Billie realised that she now had a six foot two house guest. Like buses, woes come along all at once: suddenly Herbert was a terminus.

'So I can stay? Just until I get on my feet?'

Billie glanced down at those feet. They took up most of the floor. 'Of course,' she said kindly, suppressing a scream. 'What about your sideline? Spartakiss?' Her attempt at a straight face was a valiant one.

'I gave that up,' said Sly curtly. 'It's not a job for the faint-hearted.' He shuddered. 'Hen nights . . . there are things men shouldn't know.' He looked around the beach hut, critically. 'No telly? Where's the loo? I can't see the door to the bedroom.'

Explaining gently that this was it, that there was no mezzanine level, or basement garage, Billie noticed how tired her brother looked. Usually he had that glossy, filmed-through-gauze look of American TV stars. Even his hair was floppy and disheartened. 'Hungry?' She held out her warm package. Greater love hath no sister than she lay down her chips for the man who used to call her Floss Head.

Taking the packet, Sly opened them up. 'Haven't you got any quinoa? Or something low carb?'

'Eat the chips, Slightly,' said Billie, in a menacing tone.

Lanterns off, difficult conversations over, Billie wished she could locate the mute switch for her teeming brain. A Nigel away in the bed, Sly was hunched like a small mountain range in the blue gloom. She'd been surprised when he'd accepted her offer of the bed. Perhaps she brought out the ungallant side of the men in her life. It had crossed her mind to throw herself on Sam's mercy, and use one of his opulently appointed spare rooms, but Billie suspected that Sly had come to her for more reasons than the purely practical. He'd flown to his little sister for security and sanctuary: she owed it to him to stay close. Sleep was going to be tricky.

Tears had been queuing all day, since Ed had appeared, real, touchable and smelling soooo good, up her tree. She couldn't indulge herself now. Sly was downcast enough without nodding off to his sister's sobs. She stoppered the tears, and tried to lose herself in the chanting of the sea.

'It's far too hot for a leather jacket,' Billie chided Sam when he dropped in to return her computer.

'A leather jacket is a state of mind.' Sam turned his collar up. 'It's never too hot for one.'

'Not if you're a narcissistic poser who thinks he's Spike from *Buffy the Vampire Slayer*, I suppose,' smiled Billie. She appreciated Sam more than ever now. He proved that there was life beyond relationships. With him around, Billie didn't stick out like a sore thumb. 'Did your editor like the drawings?'

'Loved them.' Sam mimed vomiting. 'Particularly the one where Tiddlywinks kisses all the other toys on the bed and says "nighty night".'

'Oh, that sounds so sweet!' sang Dot, oblivious to Sam's feelings.

'Drink tonight?' suggested Billie. 'Many drinks? Too many drinks? Far, far too many drinks?'

'I'm going to use an unusual word here.' Sam carefully enunciated, 'No.'

'I demand to see the real Sam Nolan immediately,' gasped Billie.

'Deadline, Billita.'

Absorbing this new and unpalatable professionalism, Billie saw Sly approaching the door. 'You can meet my brother.'

'Do I have to?' said Sam, predictably.

He did have to, because Sly burst in at that moment, with some of his old bravado. 'The fudge from the lady next door is quite exemplary,' he said, his face creased with admiration. 'Try some.'

Backing away, Billie shook her head. 'It's very bad for you,' she muttered.

'Is it the secret recipe?' An evil glint lit up Sam's eye as he took a square. 'Mmmmm!' he enthused, savouring it ostentatiously. 'I'd kill for that taste.'

As Dot reached out her hand, the grotesque possibilities became too much for Billie. 'Don't!' she yelped, slapping away Dot's hand.

Leaping back, Dot yanked her hand away from Billie. 'Why did you do that?'

'Yes, Billie, *why*?' echoed Sam, enjoying himself enormously.

'It's fattening. And it's a sin to eat between meals,' gabbled Billie. Only Sam would know that she was thinking, *And it contains bits of your beardy boyfriend.*

Fixing his sister with a presidential look, Sly said sorrowfully, 'Do you and Dot need to revise some of the trust exercises we explored during the Inner Winner seminar?'

'No,' said Billie, quickly. 'I'm sorry, Dot. I just didn't want you to . . . feel sick.'

'That's OK,' said the saintly Dot. 'I suppose I am overeating.' She looked uncomfortable as she added, 'I'm missing Jake, to be honest.'

As Billie knew he would, Sam leapt right in with a solicitous, 'In a funny way, do you feel closer to him when you eat fudge?'

'Out.' Billie held the door open. 'You've got a deadline.'

As Sam left, Sly said thoughtfully, 'You've got some work to do on your leadership style, sis.'

Humbly, Billie agreed. And gave him fifty pence pocket money for the afternoon.

A handful of emails waited to be read. An old sales-company colleague was announcing the double whammy of getting engaged and having breast implants, developments that had left her workmates reeling, but had little impact on Billie in her current frame of mind. The message from Jackie was erased without reading it. The last one was from James.

> Typical. Even hundreds of miles away, your latest disaster is my fault. I'd forgotten how it feels to be responsible for everything, to be in the wrong twenty-four hours a day. Thank the sweet Lord we never got married.

There was no sign-off. No jaunty news. Not even a shred of sympathy. It sounded final.

And Billie deserved it. This was just another small right hook in the endless prize-fight of her emotional life. Stowing the computer and clattering down the bare stairs, she determined to put it behind her. She and James had enjoyed a brief reprise, and now it was over. Again. Given their history, it was inevitable. Sad, but inevitable. Like Scarlett O'Hara she would think about it tomorrow.

Thirty-two

Complaining about everything, requesting special meals, tutting at the legroom in the bed, Sly was not the perfect guest. He still had the demeanour of Lord Nelson even though his life was careering downhill like a three-wheeled shopping trolley. Billie was disappointed in her sister-in-law, and not only because she had ended up babysitting her own brother. Billie had expected Sana to be more committed to Sly. This was the 'for worse' bit the registrar had warned her about.

'Just another match made in Heaven that ended up in Hell,' thought Billie, resigned now to her pessimistic rants on marriage coming true.

It was Saturday. Seven days since Billie had slept in a bed, had a moment to herself, an evening with Sam, or an email from James.

She was ratty. Perhaps that is unfair to rats. Billie was more wounded hippo-y as she charged through Sole Bay's genteel streets to the shop. One sight of Dot's pale face, soiled with worry, cranked her stress up another notch or eight. Strapping on her wings, she asked menacingly, 'Debs late again?'

'Now, don't be too hard on her,' said Dot by way of reply.

'When am I ever hard on her?' Billie's voice rose an octave. 'She's late, she alienates custom, she steals the takings and won't make me a cup of tea, yet I barely tell her off.' She slammed the post around, binning yet another invitation to take out a Capital One card. 'Dot, you look terrible.' It came out more accusing than sympathetic: Billie was at boiling point.

'Oh dear. Sorry,' said Dot, woefully. 'I'm not sleeping well. The bed. It's too big.' She shrugged, and her shoulders looked narrow in her cheesecloth smock.

'Have you thought any more about . . .'

'The police?' Dot shook her head. 'It's too early. He'll be

somewhere. With someone.' With a tiny cough, Dot asked if they could stop talking about him. 'It's better that way.'

Guilt was closing its tentacles over Billie as if *she'd* been the one in the yard with the shovel and the maniacal laughter. Debs slouched in, mobile to her ear.

'You're late,' growled Billie, calling on her inner wounded hippo to face up to Debs. 'And today I want an explanation.'

Debs held up an imperious finger for Billie to wait until she'd finished on the phone.

With a sigh that parted Dot's hair, Billie tapped a flip-flop ostentatiously until Debs clicked her phone shut. 'Thank you,' said Billie acidly. 'Now are you going to tell me why you're late? Again?'

'Gotta go,' replied Debs, retracing her steps into the street. 'Man trouble.'

Billie's mouth dropped open. 'I don't believe it.' If she'd stopped to examine her anger, Billie might have surmised that Debs was simply the straw that broke the wedding-dress shop manageress's back, and not the real problem. But she didn't stop. She charged full speed ahead. 'OI! HEY!' she yelled after Debs, who jogged off down Little Row without turning back. Billie turned to Dot. 'Right. Where does she live?'

'Hang on,' said Dot, gravely. 'Don't be hasty.'

'Hasty!' yelped Billie. 'Dot. *Where does Debs live?*'

There was only one grotty shop in Sole Bay, and Debs' flat was over it. 'Honest Bob the Bookie' operated from a dark hole, lit by one fluorescent tube. The bored men inside, smoking roll-ups and concentrating on the television screens suspended from the damp ceiling, didn't even glance at Billie as she barged through the godforsaken room and up the stairs at the rear.

'Debs!' she shouted, as she banged on the knockerless door. 'It's Billie.'

The door opened a centimetre or so, and a narrow slab of outraged Debs showed itself. 'What you doing here?' she demanded. 'I'm busy.'

'You should be busy at work,' spat Billie, weeks of frustration spewing out. 'Man trouble? Man bloody trouble? What kind of excuse is that to walk out?'

'I suppose you better come in and meet my man.' Sullenly, Debs took the chain off the damaged door, and preceded Billie into the room that constituted her flat.

It was very untidy, and very drab. The curtains at the sash windows were yellowing with age, and the carpet was past retirement age. Brightly coloured building bricks provided a splash of innocent colour on a rug in the middle of the floor.

'This is Zac.' Debs bent down and scooped up the rolypoly one-year-old. 'He's my man.' She playfully nipped his nose. 'And you give me no end of trouble, don't cha?'

Silenced, Billie stared at Zac. Gurgling and giggling, he cheered up the miserable room. 'I didn't know,' said Billie, uneasily.

'Why should you?' replied Debs, not unpleasantly. 'He's my business.' She bit her lip, before saying, 'He's got what they call separation issues. Doesn't like to leave me. Since he was born, you see, it's been me and him. His Dad ...' Debs shrugged, as she sat on the arm of a sagging armchair. 'Not interested. My family are hopeless. Bunch of drunks. So we're a pair, aren't we, Zac?' Zac said 'ploop' or similar, and Debs carried on, not looking at Billie, who stood like a totem pole. 'At college he goes in the crèche four days a week, but on Saturdays he goes next door to my mate. But he doesn't always settle. And she's not exactly patient with him, so I have to rush back.'

Replaying her history with Debs in the light of this development, Billie murmured, 'That's why you left the hen night?'

'Yup.'

Studying Zac, Billie guessed who his father was. Those ears could only be the gift of the Dumbo-like tearaway she saw attempting unsuccessful wheelies on his BMX along the front every other day. 'What are you studying at college?' she asked, sinking on to a pouffe that farted in an affronted manner.

The answer wasn't Belligerence, as Billie suspected. 'Childcare.'

Another surprise. This burly girl, with her glitter pumps and her barely there denim mini, was full of them. Billie shifted and the pouffe let out a long, slow hiss of distress. 'Listen, Debs. I know about the money.'

Debs' nostrils flared as she bent her head low over Zac. A sheen of sweat glistened on her visible flesh, which was extensive. 'What money?' she challenged.

There was no turning back: surely Debs wouldn't headbutt her in front of a baby? 'The money you've been taking from the till.'

Debs turned a flushed, angered face to her, reminding Billie of a bull about to charge. Oh God, she thought, I'm wrong. I've just accused her of stealing and I'm wrong.

'I'm sorry, right?' shouted Debs. 'I'm sorry, I'm really sorry. I didn't set out to be a thief. It's not what I want for him.' She pressed Zac's head to her bosom and he squeaked. 'I just can't make ends meet. It's driving me mad. And he always needs something. And I won't let him have the childhood I had. No cuddles, no shoes, all the kids laughing because all I had was my school uniform.' Behind Zac's solid little head, she curled one hand into a fist. 'It's not fair.'

This outpouring set off a chain reaction in Billie. She'd come here to sack her surly, useless, maddening shop assistant. Now she sat here admiring Debs for her tenacity, and her courage. For being able to hold on to this grotty flat, for making sure there were some primary colours in it, for keeping Zac fit and healthy and secure. She felt almost envious of the chubby little boy, suffocating against his mother's boob tube: Zac knew he was loved.

'Listen, I've got an idea,' she began.

'Babs knew.' Billie had reassessed that 'keep an eye on Debs'. 'But she turned a blind eye. I think it was her way of helping.'

'I think your way is even better,' said Dot approvingly.

As expected, Dot had 'Oooh'ed and clapped her hands all the way through Billie's news. From now on, Debs would come in to the shop on Thursdays, her day off from college and, luckily, a busy-ish day at Billie's Brides. The extra money would ease her financial problems, and Zac would accompany her to work, where Dot and Billie would muck in to help with him. 'But she's not allowed to use the till,' Billie warned Dot. 'She knows that, and she's cool with it.'

'She's going to earn our trust,' beamed Dot, whose belief in happy endings was unshakeable, whatever the proof to the contrary.

'Only a few days to go,' said Billie to the figure in the bed.

Annie looked a little dazed, her white curls tossed. 'I can't quite believe it's really happening, to be honest.'

'Ooh, not getting cold feet, I hope.' Billie teased. The irony was lost on Annie, who hadn't heard The Story.

'It's an awful lot to do on one day,' worried Annie. The doctors had pronounced her fit enough to undergo the operation as planned, but she seemed frailer than when she'd gone into hospital. 'Will you drop in on Ruby if anything happens?'

That shorthand again. 'I'll be dropping in on both Mr and Mrs Wolff.' Billie was having no nonsense. Annie would be alright. She had to be.

'Wheeeeeeee!' shrieked Billie, her hair trailing from under the motorbike helmet. 'Whoooooooo!'

'SHUT UUUUUUUUUUUP!' bellowed Sam from the front seat, guiding his monster of a machine down a lane so leafy and green it might have been underwater.

They stopped at the end of a track, where the woods petered out and gave way to tussocky, tangled grass. The sea shimmered coyly in the distance, and the green slopes as far as the eye could see were a long, warm bath for the senses.

Stretching out beside Sam, Billie looked up at the taut, perfect blue sky and whispered dreamily, 'This is so beautiful.'

'If you like that sort of thing.' Sam's eyes, like fallen chips from the sky over them, closed. 'I prefer to look at scenery from a car. I like glass between me and the countryside. It's dangerous.'

'Says the man who has a steel reinforced door at home in Camden.'

'You know where you stand with a zonked-out drug dealer,' argued Sam. 'These bloody insects can be up your trouser leg in a flash.'

'Still pining for litter and junkies and the congestion charge?'

'I'm also pining for street-cleaning machines that wake you up at dawn. And neighbours who would just step over the mountain of milk bottles on your mat if you were murdered in your bed. And giggly eastern European boys who don't know the English for 'morals'. And that first kiss with some bloke you've never met before, and will never see again after a speedy exchange of bodily fluids.'

'What a charming picture you paint,' mused Billie sleepily. 'Until you finish the book you'll just have to put up with all this beauty and serenity.'

'And lack of available willy,' sighed Sam.

'And that,' agreed Billie.

After lying on their backs for a while, Billie said, in a small voice, 'I'm bored.'

'Of course you are.' Sam put his hands under his head. 'The countryside is dull. It's all a myth, that garbage about open spaces being good for you. I know what's good for me and it's illegal.'

'I wonder how Heather is,' said Billie, almost to herself.

'Thrashing about, spreading the pain,' said Sam, with notable lack of sympathy. 'God, she embarrassed me that day.'

'At the shop?' Billie smiled: the episode had been so Heather-ish. 'She was excited. She'd never met a real-life celebridee before.'

'No, when she offered me her body in the Sailor's Lament.'

Suddenly highly un-bored, Billie sat straight up, as if she was on a spring. 'Offered? Body? Lament?' she clucked.

'I told you.' Sam could be infuriating. 'Oh, I didn't? You're going to love this.' Sam sat up too, his face crinkled with evil amusement. 'I was having a tête à tête with a JD and Coke, trying to ignore the stares from across the room of our beardy friend, now Missing Believed Fudged. In saunters Heather, dressed to impress. Although the only people who'd be impressed would be heterosexuals who long to see a horse dressed as Mariah Carey. Don't look at me like that.' He threw a blade of grass at Billie. 'It was you who nicknamed her Seabiscuit, not me. Anyway, she's on her own, and she sits beside me. Buys me a drink. Asks me about myself. And I realise. I'm being chatted up.' Sam threw his hands in the air. 'Me! I haven't been chatted up by anybody with working nipples since I was a teenager. So I let her down gently.'

Wincing, Billie had to ask what Sam's version of letting a girl down gently was.

'"Heather," I said, "you're barking up the wrong cock."'

'Very gentle,' sighed Billie.

'I told her I was very flattered, but the female front bottom is my sexual equivalent of Disneyland: I've never been there and I can't begin to understand the people who have. She wasn't pleased.'

'I can imagine. You were destined to be her last big fling.'

'She told me. In amongst the tears. God, you girls are good at snot. She was like a burst pipe.'

'Were you nice to her? Did you comfort her?' asked Billie, warily.

'Of course. I'm not totally inhuman.' Sam seemed affronted. 'When she'd stopped crying and saying things in an incomprehensible, mucus-heavy way, she said she hoped we could be friends.'

'That's nice.' Billie could just imagine Heather's desperate face.

'I told her I didn't have a vacancy for a friend at the moment but if one came up I'd let her know.' Sam watched Billie's expression from the corner of his eye. 'I did warn you, back at the beginning. I'm not very nice, I said. I do what it says on the box.'

'It also says on the box that you're lovely to me.' Doling out a playful punch, Billie insisted he was. 'And besides, you're the only other fearless freedom fighter facing the world with a balanced view of love and its pitfalls.'

Scrambling to his feet, Sam nodded in the direction of the bike, and handed Billie her helmet. 'Don't go romanticising us, Billificacious. That's as bad as all those self-hypnotists wandering up the aisle. We're misfits, that's all. Misfits who happened to find each other.'

Thirty-three

True to his word, Chit-Chat Charlie name-checked the shop. 'This next tune is for Billie's Brides in Sole Bay. As some of you might know, I'm jumping the old broomstick, tying the old knot any day now. Did I tell you we're expecting one Mr L. Dennis to be in the congregation? He's a mate, he's a chum, he won't want any fuss. Hell of a nice guy. So, Billie, this one's for you. That lady is spreading a lot of happiness down there in Sole Bay, ladies and gennulmen.'

Barry Manilow filled the shop. 'Spreading happiness,' scoffed Billie.

'You are,' said Dot, in her passive, insistent way. 'Look at Debs, and Sly. You've certainly helped both of them. And you're looking after me.'

'No I'm not,' said Billie, gruffly.

'You think I don't notice?' laughed Dot. 'You change stations when a sad song comes on. You check up that I'm eating properly. You even manage to talk about Jake without giving me a lecture the way everybody else does.' Dot stuck out her chin. 'And I know you're suffering, as well. I know Ed left his mark.'

'But none of this is enough, is it?' Billie sounded waspish. 'Debs is still struggling. Sly is fading away. You're crying yourself to sleep every night.' Billie sighed. 'And love solves nothing. We chase it, thinking it will solve all our problems, but all it does is ladle more on top.' Even as she said it, Billie knew she was being unfair. It wasn't love that was at fault, it was Billie's clumsy way with it that caused the problems. She could recite that last email of James's as readily as the poems she'd learned by heart at school. His cool farewell whistled sadly round her heart, proving that she couldn't even rise to the occasion when given a second chance.

'If you really, truly believe that love solves nothing, why are we organising Annie and Ruby's wedding?'

'That's different. Get on with your work, Miss Dot,' ordered Billie with a stern look at her assistant.

It was Annie's big day. Bigger than the average wedding day, as she would be a bride in the morning, and the star of her own biopsy in the afternoon.

With the shop defiantly 'clossed', the bridesmaids took off in Dot's Reliant Robin, bulging carrier bags sliding about on the back seat, giving Jenkins the white-knuckle ride of his life in the glove compartment. 'I wish I felt happier,' complained Dot, as the car belched along, taking corners at an unfeasible angle on the road to Neeveston. 'This is such a wonderful day but . . .'

'I know.' Billie was holding her door shut by hanging on to the handle, trying not to care that their three-wheeler was cutting up a Saab on the hospital roundabout. 'There's a cloud hanging over us.' A big, murky, cancerous cloud that would hover over the ceremony, no matter how much they tried to ignore it.

All hospitals smell much the same: bleach; soap; fear. Neeveston General embraced them with sterile arms as they clattered down long linoleum corridors searching for the private room the conspiratorial nurses had somehow wangled for the day. The staff loved the tiny lady in the end bed who had a morbid fear of being 'trouble', and the story of her wedding had touched them all.

Armed with scrounged finery, pots of make-up and an unwieldy set of heated rollers, Billie felt like a guerrilla as she roamed the hospital, looking for the room where she would detonate her romance bomb. She found it, and they rushed in to kiss and hug and generally embarrass Annie.

'I don't want any fuss,' was her first line, with trademark modesty.

'Boy, are you in the wrong place,' laughed Billie. 'This room is now the world capital of fuss.' She knelt in front of Annie, upright in a wipe-clean wing chair. 'I'll be on hair.' She plugged in the rollers. 'Dot, you do nails.'

There was no champagne for this bride-to-be, no French manicure. Operating-theatre etiquette insisted on nil by mouth and clean nails, so Dot would just file and shape and buff.

'Nervous?' asked Billie.

'I'm far too old to be nervous,' said Annie, whose hands were shaking so much that Dot could barely file the nails. 'I hope Ruby's alright.'

Tweaking a curtain, Billie was able to reassure her. 'I can see him down on the lawn with his best man. They're smoking cigars the size of small trees.' Sam with his shades and his pointed boots and his wraparound misanthropy might have been an unusual choice for best man, but he'd leapt at the chance. His grey velvet suit had impressed Ruby, who'd studied the lapels carefully and pronounced them 'quality *schmutter*'. For reasons of his own, hinted at only with a moody, 'They're animals,' Ruby hadn't invited his family to the ceremony: Annie simply had none.

Apart, that is, from the raggle-taggle band that had closed ranks around her in this pastel-toned private room that looked like the best en suite in a mid-priced B&B. 'It's just blusher!' protested Billie, when Annie waved her brush away. 'Give in, woman.'

Head heavy with rollers like a chrysanthemum, Annie stood up to be buttoned into her gown. It was stiff and magnificent, each pleat perfect. The bride had shrunk since her fitting, and Billie felt as if she was dressing a child. She stepped back, standing alongside Dot to survey their charge.

Arms straight at her sides, Annie was silent and still, like a tiny statuette strayed from the top tier of a wedding cake. She looked afraid of this dress she'd fantasised about for decades. She also looked beautiful. Her parchment skin was enhanced by the sheen of the material, and her regal posture made the most of the gown's design.

'I've never seen such a lovely bride,' said Billie, glad that she never cried at weddings.

'Ohhh,' was all Dot could manage. 'Oh, Annie!'

Something seemed to be disturbing Annie as Billie back-combed her fluffy, rollered white hair into a respectable, Princess Anne-ish bouffant.

306

'Have we fulfilled the rhyme?' she asked, fearfully. 'Something old, something new?'

'Well, the dress is forty years old,' mused Billie. 'Your wedding ring is new.'

Dot lifted the veil: 'Borrowed,' she said.

'Oh dear. Where's the something blue?' Annie was wringing a tissue between her hands.

Wondering why an old rhyme should be so important, Billie had to confess that there was nothing blue. Dot scrabbled through the carrier bags, and even checked her own underwear, but she couldn't find a single blue item.

'I didn't take it seriously at my first wedding,' said Annie, agitated. 'Mother warned me I'd be sorry. And I was.'

Mother must have been a bundle of laughs. 'It's just a rhyme, Annie,' soothed Billie, pinning the veil carefully on to Annie's hair.

'Oh dear,' murmured Annie. 'Oh dear, dear, dear.' This was about as sweary as she would ever get.

Taking advantage of Annie's distraction to rub some pink stain on her thin lips, Billie glanced at her watch. 'Go get Ruby,' she commanded. 'Just got to get the headdress on and this vixen is ready to roll.'

'Do you think he'll like me?' whispered Annie, genuine fear in her voice, when Dot had taken off on oiled clogs.

'You'll take his breath away,' promised Billie, arranging the veil in powdery folds in front of Annie's anxious face. 'You look divine.'

The door opened, and Billie spun round with a happy, 'Ta daa!' which melted on her lips when she met the eyes of Annie's specialist, whose arm she'd twisted so mercilessly a few days earlier. 'Oh. Sorry. Thought you were the groom.'

The consultant stood staring at Annie, glowing in white and covered by a veil, as if she was the deliberate mistake in a puzzle. 'What . . . oh, of course. The bloody wedding,' he muttered.

'Obviously,' said Billie. 'She doesn't always dress like this.'

'I'll have to move this, um . . .' The doctor whipped back the veil. 'Say aah.'

Frowning, Billie asked, 'Do you have to do this now? The registrar is already late. He'll be here any minute.'

Impatiently, the doctor replied, 'This lady is having an operation later. Would you rather I didn't check her over?' He had finished shining his tiny torch down Annie's throat and was now pointing it into her eyes, smudging the careful eye shadow Billie had just applied.

'No, of course not,' acquiesced Billie, ungraciously. It was uncomfortable watching Annie being examined, and brought the spongy cloud overhead into sharp focus.

'My patient needs all her strength. Is this carry-on really necessary?' asked the medical man, abruptly.

'Not necessary, but rather wonderful, don't you think?' This interloper was raining on Annie's parade, the only parade she'd ever had.

Finishing up, and patting Annie on the shoulder, the doctor asked, 'Remind me of the divorce statistics again?' as he headed out of the door.

Dot had crept back in. 'Sounds like you,' she commented casually.

That exact thought had occurred to Billie. She rearranged Annie's veil with a cross hand. 'Don't let him spoil your day.'

'This is the best day of my life,' announced Annie, firmly. 'It'd take more than that old curmudgeon to spoil it.' She rummaged in her borrowed bag. 'Perhaps I should take one of my tablets. I do feel a little . . .' Annie relinquished the bag, and her head sank forward.

'Annie!' chorused Billie and Dot, crowding her.

'Sorry,' croaked Annie, lifting her head, her eyelids fluttering. 'I have these turns. It'll pass.' She took the tablet that Billie was offering. 'You're such good girls.'

The good girls exchanged frowns. Always the maggot in the apple. There was no escaping the knowledge that this bride was having a most unconventional honeymoon in an operating theatre.

At last, their work was done. Annie stood, holding on to the edge of her bed, her other hand cradling her posy of blush-coloured roses. Billie tweaked everything one last time, and then had to reluctantly step back.

Chips of happiness from other big days completed Annie's wedding outfit. The borrowed shoes raised her, the borrowed veil protected her, the borrowed circlet on her head glistened like a halo. Women she had never met had reached out to wrap their arms around the little bride. Surely, with all this good-will, thought Billie desperately, nothing bad could happen?

'I'm ready,' Annie said.

Right on cue, and flanked by Sam, Ruby appeared. They were both chortling and some instinct told Billie that a dubious joke had just been shared. They straightened up like altar boys when they felt her reproving gaze upon them.

Then Ruby saw his girl. 'Look at you,' he said, his rough voice full of emotion, like an old car changing gear. 'Oh my dear, you are a beauty.' He took her arm carefully, as if it was made of china, and slipped it through his own.

Nurses crowded into the room, talking and giggling and lining the walls as they called out, 'Good luck, Annie!' and, 'What a stunner!' The registrar, a circular man in bottle-end glasses, was swept in with them, and he soon exerted his authority by requesting, 'A bit of 'ush.'

A respectful quiet fell over the guests, and he welcomed them mechanically, reading, a trifle too speedily, from a card he held in front of him. From her position behind the bride, Billie could see Annie's narrow back trembling and she was grateful that they were soon plunged into the meat and potatoes of the proceedings with the registrar's portentous question, 'Are you, Reuben Daniel, free legally to marry Anne Madeleine?'

Ruby was, and he said so.

Annie was, too.

A garrotted sniffle escaped Dot, and she delved in her pockets for a tissue. Her search yielded only a *Distressed Ducks* newsletter, on which she energetically blew her nose.

Eyes dry, Billie wasn't immune to the charm of the scene. She winked at Sam when he pretended to lose the ring, and smiled approvingly as Ruby slipped the ring on to Annie's finger, reciting the approved text, 'Anne Madeleine, I give you this ring as a token of my love and a symbol of our marriage.' He paused, before adding his own words, with shaky emphasis. 'If we have one day of married life or a hundred years, I promise to love you and look after you always.'

Suddenly, Billie was patting her own pockets, and had to

resort to wiping her eyes on those distressed ducks. Her tear glands were acting out of character, and when Ruby lifted the veil to plant a tentative, boyish kiss on Annie's lips, they let her down yet again.

Laughter and applause broke, like glass shattering. The registrar was saying, 'Grand, grand,' in a self-satisfied way, Sam was crouching in front of the Wolffs with a Polaroid camera, and Dot hissed at Billie, 'Confetti! We forgot confetti!' in a paralysed whisper.

The wedding planner had forgotten one of the most important parts of the wedding. Billie struck her forehead, just as the room filled with a swirling snowstorm of paper dots, slung overarm by a gaggle of nurses. It drifted down around the newlyweds, buoyed by the currents of laughter and high spirits, to collect about their feet.

Billie plucked some out of the air. It wasn't confetti at all: it was a slew of those tiny discs of paper from a hole punch. The nurses must have raided the office and filled their pockets. They fluttered slowly, in crazy meandering spirals, and Billie's disobedient tears fell with them.

In the midst of all this, Annie was wilting, like a lily on a stalk. Ruby noticed before anybody else and he guided her back to her chair with an ostentatious, 'Take a seat, Mrs Wolff.'

The improvised confetti had to be picked up, and Billie bumped heads with one of the nurses as they all stooped. 'Oops, sorry,' she laughed, straightening up to find that it wasn't a nurse. 'Oh! You got my text, then?'

'I crept in near the end.' Heather had lost even more weight and her face verged on sepulchral. 'This is the hospital my mum died in.'

'Oh, Heather.' Billie sucked her lip. 'I didn't know.'

'Dad used to sleep by her bed, in a chair just like the one Annie's in.'

'What did you think of the ceremony?' Billie bobbed up and down, prising up reluctant confetti. 'Not your average wedding, was it?'

'It was lovely.'

'And not a plumed horse in sight.'

The ward sister, purposeful and efficient, shooed the guests

out like so many chickens. 'This lady has another appoint-
ment today and we need to prepare her. Out.' No doubt her
experienced nose smelled a troublemaker in Sam. 'OUT!' she
roared at him, as he whispered something naughty in Ruby's
ear.

'Alright, alright, Miss Whiplash.' Sam scuttled out into the
corridor, his broad mouth in an amused line. 'That was my
kind of wedding,' he proclaimed. 'Short.'

'It's the first wedding I've ever really enjoyed,' said Billie.

They loitered, enjoying Sam's ruthless impersonation of the
registrar, until Annie was trundled out in a wheelchair in one
of those skimpy papery NHS nighties. Without her finery she
looked diminished, like a bird that had fallen out of its nest.
'Wish me luck,' she said, feebly, as one by one, her wedding
party bent to kiss her. 'I wish we'd fulfilled the rhyme,' she
fretted, her fingers clutching and un-clutching the horrible
hospital gown she'd swapped her wedding dress for. 'I can't
help thinking . . .'

His face cluttered with anxiety, Ruby was almost brusque.
'Enough about something blue, Annie. You're going to be fine.
I'll be holding your hand again in a little while.'

Cottoning on, Sam shared his inspiration with them all.
'You've had something blue all along, Annie,' he drawled.
Pointing to her sparrow-like legs, demurely clasped at the knees
on her wheelchair, he said, 'Varicose veins, darling. They're
blue. You're sorted.'

Nobody laughed until Annie did. Then they all felt free to
giggle as she was pushed down the hall. Annie waved above
her head, without turning back. Billie watched until the slender
nurse pushing the wheelchair turned the corner, and Annie was
lost from view, off on an adventure that she didn't want and
that even her new husband couldn't share with her.

It was time to go. There was no band, no first dance, no
drunken usher sliding across the dance floor on a gobbet of
cake. 'Ruby,' Billie intruded on his thoughts. 'Can we drop you
home? We'll drive you back when Annie gets out of theatre.'

Looking affronted, Ruby said, 'No, I'll wait here. It's my
place to be here when she wakes up.'

Ruby didn't say 'if' but the word needed no invitation. 'Call us the minute there's any news,' asked Billie, slowly closing the door on the old man, holding the wedding dress to his chest as if for comfort.

Trailing the others to the car park, Billie detested the profound change of mood. Half an hour earlier, they'd been celebrating, now they were waiting for a phone call. Plodding to Dot's Reliant Robin, which squatted without a hint of self-consciousness among the other cars with the more traditional number of wheels, Billie flayed herself by wondering who would sit by her bedside in hospital. A shop couldn't hold your hand through the night.

Squashing into the tiny back seat with Sam didn't bring out the best in either of them. 'Get OFF!' Billie punched Sam.

'YOU get off!' Sam punched her back.

When a queasy truce was called, and both were as comfortable as agoraphobic sardines, they set off. Heather was in the front seat, having pushed aside a tiny tank top that Dot was knitting for her favourite inmate at the hedgehog sanctuary.

'Shall I drop you at your sister's?' asked Dot, wiggling the gear stick as if it was a patient customer and she a trainee hooker.

'No.' Heather leaned back on the headrest and closed her eyes. 'Take me home, please.'

Thirty-four

One of Billie's deepest held beliefs, stronger even than her conviction that the Pope wears roller skates under those robes, was that people never fundamentally change. She knew that she would never, ever get married, and now that the Du Bois/Kelly extravaganza was back on, she knew that Heather would still hanker after the whole glossy shebang.

Lip service had been paid to the moving simplicity of Annie and Ruby's wedding, but now Heather was back off the carbs and back on the warpath. Not for her a stripped-back, bare and beautiful swapping of heartfelt oaths: Heather was yelping once more about ponies and doves and hors d'oeuvres that would 'show' her relatives.

The phone was busy. Billie knew she could do this now. These days she could confront a to-do list that reared at her like a spitting cobra, confident of her ability to wrestle it to the floor.

The only truly feared call had been taken by Dot, the day after the improvised hospital wedding. Picking up the phone, she'd muttered, 'Hello, Billie's erm, Brides things,' distracted by a pigeon coughing out on Little Row. Phone technique wasn't her strong point. 'Ruby!' she'd gasped, fluttering her hands in Billie's direction.

Dropping a customer midway through a long critical look at her underarm area in a strapless dress, Billie crossed the shop in two strides. It was hard not to wrest the phone away from her assistant, but she controlled herself and listened to Dot's uncertain, 'Ye-es,' and her anxious, 'Right,' and finally her jubilant shout of 'BENIGN?'

It was, they agreed, over a celebratory Pot Noodle, the nicest word in the language.

Benign.

* * *

In the back of her mind (as you can imagine, a rather cluttered storage space), Billie had imagined that the Debs who turned up for her first Thursday in the shop would be a subtly changed girl, meeker and less prone to comment on others, gratitude for her second chance apparent in her demeanour. Debs' first full sentence had been, 'I had a bad biryani last night so don't come too close.'

Zac settled in right away, sitting happily on the desert island of his play mat, tickled every other minute by a besotted Dot. Billie, up in the stockroom, could hear her now, chirping, 'You are so handsome, yes you are, you are, aren't you? You're handsome, aren't you? You are, you know. You're handsome.'

Fresh from a visit to the weak but recovering Mrs Wolff, with the scent from the wedding-day roses on the hospital bedside cabinet still in Billie's nostrils, her fingers twitched with the desire to email James about Annie's recovery. After the last rancid exchange she wasn't welcome in his cyberspace any more, and the only email she'd written in recent days was to a company that supplied confetti in rude shapes. Spam filters were all very well, but Billie yearned for a twat filter, which would refuse to send her dafter missives. Blaming James for the squalid mess that Jackie and Ed had made was absurd. And childish. And petty. And cruel.

And plenty of other adjectives, all of which Billie had flogged herself with as she prayed for sleep in her deckchair at night. Childish pettiness was nothing new in her life – she'd once followed a complete stranger the length of Oxford Street in order to jab her with her carrier bag as revenge for a similar shocking incident in Selfridges' food hall – but James had always absorbed her bad behaviour.

'That was back when he loved me,' she reminded herself, ticking off, 'Call re: Heather gift Angela (personalised rat-poison dispenser)' on her list. James had been patient with Billie's protracted growing-up: he'd been amused by her kicks against the constraints of a serious relationship, and generous when the inevitable tearful apologies kept him up half the night. The self-control that she'd lampooned had stopped him yelling at her when she'd rolled in hours later than she'd prophesied, and restricted his anger to a rolling of the eyes when she'd accused him of 'clipping her wings' if he asked her to phone when she was going to be late. From a distance, James's armour was taking on a white glint.

She had left James behind. It was a blessing that their wedding had been derailed at the last minute. He was pompous, bossy, detached . . . she scrabbled for her stock criticisms of him. Oh yes. He also referred to her bottom as 'our friend' and pretended to book it an extra seat whenever they flew.

These were serious crimes indeed. If tried in front of an all-female, premenstrual jury James might get life. But he could plead that he would never, ever do what Ed had done: James was faithful to the core.

The memory of James explained Billie's confidence when she'd assured Ed that not all men would have taken up Jackie's Special Offer. James wouldn't have dispensed with his trousers and his principles so eagerly.

And he would have been gallant with Annie on her big day. And he would have listened to her theory about Jake. Oh, she pinched herself, hoping to inject a little reality to her thought processes, this mythical James was faultless: at this rate he would have massaged her feet at the end of the day, fed her truffles and done the washing-up. Absence made her heart grow forgetful: the real James was no knight in shining armour, but an overworked accountant who took the mickey all through *Grand Designs*.

Billie accepted that she still had a lot to learn about the wedding-dress world, but even she, with her limited experience, knew that it was bad for business to have a boy in a blood-stained overall mooning about the shop.

Darius had it bad. He dropped in countless times a day, for change, for some sugar for his tea, to check the time, to ask what was the capital of Slovakia (Bratislava, apparently).

One afternoon, despite several nudges, hints and an outright, 'Darius, GO HOME!', he was still hanging about at closing time. 'Did I tell you I'm in the running for Junior Slaughterman of the Year?' he asked, carelessly, one gory hand on a pristine white wall.

Dot didn't answer. She was especially quiet that afternoon.

Jake's disappearance was dragging on, and her pinched look was becoming habitual.

There was little point in Billie telling Darius, yet again, that Dot was vegetarian. He simply couldn't grasp the concept. His whole life was meat, he'd been groomed to handle tripe. Out of the corner of her eye, Billie saw Zelda leave her fudge emporium and head their way, looking very like a woman hell-bent on trouble. She tensed.

'I reckon I'll win this year.' Darius nodded knowingly, reaching into his overall pocket. 'I've got a secret weapon, see.' Slowly he pulled out a long, crooked sausage. 'I call it the Dot.'

Riveted by his sausage, Billie and Dot were silent, although Billie may have gulped. Zelda's hand was on the other side of the glazed door, her expression dark.

'It's my best recipe yet,' said Darius proudly, holding the Dot so that the sunlight played on its pearly casing. 'No toes, no snout, no genitals.' If he noticed Dot gag, he didn't show it. 'Just pure meat.' Like a knight of old laying down his sword before his lady, Darius gracefully held out the sausage in both hands to Dot.

Swooping in like an avenging angel (albeit one with an Elvis bouffant) Zelda snatched the Dot. Not giving it the respect a prize-winning meat product deserves, she thrashed Darius with it. 'Take your chipolatas, sonny, and stick 'em! This girl's heart-sick. She don't need you,' Zelda punctuated the *you* with a particularly hard thwack to Darius' retreating bottom, 'and your meat bothering her.'

Cowering with Dot behind a rack of crinolines, Billie winced at each loud smack. Even for Zelda, this was extreme behaviour. She watched in disbelief as Zelda, at least a foot and a half smaller than Darius, manhandled him out of the door and on to the pavement, slinging the now detumescent Dot after him. 'Get back to your grandfather's dump of a shop and stay there!' she yelled, ostentatiously wiping her hands. 'Like grandfather like grandson. Always poking your sausage where it's not wanted!'

Coming back to Billie's Brides, she took a few deep breaths. 'I won't have it,' she puffed. 'It won't do.'

The dam of Dot's pain finally broke. 'Oh, where's Jake?

Where *is* he?' she suddenly howled, bowing under the pressure. Billie and Zelda shushed and hushed and rocked their friend as if Dot were a baby.

'He'll be back,' crooned Billie, like a mantra. She watched Zelda's face, wrinkled with concern. If there was guilt there, or regret, it was unreadable under the older lady's preferred inch of make-up.

There was never a good time to ask Sly what his plans were. He didn't seem to have any, beyond endlessly circuiting Sole Bay like a gull. Or an unemployed lifestyle guru.

It grated on Billie that Sly never offered to take the deckchair at night. And she growled to herself, like Peter the dog, when he complained about the food she managed to knock up in her shambolic kitchen. And she longed to paint eyes on her eyelids so she could snooze through his interminable tirades about how the world had done him wrong.

One word changed the way she felt about Sly, and she suspected it was one he'd never used to her before. Picking at his burnt beans on burnt toast out on Herbert's balmy deck, Sly said, out of the blue, 'Thanks.'

Looking around for the hidden camera, Billie queried, 'Eh?'

'Thanks,' said Sly, as if he said it every day. 'You've been taking the flak for me. I heard Mum giving you a hard time on the phone the other day and you could have snitched but you didn't.' He ate a bean with a fastidious shudder, and said it again. Perhaps he was getting to like the sound of it. 'Thanks.'

'It's OK.' Billie felt like bursting. Sly had noticed. He'd noticed that she'd plodded on in her traditional role as family problem, absorbing her mother's scattergun affection/abuse and protecting him. If Billie was honest, she was also protecting her mother, that other mother she'd glimpsed in the mirror. Such a fragile, vulnerable woman couldn't cope with her hero son's fall from grace. 'Thanks.' She realised that she was thanking Sly for thanking her, but she couldn't stop herself.

Another bean was speared, examined and thoughtfully chewed. 'You've done pretty well with that shop, you know.'

This was entering the realm of fantasy: Sly was praising her.

Next he'd be telling her about the alternative world he'd discovered through the back of the wardrobe. 'Really?' she goggled.

'It's ticking over nicely,' Sly conceded. 'You're making a lot of customers happy.' He hunter-gathered another baked bean. 'Well done.'

'Ooogh,' said Billie, wanting to burp with pride.

'But if I were you, I would—'

Billie held up her picnic fork imperiously. 'Let's leave it there, bro,' she said.

This was a surprise. A big one, on a par with the day Billie had realised her mother had once been a child. Scanning her in-box for a vital missive concerning the health of one of the plumed horses (there'd been worrying talk of a bad knee), Billie saw an email from James.

It was bound to be vitriolic. It was bound to be distressing. It was bound to punch holes in her already Emmenthal-like sense of self. But Billie opened it up with none of her usual prevarication. She wanted to hear what he had to say.

I don't want to leave things like this between us.

I over-reacted to your over-reaction. If I'd taken a minute to think about it, I could have imagined how hurt you were by Jackie. (I've heard the whole story since, from the horse's mouth, and even with Jackie's spin on it, it sounds dire.) You needed to lash out.

And then I felt got at. So I wrote back, just as hot-headed, just as nasty. I should have been more grown-up, and I regret it now.

Talking of being grown-up, I can't do this any more, Bill. Keep in touch, I mean. It's harder than I imagined. Some things should stay buried. I've been re-examining the past and it's confusing, depressing, unsettling – just generally bad for us, I think.

Let's wave goodbye as friends. At least we can console ourselves that we did better than last time, eh?

J

There was no change in Billie's demeanour. She didn't even reread the page. She sniffed, whether dismissively or sadly it was hard to tell. She went on to the next email that told her the horse's knee was on the mend.

'Good,' she said to herself. 'Good good good.' She closed her eyes for a few seconds. Her features sagged with sadness, heavy as the linen bag of Sole Bay pebbles that held open the door of Billie's Brides. She opened her eyes, said one more weary 'good' and went back downstairs to the shop.

A plague of disease-ridden vermin were rampaging through the stockroom. This was how Billie saw it. Dot preferred to say that some nice mousey types had come to stay for a while. Before Billie got busy with traps, Dot had begged for a chance to persuade them to leave.

Downstairs in the shop, Billie was pottering as Dot murmured at her rodent friends. Billie was an expert potterer and she was just getting into it – easing the tissue-paper pile a centimetre to the right, putting the pens in the pen tub the right way up, singing the wrong words to Abba on East Coast FM – when she turned, professional smile in place, at the sound of the shop bell.

It was a ghost.

'Jake!' breathed Billie, taking a hasty step backwards.

'Dot in?' he asked, as if he'd come from across the road and not from beyond the grave. His beard was shaggier than Billie remembered, and the bones of his face more pronounced.

'You're alive,' she gasped.

Jake frowned. 'Yes,' he nodded. 'Dot in?' he asked again, leaning forward as if dealing with a dunce.

'Where have you been?' Billie was struggling to take in this healthy, three-dimensional Jake, perfect in every detail right down to the speech impediments and the dirty toenails. He was carrying a large stretched canvas, wrapped in a sheet.

A burst of song from upstairs tugged Jake's gaze upwards. He moved slowly across the shop, as if he was sleepwalking. At the foot of the stairs he turned and said, 'Wish me luck.'

Perhaps, thought Billie, he *is* a ghost. The original Jake would never have admitted to needing anything so mundane as luck.

Now that Zelda was suddenly exonerated of murder most foul (albeit most understandable), Billie nipped next door to bring her up to date. Deserting her post, Zelda waddled back to Billie's Brides.

When two people share the same vice there's no need for polite pretence, so Zelda and Billie eavesdropped shamelessly, huddling together by the stairs and straining to hear what was going on above their heads.

Unfortunately they couldn't discern words, just a low murmur. And then tears. A deluge of tears.

'I'm going up,' grunted Zelda, setting one support stockinged foot on the stairs.

'No, listen,' grinned Billie. 'They're happy tears!' The next moment she and Zelda had to fly across the floorboards and affect nonchalance by the till: Dot and her prodigal boyfriend were coming down.

'He's back!' Dot's innocent happiness was almost catching.

Almost. 'So I see,' sighed Zelda, looking Jake up and down as if he'd just applied for the post of Chief Handbag Stealer. 'You took my advice, then?' She nodded at the canvas that Dot was clutching.

'Yup.' Jake was taciturn. He was greedily, hungrily, *desperately* focused on Dot.

She was something to see. The pallor had disappeared, her posture had straightened and her hair had somehow perked itself up. She was displaying all the attributes Cruft's looks for in a puppy: sparkling eyes, rude health and a loud yap.

'Look at this! Just look at this!' she squealed, spinning the painting round.

A respectful hush fell over Zelda and Billie, two women not prone to silence. The full-length portrait of Dot was more realistic and straightforward than Jake's usual tricksy style. She was wearing a gauzy gown through which the slender lines of her body could just be glimpsed, and her gaze out at the viewer was direct and frank and loving. He had caught the sweet expression in her eyes perfectly.

'It's beautiful,' said Billie, unable to keep the amazement out of her voice. Where was the mud? The blood? 'I didn't realise you could paint like this.'

'I don't normally have a subject like Dot. I've never felt so inspired.'

Billie checked Jake for telltale signs of facetiousness but couldn't discern any: he'd given Dot an honest compliment, the very one she'd been yearning to hear for years. 'Why don't you trot home and hang the picture?' she suggested. A reunion is an intimate thing, and besides, Jake smelled like a cabbage-processing plant.

'What did you mean,' Billie asked Zelda as soon as the intertwined pair left, 'when you said he took your advice?'

Zelda rested her zealously insulated bottom on a chair. 'The night Dot threw him out, he banged on my door,' she elucidated, tucking a stray wisp of coal-black hair out of her eyes. 'What a state. Soaked through. Sobbing. Wittering about killing himself.' She pursed her carmined lips. 'I was tempted to encourage him, or even drive him to Beachy Head meself. But then I thought of Dot, and I tried to help. Said he had to value her. Appreciate her. I gave him a good telling-off.'

'That was brave,' muttered Billie.

'Oh, I don't want for courage,' said Zelda, complacently. 'I enjoyed it. Got a lot off me chest. He was whining about how he couldn't tell her how he felt and he didn't have the right words. Oooh, he was right wet. So I told him to paint her. To get off his arse and paint her. To show how he felt through his art.' She exhaled noisily, and none too happily. 'I would never have suggested it if I thought the mucky bugger was going to take me seriously. She's better off without him. The little sod wouldn't tell me where he was going, wouldn't say when, if, he'd be back. He ran off so fast he left his stupid hat behind.'

'Did you see how happy Dot looked?' asked Billie, wonderingly. 'As if she'd glimpsed Heaven.' She folded her arms, mirroring her older neighbour. 'It won't last, of course. He'll start insulting her again. Bullying her. Walking all over her.'

'It won't matter,' said Zelda, with a kind of resigned serenity. 'She loves him. What I didn't know before today, is that he loves her.' She shrugged. 'Who would have thought he could paint like that? Beauty in every brushstroke.'

That was inarguable. 'It's easy to believe that Jake loves her: Dot's so completely and utterly nice. But what does she see in him?' Billie was tussling with an old topic again. 'He doesn't deserve someone like Dot.'

321

'People don't deserve love,' said Zelda placidly, as if this was something Billie should have learned long ago. 'If that counted for anything, half the world would be on their own. You can't explain it. We just choose to love somebody and that's that. I've loved the same man for fifty years but I'd happily run him over with a tank if I got the opportunity.' Zelda fixed Billie with a searching look. 'People choose love. They always do. You're a smart girl, Billie. You knew that, didn't you?' she didn't wait for an answer, but slid one plump hand into the pocket of her apron. 'About time you tried my special recipe.'

Shooting out an eager paw, Billie took the fudge with a clear conscience. 'Oh. My. God.' She leaned back on the counter, cheeks flushed. 'I'd rather eat that than invite Brad Pitt to buy me at auction. What's in it?' Now that she knew it was Jake-free, Billie was as curious as everybody else.

Ignoring her, Zelda mused further on the subject of the day. 'On paper, you should have loved that Ed.'

Chewing more slowly, Billie looked down at her feet.

'Handsome. Polite. Went like a rocket in bed, no doubt.'

Billie looked up to raise her eyebrows: Zelda never could stick to approved topics for her age group.

'But you didn't love him.' Zelda suddenly turned a sharp eye on Billie. 'And you never would. I knew that.' She half smiled. 'Did *you* know?'

'Yes.' As soon as she said it, Billie knew it was true.

'Your heart is already taken. Hearts aren't like heads, they're not fickle.' Zelda paused, and changed the subject. 'Nip next door and fetch me emergency gin, darlin',' ordered Zelda, with the same expectancy of obedience dictators enjoy.

Billie nipped, the emergency gin was opened, and the two women settled down in Billie's Brides with a glass each to mull over the surprising day. Billie savoured the sharp taste of her drink, but not as much as she savoured being so close to finally solving her Sole Bay mystery. 'The night of the storm—' she began.

'Oh, that evil night!' wailed Zelda, grabbing centre stage immediately. 'The night that wrenched my Raven away from me.' She hung her dyed head, after a fortifying sip of Mother's Ruin. 'I didn't let on about Raven's death. I know how Dot felt about him and I didn't want to burden her. She had enough to worry about. To know that cat was to love him. I buried him in the garden, you know, so he'll always be close.' She raised her eyes to Billie's, and they were twinkling at their usual warp speed. 'I had to do something to keep me mind off him, so I finally got round to making my extra-special, tip-top fudge.' She nudged Billie. 'Bet you can't guess what's in it.'

Billie couldn't. But now that she knew who wasn't in it, she could happily eat her own weight in it. 'You'll laugh, Zelda, but I used to think you were a witch.'

'Well of course I'm a witch. That's how I kept me looks.' Zelda smiled and her dentures slipped. 'Pour us another gin, there's a good girl.'

Approaching Herbert's Dream II, Billie could hear voices. Not the babble of Chit-Chat Charlie, nor the 'Listen, I'm talking' tones of Radio 4. Sly had a woman in there.

Crouching, Billie tiptoed towards the tiny window and peeped in. She could see Sly standing with his head in his hands, and she could make out the shoulder of a smaller female standing in front of him. That shoulder gave the game away. Only Sana could wear linen so uncrumpled in a heatwave.

'About time!' laughed Billie, flinging the door open and crossing to kiss her sister-in-law. 'Have you managed to forgive him?'

'Nearly.' Sana shook her head in a kind of horrified awe. 'Honestly, Billie, men . . .'

Head now out of his hands, Sly's face was a medley of differing emotions. He looked ashamed, relieved, happy and suicidal all at once. Billie realised just how much he'd been holding in during their enforced hut share. She felt for him, suddenly glad not to be a slab of testosterone, afraid to show weakness. 'Maybe now you can show him that money isn't everything.'

'Oh, it was never the money.' Sana sounded impatient: possibly she was sick of being misunderstood. 'It was the lies. Leaving the house for the office every morning. Saying he was holding a seminar when he was dancing about in a loincloth.' She turned despairingly to Billie. 'Spartakiss! If only he'd trusted me, I could have come up with a much better name.' This seemed to annoy her more than the bankruptcy. 'I've got a job now,' she said, calm again.

'No. I told you the day we got married you'd never have to work,' said Sly vehemently.

Interrupting, Billie said glibly, 'People say all sorts of crap on their wedding day, Sly.'

Interrupting the interruption, Sana said forcefully, 'I meant every word. I said I'd stand by you in sickness and in health, and you're certainly sick in the head, Slightly Baskerville.' Sana stood a little taller, 'And yes, I know you don't like your whole name, but I don't like being treated like a child by my own husband.'

Beneath the hut, tectonic plates were shifting. The power in this marriage was transferring. Billie stayed very quiet, as Sana told Sly that she had already taken up a position as PA in a large fashion importer's. 'The money is nothing like what you earned. Life won't be fabulous,' she said, 'but it will be OK. And as long as you and Deirdre and Moto are there, that's enough for me.'

The Inner Winner hugged his landlady, who was already eyeing her bed greedily, and sat in the passenger seat as his remodelled wife drove him away.

Despite the pleasure of being able to lie down at last, the hut felt very small that night. Around Billie, souls were pairing off again. She was the outrider once more, flying the flag for independence and freedom. And for leaving the radio on all night because the silence of her four walls was just too much.

Thirty-five

The Big Day had arrived.

For most humans in the land, it was another ordinary Saturday. The twenty-third of August. A day off, perhaps. A day to mooch around H&M, trawl the supermarket, or stay in bed eating Munchmallows and trying not to think about the state of the garden.

In Herbert's Dream II it was D-Day, the Day of Days, a Day To Remember. It was a Red-Letter Day, the day Billie's Brides earned its stripes. It was Doomsday.

Billie had been up since first light, dosing herself with strong coffee in preparation for the trials ahead. She considered taking up smoking, or possibly crack, to get her through the next few hours. She'd last heard from Heather at midnight when the bride-to-be had woken from her beauty sleep to fret about the registrar's breath.

Accessorising an oyster silk slip dress with Reeboks, Billie slipped her heels into a capacious shoulder bag. Half wedding guest, half slave, the final sartorial touches would have to wait until her final 'to-do' list had been ticked into submission.

Ringing the doorbell at Heather's house at ten a.m., Billie had already looked in at Homestead Hall, double-checked the arrival time for the open carriage, and bought a new pair of nude thirty-denier tights for bridesmaid number four.

The tiny house, bursting with people, was unrecognisable as the pristine home Billie had spent hours discussing place cards in. Dean had been banished to Ed's, and both storeys were awash with women. The twelve bridesmaids were downsized to eleven (one had booked a week in Miami when the cancellation was announced) and they were all darting in and out of rooms, thundering up and down the stairs, and conducting whispered conversations asking what they had ever done to

Heather for her to put them in drop-waist cappuccino taffeta with matching marabou boleros.

The sole male in the house, Hamish the weeny pageboy, had to be inserted into his cappuccino knickerbockers by Heather and three of the heftier bridesmaids. Tears of shame had dried on his cheeks and now he sat with his Game Boy at Granny's feet in the sitting room.

'WHAT TIME IS IT? I NEED THE BOG!' Heather was screaming at the closed toilet door, face half made up and rollers in her hair. Her slip hung loosely on her bony frame.

Passing the smallest bridesmaid having a sneezing fit into her marabou on the stairs, Billie approached Heather with cautious professionalism. 'Open your mouth.' She threw two tablets down the bride's throat. 'Headache tablets. No calories.'

Obediently, Heather swallowed the capsules. 'Have you checked the—' she began.

'Whatever it is, yes. I've checked flowers, I've checked place settings, I've checked Dean's choice of underpants. If I could, I would check your blood pressure, but something tells me I wouldn't like it.' Billie had become very bossy since the wedding had been raised from the dead. The only way to deal with a bulldozer, she'd concluded, was to drive another straight at it. Now that she matched Heather strop for strop they got along just fine.

'What time is it?' asked Heather, before banging on the toilet door again. 'GET OUT OF THERE! I AM GETTING MARRIED IN THREE HOURS! DOESN'T ANYBODY CARE?'

'It's one minute since you last asked,' Billie told her calmly. 'We've got oodles of time.'

The toilet door flew open, revealing Angela, who was bundled out of the way by her impatient sister. 'Thank you for completely ruining my poo,' huffed Angela, tramping shoeless back to the master bedroom, her taffeta skirt bundled up around her knees.

There were shouts coming from inside the loo. Pressing her ear to the door, Billie could hear Heather caterwauling, 'BILLIE! SORT OUT GRANNY'S HAT!'

Stepping over a bridesmaid blowing her nose on her sash, Billie sought out Granny, chain-smoking down in the sitting room. 'I understand there's something wrong with your hat?'

As far as Billie could see the hat was fine: the face under it was the problem. Arch, brittle Granny was like a human scythe. All around her were cut off at the knees.

'I've gone off it,' announced the well-preserved woman, skinny as dental floss and about as much fun. 'It needs a flower on the brim.' She tossed the plain white boater across the room.

'I'll pick one from the garden,' said Billie, optimistically, bending down to retrieve the hat.

'I'm a martyr to hayfever.' Granny took a long, somehow malevolent drag on her cigarette. 'You can make one.' She put her head on one side. 'For three grand, dear, you can make me a flower, surely?'

So this was where Angela got her charm. 'It'll be my pleasure,' Billie assured her, backing out on her trainers and pulling some swift, evil faces behind the door.

The kitchen was full of gossiping bridesmaids, swapping diet tips and dunking chocolate biscuits in their tea, so Billie shut herself in the utility room. The hat stared unhelpfully back from the top of the washing machine. Plain, white, unremarkable, it certainly needed something to cheer it up. Billie racked her brains.

Many times over the years she'd seen her mother fashion props out of the most unprepossessing raw materials. A cheap glass they'd got free with petrol had been reborn as a poisoned chalice. Billie's skipping rope had found fame as Annie Oakley's lasso.

'What would Mum do?' Billie asked herself, as she head Heather yelling, 'WHAT TIME IS IT?' She rifled her bag, pouncing on and then discarding various tat. A packet of tampons lay at the bottom, among the chewing-gum wrappers and receipts. Billie took one out. It was white. It matched the hat. And there would be a certain grim justice in sending Granny Du Bois up the aisle with what chemists coyly term 'feminine hygiene items' on her head.

It takes determination to make a credible flower out of a handful of tampons, but by unwrapping them, tying them all together, adding a few leaves cut from the green plastic lid of a detergent tub, and tweaking them carefully, Billie achieved a bold, modernist chrysanthemum. Proud of her handiwork, she fixed it to the band of the hat with bendy tags filched from Heather's impressive selection of sandwich bags. 'Thanks, Mum,' she whispered.

Surprised, Granny managed a grudging, 'Very pretty,' as she admired herself in the mirror over the pebble-effect fireplace.

And so absorbent, thought Billie, rushing back up to investigate loud bridal screams.

'Look at this make-up!' Heather pointed with both forefingers to her own face as if it was a stranger's. 'I look like Lily fucking bloody Savage.'

The make-up artist, who had already endured a grilling about her experience and her attitude to lipliner from Angela, looked near to tears. 'I've exaggerated it a little for the photographs,' she said, in a wobbly voice.

'You look gorgeous.' Billie knew only superlatives would do. 'Fabulous. Dean will be knocked out.'

'If he notices,' said Angela, arms folded, looming over the scene like a bad fairy. Her sister's wedding wasn't bringing out the best in her. She buttonholed Billie. 'You've made sure Ed's sitting next to me, haven't you?'

Having already reassured Angela twice about this, Billie simply nodded, before returning her attention to Heather. The bride's chest was scarlet, and her nostrils were flaring. 'Everybody out!' ordered Billie, clapping her hands. 'Heather needs some time to herself.'

The hairdresser, the make-up girl, sundry bridesmaids and the woman next door who had never liked Heather and was there to gather information on the calibre of her soft furnishings were all shepherded brusquely out of the room. Billie tugged the curtains across and left Heather alone on the bed, feet higher than her head, with orders to breathe deeply.

Sniffling slightly, the make-up artist was powdering Angela's upturned face in the spare bedroom, where two bridesmaids lay across the bed like overdressed corpses. As Billie passed the open door an, 'Oi!' from Angela called her back.

'Are you bringing a plus one?' Angela wanted to know, her head uncomfortably tilted back.

'No.' Billie smiled. 'Thank God.'

'For a while there,' said Angela, closing her eyes as they were powdered over, 'I thought you had your eye on Ed.' She opened one eye. 'Did you?'

How to answer? Billie flirted with honesty – 'I didn't have my eye on him, Angela, I had every inch of skin on him. I was shagging him senseless while you were combing carpet for rat droppings' – but ditched that for a circumspect, 'Don't worry, he's all yours.'

Succumbing to eyeliner, Angela said complacently, 'We'll have matching tattoos by Monday.' She lowered her voice. 'How's my sister doing? Do you think she'll be alright?'

'Of course.' Billie seemed to know Heather better than her sibling did: all this hysteria would morph into glacial calm the moment she hit the church. 'This is the day she's been waiting for.'

'For some reason. I mean . . .' Angela pulled a face and a zigzag of eyeliner streaked across her temple. '*Dean*. Would you?'

'I wouldn't, to be honest.' Billie couldn't pretend: she'd seen Dean at seven a.m. that morning and he'd looked like a fresh bruise. 'But Heather would. She loves him.' Billie trotted out. She was too busy to discuss the basics of life with Angela. Heather's love for Dean was Heather's business. Just like Dot's feelings for Jake, they didn't need to be explained or justified. People fell in love, and they expressed it in different ways. Billie knew she would never want to celebrate love by dressing up in white and hiring a Rolling Stones tribute band, but she no longer scoffed at Heather and women like her.

No. Billie had realised, during the recent long nights alone in Herbert, that she envied those women. She envied them their singlemindedness and their self-knowledge and the way they knew what to do when love came along. They treated it with respect. When Billie had been handed love she'd jiggled it and tossed it and left greasy fingerprints all over it.

She knew better now.

'I have to get back to the shop,' Billie told Heather, who had been deep-breathing in the dark for half an hour.

'You can't!' whined Heather. She sat on the edge of her bed, half dressed. Her underskirt puddled on the sisal around her feet. 'I need you.'

'You've got all the help you need. I'm only in the way here.' Billie was expected back at Billie's Brides so that Dot could visit Annie, who was still in hospital: under the new regime Debs couldn't be left in charge of the shop. She reached out and hauled in a passing bridesmaid. 'Lyndsey here will look after you. Won't you, Lyndsey?' she asked, nodding encouragingly.

'Of course.' Lyndsey patted Heather's arm as if she was a forgetful nonagenarian in a day centre. In a broad Irish accent she gushed, 'All you have to do is sit back and enjoy your day. Things will go wrong, of course they will. Doesn't matter one bit.' Lyndsey bared her Du Bois overbite as she squeezed Heather's hand. 'As long as you enjoy yourself, that's the main thing.'

'Are you trying to kill me?' Heather shouted so loudly that Lyndsey leapt back and trod on Hamish. 'Do you want me to drop down dead in front of you? Things will go wrong? THINGS WILL GO BLOODY WRONG? Thank you oh so very much! Have you any idea how much I've spent? I could have bought a street in Wales for what this fucking wedding has cost me!'

Blubbering in pain from the stab of Lyndsey's cappuccino stiletto, little Hamish blundered backwards on to the hem of Heather's underskirt.

'No!' gasped Heather, darting down to examine the fragile silk. 'GET OUT YOU TROLL!' she bawled, an inch from the terrified pageboy's face.

Hamish was a blur as he sped down the stairs. Before she left for the shop, Billie gingerly placed his knickerbockers in the fast cycle of the washing machine.

'Is that what you're wearing?' asked Debs, frowning at the oyster-coloured slip dress.

'Why?' asked Billie sharply.

'Nothing. Just . . .' Debs seemed to reconsider. 'Nothing.'

It wasn't deliberate, Billie told herself, this unfortunate effect that Debs had. Her assistant was a courageous, resourceful, deep woman of today. 'It looks better with the shoes,' said Billie, hopefully, doing up the delicate straps of her gold sandals.

'Yeah,' agreed Debs, with unmistakeable doubt. 'Looks a bit less like underwear now.'

'Zac looks smart.' As smart as a doorman at a dodgy night-club. Zac's baby tufts had been gelled into a Mohican, and he was wearing a bow tie over his Babygro. Billie had been surprised when Debs received an invitation, but Heather had scattered them like, well, confetti. Zelda was a guest (apparently she was a bingo crony of some aunt or other), as was Mr Dyke. 'It was nice of Heather to invite you and the baby, wasn't it?'

'S'pose.' Debs pulled a gift voucher out of Zac's damp grasp. 'Oh, look, it's your poof.'

Sam's suit was getting another outing. His hair was shorter, less punky.

'You've been clipped,' said Billie, approvingly. She was proud of Sam's looks in a maternal way, as if his broad shoulders and even teeth reflected well on her.

'We need to talk.'

'Blimey.' Billie was taken aback, both by the way his drawl had dropped a few rungs and by the phrase itself. 'If we were going out I'd assume you were going to chuck me.'

'I'm serious, Billie. We need to talk.'

'You called me Billie,' said Billie, slowly, studying him. 'You've never called me that before.' She drew away from him, not liking the smell of this one little bit. 'Why are you so serious? You're like a newsreader announcing the death of a royal.'

'Can we get out of here?' He was nervy, glancing around as if paparazzi might be lurking in the kitchenette.

'Sure.' Billie could tell that Sam meant business. She turned to Debs, and did something unusual, something she'd normally attempt only in armour. She took Debs' hands in her own. 'Can you look after the shop while I talk to Sam?'

'But you said . . .' Debs was silenced by a squeeze from Billie's fingers. She thought for a second, then said, 'Yeah.' She squeezed back, and a tiny laugh slipped out. A laugh unlike her usual sullen snorts. 'And don't worry.'

'I'm not worried.' Billie enjoyed the little smile they shared, before turning back to Sam. 'Let's go, so you can tell me that you only have two weeks to live or whatever it is that's on your mind.'

His arm through hers, Sam marched Billie through Sole Bay. She'd never been marched before, and it wasn't comfortable.

Especially on new, vertiginous heels over uneven paving stones. Breathless, she looked up into his face. He'd slipped his dark glasses on. They added to his look, but detracted from her peace of mind. 'Oh God,' she suddenly shrank. 'You *aren't* going to tell me you have two weeks to live, are you?'

They passed Dykes, and the chip shop. Rounding the corner of Tesco Metro, Sam said, woodenly, 'You're not going to like this. Any of it.'

'I already don't. Quit with the mysterious utterances, Sam.'

Passing the Sailor's Lament, the whiff of last night's beer on the breeze, Sam said, 'I'm leaving. I'm off to London straight after the wedding.'

Mid-march, Billie halted. Her heart was sideways in her chest. In a very small voice, almost too low for him to hear, she said, 'Sam, you can't go.' She was losing her partner, her buddy, the only other soul in Sole Bay inoculated against love.

Refusing to stop, Sam forced her to scuttle after him. 'I've got to go. The book's finished. I need to see London again. I tried, but I can't live without casual sex and people being rude to me on public transport.'

Crushed, Billie noted the ease with which her Siamese twin could leave her. 'Oh. OK. Right.'

'Obviously I can't leave you on your own.' They'd zoomed past the burned-out tea shop, and Billie's new shoes slowed them down a bit on the cobbles of the square. Sam hurried her on until they were at the bandstand. Whisking her in, he plonked her down on the rotting bench, and swung one foot up beside her. Leaning down into her face, he told her, 'I've found you a replacement.'

Now Billie guessed why he was so nervous. And she reckoned he was right to be. 'Don't you dare inflict a cat on me, Sam,' she warned heatedly. 'I've got a few years left before I give in and get a cat.'

'It's not a cat, you fool.' Sam almost smiled. 'You've got to trust me, Miss Baskerville. I'm doing this for your own good, even if you hate me for it.'

'Will you stop being so damned cryptic!' Billie was ready to fly apart. 'What is this about?'

'Secrets.' Sam cocked an eyebrow. 'Know anybody with a secret?'

'Well, no,' blustered Billie, not liking this swerve of direction much.

'Somebody with a little white lie on their conscience perhaps?' Sam loaded the question with meaning.

Harrumphing, Billie tried an affronted, 'I hope you're not talking about me, Sam Nolan. I'm an open book.'

An eloquent look suggested that Sam didn't believe her. 'It's home truths time. I could have just buggered off back to London without any of this, but I couldn't because . . .' Sam faltered. Sam, who always spoke his mind, who was never lost for words, faltered. 'Because I love you, I suppose.'

'Aw!' Billie relaxed, looking up at him soppily from her splintery seat. 'Do you? I love you, you know.'

'Alright, alright, enough.' Sam looked as if he'd been confronted with an army of Tiddlywinks toys. 'I'm going to give you some advice now, even though I don't believe in the stuff. Don't ignore me, doll. Once, a long time ago, I ignored somebody who was trying to help me. And I regret it.' Sam swallowed. 'I've never said that out loud before.'

'What do you regret?' Tense again, Billie sat up straighter.

'Years ago, a family friend spoke to me the way I'm going to speak to you. They knew I was planning to do something disastrous, something that would resonate through the rest of my life. They were blunt, they told me things I didn't want to hear, and I pooh-poohed it. Just like you will.' Urgently, Sam repeated himself. 'But don't you ignore me.'

'What advice were you given?' A door into Sam's past was creaking open.

'A friend of my dad's took me to one side. I was so young. Eighteen. With hindsight I can see that he was gay. And he told me to think. To think very hard about what I was about to do. He knew about me, you see. He knew I wasn't the clean-cut young hetero my parents boasted about at the golf club. He saw the signs.' Sam smiled. 'Smelled the cologne. But I pretended I didn't know what he was on about. So I went ahead as planned. And I got married.'

'NO!' barked Billie.

'The works. A shit suit. A white dress. Our first dance was "Love Is All Around" by Wet Wet Wet.' He shuddered, repeating, 'Wet Wet bloody Wet,' as if to himself.

Eyes wide, Billie muttered, 'You were married.'

'I *am* married.' Sam nodded at her renewed amazement. 'She won't divorce me.'

'This is . . .' Billie shrugged. 'But you're . . .'

'Gay? Just a tad.'

'Who was she?' Billie was avid for detail. 'Where is she?'

'She was the girl next door. Literally. I didn't have much imagination when I was a teenager. She chain-smokes in Guildford now. She never got over it either.' Sam shivered.

'So what was the marriage like?'

'The worst sex and the loudest rows in the history of the Home Counties.' Sam shrugged, too. 'It was a farce, and it was all my fault. I broke her heart. My first trophy.' He swallowed. 'One I didn't want. One that still makes me fucking hate myself. All because I didn't listen.' He held up a long finger. 'So you listen to me, and you listen good.'

'OK.' Billie shrank a little.

'Don't hate me.' Sam took a deep breath. 'I read all the emails you and James sent to one another.'

'You what?' Billie spluttered and blithered and blathered and tried to jump up, but Sam put a strong hand on her shoulder and held her down. 'How? When?'

'Spare me the moral outrage. You know I'm lacking in niceties. I saw them when I borrowed your computer. Can we get over the fact that I read them and move on?' His eyebrows, so much darker than the processed nest of his hair, showed over his shades.

A few more damp noises escaped, then Billie nodded. She was uncomfortable, as if Sam had been elbow-deep in her knicker drawer, but she was also curious. 'Go on.'

'Every one of those emails was a love letter.'

'Oh come on!' Billie folded her arms. She was feeling hemmed in, by that long velvet-clad leg, by that handsome face, by the ridiculous turn the conversation had taken. 'They were just badly typed nothings.'

'His weren't badly typed. And just like yours, they were love letters.'

Billie was having none of this. 'If you remember, he only got in touch to tell me he'd found somebody else.'

'Yes,' drawled Sam. 'Funny that. I mean, why bother? If he was sooooo over you, why bother?'

'To hurt me, I suppose.'

'To get a rise out of you. To rattle your cage.' Sam took off his glasses and looked at her pityingly. 'To get your attention. Obviously.'

'He called her his significant other.'

'And you waxed lyrical about your brave fireman.'

'Exactly,' said Billie, definatly.

'The very same fireman you couldn't bring yourself to sleep with. Why, I wonder?'

'That was definitely nothing at all to do with James,' said Billie.

'Of course not. And he sorted out your VAT,' Sam went on.

'Exactly,' said Billie, adding, 'again,' slightly sheepishly.

'Love bloody letters!' Sam almost shouted. 'Two stubborn fools who couldn't type what they really felt, pussyfooting about like Edwardian spinsters.'

'You're wrong.' Billie shook her head, wondering where this meandering conversation was headed. Was Sam going to suggest some sort of reconciliation? He wouldn't say that if he'd seen James's last email. 'If you remember, he advised me to hang on to Ed.'

'Jealous. Covering it up.' With an air of finality, Sam spoke as if there could be no possible argument.

'If he was jealous he would have been upset when I told him I was falling for Ed. Instead he went all snooty on me.'

'Duh,' said Sam. 'Double fucking duh. Of course he went snooty. I'm betting he always used to when you got him where it hurts? Yes?'

That was true. Billie recalled how James would suddenly morph into Prince Charles if she laughed at his tie. Which she did quite often. 'So what?'

'So what?' shouted Sam. 'So the poor guy was trying to build a time machine in every single email. All those *do you remember?*s He was trying to rekindle the old feelings. He was testing you. And what do you go and do, you daft lump?'

'I blame James for Jackie and Ed sleeping together.'

'Exactimundo.' Sam folded his arms, satisfied.

'But it doesn't matter. I don't know where you think this is going, but James and I have nothing more to say to each other.'

'Stick that chin any higher and a gull will land on it,' scoffed Sam. 'Are you telling me you didn't get a glow all over you when he said he'd fetch Blankie?'

Billie wasn't telling him that.

'And as for that last little exchange. Yours was a doozie, managing to blame him for Jackie's dropped knickers.' Sam unfolded his arms, and poked her in the shoulder. 'The biggest, baldest love letter of them all. You might as well have typed COME AND RESCUE ME!'

'Rubbish,' insisted Billie, her head beginning to spin with the ramifications of what Sam was forcing her to confront. 'And he replied by thanking God we never got married.'

'Anger. Fear. The usual male stuff,' decreed Sam.

'You didn't see the last one,' said Billie, quietly. 'James told me he couldn't stay in touch. He killed us stone dead. Again.' She kept her face carefully composed. It wasn't easy.

'And what reasons did he give?'

'Erm, confusion, or something like that.'

'You people . . .' Sam sighed. 'Thank God neither of you are detectives.'

'What are you saying?' Billie's umbrage took off well, with volume and defiance. But then it tapered off. 'That I'm in love with James?' She swallowed. 'Still?'

'You've misdiagnosed yourself all these years. You're not allergic to love, or commitment, or even marriage.' Sam spoke rapidly. She could tell he was anxious about how she was taking this. 'You're allergic to big, fuck-off, fancy weddings, that's all.' He folded his sunglasses fastidiously and tucked them carefully into his breast pocket. Sam seemed to be stalling, but at last he got it out. 'You don't think you had a lucky escape at all. You wish you and James had got married,' he drawled.

Mouth dry, Billie longed to vault over the bandstand rail and throw herself in the sea. She didn't want to answer. She'd been running from that thought since August twenty-third last

336

year: today was its anniversary and she was tired of running. She knew Sam well enough to know that he wouldn't let her wriggle off the hook. 'There's something you don't know,' she began, feeling older than Annie. She had an ugly confession to make to a man whose high opinion she treasured. She told him as simply as she could. 'There's one detail I always fudge in The Story.' She sighed, and a gull answered her with a scraping laugh high over the bandstand.

Shutting her eyes, Billie remembered the plush cell that her hotel room had become last August. She'd been primped and prepared and deemed ready. Her dress was an extraordinary construction, designed to elicit a 'Wow!' from the hundred or so guests already gathering at St Bugga's.

Decisions about cake, about colour schemes, about flowers, about hundreds of things Billie couldn't care less about had been extracted from her over the previous weeks. She'd flailed, not waving but drowning: nobody had noticed. Her mother was up to her haunches in estimates and invoices, her girlfriends couldn't wait for the reception, and James seemed to be living in a parallel universe.

James's days were unchanged, whereas Billie had veered off the track of everyday life some time ago. Her waking hours (and even her lurid dreams) were dominated by marquees and honeymoon packages. James was going to work, playing tennis badly, watching indescribably boring documentaries about the Nazis, and suggesting sex at the exact moment she was too tired to contemplate it, just like he always did. He was way off on the horizon, with the normal folk, while Billie was marooned down in the valley with the crazy wedding tribe.

That girl in the mirror, around whom the bridesmaids were fussing and crying as if she was the Second Coming and not just a scared bint wearing way too much make-up, had looked as unfamiliar to Billie as James did.

Back in the present, with Sam invading her space, Billie bit her lip and said, 'James didn't jilt me.' She frowned at the truth as it belatedly made an appearance. 'I jilted him.'

'Yeah, I know,' Sam said glibly. 'He told me.'

Eyes wider than her mother leaving Harley Street, Billie yelped, 'You've spoken to him?'

'Oh dear. I knew you wouldn't like it.'

'Wouldn't like it?' Billie was horrified. 'So you know. You know I lied.' She was hot with shame.

'And I still love you,' Sam reassured her unsentimentally. 'More to the point, so does James. Now *that's* forgiveness.'

'Please, Sam, tell me what this is all about,' groaned Billie.

'I told you. I've arranged a replacement me.' Sam grasped her hand and tugged her off the bench. She pulled back, but he was stronger. Laughing now, his nervousness had evaporated. 'Come on!'

Dragging Billie along the front, Sam steered her towards Herbert's Dream II. Imaginative insults couldn't dent his determination, and her demands to know what was going on were ignored.

Her hair was in her eyes and the sun was glancing off the pebbles, but Billie could see a figure on Herbert's veranda. Busy shouting and lashing out, she couldn't place it.

'You're a year late.' Sam suddenly stopped. 'But you're finally here. Go get him.' He propelled Billie towards her beach hut, where James waited.

Like a sleepwalker, Billie put one unsteady foot in front of the other. She pushed her tangled hair out of her eyes and took him in as she drew nearer. James was the same as she remembered. Exactly the same. Fair. Solid. A firm jaw. A crooked front tooth. Green eyes that didn't waver. Arms open wide.

Her James.

They held on to each other for a long time.

'I'm sorry,' croaked Billie.

'No, I am,' said James, his breath hot in her ear. 'I should have noticed.'

'No, I am,' insisted Billie. 'I was cruel.'

'You were scared.'

'And cruel.'

'OK.' James laughed into her hair. 'I give in. You can be sorry. But only if you let me be a bit sorrier.'

Pulling away, but no further than their arms would reach, Billie said, 'We were very far apart, weren't we? I was drowning in the wedding, and you seemed so distant.' Hastily, she qualified that with a, 'I'm not blaming you. It was me, all me.'

'Let's never get that far apart again,' said James, soberly.

'Can you really forgive . . . what I did?' Billie had spent a year believing she was a monster.

'The minute I understood you, I forgave you.' Perhaps aware that he was coming on like a saint, James added, 'But it took a hell of a long time to understand you.'

With too many tears for glamour, Billie asked, fearfully, 'What about your significant other?'

Shaking his head, James dismissed the poor girl. 'Not that significant. She wasn't really like you.' His voice faltered. 'Nobody's like you, Billie.'

Feeling as if she might take off from the veranda and whiz around Sole Bay like a punctured balloon, Billie laughed giddily. 'I hope that's a compliment.'

'It is,' said James, 'and then again it isn't.' He kissed her, despite the wayward hair that was determined to come between them.

That kiss took her home. 'James, James,' she whispered, panic-stricken and enjoying it. 'I love you, I love you, James, I've always loved you, James.'

'It's alright, it's alright,' soothed James. 'I've always loved you, too. It's over.'

'Are we back together?' Conscious that she was talking like a teen romance novel and not caring one bit, Billie double-checked. She needed the i's dotted and the t's crossed.

'At bloody last,' nodded James.

'Oh my God, I've got a PLUS ONE!' yelled Billie, and she kissed him again, with a little more intent. Romance could only do so much: she had saucy plans for James.

A cough interrupted them. Sam had joined them on Herbert's deck. 'We've got to find a way of gluing you two together so you don't come apart again,' he said, mock grave.

'No wedding!' wailed Billie, putting up an arm as if to fend off Zelda's evil eye. 'I admit I'm in love but I haven't changed my entire personality. I'd rather slash my—'

'Yeah, yeah, yeah.' Sam flapped his hands to calm Billie down. 'We know. We get it.' He leaned towards her and

spoke slowly and loudly. '*You don't like weddings.* Got it.'
He took a piece of paper out of his pocket and waggled it.
'James and I have had an idea,' he said, grinning that satanic
grin of his.

Billie had had a recurring nightmare along these lines. She was
standing in all her bridal finery, and the entire congregation
was staring at her. Just as they were now.

Unlike her dreams, the congregation consisted of just two
people, Sam and James. Her finery was different, too. The bridal
bouquet was a sprig of plastic roses filched from the window
box of Herbert's Dream II's neighbour. The veil was Blankie,
tied under her chin and making her ears rather hot.

'Are we ready?' asked the minister, raising his voice so they
could hear him above the wind off the sea which was rattling
the hut's veranda.

'Well?' James inclined his head doubtfully down at his
blushing bride. 'Are you? This time?'

'Ready,' whispered Billie, pushing Blankie up her forehead.
He was beginning to itch.

'Then I'll begin.' The minister was new to his job. Until the
previous evening he'd just been a millionaire illustrator with
peroxide hair and an attitude problem. Now, thanks to an
internet payment of fifty-five dollars, he was a fully paid-up
minister of the Church of Jesus Christ Megastar. As he'd
explained to Billie, 'We're an LA-based church, not as popular
as our Catholic rivals but a lot more easy-going. We're very
big on forgiveness.' Here he had fixed Billie with a glare over
his shades. 'Which is just as well,' he had said.

Now Sam was solemn with the gravity of what he was
about to do. 'Brethren,' he began, 'please take each other's
hand.'

After a bit of tussling, Billie's hand lay prettily in James's
larger one. She looked down at them, dewy-eyed, and regretted
writing the phone number for the dry-cleaner's along her thumb
that morning.

'Billie and James,' boomed Sam, over the wind and the sea
and the gulls. 'I now pronounce you bird and bloke. Don't split
up again. Amen.'

Little White Lies

'Ayyyyyyymen!' whooped James, whose accountant friends would not have recognised him.

'Amen!' blubbed Billie, who was becoming reconciled to the fact that, after years of believing the contrary, she was *exactly* the sort of girl who cried at weddings.

Thirty-six

The last to arrive, Billie and Sam tiptoed like naughty children into the private chapel in the grounds of Homestead Hall. The clamour of the bride's carriage could already be heard outside on the lane.

Glancing collusively at each other, the smirking pair slipped into the back pew, skating down it on their bottoms to find the middle. Like a shaken can of Lilt, Billie was ready to explode, and fizz in a wide parabola over the heads of the congregation. She had never been so joyous, and so restless, nor less inclined to sit still and listen to a vicar.

Wiggling on the hard bench, she squeezed Sam's arm. The 'Ouch!' only made her squeeze it again. She giggled. She sighed. She shrugged. In short, she was hugely irritating, just one side effect of love that she'd forgotten about.

'Do you adore James? Isn't he fantabulous?' Billie asked Sam, in a penetrating whisper.

'He's a good bloke.' From Sam, this meagre compliment was meaningful.

'Yes, he is. He's a good bloke. The goodest ever bloke in the history of blokedom,' simpered Billie, wiggling again. 'Dot!' She noticed the sleek waterfall of strawberry hair in the next pew. Jake had earlier announced that his principles wouldn't allow him to enter a house devoted to the empty promises of a dead deity, and Billie had passed him in the churchyard stretched out on a tomb like a martyr in fancy dress. She leaned forward to yank Dot's hair.

Spinning round, Dot gave Billie a thumbs up. 'Everything looks great, well done!' she mouthed, reminding Billie to look about at her professional handiwork.

Everything did indeed look great. The small, mellow-toned stone chapel was all gussied up, its columns garlanded with freesias, its altar draped with ivy. Tasteful, rustic and charming, it resembled a still from one of the wedding magazines Billie flicked through with gritted teeth and heaving stomach: and it was all her own work.

'Gosh,' thought Billie, her vocabulary distinctly Sole Bay. 'I'm a *good* wedding planner.' It was indisputable: after a decade of avoiding the sack by judicious use of revealing tops and diligent buck-passing, Billie Baskerville was good at her job.

'Have you redone your make-up?' whispered Dot, twisting in her seat to steal a good look at her boss. 'You look about twelve.'

'I've redone my soul,' claimed Billie ebulliently, to a theatrical sigh from Sam. She wiggled again, and almost slid off the polished wood.

'Calm down,' hissed Sam, crossly. 'People will think you're on drugs.'

'I am!' Billie sat on her hands, as if they were belligerent drunks, and tried to focus on the other guests. The wiggling stopped when her eyes found the back of Ed's head.

Stiff in his best-man finery, he was talking to the vicar at the front of the chapel. Billie took in the sexy cap of curls on his gracefully modelled skull, tamed today by some gel-wielding hairdresser, and the expanse of shoulder in a well-cut morning coat. She sucked her teeth, as intimate memories, too explicit for a holy place, tumbled through her head. He was so inescapably graceful, holding his top hat as if he wore one every day down at the fire station, and yet he'd behaved so badly. There was no tug of desire, no tidemark of regret. When Billie looked at Ed, she saw a handsome, weak man. Not a bad man, and not a man she mourned. She had achieved the cliché of closure: she felt *terribly* modern.

The groom was bubbly, for one standing so close to the gallows of his personal freedoms. Dean was chatting affably, like a stand-up comedian working the crowd. Billie couldn't hear what he was saying, but from the way he was bobbing up and down and looking pleased with himself she guessed that he was showing off by farting the Wedding March, a flatulent tour de force outlawed by the fragrant woman in white currently to be heard intimidating her father out in the porch.

In the front row, Granny Du Bois leaned ostentatiously away from Dean, the tampons on her hat shuddering with outrage. The chic little lite-flow flower looked neat and tasteful, but if it rained Granny would find herself with an overblown rose weighing down her millinery.

Another formidable woman in a strange hat was nearer to hand. Zelda took up an awful lot of pew beside Dot, a glittering black confection of feathers and bows clamped to her head. She was chewing, her powdered and painted face sucking and chomping in a bovine way. Billie watched her waggle her bag of fudge across Dot's lap in Mr Dyke's direction.

Half turning, he shook his head genially. Zelda's loud tut echoed in the chapel, and a hazy notion glimmered in Billie's head. A penny didn't drop, but it teetered on the edge. Mr Dyke's and Zelda's profiles faced each other, like cameos, over Dot's innocent head; cogs, dusty and surprised to be called on, began to whirr in Billie's mind.

A wet wipe hit her squarely in the ear. Zac's chubby hands applauded his own aim, from the far end of the pew in front. Debs scolded him absent-mindedly, and Billie leaned across Sam's lap to ask her, 'Lock up OK?'

'Yeah.' Debs, her lobster décolletage contrasting vividly with her lime-green sundress, added, 'I cashed up an' all.'

'Good.' Billie's radiance must have lapped out as far as Debs, because the girl smiled, really smiled, in response.

Under his breath, Sam hummed the *Crimewatch* theme, but he was drowned by the Wedding March, not, this time, from Dean's bottom, but from the more traditional church organ.

Everybody stood up at once in their new clothes, as if facing a chic firing squad together. A fluttering excitement perked up the congregation, as if an unseen hand had goosed them all. Creaking double doors at the back of the church opened, to let sunshine stream through the dusty chapel.

Heads turned to get their first view of the cosseted queen bee at the centre of the day, but before Billie craned her neck to see Heather, she intercepted the look that Zelda threw at the oblivious Mr Dyke over Dot's head, as the familiar, evocative music swelled.

That look was an eloquent one: it gave away decades of

Little White Lies

secrets and spells and longings. It was the look of a woman who had chosen to love a man decades ago, and who had never wavered, despite more rough patches than Billie's heels. Perhaps happiness rendered Billie super-perceptive, but suddenly she saw that if she was to make a jigsaw out of Zelda's eyes, Mr Dyke's nose, Zelda's complexion and the butcher's affable air, the picture on the box would be Dot.

Oh Zelda, groaned Billie inwardly. The eccentric little woman had made another painful choice a long time ago: she'd given up her baby and watched her grow up unloved, but respectable. And now Zelda was looking over her granddaughter, her ferocious pride intensified by secrecy. The little trio in front of Billie was a family unit, but only one of them knew it.

Reaching out to surprise Zelda with a kiss that couldn't communicate one tenth of what she wanted it to, Billie was rewarded with a mouthful of feather from Zelda's hat. Picking fluff from her lips, Billie realised that the bride had reached the end of the pew, and Billie paused in her ape-like grooming to look at her.

Head down, her long neck gracefully bent over her lilies, Heather took Billie's breath away. Horsey, gurning Heather, patron saint of the pretentious and spokeswoman for castrators everywhere, was a goddess. Ruby's forty-year-old gown worked its white-dress magic on her, and Heather was transcendent, transformed. Even the Chinese burn she was grimly administering to her nervous dad's wrist in an effort to slow him down couldn't dent her perfection.

Clasping her hands together to stop herself applauding, Billie beamed. Even Sam was smiling, she noticed approvingly. Today she was indulgent, enjoying the gasps and grins Heather provoked as she passed by, truly gorgeous for once in her life. This was Heather's perfect moment and Billie watched without any of the rancorous postscripts on matrimony she normally scribbled to herself.

Sitting down, and standing up, and singing, and responding to the prayers, Billie never let go of Sam's hand. She was making the most of him while she had him, knowing she'd soon lose him to the lure of Kentucky Fried Chicken and same-sex adventures of the flesh. The readings, nervously gabbled by the more

345

photogenic younger relatives, stressed love and fidelity and not coveting thy neighbour's ox.

'Thy neighbours' cocks?' queried Sam innocently, but quite loudly. Mr Dyke, or Dot's Grandpa as Billie now thought of him, turned around with a quelling look, but Billie saw Zelda's shoulders quake.

Dean's vows were long and comprehensive, especially when compared to Heather's blithe promise to 'love, honour and occasionally cook for'. An interminable poem extolling understanding and harmony was read out by a third cousin once removed who wanted to be an actor, allowing Sam to fit in a short nap. Nobody slept through the Italian screechings of the opera singer Heather had insisted upon, even though her musical preferences stretched only as far as Girls Aloud.

'It's the doves next!' Dot swivelled round to remind Billie, like an excited pantomime-goer.

'Doves?' hissed Sam, in some alarm. Next moment, the doves, dyed pink at great expense, had been released by the Dove Master, as Billie had privately labelled the myopic little bloke in a Motörhead tee shirt who'd delivered them in his estate car. Flapping, fluttering wings filled the chapel, and eerie coos echoed in the stone rafters. Tiny, vicious claws darted overhead, and the congregation ducked and clung to each other as the birds swooped and squabbled in mid-air, confused by the lack of space. Feathers drifted down on to Granny Du Bois' tampons, and Hamish's screams drowned out the uplifting medieaval tune a step-cousin was gingerly picking out on a lute.

Billie bit her lip as she whispered to the cowering Sam, 'Not *quite* the effect Heather was after.' Thankfully, the bride was unaware of the perfect circle of dove plop on the train of her gown.

A triumphal organ struck up again, and the ceremony, agonised over for months, described in pie charts and schedules, anatomically dissected in a beach hut and debated more than the war in Iraq, was over. Heather was married, and, less vitally, so was Dean. They stormed down the aisle as if debt collectors were after them, tailed by their guests, in a tempest of confetti.

The bells were ringing. Children were laughing. The sun was

highlighting the new glints in the ladies' hair. Heather was crying with happiness. Taking Billie's arm as they processed out of the church, Dot challenged her, 'Go on, take the mick. What do you want to make fun of?'

'Nothing.' Billie shook her head, regretting that her hair didn't swish like Dot's when she did this: Billie's hair kind of trundled. 'It's perfect.'

Dot looked suspicious.

'Honestly. It's perfect. It's exactly what Heather wanted.' Billie smiled, wryly. 'I can't pretend it's what *I* would want, but that doesn't matter.' She had already had what she wanted. An elastic band wound tight around the third finger of her left hand reminded her that James was waiting for her, that from now on he would always be there to go home to. Their ramshackle wedding hadn't been legal, but it had been binding. 'Each to their own,' she ended sunnily.

Inserting himself between them both, Sam informed Dot, 'She's been through a cynicism-rinse. It's all gone, every last drop. She really is the wedding fairy now.'

'He's exaggerating,' laughed Billie, playfully hitting Sam on the arm and leaving a bruise that would last for weeks. Heather could be heard, inviting people to get into their places for photographs with a gracious, 'OI! MOVE IT!' Billie whispered in Dot's ear, 'I'll tell you later.'

'You'd better,' said Dot dubiously, turning to hurry Zelda up. 'Come on, we're being summoned.'

Zelda had a tight grip on Mr Dyke's arm, and obviously had no intention of speeding up. The sight of them strolling along together, and the thought of all the might-have-beens as they followed their granddaughter across the church yard, stopped Billie in her tracks.

Until Sam propelled her, with the use of both hands on her well-cushioned behind, towards the photographer. Heather's hands sliced the air as she marshalled everybody, evidently not trusting the professional to do it to her taste. Billie knew exactly what her client was up to – the less attractive family members were being massed on the ends of the rows, so that Heather's scissors could edit the big-nosed, the bald and the bad-hatted out of her perfect day. It was unlikely that any of Dean's family

347

would make the final cut. Even the toddlers looked like sumo wrestlers, and trying to tell the sexes apart was an interesting puzzle.

Sauntering over to join them in his wedding finery of a suit made from tea towels, Jake scoffed, 'Our wedding won't be like this.'

'Our what?' asked Dot, amazed.

'You heard me.'

'Yes, we did,' murmured Billie, wondering whether to be pleased or horrified. Jake had made certain promises, had accepted certain changes since his return: he washed up, he made the bed, he tolerated Billie, and she had noticed that he was now only misogynistic on Tuesdays. Despite all this, Billie was suspicious. Just as a leopard can't change its spots, Billie suspected a Jake can't change his possessive ways. Billie took in Dot's face, shining like the lighthouse, and plumped for pleased. For now.

The photographs took longer than the service, an irony not lost on Jake. Tuning out his morbid meanderings about the plasticity of romance, Billie watched Ed, dutifully smiling with each new permutation of guests and family.

Eyeing her, Sam said provocatively, 'You've got to admit, the boy's a beaut.'

'If you like that sort of thing.'

'Billifer, who doesn't like that sort of thing?' laughed Sam. 'I wouldn't kick him out of bed for eating crisps.'

'Been there.' Billie lifted her nose, smug. 'Done that.' She let her gaze linger on Ed's taut body, screaming to be heard even above the conservative drone of his traditional morning suit. 'I'm sorted for snogs, thank you very much.' She looked away, eyes wide, plucking at Sam and hissing urgently, 'Look at Angela. *Look at Angela!*'

Sam stared openly, hands on hips, enjoying the floorshow of the bridesmaid's pursuit of the best man. 'If she gets any closer to him they'll be sharing vital organs.'

'Is he red at all?' Billie asked, still averting her gaze.

'If anything,' Sam decreed, 'the poor bloke's rather pale.'

'Hello, Hamish!' sang Billie, as the pageboy, no doubt seeking sanctuary from the ordeal of death by photograph, sauntered up to them. 'Oooh, Hamish,' she grimaced, as the wind changed direction. 'Go and see the nice lady over there. She's called Dot. She'll play with you.'

The very last photo was Heather and Sam, 'My famous writer friend.' She beamed like a soap star accepting an award, and he made bunny ears behind her head.

Meandering along with the other guests in the wake of the carriage along the stony path to the main house, Billie warned Sam of what lay in store. 'It gets worse,' she said. 'There's a harpist.'

Screams floated out from within the carriage, and Heather's head, the veil slightly askew, appeared, shouting, 'Pass by, everybody, pass by! DON'T LOOK!' she yelled at an ancient relative who had slowed, startled by the immense, steaming turds one of the fairytale white horses was dropping on to the path.

As Billie hurried past, Heather leaned a little further out to hiss, 'I'll want a discount for this!'

The tinkling notes of a harp lured them to Homestead Hall. Billie scanned the terrace, saw what she was expecting to see on a stone bench, and relaxed. 'He's there,' she said to Sam.

Sam bent himself far enough out of character to say, 'Of course he is.'

A flute of champers greeted every guest in its indomitably fizzy way as the guests filed through high French windows into a sunny white and gold reception room.

'Posh,' said Sam, not entirely admiringly.

'Upper-class grotesque,' damned Jake.

'Nice curtains,' simpered Dot.

'Another champagne?' asked Billie.

The seating plan was attracting a lot of attention. Billie knew it by heart, but the others checked it anxiously. 'Oh we're together, Jakey!' Dot was relieved.

Sam was less pleased. 'I'm between a Charles Harrington-Badweather and a Millicent Broadstairs.' He loosened the fat knot of his silk tie. 'Probably a stockbroker and an airhead housewife, who'll discuss fucking mortgages all through the meal.'

'Maybe,' said Billie, who knew that Heather had put Sam on the children's table. 'Let's hit the food before the rush.' Weddings, rediscovered exes, incontinent stallions – nothing could distract Billie's tummy from its punishing timetable.

Heading for the buffet, Billie found herself picked off from the herd: she was that knock-kneed antelope familiar from BBC wildlife programmes. The lion was Ed, and he stood purposefully in her way.

'Ed.' She stepped back as if he was contagious.

'You,' said Ed, quietly. 'Don't throw your drink over me, will you?'

Billie shook her head and laughed, a little more energetically than his anxious joke deserved. 'Don't worry. I promise not to go all *Fatal Attraction* on you. I know how much that gear cost to hire.'

'You alright?' he asked. He'd found a way of phasing out everyone else in the room.

'Fine!' Billie was being bright and perky and distant, defying Ed's attempt to draw her back into that bubble of intimacy that ex-lovers can always recreate. She didn't want to be intimate with Ed ever again. 'Watch your back. Angela's on a mission.'

'She's wasting her time,' said Ed, twitching slightly. 'She smells of Chanel Number Five and fatal chemicals. Anyway, I'm off women.' He looked at his feet. 'Most of them. There is one, but . . .'

Billie stood on tiptoe to kiss Ed's cheek. Smiling at his surprise, she said, 'Thank you, Ed.'

'For what?' He looked puzzled. 'Why don't you want to stab me?'

'Oh don't get me wrong,' said Billie, sweetly, 'I do. But you've been an important part of my journey.'

'Is that girl speak?'

'Yup. Good luck with the speech.' Billie left him and his patronising references to girl speak behind. *Forever*, she thought, melodramatically. She felt she was owed a little melodrama, after what Ed had put her through. Turning, she almost bumped into the newly minted Mrs Kelly. 'Heather!' she squealed, throwing her arms around her.

'Mind the dress,' snapped Heather, before relaxing into the hug that Billie was determined to give her. 'How do you think it's going?' Her face, powdered, blushered, shadowed, highlighted, plucked and glossed, suddenly puckered like a squashed tennis ball. 'Is everybody happy? Did the doves work? Was the lute too much? Has somebody washed Hamish? Does Dean look like a monkey in his tailcoat?'

'Heather.' Billie took her squarely by the shoulders, wondering if she would ever get to the bleeding buffet at this rate. 'Your wedding is going fantastically well. Listen.' She cocked an ear, exaggeratedly. 'Laughter. Chatter. The chink of glass. The ceremony was wonderful. The photos will be beautiful. You look like Gwyneth Paltrow with a push-up bra. Your guests are happy.' Billie paused. 'Are you?' She asked, urgently.

Seeming surprised at the question, Heather thought for a minute. 'I suppose I am,' she laughed.

'I know you didn't believe it this morning, but that really is all that matters.' Billie braved the billowing veil, the lacquered curls and the make-up that could deflect bullets to kiss her client on the cheek. She said quietly, 'Your mum would be so proud of you today.'

Nodding silently, Heather pursed her lips and took a breath. She recovered to say, covertly, 'If Dean's nan tries to instigate the hokey-cokey, hide her Zimmer frame, will you?'

At last Billie made it to the buffet, where thousands of calories were patiently awaiting her attention. From behind her, she heard Heather bawl, 'OUTSIDE, EVERYONE! I'M THROWING THE BOUQUET!'

Billie was caught up in a stampede of new heels. Tutting inwardly, she gave up all hope of getting the wrong side of a vol-au-vent as she positioned herself on the lawn among the other hopefuls, all jostling like rugby fullbacks in their chiffons and linens.

Hurling overarm, Heather took a good run up. 'YNUUURGH!' she snorted, as East Anglia's most discussed bunch of flowers left her grasp and headed for Billie's face at top speed.

Flattened by the lilies, Billie heard Dot say, as she helped her up, 'Billie's next! The wedding planner's going to get married next!'

Dusting herself down, Billie handed the bouquet to Dot. 'Too late!' she grinned.

'Eh?' asked Dot, with a daft look.

'I owe you a million pounds.'

'Eh?' repeated Dot, before evidently remembering the bet

they'd made a long time ago when they were refurbishing the shop. 'You're married?' She gaped, a picture of befuddlement. 'But how? That's not possible!'

'Get me another champagne and I'll—' Billie saw James striding across the lawn. '*We'll* tell you all about it.'

'A million pounds,' marvelled Dot. 'You'll make a lot of badgers very happy.'

'And that,' said Billie, 'is the main thing.'

POSTSCRIPT

Billie and James

do not request the pleasure of your company
at the non-wedding
that already took place.

Please join us for the non-reception
at Billie's Brides
on 22nd September at 8 p.m.

No presents
No hats
No speeches
No top table
And <u>definitely</u> no white dress

Dear Great Aunty Babs,

A whole month since the most discreet wedding in the history of the world and we finally got round to throwing a party. I know you're having the time of your life with your sheep shearer, but I wish you could have been there – it's all down to you and your bonkers offer of this shop. There were no gifts, no vows, lots of kissing, some woeful dancing and a lot of love.

It was a double celebration – Billie's Brides is in profit! Real, proper profit at last. I did what I guessed you'd want me to do in this situation: I gave Dot and Debs a raise. Dot did the catering for our bash, so we had quite a few tofu 'n' marmalade kebabs left over, but James's punch took the guests' minds off the food.

The bride wore red. A Ruby Wolff creation made

especially for me! Annie sewed a tiny blue bow just inside the bodice – as she said, I can't be expected to supply my own varicose veins just yet. She seems much better, although Ruby enjoys fussing over her so much that Annie admitted to me (after a sip of punch) that sometimes she pretends to be tired so that he can tuck cushions under her feet and bring her cups of tea.

Our picture went up in the Gallery of Happiness. A Sam Nolan original, it's a biro sketch of me and James, laughing on the beach and showing off our elastic-band rings. At least, I think we're laughing – my hair is obscuring my face, and, sadly, most of the groom's face, too. Those rings are still firmly on, albeit a bit grubby by now. Gold is so *common*, don't you think?

Well, back to the party. The new husband was resplendent in jeans that looked as if they'd lived in a trouser press for a year and a daringly casual tee shirt (ironed, but not by me, obviously). He's a bit tired these days (that commute is a killer) but no less handsome. Not to me. But then, he'll always be handsome to me. Hopefully James will find a position in Neeveston, or somewhere nearby, before too long. Living in Zelda's top-floor flat is rather different to his apartment – the carpet can make you faint if you look into its swirls for too long – but I appreciate all the little luxuries I'd been living without. James doesn't raise his eyebrows any more when he catches me hugging the power shower or snogging the washing machine. Mind you, I still wake up in a panic because I can't hear the sea . . . good old Herbert. Apart from James, he was the only man who's never let me down.

The shop was packed with friends and family and customers, all trying to chatter over the music that Debs insisted on turning up every time my back was turned. Sam came all the way from London, leaving (according to him) a small taxi driver locked in his flat.

Like all the best parties, things got a little out of control. After drunkenly confiding her fudge's secret ingredient (tomato ketchup! Who'd have guessed?), Zelda forced Mr Dyke to sip home brew out of her slipper, and Jake stripped off to reveal the epic poem about the nature of love he'd daubed on his body in woad. Intervention by Debs ensured his underpants stayed on, and we never did get to see what he'd rhymed with 'sociopathic'. Or, thankfully, where.

Clicking her red shoes together, Mum was in character for her latest starring role. She treated us all (unasked) to an a cappella 'Over The Rainbow' which made Julia cack herself by the trifle. She spent most of her time keeping Dad's Cowardly Lion mane out of his punch, but she took me aside to let me know how furious she is with me for getting 'married' without her. 'I've still got the bloody hat from your first crack at it!' she complained. But she loves James, and something has changed since the non-wedding. I can't explain, but she looks at me differently, as if she's really seeing me. As if I've finally, officially, grown up and she's still getting used to it. I look at her differently, too – I've stopped blaming her for everything. She's just a woman, a funny, lively, disappointed woman trying to make the best of things. Like the rest of us. I kiss her more, and I like the way her cheek smells. Dropping her Dorothy accent, she said to me, 'I'm so relieved you've settled down at last.' What an expression! I don't feel as if I've settled down, I feel as if I'm at the top of a slide in greased knickers. I have a man to ravish (excuse the language, Great Aunty Babs) and a shop to run and fudge to eat and oh, far too much going on to call it settling down.

Debs' nylon tracksuit matched Zac's. Did I tell you she's cashed up twice now, and we're still solvent. *And* she's paid back every penny she stole: if only she could stop pointing out the customers' cellulite she'd be perfect.

As Ruby and Annie defiantly waltzed to the Eminem that Debs insisted on playing, another past customer, Ivanka, attempted an us-new-brides-together chat with me. 'I thought marriage would be like owning pet,' she said, in her accent thick as Jake's soup. 'But is like being stuck in lift with . . .' She couldn't find an analogy bad enough, and instead she just gestured at her husband, who was explaining the ins and outs of caravan insurance to James. 'Well, with Clifford.' Before she left, she said casually, 'Perhaps I poison him.'

My first big client was there, all brown from her honeymoon in Goa. Dean wasn't quite so brown; having caught a tummy bug from the in-flight catering, he spent his two weeks in paradise sellotaped to a toilet. Heather took me to one side to tell me that I'd helped make her wedding the best day of her life, and I hugged her and said, funnily enough, it was the best day of mine, too. When somebody thanks you, with tears in their eyes, for making their childhood dreams come true you'd have to have a heart of stone not to feel something. No wonder you love this silly old shop so much, Great Aunty Babs.

If you hadn't chosen to explore Australia, I would never have found this magical town. Thank goodness I accepted your offer. If we say 'yes' to life, it usually works out, doesn't it? Perhaps that was what Jackie was trying to say – or shout – when she delivered a character assassination instead of an apology. I'm starting to think she was right, that people's choices shape their lives. It's what we say 'yes' to that matters in the long run.

Sorry if I'm starting to sound evangelical and scary – a bit like one of Sly's seminars – but love finds a way, doesn't it? It pushes round the bricks and through the doors.

I mean, look at Debs and Zac – everybody shook their heads at another teenage single mother adding to the statistics of doom, but she's bringing him up the best she can. I shook my own head when Dot took Jake back, but it was the right choice for her: for some reason, a dyspeptic scarecrow with enough facial hair to stuff a duvet is essential to her personal happiness. You'll be glad to know he's behaving himself. So far.

Choosing amateur dramatics is also unfathomable to me – especially as I had to endure a childhood with different parents every month. I have happy memories of the weeks that they were the King and Queen of Toyland, but talking to my mother through the wardrobe door when she was rehearsing for Anne Frank was less fun.

Their son chose success. It didn't repay the compliment, and now Sly is washing up in Colonel Cluck's Chicken Parlour – but he is the *best* washer up they've ever had and he's finished in time to collect Deirdre and Moto from school. Deirdre is very impressed with her mummy's new job – perhaps she'll ask Santa to bring her a Career Barbie for Christmas.

Some choices can hurt others, but people make them anyway. Ed chose the path of least resistance, and Jackie chose the nearest shiny man, with dumb old me caught in the crossfire.

And sometimes, our choices hurt ourselves most of all. Great Aunty Babs, I know about Zelda. I guessed. I would never have imagined that such an epic story of love and sacrifice and fudge was playing out next door to your shop. Zelda's my new heroine – she gave her baby away even though it must have broken her heart, she looks out for her granddaughter (even seeing off a potential incestuous suitor), and protects the good name and marriage of her lover. And *continues* to love him. No wedding for Zelda, but a lifetime of commitment – I hope I can be as loyal to James.

Well, the party eventually wound down. James, making a play for the title Eerily Perfect New Husband of the Year, picked up empty glasses, rooted out abandoned quorn puffs from various hiding places, and straightened the dresses that the conga line had disturbed. As the lights were flicked off, one by one, I found myself staring up at the Gallery of Happiness.

All those women made a choice, too. One that was beyond me. They chose to stand up in public, in a church or a registry office or a hotel, point to their man and yell, 'I LOVE HIM! AND I ALWAYS WILL! AND DON'T I LOOK GOOD IN WHITE!'

My wedding wasn't cut from the template supplied by the glossy magazines, but I do love him, Great Aunty Babs, and I always will. And I look pretty shit in white, to tell the truth.

I'd better sign off now. James is perfect, but not so

perfect that he'll let me get away scot-free with the washing-up. You'll love him, I know you will, and he hears so much about you from Dot and me that he feels like he knows you already. Write soon, and let Sole Bay know how their ambassadress to the Antipodes is getting on. But much as I love you, my darling Great Aunty Babs, please don't come home too soon . . .

BERNADETTE STRACHAN

Diamonds and Daisies

Novelist Sunny Parkinson might write scorching romances, but her own life is decidedly lacking in passion.

A knicker-snatcher is at large in her block of flats. Her best friend's marriage is crumbling over a luncheon-meat scandal. She lives with a spherical couch potato and a workaholic virgin. And an Irish nun has just moved in to their spare room.

But one night at the launderette she meets Count Fabio Carelli – a man so traffic-stoppingly sexy he could have stepped straight from the pages of her latest novel . . .

Candlelit dinners, luxury spa dates and weekends in Paris are a far cry from the weekly pint and pork scratchings with her ex-turned-TV-gardener. Sunny is understandably dazzled.

But is this the happy ending she's always craved or is it too good to be true?

HODDER

BERNADETTE STRACHAN

Handbags and Halos

Nell Fitzgerald suspects there must be more to life than pampering celebrity egos at the theatrical agency where she works. Especially when she's blackmailed into playing girlfriend to a closet gay, perma-tanned TV presenter with a penchant for wearing leather chaps.

Vowing to inject a little depth into her existence, Nell enrols at a local charity. But when her various red carpet appearances spark embarrassing tabloid headlines that raise eyebrows at the volunteer centre, Nell realises doing good isn't easy.

Chaos reigns as she tries to juggle these two very different worlds as well as her eccentric family and perplexed girlfriends. And there's an added complication: Nell's growing feelings for her boss at the volunteer centre – a very grown-up, frighteningly sexy single dad . . .

HODDER

BERNADETTE STRACHAN

The Reluctant Landlady

Actress Evie Crump *seems* to have it all: glamorous job, beautiful man, and now – thanks to an unexpected inheritance – a lovely big house.

In reality, Crump isn't the name-in-lights to get Hollywood producers banging on her door; the man is her best friend, Bing – more likely to borrow her kinky knickers than buy them for her – and the house is a rambling ruin, complete with lodgers from hell.

Then Evie gets her big break – in a dog food commercial. Suddenly she has two roles to play: leading lady to her gorgeous leading man, and reluctant landlady in the real-life soap opera of 18 Kemp Street – where the plot is about to thicken . . .

HODDER